NO REGRETS

To
Aunt Dot,
There will always be
a place in my heart for
you — I love you very much —
Hope you enjoy the book —

Donna
10/2003

NO REGRETS

The Forgiving Heart of Allyson Porteus

Donna Lynch

iUniverse, Inc.
New York Lincoln Shanghai

NO REGRETS
The Forgiving Heart of Allyson Porteus

iUniverse, Inc.

For information address:
iUniverse, Inc.
2021 Pine Lake Road, Suite 100
Lincoln, NE 68512
www.iuniverse.com

ISBN: 0-595-28759-X (pbk)
ISBN: 0-595-74876-7 (cloth)

Printed in the United States of America

I dedicate this book to my husband, Bob, who means everything to me. Your patience and understanding has carried me. Thank you. I love you.

In loving memory of Edna May Kelley (Prue) Charlton
(December 3,1934–November 24,1994)

"The fragrance the violet sheds on the heel that has crushed it."

—Mark Twain

ACKNOWLEDGEMENTS

A very special thank you to my friend, Jack Pettey, Dell editor. Finally, Jack. I couldn't have done it without you. Agent Carol Bodey, you saw what my eyes refused to. Thank you. Agent Debbie Fine and Agent Kelly O'Donnell thank you for trying.

Mystery Author John M. Prophet and his wife Ellen...you two are the best. Much thanks for all your help. Best wishes in your success, John.

Charles Corkum, my high school teacher, thank you for helping me in the beginning by setting up a program for writing this. My friend and author Tanny Mann, you inspire me. Children's author Richard Wainwright, Rose Krikorian and Agent Elizabeth Weed, thank you all for taking time out of your busy day to read my novel and giving me the feedback I needed. It was deeply appreciated.

My wonderful friends, Dawn Bobal, Anneliese Richter, Deirdre Weeks, Donna Mackie and Sue Sullivan, I thank you for the encouragement and believing in me. I'm fortunate to have you all as my friend.

PART I

CHAPTER 1

One chilly, rainy night the cablevision went out. They set the candles up when the lights flickered and started a fire in the hearth. Allyson Porteus snuggled up in a sleeping bag near the fireplace, and gave her Aunt Edith a woolen throw blanket to cover herself while she rocked in the old chair.

"I miss him so much," Allyson divulged quietly, gazing gallantly into the crackling fire.

"Believe me, I understand. Do you want to talk about it?" she asked softly.

"He's married, Auntie," she blurted out, still looking into the fire.

Allyson felt this heavy weight lift instantly off her chest after confessing the awful reality, but she feared her aunt's reaction. She couldn't turn her head and face her.

"I thought this might be the problem," she responded wisely.

"How'd ya know?" Allyson asked, turning slowly to face her now, with tears starting to form at the corners of her eyes.

"Listen, honey, you forget your dear Aunt is older than you are," she said smiling.

"This wasn't something I planned. It just happened," Allyson uttered.

"There's no reason to explain. I'm not going to condemn you. We're all human, and that in itself can make us vulnerable."

"When his wife found out about us, she threatened to cut him off financially. After that, he ran like a scared rabbit," Allyson added.

"Does he have any other children?" Auntie asked.

"No. At least not that I know of."

"Well, that's a blessing. Give him time. Men don't think like us. And they don't get that maternal bond either. This may be overwhelming to him right now, but if he's any kind of a decent human being—which I'm sure he is, he'll want to have some sort of contact with his son," she concluded, as her eyes closed slowly.

Allyson kept her invigorating words in her thoughts as she crawled upon the couch and drifted off to sleep, dreaming of the night when she first met Kyle. She had been walking arm and arm into the black and white marble foyer of the Caldwell mansion with Harold Elliott, an acquaintance from the firm where she worked, Cape Cod Realty.

Greeting them upon entering the ballroom was the ravishing Janice Caldwell, slim with willowy movements, and silvery blond hair pinned up neatly and elegantly in the back of her head. When she extended her hand towards her, her long thin fingers set off by large diamonds sparkled so brightly they nearly blinded her. There was a look of evil, though, behind those gorgeous deep green eyes of hers, a look that dared her to trespass on forbidden premises. It frightened Allyson momentarily.

Janice's gaze shifted quickly to her companion, the handsome and charming Kyle Riker, who gave her an inviting once-over with his kaleidoscopic eyes of blue. Her body tingled from head to toe when he held her hand in his. Allyson felt Janice's eyes upon them, and she immediately withdrew her hand from his. Yet every time their eyes met during the course of the evening, they locked.

She polished off a glass of white wine, and when Allyson looked around everyone seemed to be standing still in time. Without any warning and much to her shock, Kyle appeared from behind her and swept her up into his Herculean arms and carried her out onto the patio. Mesmerized by his enchanting smile, Allyson became speechless as he planted his warm lips upon hers.

Then Janice came into view from out of nowhere, her dark eyes shooting daggers at them. Her gaze was so powerful, Kyle dropped her. It was then that Allyson awoke instantly, on the living room floor, still wrapped in the sleeping bag. It was 3:00 A.M. Aunt Edith was still asleep in the chair but was aroused when she heard the big thump, as Allyson, hit bottom.

"Are you all right?" she asked sleepily.

"I'm fine, Auntie. It's almost time for another feeding. Will this ever end?" Allyson mumbled.

"What?" Aunt Edith asked, still half asleep.

"Would you like a cup of coffee?"

"Sounds good to me," Aunt Edith said, as she stretched her arms forward, yawning.

Allyson couldn't believe that the day after tomorrow Aunt Edith would be leaving already. The time had flown by so quickly. Then again, it always did when her aunt was with her.

There was still no word from Kyle. Not even a phone call since the plush accommodations of the limo service he had most generously provided for their welcoming home present. Allyson wondered if he was still out of the country, or if he was avoiding them.

"Auntie, I don't understand him," she said, as she looked into her son's eyes while feeding him the bottle. "Here lies this beautiful baby boy who looks so much like his father, yet it appears Kyle could care less."

"I'm sure when reality sets in, he'll come around. Out of curiosity, if nothing else. Once he sees his son, I'm sure he'll want to be with him," Aunt Edith said with encouragement.

"I hope you're right. For my son's sake. Janice keeps Kyle under her control, and she has the money and power to do it. He would be totally dysfunctional without money. He's just another spoiled rich boy with a pretty face. Janice, being quite a bit older, takes the place of his deceased mother—I think. He makes Janice feel young, and she loves the attention she gets from her little social circle. Most of them are much older than she is, and they drool with envy when she promenades in front of them with her young stud under her fin," Allyson ended with long sigh.

"That coffee perked you up," Aunt Edith said as she poured her another steaming cup. "If you know all this about him, what attracts you to him?"

"Chemistry. Lust. Call it what you like. It's a fatal attraction I can't resist. My head knows what he is, but my emotions speak differently, and I can't stop thinking about him. Now that I have his son, it's harder for me to forget him. I can't break the ties with him…I think I still love him."

"It may seem like a tough road ahead, Ali, but your heart will guide you down the right path. Your main concern now is Benjamin. Give him lots of love, and in the end things will work out for the best. You'll see," Aunt Edith said with a loving smile.

CHAPTER 2

It was a Monday morning. Aunt Edith was packing to leave. As Allyson watched her fold her clothes neatly into the suitcase, she was already feeling a gnawing sense of loss. She knew she would miss her terribly. She was the only family Allyson had left, since she had lost contact with her dad. Allyson still had Felicia, her roommate and best friend, but it wasn't the same.

"Thanks for everything," Allyson said, as she hugged her tightly, not wanting to let her go.

"You be good, and take care of that precious son of yours," Aunt Edith said, still boasting over her new great nephew. She kissed her on the cheek, and brushed the hair from her wet eyes.

"I will," Allyson said dolefully, trying to hold back her tears. She stood in the doorway waving good-bye until she could no longer see her. In the meantime, Benjamin woke from his nap and was fussing.

She held her little baby in her arms, and for the first time he began to coo. She cooed back. He smiled. She fed him and dressed him in the sailor's outfit that Aunt Edith had bought him. With his long dark hair, deep blue eyes and rosy lips he looked like a baby model, ready for his first advertising pose. Allyson was so happy, yet she felt so lonely and unloved, and terribly sorry for her son who had no father in sight.

"I'll make it up to you, my beautiful Benjamin. I promise," she said softly, as she placed the rattle in his pudgy hand and tickled his chubby little belly.

Being another nice day, she decided to bundle up Benjamin and take him for a walk in his carriage. He stayed alert for quite awhile, looking all around, but after encircling the same area numerous times, he eventually dozed off. Most of the small vacant homes she strolled past were summer cottages—many of which were boarded up for the long winter. With no sounds of automobiles, children playing or birds singing, it was a desolate place sometimes. She figured she'd have to return to work sooner than she had originally anticipated.

She parked the carriage at the front doorstep and carried her sleepy Ben into the house. It was close to four, almost time for his dinner. After she laid him down in his crib, and walked through the small hallway into the kitchen, she noticed the answering machine blinking. There were three calls.

"Hi, Ali. It's Aunt Edith. Everything is okay. Just want to let you know I arrived home safely. Talk to you soon."

The second call was a hang-up call. The third one was from Kyle.

"Allyson, it's me. I called earlier, but hung up when you didn't answer. If you get this message, I'll call you tonight around eight."

Her heart was beating so hard when she heard his voice, she thought it would beat straight through her chest. She couldn't believe it was him. Her head began to whirl. "What if he wants to see us tonight?" she said aloud. The place was a mess. She was a wreck! Allyson instantly became a ball of energy. She began picking up everything in sight. Clothes were strewn across chairs, and Ben's toys were scattered everywhere. But not for long. She whipped through the house vacuuming, dusting, and she even washed the kitchen and bathroom floors. After she fed Benjamin dinner, she dressed him in his best outfit. And then she remembered he would be sleeping by eight o'clock, so she put on his pajamas. After all, they weren't entertaining the President. They didn't need to impress this man with clothing, or anything else for that matter. Ben was his son. Kyle should automatically love Ben as he is.

The phone rang at exactly eight. Even though Allyson was expecting it to ring, it startled her. Her nerves had been on edge ever since she heard his voice on the machine. That was one plus for Kyle; he was seldom on time. She didn't hurry to answer it.

"Hi, Ali. How ya doing?"

"We're fine, Kyle. How about you?" she responded lightly.

Allyson wondered where this conversation was headed. Someone had to break the ice, and she had a feeling it would be her.

"It's been awhile. I thought I'd hear from you sooner?"

"I tried, but I heard through the grapevine your aunt was visiting," he explained.

"We have a beautiful son!" she blurted out, her blood beginning to seethe with anger.

"That's why I'm calling. I was hoping to come by, if it's convenient for you, of course."

"What do you mean, convenient for me? I have all the time in the world. You have the issue with time—remember?" Control yourself, she thought. She didn't want to drive him away.

"Oh, Ali, I see I'm upsetting you. Maybe this isn't a good idea."

"No, I'm fine," she said, fuming inside. "When are you coming?"

"Is tomorrow at 1:00 P.M., all right? Janice will be at a meeting until 4:00 P.M."

Just hearing her name made her skin crawl. Janice Caldwell still had the upper hand.

Would she always?

"Yeah, see you then. Good-bye, Kyle."

Allyson had so many mixed emotions after speaking with him; she couldn't tell if she was coming or going. This man did something to her; no matter how often she told herself the situation was hopeless.

CHAPTER 3

Allyson tucked Ben into his crib, with his Pooh bear, around seven o'clock. The fresh air had pooped him out, and he fell asleep as soon as his precious little head hit the pillow. She must have dozed after that, because she didn't become conscious until Felicia came strutting through the front door.

"Hi. How was your night?" Felicia inquired, with sincere interest.

"Quiet with Aunt Edith gone. Benjamin fell asleep early." Allyson knew Felicia was waiting to hear something juicy. She couldn't wait to drop the bomb.

"Nothing exciting, huh?"

"Well…Kyle called. If you call that exciting," she quietly boasted.

"You're kidding!"

Allyson shook her head.

"Tell me more. Tell me more."

"Hey, what do you think this is? Tell you more. Tell you more. This isn't something from out of the movie, *Grease*."

"Isn't this the first time he's called since Benjamin's been born?" Felicia asked with great enthusiasm.

At twenty-four, the prime of Felicia's life, a year younger than herself, Allyson wondered if she had any desires to be with a man. She devoted all her free time to the school, tutoring those children who fell behind because of illness or some other disability.

There was one boy named Kevin she talked about a lot, but she didn't remember her having a long-term relationship with anyone, much less a brief love affair. There was never anyone special—at least not that Allyson knew about.

"We have a date tomorrow at one," she answered, taking a deep breath, smiling dreamily.

"I betcha he can't wait to see Benjamin. He'll adore him," she said excitedly.

"He sure will," Allyson added, noticing how bubbly Felicia got whenever they spoke of Kyle. She wondered if she had an eye for him. He had charmed many, by far—her included.

Felicia rambled on about what outfit Allyson should wear, and what she should dress Ben in. In spite of the conservative person Felicia was, she kept up with style. Allyson wasn't quite as reserved as her. She liked dressing provocatively, dangerously revealing all that her friend kept hidden.

"I think Benjamin would catch his daddy's eye with his sailor's outfit. And you…in your knit dress—the peach-colored one."

"I thought you were my friend. That thing has had it. It's ancient," Allyson said, rolling her eyes at her.

"That dress may be old, but it still looks great on you. And the color goes well with your skin tone. You look absolutely sexy in it," she said, with what Allyson thought might be a touch of envy.

"Maybe you're right. That old knit does flatter my womanly curves," Allyson said with a smile.

CHAPTER 4

As Allyson sat tensely on the tattered earth-toned sofa looking like a prima donna, she wondered why she was trying so hard to impress this man? A man with whom she'd already had a compelling affair, and was now the father of her son. Probably because she knew she never really had Kyle from the start. Janice Caldwell was the only one who truly had him. She still did, and probably always would own Kyle.

The phone rang at 1:10 P.M.

"Hello."

"Hi, Ali. It's me. I'm not going to be able to make it."

"What do you mean? You said you'd be here at one."

"I know. I'm sorry. The plans have changed. Janice's meeting was cancelled."

"Your son is waiting to see you."

"Listen, I'm going to try and get away," he said, in his usual charming and soothing voice.

"Yeah, sure. See ya later, Kyle," she said with obvious disgust, trying to disguise her immense disappointment and profound hurt.

Allyson plunked down hard on the couch, stewing. She tried to concentrate on "All My Children" hoping he would show, but she knew deep down it was unlikely. When the soap ended, she took off her dress and threw on her jeans and T-shirt. Ben had spit up on his clothes, and his diaper needed changing. Ben's good nature turned instantly, and he was crying for another bottle before his afternoon nap.

She wanted to run on the beach so badly. She needed desperately to sort out her feelings. Nevertheless, she couldn't just pick up and run like she used to. This was the first time she felt confined. She was very much aware that Ben was her main priority, but she felt selfish and a bit resentful. She realized that she had a little person, and she was responsible for him. Her life would never be the way it used to be.

As she moped around feeling sorry for herself, she got some Perrier water from the fridge. There on the second shelf sat a large bar of deep rich chocolate. Her weakness. She closed the refrigerator, and then she poured the water into a tall glass. Then she ambled back to the couch. As she looked around the small living quarters, she noticed that everything was spotless, and in its place. Ben was sleeping. The television couldn't hold her attention. She had read all the novels in the small bookcase. The more she thought about Kyle, the more upset she became, and the more her thoughts drifted to that chocolate.

Dark, light, or any kind of chocolate had been her downfall, and the reason she had gained so much weight when she was a teen. But that was then, and this was now. Finally, she couldn't control herself any longer. She sheepishly opened the door to the fridge, looking around to make sure the coast was clear, then she scoffed the chocolate like a vulture. She curled up on the sofa and indulged in it as if she were a deprived child.

At this point, Allyson knew he wasn't going show. Another disappointment written off in her memoirs. Although Kyle was debonair and bodacious, he was also very manipulative and arrogant, yet that still didn't stop her from wanting to be with him. She didn't care if he was married; she could only think of satisfying her own needs and desires. Besides, it was evident his was only a marriage of convenience. He had told her many times he didn't love Janice. The sad reality, money prevailed over their love.

❦   ❦   ❦

Allyson heard the raveling of the small blue stones when the Volvo pulled in the driveway. She looked out. She saw Felicia unfasten her seat belt. She couldn't get out of the car fast enough. Allyson thought she was going to fall flat on her face. She raced in.

"Hi, Allyson. Well…how'd it go?" she inquired with great animation, slightly out of breath.

"It didn't go."

"What happened?"

"He didn't show. I should have expected that from him."

"Oh, that's why you look so gloomy."

"It shows? It's my own fault. I should have known. I mean how many times has he done this to me in the past?"

"Is Ben still sleeping," Felicia asked.

"Yup, but he's about due to get up."

"I was thinking, being a beautiful day and all, I'd like to take Ben for a walk in his carriage. If it's okay with you?"

She looked at Felicia and nodded. Felicia looked so sweet in her frilly cotton blouse and pleated wool skirt. If she raised that hemline and revealed some cleavage, Allyson would have some serious competition to worry about. Nevertheless, she'd always been a good friend, and Allyson knew she could trust her completely, even with the man she loved.

"Sure. Why not. But before you go, can I take a quick run on the beach?" Allyson implored. "I won't be long. I promise."

"Go ahead," Felicia said, waving her hand, shooing her out.

"Thanks. I love ya." Allyson grabbed a sweater and flew out the back door.

CHAPTER 5

The next morning Allyson was up at six, raring to go. But to go where? She was like a ball of energy, but she had nowhere to expel it, except in this small cottage, and on her child. She didn't regret this. Her baby meant everything to her, but she needed more. She wasn't getting any compensation for keeping a clean house, or from the constant changing of diapers. She was smart, and she was educated, and she had a lot to offer.

She made Felicia her favorite cranberry muffins. In spite of how she felt, she was becoming a real homemaker—which included baking.

"What's the occasion? Should I dare ask?" Felicia questioned, eyeing her with curiosity, as she took a bite into the muffin. "Yummy. This is really good."

"There's no occasion. I just wanna show my appreciation for all the nice things you do for me," Allyson said.

"If you say so. But now I'm gonna start to worry. There's got to be a motive behind all this," Felicia said, as she eyed Allyson suspiciously, taking the last morsel of the muffin.

"What do you think of the idea of me going back to work, part time that is?"

"That's great, I guess," Felicia said as she stood up, swishing down the last drop of coffee. "If that's what you want. But who will take care of Benjamin?" she asked, as she picked up her briefcase.

"Well…I was thinking, maybe a day care center. There are some good ones around, Felice."

"We'll talk later," she said, as she turned for a split second before going out the door, giving her an uncertain look.

Allyson didn't think it mattered what Felicia thought. This was her life, and she was going to do what she felt was right, for her son and her.

CHAPTER 6

❀

"Good Morning. Cape Cod Realty. Taylor speaking. How can we be of service to you today?" the secretary asked, with a long sigh.

"Wow, that's a mouthful. How's it going?" Allyson asked.

"Wait a minute. I know this long lost voice…Ali, is it really you?" Taylor asked excitedly.

"It's me."

"It's so good to hear from you. What have you been up to?"

"Uh…playing Mom and all that good stuff."

"By the way, how is the little one? I'll bet he's getting big."

"He's almost six months."

"Wow. I wish you'd bring him by one of these days."

"I will."

Taylor had no children of her own, but she had a magical persuasion with those denizens of the small world. Whenever they cried, she'd make them laugh by making funny faces. She kept the kids entertained, and if she was busy, she'd give them some paper and a pencil so they could amuse themselves. The brokers and salesmen in the office adored her because they could conduct business much easier with their clients.

"We all miss you, Ali."

"I miss you guys too. That's another reason why I'm calling. I'd like to come back to work. Part-time that is, until Benjamin is older."

"That's wonderful. That's the best news I've heard today. Jack and Harold are out of the office right now. But Jack's expected any minute. I'll tell him the good news as soon as he walks in. I got your number here somewhere," she said. Allyson could hear her thumbing through that old Rolodex. "It hasn't changed, has it?"

"Nope. Thanks, Taylor. Talk to you soon."

"Hope to see you soon."

"Me too."

CHAPTER 7

"He looks just like Kyle," Felicia boasted. "Look at these tiny fingers and toes," she said excitedly, as she counted them, as if taking a count of each student in her class.

"There's really no way of knowing just yet who he'll look like. He's still too young. And all babies have blue eyes."

"Yeah true, but he's got his daddy's dark hair."

"I suppose," Allyson concluded.

At that moment in her reverie, the persistent ringing of the phone shattered thoughts of Kyle.

"Hello," she answered with considerable aggravation, at this disruption of her erotic and blissful musings.

"Are we having a bad day, today?" Harold Elliott asked. Her ex-boss. One of the owners of Cape Cod Realty.

"Oh, no. Everything is fine, Harold. How you doing?"

"Great. I got word you were interested in coming back to work. Am I correct?"

"You certainly are. That is, if you'll have me?"

"We'd love to have you back, Allyson. You were a great asset to our agency."

"Thanks."

"When would you like to start?"

Uh…as soon as I find a reputable day care for Benjamin, she thought. "Is next Monday okay?"

"That will be fine. See you then."

Allyson needed an escape from being solely a mother. She found herself slowly vegetating being at home, while constantly raiding the refrigerator. She did not want to fall back into the rut she was in when she was a teenager. The thoughts of becoming obese again terrified her. This is why she decided it was time to expand her horizons, and go back to work. Running, her favorite past time, just wasn't enough for Allyson. Sitting home day after day with Benjamin gave her excuses to fill her face, and this was beginning to depress her. She couldn't continue like this.

CHAPTER 8

After thoroughly investigating five-day care centers, Allyson finally chose Fairview Acres Day Care Center. Not only was it attractive to her because it was handy to where she worked, but it came highly recommended by Taylor Hart, their secretary at Cape Cod Realty. She knew the proprietor, who was also the schoolmaster, very well, through her family. And since Taylor had always been a good friend to Allyson, she trusted her judgment.

Fairview Acres was impeccably clean and had much to offer as far an enjoyment for the children. But most importantly, Allyson had a good feeling about the teachers. After speaking with them separately, she felt quite confident leaving Benjamin in their charge. They seemed to have a rich fondness for children. She felt strongly that Benjamin would be safe in this caring environment, enabling her to work to her full capacity without worrying about his well being.

Departing from her baby was harder than she had ever imagined. He clung to her dearly and wouldn't let go. His little hands were clenched tightly around her neck, as he buried his head into her chest and cried his heart out. When she attempted to release him, he howled even louder.

Most of the time, it had been only the two of them. They had become extremely attached in the short span of his young life. Allyson didn't realize it would be so difficult to let go of him that first day. This was a whole new experience for him and her. They really hadn't been apart since his birth, except when she had left him for a few hours here and there with Felicia or Aunt Edith. Her baby just wasn't used to being around strangers. She had no idea how upsetting it would get, for the both of them, to be separated. Allyson actually felt utterly cruel as she unfolded his small hands from her neck. But she knew she was doing the right thing. Her own eyes filled as she reluctantly handed him over to Karen, his new caretaker.

"Don't worry, Mom. He'll be fine. Trust me," she said, with much compassion, while taking Benjamin from her arms.

Allyson walked away slowly, and she didn't look back until she reached her car. A drop of water fell from the corner of her eye. Already she felt a condensed sense of what mothers felt when their children leave home to venture off on their very own. Even though she knew she was a long way from that scenario, she was experiencing an early taste of what it would feel like when it came to that inevitable moment in time. But now it was time to return to work.

CHAPTER 9

When she first passed through the double-glass doors of Cape Cod Realty, the first thing that caught her eye was this huge fluorescent banner, supported by a large beam, in the middle of the room, reading: "Welcome Back Allyson." A few of the guys were busy on the phones with business as usual, but the rest greeted her with a warm hello and a friendly handshake. Some even blew her a kiss.

"I'm so glad you're back," Taylor said, embracing her.

"Okay, enough of the mushy stuff. Let's get to work."

"Same ole Ali," she grinned.

When she sat down at her old desk, it felt almost as if she had never left. The official first day back seemed to hurtle past. She showed three houses to a prospective buyer. Later that afternoon, he returned with a binding deposit and an offer.

When she attempted to contact the sellers, there was no answer at their home. So she left a brief message on the answering machine, telling them she had someone interested in their property, but she received no response from them by the time she was ready to leave for the day.

She couldn't wait to see her Benjamin. She started to become apprehensive as she drove toward Fairview Acres. She prayed his day was as successful as hers for when she had left him in the morning, he had been so distraught. Putting her doubts behind her, she strolled confidently up the steps to the front door of the center. She wondered if he would be angry with her for leaving him in a strange place, filled with so many new faces. Her fears subsided when she peeked in and saw him settled in rather nicely amongst the other children, playing ardently with a medley of toys.

Once Karen spotted her, she immediately picked up Benjamin, from the play circle, and brought him to her.

"Hello, Mother. All went well, as you can see for yourself."

"Thank you," she said, taking him from her arms and smothering him with kisses.

❀   ❀   ❀

Allyson had slightly over an hour to be with her Ben alone before Felicia got home from school. She held him in her lap, and they played for awhile. But when he rubbed his eyes, she knew he was getting tired, so she put him in his playpen until she could fix him a bottle. But before the water was heated, he fell asleep. She covered him with his blanket. And just as she was walking away from his playpen, the phone rang, rather loudly. It was so earsplitting that Ben awoke, crying uncontrollably. She picked him up quickly, coddling him as she hurried to answer the disturbing ring.

"Hello," she all but yelled, unable to hear above Benjamin's wailing.

"Ms. Porteus, this is Mr. Hamilton."

"Who?" she shouted, above Ben's cries.

"It sounds like my timing is poor. Maybe I should call back?"

"No. Please wait. Just give me a minute," she pleaded.

Allyson put Benjamin in his crib this time, reassuring him of her presence and giving him quick pecks on each cheek. Then she gave him his bottle. He took it gratefully, closing his eyes, calming himself.

"Sorry to keep you waiting, Mr. Hamilton."

"It seems like you got your hands full, young lady."

"He's worth it. Believe me."

"I'm returning your call to let you know I can't go $10,000. less."

"Do you have a counter offer, Mr. Hamilton? I know you've been trying to sell this house for over a year. It's not in the best location, you know."

"Yeah, you're right. I guess I can drop it another $5,000. But that's my final offer. I can't let it go for less than $145,000."

"All we can do is keep our fingers crossed. I'll get back to you as soon as I hear from Mr. Jones. Talk to you soon."

After hanging up the phone, Allyson hurried into the bedroom to check on Benjamin. He was sound asleep. He looked so peaceful. His body was very long in this early stage of his young life. He was an incredible baby; no one would ever believe he was once in an incubator, so small and frail, clinging to life. She remembered the kind woman who stood next to her at the nursery's window in the hospital, trying to convince her that her son would be as healthy and as tall as her son turned out to be after being in an incubator.

Knowing Ben was fine, safe in his crib, she called Calvin Jones. On the first ring he picked up the phone.

"Mr. Jones, Ms. Porteus here. I just got off the phone with Mr. Hamilton. He's willing to come down $5,000. more. But that's his final offer. What do you think?"

"No. No. That's still too much money."

Sure, she thought. He's one of the wealthiest old-timers in the town of Eastham. But then again, that's probably why he's loaded.

"Let's try and negotiate one more time. How about if we ask him to split that difference, reducing the price another $2500. Does that sound reasonable to you?"

"Yeah. Yeah. That will do," he said, in his scratchy voice.

"I'll try to reach him tonight. If not, hang in there; he's a very busy man. I'll get back to you one way or another first thing in the morning. You'll be on the top of my list. Sound good?"

"Yup." Clunk went the receiver in her ear. I need clients like this, she told herself. He's so sweet and understanding.

By this time, Allyson was wiped out. It was four thirty, and Felicia still wasn't home. She began supper. It was a good night for hot dogs and beans. She could hear Ben playing with his mobile above his crib. She was glad he was awake and playing quietly. Allyson knew if he slept any longer, he'd be up half the night. Just then, she heard Felicia's key in the door.

"How'd it go today?" she asked.

"Not bad. Not bad at all. I'm beginning to feel it now though. But once the routine sets in…. Actually, it felt rather good, getting back to the old grind again. It was tough leaving Benjamin, but once I saw how happy he was when I picked him up, I felt much better."

"That's good. I'm glad everything turned out well for the both of you. What do I smell burning?" she asked, sniffing.

"Oh, no!" Allyson shrieked, running over to the stove. They were hot dogs," she cried, lamenting over the pan of dried up, black sticks.

"I wasn't all that hungry anyway," Felicia said, with more than just a touch of mirth in her voice.

"Think it's funny, huh? I never proclaimed to be a cook," Allyson said, grinning.

After Ben was asleep, they spent a quiet evening together. Felicia worked on some assignments for the following day, and Allyson watched an old mystery on TV. Periodically, during commercials, she called Mr. Hamilton, but couldn't reach him.

CHAPTER 10

The phones were ringing off their hooks at the office. Everyone seemed to have spring fever. Mr. Jones had called twice already, but Allyson had no answer for him yet. Other than the fall, this was the best selling season. People seemed to come out of their shells after the long drawn-out winter. Owners would flock down from their winter homes to reopen their cottages, and contemplate on whether to sell their property in order to purchase something new.

"Allyson, line two. Mr. Hamilton returning your call," Taylor announced.

"Hello, Mr. Hamilton. A lovely day today. Did you get my message?"

"Yes. I would have called you sooner, but I wanted to consult with my attorney first."

"And?" She waited patiently, with her fingers crossed. She needed this commission. She had used up practically all of her savings on hospital bills that were still coming to her.

"He said go for it."

"That's wonderful news. Mr. Jones will be pleased to hear that," she said, giving Taylor the thumbs up signal as she walked past her desk.

The closing was set for three weeks from now, after the termite and septic system inspections had been completed, and approved. If all went as expected, in a few short weeks, she could count on a big check!

One of their salesmen was out ill, and Allyson was elected to report to the registry of deeds in Barnstable for a closing. She didn't object, since there was a small fee in it for her.

Allyson arrived promptly at 11:00 A.M. with all the paper work needed to proceed with the closing. She was to meet with the buyer and the seller.

Stupidly, she'd forgotten to get a description of the two. She had no clue as to who she'd single out from the cluster of people standing around, waiting to meet with their agents. She had just assumed they would be well dressed since this was a half a million-dollar sale. The home wasn't worth a quarter of its asking price, but its excellent location was the contributing factor. This old house stood lopsided on a bluff, overlooking the boundless ocean. Despite its deteriorating condition, the breathtaking view from the old Cape home was worth every penny.

After examining each long table carefully, in the large room where agents and clients, along with their lawyers, sat to finalize their business, Allyson came to the ultimate conclusion that her clients were not present. No one seemed to look out of place. There was a clan of lawyers conservatively dressed in dark suits hovering around a rectangular table, which had incredibly large books, containing thousands of deeds and maps of sundry properties.

Other counselors stood patiently, waiting to be served at the counter, where aides would assist them in establishing new deeds, accepting filing fees, or help them with other pertinent information needed to complete their transactions.

Each time a new face entered the room, appearing confused as to which direction should be taken, Allyson hoped she was the one the person was looking for. But every time she graciously approached a distressed-looking gentleman, he'd glare at her, looking somewhat annoyed, and would simply shake his head negatively. She kept pacing the floor, frequently looking at her watch. The men and women who identified with one another from the start and were seated at the long tables lined up on one side of the room near an array of windows were now shaking hands, indicating they had summarized their business.

At 11:15 A.M., Allyson strolled back into the foyer, where she sat on a sturdy wooden bench. She pulled the purchase and sale agreement from her briefcase to verify the date and time of the closing. She was correct. It read: June 16th, 11:00 A.M. Her clients were late. Both parties. She reached into her purse to find a dime to call the office, hoping to get an explanation as to why no one showed up. At the same time, she could get a basic description of who she was supposed to be representing.

When Allyson found that she had the opportunity, she walked swiftly over to the pay phone. Her pocketbook dangled from her left shoulder, and she was carrying her briefcase in her right hand. Just as she was about to place the briefcase on the floor in front of her so that she could make the call, someone tapped her lightly on her right shoulder. She jumped!

"Excuse me. I didn't mean to startle you."

"No problem. I guess I'm just a little on edge."

"Are you Miss Porteus?"

"Yes. How may I help you?"

"Hi, I'm Marc Kelsey, I'm representing the bank, on Mr. Schuller's behalf," he said, extending his hand.

"I was just about to ring my office to see what happened. I'm just filling in…. The person who's been handling this sale is out today."

"I know. I called Cape Cod Realty. I was just informed myself—there's been some minor complications. Mr. O'Neil had a heart attack last night. The closing has been postponed."

She stood in bewilderment for a few seconds, amazed at how deep and manly this guy's voice was, after staring into his apologetic, boyish face. "I'm not sure it's a minor problem, for them at least. A heart attack is a very serious thing," she said coolly.

"Forgive me. Of course it is. I didn't mean to sound so ruthless. What I meant is—the deal will go forward anyway. Mr. O'Neil has had a history of heart disease. His wife has agreed in writing to take care of things. In the last three years, knowing his health was failing, he liquidated many of his assets so that she'd have enough money to take care of their property if something should happen to him."

"I see. Well, that's too bad. I hope he'll be all right," she said, grimacing.

Mr. Kelsey looked at his watch. "It's nearly twelve. Lunch time. Can I interest you in a light lunch? Do you have time?"

He was a typical lawyer in the way that he dressed, with his dark gray suit, and also in the manner in which he verbally expressed himself. His conservative mannerisms also fitted his highly respected profession. But there was something more appealing about him than his stuffed-shirt attitude and boyish face, spotted with dozens of pale freckles, which attracted her to him.

"Why not," she said, smiling up at him.

CHAPTER 11

They crossed the street to a small but quaint restaurant. The solid structure had an authentic look and wafted a musty odor, but it was warm and attractive. Many of the bigwigs from the courthouse complex had their lunches here so she figured the food was good.

Here she was sitting directly across from this complete stranger, whom she had just met only moments before, and was about to have lunch with him. And to her incredulity, she seemed to be totally intrigued with Mr. Marc Kelsey. Allyson was actually enjoying herself for the first time in a long time. He made her laugh by telling her hilarious jokes about lawyers and their clients. He tried to lower his deep voice, nearly bobbing his head against hers from across the table, so that no one could hear, because his peers surrounded them, and he wasn't sure they'd appreciate his humor. He was the exact opposite of Kyle, but she liked him nevertheless. He had an open sincerity that attracted her to him.

"I see no wedding band," he said, looking at her hands.

"How observant you are, Mr. Kelsey."

"You can call me Marc—especially now that we know each other so well," he said, glancing at his watch. "After all, we've been together just shy of thirty minutes. And since life is moving on, why wait? I'd like to take the liberty—in case I don't get this wonderful opportunity again—to ask you for a real date," he implored her with his dark brown eyes. "Unless, there's someone else?"

"First of all, there is no one in my life right now."

She thought about Kyle for an instant, but he had made no attempt to see his son. What was he to her anyway? Whatever they once had together had fizzled when she got pregnant. Kyle had no claims on her, and it was becoming quite obvious he didn't care about her—or about his son.

"And second of all, I'd be happy to have a real date with a real man," she said soberly.

They tried to restrain themselves from chortling, but just as the waitress brought the check over to their table, they spontaneously burst into a chorus of full-blown laughter.

"Will there be anything else?" she asked, looking at them rather strangely. Neither one of them could answer they were chuckling so. They just shook their heads and hands, indicating a no response.

She placed the check in front of Marc and walked away, shaking her head.

It was a terrific lunch. Allyson had never felt more relaxed with anyone. Her date made her laugh, and he was easy to talk with. He walked her to her car, and they exchanged their business cards. This was like an informal invite to a nice friendship. In any event, she knew she wanted to pursue it. He kindly shook her hand, thanking her for her 'sweet hospitality,' and she expressed her gratitude in return. He said he would call her as soon as he checked his schedule, and she believed him.

CHAPTER 12

Days passed and weeks followed, and there was no word from Marc Kelsey. Allyson wondered if he was no different than Kyle. She didn't need the aggravation, or the torture. She still had his business card with his phone number on it, but she was resolute not to make the first move.

One Saturday morning, around eight o'clock, as she was getting ready for work, the phone rang. She was never in a hurry to get to the office too early on the weekends. Even though they were busy days for the agency, vacationers liked to sleep in.

"It's for you. Some gentleman, with a deep voice, asking for a Miss Allyson," Felicia said with a grin, trying to imitate his voice, while cuffing the receiver, so he wouldn't hear her mock him.

"Cute. Real cute," Allyson said, yanking the phone from her.

"Miss Allyson Porteus here. With whom am I speaking?"

"Sorry to disturb you so early—knowing the real-estate business as I do, the weekends are usually the craziest."

"So very true. But those tourists seldom rise before mid-morning. I'm still not sure with whom I am speaking," she said, bantering him. "Announce yourself, please."

"My apology. Mr. Marc Kelsey reporting to Miss Allyson Porteus," he said.

"I'm sorry. Why, it's been so long since our last encounter, I nearly forgot the sound of your voice," she said quite soberly, with just a touch of a southern drawl.

"Ah, you're too much," he said with a small chuckle. "You probably think I'm like the rest of them—never call when they say they will. The truth is—I've never stopped thinking about you. This is not a line. I had to contend with some family matters. I've been out of town for awhile."

"I hope everything is all right?" She didn't want to pry, but she didn't want to give him the impression she was heartless either.

"Well…it was something that required my attention. Things are stable for the time being, which is why I'm calling. Would you be free tomorrow night—to join me for dinner—at the Sea Breeze Inn in Chatham? And maybe later—we could catch a movie?"

"Wow, that's my favorite spot. I'd be delighted to join you."

"Phew. I was afraid you'd turn me down. Somebody up there is being good to me."

"I think I'm too particular."

"I hope it's to my advantage? Is 7:00 P.M. all right?"

"That's perfect," she said, knowing Benjamin should be asleep by then—or pretty close.

"Let's see…12 Beach Road must be somewhere near the beach."

"Yup. Take a sharp right down by Irwins Shack off 6A, and follow that back road till you come to Beach Road. We're the fourth house on the left. It's the red one with black shutters. You'll see my Saab in the driveway."

"Until then—so long, Allyson."

"So long, Marc."

"What was that all about?" Felicia asked with open cat ears.

"Well, I didn't want to say anything, until I knew for sure myself."

"What? You used to tell me everything," Felicia said wryly.

"Yeah, well…that was before my life became so screwed up. My track record with men hasn't been the greatest."

"At least you're getting them. There's still no excitement in my life," Felicia said pensively.

Allyson didn't have the heart to tell her that if she dressed a bit more provocative, they'd be swarming around her like bees on honey. She had hinted to her once about changing her appearance, but Felicia was appalled by her gesture. From that day on, she decided to keep her opinions to herself.

"Oh, come on. Don't be that way. How does the saying go? Those who wait…I forget how it's worded, but you'll find somebody—real soon. You'll see. Some gorgeous hunk of a man will be seeking to find a wonderful teacher, like yourself, to be his wife…and the mother of his children."

"Oh brother…in my dreams. It sounds good except for one thing."

"What?"

"I prefer to have my own children, but I'll take his kids too—if I have to. At the rate I'm going, I can't afford to be too fussy."

"Dreams keep us bound. Nevertheless, it doesn't sound so far-fetched to me. There's someone out there for everybody," Allyson said rushing around, trying to get ready.

"You guys mean a lot to me?"

"Ditto. I gotta go," Allyson said, hugging her quickly. "Give Benjamin a kiss for me. Thanks, Felice. And don't give up the ship. Your dream boat may be the captain," she said, smiling at her.

CHAPTER 13

Saturday morning, as usual, was purely hectic at the real-estate office. Before Allyson realized it, it was running close to five. Marc was picking her up at 7:00 P.M. Thank goodness for Taylor. She told her confidentially that she had a date with Marc, and she helped her as much as she could with summer rentals. Taylor had directed many of the common tenant complaints to some of the idle agents, who were sitting around dreading the unavoidable. And Allyson was grateful for her cooperation in assisting her with the overload of paper work. At 5:40 P.M., she winked at Taylor and barreled out of there.

When she got home, all was calm. Ben was playing quietly in his playpen with his toys. As soon as he saw her, his little arms stretched out to her, and he began to whine. She hurried over to him, picked him up and hugged him snugly. Then she kissed his forehead.

"I missed you, Benjamin. What did you and Felicia do today? As if I don't know. These dark stains on your shirt are all the evidence I need."

He smiled tiredly, his little mouth working in silent motion. He tried so hard to express himself, but only cooing sounds emerged.

"We went for a long walk down by the beach, and then we skipped over for an ice cream at the Ice Cream Parlor. Delicious creamy chocolate. Hmm...two big scoops."

"Make my mouth water, Felice. Go ahead, rub it in. And while I drool, tell me what to wear tonight."

"How about your black twill pants and your white sleeveless blouse. That always looks so pretty on you. Especially with your dark hair. You've got enough color already, so the white will look dashing, and the dark pants will make you look slim. Not that you aren't anyway."

"Good choice. He mentioned a movie afterwards. The nights are still chilly, maybe I should bring a sweater."

There wasn't much time to dilly-dally. She surmised that Marc was a man of promptness. And sure enough, her calculations were right. She was touching up her make-up, when she heard his knock at exactly 7:00 P.M.

He looked fantastic. He wore beige Dockers pants, a casual striped polo shirt, covered with a black V-neck sweater. He wasn't drop-dead handsome, but he was very cute with his freckles and his small reddish-blonde mustache. He reminded her of Michael J. Fox, but a taller version.

She introduced him to Felicia, and for a split second she almost skimmed over her son, who was right there in plain sight. Allyson wondered at first if he would be interested in her, if he knew she had a son. She wondered if he would have called, if she had told him from the start. But hell, her son meant everything to her, and if Marc Kelsey had a problem with that too bad. It would be his loss, not hers. At least that's what she kept trying to tell herself.

"Marc, I'd like you to meet my son, Benjamin," she said proudly.

"Very nice to meet you, young man," he said, while lifting Benjamin's little hand delicately into his own, giving him a gentle shake.

Ben smiled at first, and then eyed him suspiciously, as he started to wail. He cried for such a long time, she thought her evening was ruined. This stranger was intruding on his privacy. No man had trespassed through their front door since Benjamin was born, and hearing Marc's deep male voice frightened him. Just Marc's presence was threatening enough.

Allyson gave Ben a kiss and smiled assuredly to show him that his mommy wasn't afraid of this man. Then she shook Marc's hand, smiling warmly, to let Benjamin know Marc was an all right person and wasn't there to harm them.

Once Ben felt secure again, he lay down with his bottle and dozed off. Marc looked a little awkward standing there. He was in an uncomfortable situation, not knowing she had a son. And the scene Benjamin had just displayed would have scared any man who wasn't used to children. Fortunately, Marc didn't seem bothered by Ben's conduct, or else he was a fabulous actor.

It was time to escape while they could. Felicia gave her her approval with a nod, and they tiptoed out of there, closing the door quietly behind them.

Allyson waited nervously for Marc to fire out the first question concerning Benjamin. With the quietness lingering heavily, she cracked her window and inhaled slowly the cool fresh air. What was she supposed to tell him? The truth? Or fabricate, and tell him Benjamin was left on her doorstep?

"You have a beautiful son, Allyson. He looks like his mother."

She knew he didn't, but she answered with a simple, "Thank you."

"You must be proud."

"Very," she said smiling, as she took a long sigh of relief.

"I would like a son someday. Children make the world go 'round."

He made her feel good, and right from that moment she was at ease with him. She never said anything about Ben's father. There was no reason to mention him, and Marc didn't inquire.

CHAPTER 14

The Sea Breeze Inn was packed as usual. Being a weekend night and being the most popular place around, they had a twenty-minute wait before being seated. The bar was crowded with all the locals. The preppy businessmen were socializing and sniffing out their prey for the night. Allyson couldn't help but overhear some of their lies. Some women were so desperate, they'd believe anything.

This was the place where Kyle and she had met secretly, on more than one occasion. However, they weren't fooling anyone here. She thought the majority of people in town had speculated they were having an affair, but that knowledge somehow stayed subdued. She caught a few women whispering when they thought she wasn't looking. When she would turn to glare at them, they'd snicker, then mosey on with whatever they were doing.

Once they finally got seated, at a table for two, Marc ordered a bottle of red wine.

"I wanna know all about Allyson Porteus. Where she's from? What she likes and doesn't like? What her dreams are? Her expectations?"

He leaned toward her with a broad grin that resembled a young boy's. Only that deep manly voice of his hinted to her that she really wasn't keeping company with a boy. There was someone awfully mature and very much worthwhile behind that young looking face.

"There's really not much to tell. I grew up in New York. I studied journalism at New York State. I'm Irish and Greek. My mom was Irish, and my dad is Greek. I was a chunky teenager. I love to run the beach. And…that's about it," she said smiling.

"Uh, but I detect there is much much more. But in due time, my dear Allyson. In due time," he said with dancing eyes.

Marc was so different from Kyle, but in a preferred way actually. He had an amiable flair about him.

The waitress approached their table and took their order.

"You haven't told me anything about yourself. We've only chatted about me. I need to know what type of man I'm dining with. Is he wild and crazy beneath his subdued exterior? Could he be a subtle serial killer?"

"I could keep you in suspense, but since you must know—I'm Superman in disguise," he grinned broadly. "But seriously, I have two older sisters, and one younger than myself. You can imagine what that was like growing up. I went to parochial school for eight years, until I couldn't take it anymore. Then I broke loose like a stud horse, and enrolled in a heterosexual high school. I courted every girl who would have me—which wasn't too many. I never found my true love," he said gravely.

"How sad," she said, while resting her elbows on the table, her hands holding up her chin, looking deeply into his mischievous brown eyes. His dry sense of humor made her grin.

After Allyson had gobbled up the bowl of salad and the banana bread, she wasn't sure she'd be able to touch her entree dinner. When it finally came, she had no trouble finding room for the tasty Alfredo and tender chicken.

She excused herself and headed for the ladies room, hoping to relieve some of the pressure from all that delicious food. Allyson had to channel through the crowd and past the bar area. To her amazement, she saw Kyle sitting on one of the high-chaired stools, drinking with his friends, and flirting with a bleached blond. She hurried into the bathroom, hoping he wouldn't notice her. The old feelings were stirring up again. Her knees felt weak, and her hands were trembling.

What's happening, she wondered? He had that much effect on her still? This is ludicrous, she kept telling herself. "Why am I letting this man upset me so?" She wondered. Allyson knew when she accepted Marc's invitation to dinner that there would be a possibility of Kyle being there. The Sea Breeze Inn was one of his favorite hangouts. But she never thought he'd still have this much influence over her. She stayed in the powder room till she regained her composure. The trembling finally subsided. And after combing her hair numerous times, she knew she had to get back to Marc. He had to be getting concerned. So she scurried out of there, aimed in one direction only. She wanted to reach their table as quickly as she could.

But as soon as Allyson approached the bar section, which was in her trail back to their table, she became inert. Kyle was lighting a cigarette for a bleached blond in a fire engine red dress. Her gross, oversized bosoms were practically sitting on the glossy bar. He never even noticed her till the woman whispered something in his ear, whereupon he slowly turned around. Her eyes met his and locked. A moment later, he jumped off the stool and ambled over to her.

"Allyson, what are you doing here?"

"What do you mean, what am I doing here? I have a life too, you know. By the way, who's the bimbo?" she asked, glaring at the woman, who was taking a surveillance, while smirking cunningly at her.

"Nobody special. Just somebody I met at the bar. She's married."

"So—what difference does that make?" Allyson asked angrily. She was acting like a jealous shrew, but she couldn't help herself.

"We need to talk," he said, smelling of liquor.

"How many times have I heard that? All the times you said you were coming and never did," Allyson said, seething with even more anger now.

"How's our son?" he asked nonchalantly.

"Our son! You have the audacity…. You haven't even seen him," she said, raising her voice above the noise.

"It hasn't been easy."

"Oh, I can see that," she said, waving the dense cigarette smoke out of her face, as she peered over his shoulder at the blond woman in the red dress, who was still waiting for Kyle to return to her. "You son of a b…" she said, lashing out at him with her hand. He seized her wrist just as she was fixed upon slapping that deceptive face of his.

"I like feisty women. Did I tell you, you're looking mighty good these days?" he said, grinning from ear to ear.

This really turned him on, and she was ready to kick herself for giving him the satisfaction. But when she looked into his eyes, she began reliving all those past emotions—so crazed and powerful, stirring up in her all over again. And the sad thing was, he knew exactly what he was doing to her. That's what irritated her even more.

"Believe what you want, Ali, but I do think about our son. I know you don't believe me, but I do. I wanna see him. Really," he said, looking sincere.

"Prove it. I gotta go," she said, when she saw Marc heading towards them. "I'm with someone," she emphasized, walking away.

"With who?" She heard him yell. However, she continued walking through the heavy traffic of people, standing around the bar, and she didn't look back.

Marc could sense she was upset. He had to have seen them. He asked her warily if she wanted dessert, and she just shook her head. He motioned to the waitress for the check.

"I thought you deserted me," Marc said.

"I'm sorry. I bumped into an old friend. I got a little carried away," she explained, as they were walking to the front door of the inn. Allyson took one last glance at Kyle before leaving. His eyes were, unmistakably, focused upon them. Good, she thought.

"Was that Kyle Riker you were speaking to?" Marc asked, when they were safe in the car.

"Yeah, that was him. You know him?"

"I was his wife's attorney for a short time. She bought some land in California."

"Really," Allyson said, greatly intrigued now.

"She's the kind of woman who wants things done yesterday, if you know what I mean. I was temporarily filling in for Alex Gordon—her family's attorney—for years. He's getting up there in age. It was too much for him to travel that far to clear a title. I didn't mind—it was easy money. And that's when I got the pleasure of meeting both of them, briefly.

From what I could see—you and Kyle seemed pretty intense over something."

"You're going to find out eventually, so you might as well know now." She paused. "Kyle Riker is my son's father," she announced meekly.

"I sort of gathered it was something more than just a casual acquaintance, between you both. I compiled all the circumstantial evidence I needed, during your fired-up rage."

"A typical lawyer's conclusion. We did have something special once, but it's over now."

"Is it, Allyson?"

"Yes. He owes me child support. I'm just angry about that."

She must have sounded unconvincing, because he gave her this disbelief look. Plus, her face couldn't navigate a lie without deceiving her. And she was thankful when the subject of Kyle was quickly dropped.

They still had time to catch a flick. They missed the first fifteen minutes, but they soon figured they were only missing the advertisements. She was determined not to let Kyle Riker ruin her evening—or her life! Her concentration was solely on the scenes on the screen. Not that she was unaware of her companion sitting closely beside her—a man who still brought her here, in spite of the touchy situation they had just left.

They were perched in their theater seats like two teenagers, chomping away on popcorn while sipping a Coke through a straw. Marc put his arm around her a few times to comfort her, when he saw her rise from her seat during some of the unexpected horror scenes. He was not too forward, and she respected him for being a complete gentleman. Regardless, Allyson wasn't ready, by any means, to jump into anything right now.

On the way home, she wondered what Marc was feeling. And if he would ever want to see her again? He had been a good sport for not backing out of the date after learning about Benjamin and then her involvement with Kyle. This man had discovered too much too soon. He hadn't even gotten the chance to really know her. And he already had enough of a glimpse of her life to scare him away for good.

Marc was quiet as they drove back to her place. Of course, it was late and they were both very tired. Then, unexpectedly, he asked what she had hoped he wouldn't.

"Are you still in love with him?"

She hesitated before answering. "I don't know. I don't think so, but I'm not sure. I don't want to be," she admitted, with a tear escaping her eye.

"That's all right. I got time. I'm not going anywhere," he said.

She wondered how much time he was talking about. Would those ceaseless pains that Kyle had inflicted on her ever go away? Allyson thought she was getting over him. She thought she would hate him for abandoning her and his son. She thought that after all the time that had passed there would be nothing left, but instead seeing Kyle again only added fuel to the burning desire she obviously still had for him.

Marc pulled slowly into her gravel driveway, put the car in park and turned to look at her.

"You're home. You're safe," he said with a slight smile. A smile that seemed forced.

She wasn't ready to divulge her deepest thoughts to him. It would only dampen the little they already had together. He bent over and kissed her. And when his warm lips met hers, she felt something. It was a delightful sensation, but she didn't know if it was her hunger for affection, or if she was truly attracted to this nice man. All she knew was that she didn't want to release her lips from his.

"Thanks for everything. Call me." she said, hopping out of the car and closing the door.

"I will," he said through his open window. "And take care of that little guy. He's special." He waited until she got in, then drove away.

She sat in the dark for a long time thinking about her life, wondering where she went wrong. Flashbacks of various stages in her childhood tumbled into focus. She saw her dad trying to catch a snapshot of her on a decorative horse as the carousel circled hooplike, round and round. He looked so young and debonair. Allyson was proud to have him for her dad.

She remember vividly when they would walk to the local bakery, a quarter of a mile from their house. It made no difference what the weather was like; he and Allyson would stroll, hand in hand, every Saturday to Sam's bakery. Her dad would always buy bread for her mother, freshly baked that day, sometimes still warm from the oven. Then he'd pick out the biggest and most delicious eclairs ever. One for him, and one for her. And they'd delightfully devour them before they got home. They made a promise not to tell mother, for she'd say they were spoiling their dinner. It was their little secret.

When she was small, she told her dad once that she was afraid of the bogeyman. He had comforted her, by telling her no beast, or bully would ever harm his precious little sweetheart, as long as he was around. And the following day, he purchased a night light for her. Allyson believed in him, and eventually her silly fears vanished. She no longer needed a light in her room. She felt safe just knowing her dad was there to protect her. And she wished he was sitting beside her now, telling her how he'd chase away that ubiquitous bogeyman of her childhood.

Felicia quietly emerged from her bedroom in her stocking feet.

"I thought I heard you come in. Why are you sitting in the dark?"

"I don't know. Just thinking."

"How was your night?" she asked in a low voice.

"Pretty good, until I ran into Kyle. That screwed up everything."

"Are you serious? Where? What happened!"

"You know we went to the Sea Breeze Inn for dinner?" she asked, with a long deep sigh.

Felicia nodded.

"Well, I went to the ladies' room—and there he was, sitting at the bar—with some bleached-blond bimbo."

"What happened?"

"I lost it."

"Yeah…. What'd ya say?"

"I just mentioned the fact that he hasn't taken any interest in wanting to see Ben. I didn't want him to know how much it bothered me, but he ticked me off so much after seeing him with that woman, I blew it."

"Did he know you were with Marc?"

"Yeah. I'm pretty sure."

"At least you showed him that you're not just sitting around waiting for him. And just because you're a mother now, doesn't mean you don't have a life."

"Then why can't I just forget about him and go on with it?"

"Do you still love him?"

"I don't know what I feel anymore. Marc asked me the same question."

"What'd ya tell him?"

"The same thing I'm telling you. I'm confused, Felice. All I know is—Marc's a wonderful person—I don't want my screwed-up feelings to hurt our friendship," she said, as she rose from the sofa and walked toward her bedroom.

"Goodnight, Felice."

"Nite."

CHAPTER 15

It was a very warm summer morning. Allyson unlatched the screen door and picked up the Sunday edition. Felicia was still asleep, and Benjamin was in his crib wrestling with sounds, trying to form words. She sat down with a mug of strong, steaming coffee. After she disposed of the circulars, the comics and the classifieds, the bulky newspaper was now quite flimsy. In the worldly news, there was an article about the AIDS virus. She skimmed over it. It made her shudder, but she knew they had nothing to worry about. As she quickly glanced over each page, her attention was soon drawn to an article written by a man named Carlos, who wrote in the town's best interest. Emphasized in large bold print was:

"Elect Janice Caldwell for your local Representative." Born and raised in Chatham, and only daughter of the late honorable Henry Caldwell of Chatham. Janice is married with two grown children, Sarah and Jennifer. She was educated at Harvard University and graduated third in her class, earning a degree in business administration. She also served as town selectman for three consecutive terms, beginning in 1975.

She felt nauseated as she continued reading, but she couldn't put the paper down. I could never compete with this woman, she thought. No wonder Kyle would never leave her. Why would anyone give up a life of luxury, and the opportunity to be recognized and respected by people from the upper crust? So absorbed in the article, she never heard the phone ringing till she saw Felicia wandering aimlessly into the kitchen, rubbing her eyes.

"Good morning," she answered cheerfully, amused by Felicia's frazzled hair, flying off in all directions.

"Allyson, I need to see you," Kyle said, sounding desperate.

"My time is valuable too, you know. Who is this?" she asked.

"Okay, Allyson, let's cut the bull," he said, sounding fed up.

"Who gets the bigger piece," she bantered, knowing the game was in her ballpark for once.

"Okay you win. I'm sorry about last night. About everything. Give me another chance," he implored.

It was all right for him to be a gigolo...a philanderer...a Casanova.... But when the shoe went on the other foot, it became a completely different scenario.

"Just like that, huh Kyle. I should give you another chance? Should we begin where we left off?"

"We are a family, Ali."

"How do you figure?"

"Can we start over, Ali?"

"When did you say you were divorcing Janice—and marrying me? Are those your intentions?"

"Ali, we'll talk about it tonight. Can you meet me at the Shady Tree—around eight?" He didn't wait for her to answer. "Please be there. Gotta go," he said, and then he hung up.

She didn't know if he couldn't accept a rejection, or whether Janice had just entered the room. Every opportunity Janice got, she would spy on Kyle. Not that there were too many of those opportunities, because her political involvement played a much greater part and took much of her time. She had alleged to care for Kyle, but it was apparent, to Allyson anyhow, that he was nothing more than a commodity that came second in her life, politics being the first.

She'd flaunt her young stallion in front of her cliquey group of women friends, and they'd virtually water at the mouth, green with envy. Allyson and Benjamin had much more to offer Kyle than this phony circle of BS. But money, and all the prestige that accompanies it, was much more appealing to Kyle, than all the love that they could possibly give.

CHAPTER 16

It was a slow day at the office. She thought she'd be grateful for that, but it gave her too much time to think. Her jumbled mind kept racing from Kyle to Marc, Marc to Kyle, like a large pendulum swinging freely to and fro, weighing their differences. Since Kyle was Ben's father, he would automatically love and care for him more than Marc would. But she wasn't confident in that evaluation—whatsoever. Marc was more compassionate and understanding. And the big plus was—he was not married! She had a headache by the end of the day, from all the heavy shuffling her poor, battered brain was trying to negotiate. She was trying to determine which man would be the best for them, when she didn't even have the final word on the situation.

That evening, she drove to the Shady Tree to meet Kyle. She didn't want to give in and show up, but he knew she would. And regardless of what the end results might be from this colloquial exchange, a compelling force seemed to pull her along with barely any resistance. She had to put to rest the agony of not knowing where she stood with him. Was there a chance to find happiness together, or was he going to string her along all over again, making her believe there might be a future for them one day?

The moment she saw Kyle she was succulently whisked into his arms, after being captivated by his deep-blue kaleidoscopic eyes, and his award-winning charm. He knew exactly what turned her on, and using his playful tactics he lured her into the back seat of the stretch limo with a bottle of wine. When she got inside, everything was set up, perfectly, for a convenient seduction. The two wine goblets. The crackers and cheese. Soft music. The whole nine yards. She was his puppet, and she let him work her strings. What did she expect?

"How quaint. Anything in mind, here?" she asked, with a touch of sarcasm in her tone, very much aware of what his intentions were.

"No. I just thought it would be a good place to talk."

And what else? Kyle was not the kind of man who could express himself openly. He thought making love resolved any conflict. It's what he believed he did best, and she couldn't argue with him there. His lovemaking was so robust sometimes, nothing else seemed to matter. Any problems they had together were conquered, at least temporarily.

"How you been?" she asked sardonically, pouring a glass of wine.

"I wish you wouldn't be so hard on me," he said, gently stroking her hair with his fingers.

"I have every right to be. You deserted your son and me. Why haven't you come to see him?"

"Guilt, I guess. I'm afraid that once I see him—I won't be able to turn away."

"Is that so terrible? Don't answer. I don't want to hear what you have to say."

"What'd ya doing with Marc Kelsey?"

"Oh, so, this is what it's all about. You can't have me when you want anymore. I don't belong to you," she said in anger, and with tears.

"I was wrong—I admit it. I can't change what has happened—I can make it up to you and Benjamin."

"Do you mean that?" she asked, looking into those cunning eyes—which were now telling her to trust him. The elevator music and the wine not only had set the romantic ambiance, but they provoked old feelings. Kyle was making promises she knew he couldn't keep, but she listened to him, nonetheless, and for some crazy reason she believed he was going to follow through this time.

They made love, over and over again, in the limo, until they fell wearily into an unconscious state. At 1:00 A.M., closing time for the Shady Tree, they were aroused abruptly by some boisterous commotion in the parking lot. A rambunctious crowd had just exited, or was bounced out from the tacky joint nearby. One belligerent drunk banged on the limo's tinted windows, looking for a ride home. Kyle told the creep to wait a minute, but the man was persistent.

They got dressed in a flash. Then Kyle rolled down his window to tell the intoxicated creature to knock it off. He asked him politely to take a hike, but the fellow wouldn't leave. The longhaired, unshaven offender became increasingly obnoxious, and Kyle's patience was wearing thin. The second time Kyle rolled down the window to try and reason with the nasty drunk, the man took a swing at him.

He jumped out of the car enraged, and gave the guy one big slug in the gut. And considering the size of him, it was a surprise when he fell backwards. But this irritated him even more. Just as Kyle was turning away, to get the keys out of his pockets so that they could get out of there, the staggering drunk lunged at him with a pocketknife.

Allyson screamed.

"Watch out, Kyle! He's got a…knife," she yelled. And Kyle turned just as the blade gouged him.

She let out another loud scream for help, but the few people that had been loitering had already split. The scene was becoming violent. Too violent. This was something that happened in the movies or in other parts of the state, but not on Cape Cod. Here she was in the midst of it all.

Kyle, angrier than ever from the repercussion, swiftly kicked him in the crotch with his foot, and the assailant dropped like a swatted fly in sheer agony. In the meantime, Allyson wasted no time scooping up the keys that Kyle had dropped on the ground, and nervously turned the ignition key. As the limo's motor droned, she shouted to him to get in.

Suddenly, she became stupefied, spotting the blood dripping from his arm. Then something like a rock or a pebble struck the side of the car. That quickly shook her from her trance, and she pressed the gas pedal to the floor, all the while keeping one eye on the bad guy through the side mirror as he chased them on foot. Then as they turned the corner to exit the parking lot, she saw him fall flat on his face. Evidently, he had fallen into one of the ruts in the road. They kept moving.

Once they were safely out of sight, she pulled the limo over to tend to Kyle's wound. He saw the blood gushing out of his arm and passed out. She tore her blouse to make a tourniquet for his arm, hoping it would stop the bleeding, at least until they got to the hospital.

She chose the highway, the fastest route to the Cape Cod hospital. They had the double lane highway to themselves, and she pushed the gas pedal almost to the floor.

About halfway there, a dark colored Dodge Charger, probably a 1970, appeared from out of nowhere. The Charger was in the passing lane, but wasn't attempting to pass. The car stayed in line with them, keeping the same speed.

When she looked down at the speedometer, she found she was cruising at a speed of seventy-five miles per hour.

Allyson slowed a speck to allow the Dodge to pass, but when she did, he also reduced his speed. She tried to ignore whoever it was driving that cream puff, but as soon as she sped up, so did he.

She thought they were playing. Actually, she was convinced of it. Then suddenly, the other car began to sway.

"Oh God, they're drunk," she cried aloud. They were getting too close. She freaked. Not wanting to get sideswiped, they forced her into the breakdown lane. She nudged Kyle and called out his name, hoping he'd awake. But it was of no use. She was alone. She kept wondering if it was that creep they had left back at the Shady Tree. Could it be, he was seeking revenge?

Allyson stole a quick glance to her left and saw the passenger's side window being rolled down. Her heart jumped into her throat. What if they have a gun? I watch too much TV, she kept telling herself. She refused to look at them again.

They tooted their horn to get her attention, or to annoy her, and she practically jumped out of her skin. She took another quick glimpse out of the corner of her left eye, and saw they were still aligned with her. This time when she looked, she saw two juvenile heads sticking out the windows. Teenagers raising hell in the middle of the night, but they scared her.

They were minutes away from the exit. She prayed they wouldn't interfere with her entering the ramp. Fortunately, a blue flashing light with a siren appeared and pulled them over.

By the time Allyson reached the hospital emergency room, her hands were glued to the steering wheel. But there was no time to waste, Kyle was bleeding profusely. She rushed into the waiting room, disheveled and frantic. There was one patient waiting to be cared for, and it didn't look as though his problem was urgent.

She hurried to the front desk and demanded assistance. It was out of fear that she reacted so forcefully. And she thought the hospital staff understood that, because they were very accommodating. A large male nurse in a spotless, white coat pushed a wheelchair to the limo with her. He lifted Kyle, as though he was lifting a feather, put him in the chair, and wheeled him in.

Somebody from the medical staff had already been instructed by the doctor to call the police, since stab wounds were a criminal offense. Kyle came around slowly as the doctor began working on him. But since his wound was so deep, the doctor sedated him. It wasn't nearly as bad as it looked. Kyle escaped with a total of fourteen stitches.

Two patrolmen arrived within minutes after the hospital informed them of the stabbing. Officer Herman was short, stout, and middle-aged. Officer Crowley was tall, slender, and young—early twenties, a rookie with a marine haircut. Crowley took her statement, and Allyson gave Herman a brief description of the suspect. It didn't take the officers long to figure out who he was. He was well known by the police. His name was Alex Kimball, and he had a record of misdemeanors.

"We've been trying to put Alex away for a long time—to get him out of circulation, before something like this happened. Unfortunately, every time they bring him to court, he's got a sad story to tell the judge. The last time he was arrested, he told the judge his mother was dying, and his sister was handicapped, and he needed to be home to help them, and the judge bought it. Can you believe it?" asked Officer Herman.

"That's too bad. People like him shouldn't be roaming the streets. He's a menace to society," Allyson murmured.

"Will your friend testify against him in court?" asked the young rookie.

"I'm sure he will, but you can ask him yourself," she said.

Kyle did not press charges. The police didn't submit to it well, but the system had already showed signs of failing them, be that as it may. Alex would no doubt tell the judge another sob story, get a slap on the hand, and be sent on his pitiable way. Kyle said he was going to tell Janice he ripped his arm on some rusty old barbed wire somewhere. He said she was very intelligent but extremely gullible, and she believed anything he told her. Was she merely patronizing him for her own amusement?

CHAPTER 17

Allyson crawled between the cold sheets around 4:45 A.M. Dawn would be there within the hour. With her body and mind so fatigued, she fell asleep almost instantly. The next thing she heard was Benjamin crying. She wanted to shut him out—block the noise. She put her pillow over her face, wrapping it over her ears, but his crying was persistent. So, she pried open her eyes and peeked at the clock radio on her dresser. It was 6:35 A.M. She stumbled from her bed. By the time she had reached Benjamin's room, Felicia was already in charge, changing his diaper.

"I'll make it up to you, Felice. I promise."

"Promises. Promises. I'm just jealous. Tell me what happened last night."

"You won't believe it. Let me feed Ben. You fix the coffee, and I'll tell you all about it."

Allyson dressed Ben in an adorable jumpsuit and put on his Weeboks. She melted each time she looked into his big blue eyes, so full of innocence. She wished he would stay this small indefinitely. She felt guilty not being with him as much as she used to, but the time they spent together now was much more of a quality time. It was far more meaningful for her, and she thought they appreciated each other more too.

Felicia sat across from her at the kitchen table, waiting eagerly for her to fill her in on the scoop of the previous night's events.

"You look like hell," Felicia blurted.

"Thank you. That makes me feel so much better," Allyson said, warming her hands around the coffee mug.

"I'm sorry," Felicia said earnestly, while searching Allyson's eyes for the tangy details of the night before.

"To make a long story short—some creep stabbed Kyle last night."

"Oh my God! Where—where he'd get stabbed?"

"In the arm.... Well anyway, Kyle got away from him. I drove him to the hospital—he passed out on me. Then some drunken teenagers started harassing me on the highway. They wanted me to race them. They almost forced me off the road. A cruiser saved me—thank God, by pulling them over. But then, someone from the hospital called the police when he saw the wound. Kyle didn't press charges—he was afraid Janice would find out. He ended up with fourteen stitches. It was one hell of a night, I'll tell you."

"I can't believe this," she said, with her mouth wide open. Her eyeballs bulging. Allyson thought if that mouth of hers stayed open much longer, it might freeze up.

"I told you, you wouldn't believe it," she said smiling amusingly.

Her short explanation wasn't enough. She could never satisfy Felicia. She always thought there was a lot Allyson wasn't telling her. Of course, their lovemaking was private. There was no chance of Felicia siphoning those intimate particulars out of her. She wanted to bury last night's nightmare, but Felicia hounded her until it was time for her to leave for school. As much as Allyson adored Felicia, she was ever so glad to see her go.

CHAPTER 18

Allyson was thankful she had the day off. Mondays were always slow after a long weekend. When Benjamin takes his morning nap, I'll lie down, she thought. That concept was overthrown when she received an unexpected phone call from Kyle, thanking her for all the support she had given him again. She had the strong impression that he truly wanted to pursue a relationship again. He told her he'd be over around noon, and he made it quite convincing that he wanted to see his son. She was elated, in spite of the fact that she kept telling herself that she should think about Marc.

She jumped into the shower when Ben fell asleep, and when he awoke she gave him a bath. She dressed him in a pair of blue jeans and a canary-yellow Izod sweater. The color looked ravishing on him with his olive skin and dark hair, bringing out his big blue eyes. His father couldn't help but love him, although deep down she had her reservations about the matter.

As they sat on the sofa awaiting Kyle's arrival, she wondered if he was going to disappoint them again. Her qualms were practically confirmed when the cuckoo clock struck noon, and there was no sign of him. Ben was fortunate to be young enough not to be affected by his father's broken promises.

By 12:15 P.M., she was about to give up all hope of seeing him. Ten minutes later, his red Porsche was outside. Better late than never, she thought—even though she wasn't so certain about that. She was nervous, not knowing how things were going to turn out. This was the very first time Kyle would see his son. If he wanted to bail out, Ben was young enough not to perceive the loss. Yet, there was still plenty of time for them to become acquainted, without any bad feelings between them.

"Hi," he said in a low timid voice, as he came through the door, with a red rose and a rather large wrapped gift.

"Hi back. It's all right. He's awake. Voices don't frighten him."

"This is for you," he said, handing her a budded rose encircled with baby's breath.

"Thank you. It's lovely," she said, taking a deep whiff. I'll put it in water," she said, walking away.

Allyson watched Kyle from where she stood at the sink. He peeked over at Benjamin while removing his jacket. Then he sauntered slowly over to him with the present in his hand, but as soon as Benjamin spotted him, he began to wail.

"Your face isn't familiar to him, that's all," she said, walking back into the living room, with the rose in a vase of water. She placed it on the coffee table and walked over to the playpen. Ben's little arms were reaching up, for her to rescue him, from this total stranger.

"Once he sees you're not a threat to us, he'll accept you. It won't be long," she said, putting Ben between them on the sofa.

Kyle put the gift he had brought on Benjamin's legs. Ben smiled up at her, and then he looked over at Kyle, timidly. But after they helped him open his gift and he saw it was Big Bird from Sesame Street, Ben smiled at both of them. He seemed to recognize the bird immediately, or else he was attracted to the vivid colors. He was content with his new stuffed animal, and he made the first real connection with his daddy.

Kyle barely took his eyes off his son. He appeared hypnotic as he gazed whimsically at Ben. A super blend of melancholy and bliss. Tears engulfed her as she watched them. Instantly, they became a pair. They were the mental photograph she had wanted to capture from day one, and now she could actually keep this lasting memorabilia of a daddy and son, smiling happily at one another, in her memory and in her heart.

"He looks like me—he's got my chin—my eyes," Kyle said excitedly.

"Would you like to hold him?"

"Huh, me?"

"Yeah, you, Daddy."

"Uh, sure. Why not," he said, squeamishly.

Ben settled into Kyle's arms almost naturally. Almost as though he knew he belonged with this man. They became so acquainted that after awhile it was hard to believe they had only met a few hours ago. They played well together.

Allyson went for a run on the beach, and they didn't even miss her. Kyle really seemed to be enjoying every moment.

When the two of them finally began to unwind, around three, Ben fell asleep contentedly in Kyle's arms. It was a beautiful sight. She never thought she'd witness the day when Kyle would be holding and loving his own son. Her eyes began to well up, so she walked into kitchen. Kyle put Ben in his crib, and then he came into the living room and sat down beside her. He gave her a sweet kiss, and thanked her for doing such a superb job—bringing up their son. Then he began kissing her more passionately.

"Felicia will be home soon—within the hour."

"Plenty of time. Let's call it a celebration of our new beginning."

She let his noncommittal comment slide for the time being. She didn't want a heated argument after an almost perfect reconciliation.

He guilefully rubbed his hands across her sweatshirt, arousing her. "See, you want me already," he said, caressing her taut nipples, protruding beneath his warm touch.

"I'm yours," she said, with cupidity.

At that remark, he picked her up and carried her into the bedroom, where he laid her down. With their erratic breathing and their hearts skipping beats, there was no time for him to undrape her romantically, or for her to unclothe him. She longed to feel their naked bodies touch once more—wrap together as one, and escalate their lovemaking to the greatest peak.

After almost an hour of fervid passion, they had just enough time to compose themselves, before Felicia came racing through the front door; her pace accelerated, after seeing the red Porsche sitting out front.

"I think she's got an eye for you," Allyson smirked.

"Who?" he asked, frowning.

"Felicia."

"What can I say?"

"Don't be so cocky. What happens when you're old and gray?"

"I'll still be fighting them off," he said, grinning.

At that moment, the phone rang. It was Marc.

"Can I call you back?" she said rather flatly.

She could tell he knew who was around. She felt badly after she hung up. Kyle didn't ask who had called. Maybe he figured it was a business call, or he was secure enough with their new beginning.

Just as Kyle was getting ready to leave, Felicia bounced in. Allyson never saw anyone excite her as much as Kyle. It seemed he had that effect upon every woman he met. Felicia must have seen the gleam in her eyes.

"I hope there wasn't any hanky-panky going on here," she said with a small chuckle.

"Not I," said Kyle, slyly.

"Said the cat," Felicia replied back, rehearsing quotes from a children's book.

She looked at Allyson, and Allyson patted her chest lightly.

"Nothing going on here."

"Okay. I get the message. MYOB."

They both looked at her and said, "You got it."

They all laughed.

Kyle quickly kissed Allyson on the lips and said, "I'll see ya in a couple."

Whatever that meant. Two days? Two weeks? She stood at the door and watched him get into his car and drive off. He never looked back. And from deep within, she felt that all too familiar emptiness emerging once more.

CHAPTER 19

Ben was cranky and felt feverish. Allyson took his temperature, and it was one hundred and one. She had warned the crew at work, if her son should get sick, she would stay by his side until he was better. They were very understanding at the time. They had said that family mattered first. However, when she called them, she was hearing something very contrary. Taylor relayed a message to her from Stan Wright, one of the younger hotshot brokers in the office, who always took on more than he could handle.

"Stan wants to know if you'd come in for a couple of hours—to wrap up a deal. He said there'd be something in it for you. We're sort of short-handed today," Taylor said wearily, knowing that in the long run she'd get stuck helping out.

"Sorry to hear that. I feel bad for you, but I have no sympathy for the rest. And as for Stan, tell him—my son is more important."

"Right on! Give Ben a big kiss for me. I hope he's better soon. You take as much time as you need."

"Thanks, Taylor. See ya soon."

After Allyson hung up, she called Ben's pediatrician and described his symptoms. The doctor told her not to worry that all sorts of viruses were spreading around. She said to get some Tylenol in him every three or four hours to reduce the fever. And if Allyson had any other concerns, not to hesitate to call.

"Try and relax, Ms. Porteus. This is what motherhood is all about," she said.

"Easier said than done, Doc."

"I know, believe me. I have three of my own. But there's no sense in getting yourself all worked up unnecessarily. That's why I'm here. Now, if the fever continues for more than three days—I'll want to see him. But in the meantime, if you have any questions—whatsoever, call me."

"Thanks. Good-bye," Allyson said, wishing she could keep the doctor on the line; she was very nervous about him being sick.

"Bye."

Allyson took his temperature every half-hour to make sure the fever hadn't risen. It had, slightly, but then it stayed low grade. She fed him his lunch, and he threw it up. She began to panic because nothing seemed to stay down. She wanted to call the doctor back, but she didn't want to appear like the overly protective mother that she really was. Ben was everything to her, and she hated to see him so sick. It broke her heart in two, seeing his body so limp—the way she so vividly remembered him, lying in the incubator at the hospital, the first few days he was on this earth.

At 4:00 P.M., his fever had risen to a scorching 104 degrees. She immediately called his doctor again. Knowing Allyson was an anxious new mother, she responded to her call right away.

"Doctor Pelletier, his temperature is 104 degrees," Allyson said, with her voice cracking, and tears welling up in her eyes.

"Ms. Porteus, please try and get hold of yourself as I explain. This is normal. A child's temperature most often rises at this hour of the day. This is a high temperature for an adult, but fairly common for a child. If it'll make you feel any better, I'll take a look at him."

"Could you? Would you?" she cried.

"Yes. Get him dressed and bring him in."

"Thanks. Thanks so much."

It made a major difference to Allyson knowing the doctor would see him, instead of just diagnosing her professional opinion of his illness over the phone. And she certainly felt much more at ease after seeing her, even though the examination was the same prognosis she had described when she first spoke to her. His lungs were clear. There was no ear or nasal infection. It was just a nasty virus. But it was a tremendous relief to Allyson, just knowing for certain, that's all it was.

It wasn't easy being responsible for another human being, but Benjamin was well worth every bit of the price one had to pay—worrying about a child. Kyle should have been there with them as a family, helping with the responsibility of Ben—but more importantly, just being there for him so that Ben would know that he was loved by two parents—not just one. Kyle had the option to come and go as he pleased, and he didn't have to deal with the tribulations that she faced each day, during Ben's growing years. Somehow, it didn't seem quite fair. But then again, life wasn't always fair either, was it?

Allyson telephoned her aunt for some moral support. After Allyson told her of Ben's sickness, Aunt Edith made her feel so much better by telling her how this wasn't unusual for young children. Aunt Edith sounded like Doctor Pelletier, yet it was always nicer hearing it from someone who really cared. Allyson wondered how she knew so much about kids, when she never had any of her own.

"Your mother would curl up at the bottom of your bed at night—when you were burning with fever. She would bathe you in tepid water, or rub you down with alcohol. Anything to cool you down. I could just imagine what she was feeling. It was an incredible sight—the two of you. I was envious of her then. She loved you so very much, Ali."

"I know—and I loved her too. I miss her, Auntie. She would have loved Ben—with all her heart," she said, teary eyed. Even though they weren't terribly close because Sandra Porteus was a very private person, Allyson didn't love her any the less.

"I hate to bring up a sore subject—have you heard from your dad lately?" Aunt Edith asked warily.

"No. It's been awhile—a long while, actually. He's probably packaged up with some young thing again."

"You sound bitter. Even though you feel as though your dad has deserted you, I know he loves you. You will always be his little girl—no matter what. He's always been very proud of you."

"Yeah, maybe at one time. That's in the past now. I'm a grown woman, with a child of my own. He's a grandfather—he doesn't even know it. He hurt Mom and me so much. Will that pain ever go away, Auntie?"

"I'm sorry you've had to endure this hurt, Ali. Some men are just creatures of habit. They have to keep filling their egos—to keep them going. It's unfortunate Alexander has to fit that mold, but that doesn't mean he didn't love you both. I think your mother knew that."

"I always feel so much better when I talk to you. Thanks for listening. I love you, Auntie."

"I love you too, Ali. Keep in touch."

"I will."

CHAPTER 20

Allyson kept a close eye on Benjamin. She jumped up every time she heard him moan or utter a small cry in his sleep. When Ben's fever finally broke completely one night and she was confident he was on the road to recovery, she called Marc to apologize for her rude abruptness during their last phone conversation. She had just managed to get back together with Kyle then, at least that's what she thought, and he was on his way out the door when Marc phoned.

She wanted to say good-bye to Kyle that day, with hope there would soon be another hello—but deep down she knew it was just another meaningless scene added to her very own pitiable comedy. Marc's timing just happened to be poor, but it wasn't his fault, and she had to let him know that. However, when the answering machine clicked on, she was eager to hang up. But as soon as she heard his deep beguiling voice, she felt compelled to listen to his announcement.

"If you dialed my number wishing to speak with me, then your call must be of some importance. Therefore, don't hang up leaving me in suspense. Feel free to express yourself when you hear the beep—I'll return your call as soon as I'm able."

Allyson was ecstatic when she heard the message. She hemmed and hawed after she heard the last beep. She told him it was her, and she wouldn't blame him if he didn't want to call her back. Then he shocked her by picking up the phone. He was there all along. He just wanted to hear what she had to say before responding.

"Marc, umm…. I was afraid you wouldn't want to talk to me."

"Why would I not want to speak with the lovely Miss Porteus? Just because she dumped me for someone else, and left me lonely—is no reason to be mean and not speak to her. Right?"

She smiled. "I have to be honest with you."

"Careful—I have a weak heart."

"Seriously, I never meant to hurt you. You're my friend."

"I'm everybody's friend. I'd like my life to have a new story."

"If you're looking for sympathy, you're not going to get it from me." She paused. "You're very special to me."

"I am? Gee, how come I wasn't aware of that?"

"That's what I like about you. You're not full of yourself."

"Hmmm," he murmured. "Is that so? That could change."

"I hope not. Marc, seriously, though, I want to apologize for not calling back. I really have no excuse—except that Ben's been sick, and I haven't left his side."

"Oh, no. Is there anything I can do?" he asked earnestly.

"Thanks, but he's okay now. His fever finally broke tonight. I think he had the flu or some virus. Doctors never really give names to these bugs, but he's recuperating just fine."

"Well, I'm glad to hear that. I'm here if you need me. I'll wait, though, until I hear from you—I 'd hate to intrude at the wrong time again. I hope Ben gets better real soon."

"He will. Thanks. See ya, Marc."

What more could she say? He could tell so much from her voice.

❦   ❦   ❦

And as the weeks moved on, there was still no word from Kyle, except for the support checks that came regularly now. Maybe he thought money would make up for his absence. He had her completely fooled, after remembering the clear picture of attachment she saw between his son and him, the last time he came to visit.

And their lovemaking had been as sparkly and electric as ever. But this was the way Kyle was. Everything was hunky-dory, but only for brief moments. Kissy and lovey, and then no word from him for months. Maybe he believed that the once-in-a-blue-moon affection he gave Benjamin and her would make up for all the time that he lost in between. But he couldn't be more wrong. He couldn't burn the candle at both ends and think that he was going to make everyone happy. It just didn't work that way. Not for her.

Sometimes Allyson wished she could obliterate her blunders and make a perfect world for Ben. But if that were to happen, there'd be no Ben. And he was hardly a stupid mistake. He was a lasting treasure. And since perfect worlds didn't exist and never would, she planned to do the best she could with their actual situation.

CHAPTER 21

Allyson peeked out the window before answering the door. She saw a blue Mazda in the driveway. She didn't know anyone who drove a Mazda.

"Who is it?" she called out, before opening the door.

"Your dad."

"Just a minute," she said. Her heart began to race. She straightened her clothes, took a quick glance in the mirror, and looked around to make sure the house was presentable. She picked up a few pieces of clothing which were strewn over a chair and hid them under the cushions of the sofa. Then she tossed Ben's toys back into the playpen. She took two deep breaths and slowly opened the door to let her long lost father come inside.

"What took you so long? I thought you'd forgotten about me," he said. You took the words right out of my mouth, Dad, she thought, as she stood staring at him.

"Well, aren't you going to invite your ole dad in?"

"Yes, of course, forgive me. Come in."

"You look as beautiful as ever," he said, smiling, reaching out to give her a hug and a kiss.

She responded back, naturally, but with a cool embrace, and a quick peck on the lips. She felt as if she were hugging a stranger. Those feelings of betrayal were deepening. It had been over two years since her mother had died, and there had been no word from him until now. She had no idea where he was living, or what he was doing. Now here he stood in front of her, expecting her to smother him with affection.

"Dad, it's been a long time."

"Yes it has, sweetheart. I hope you can find it in your heart to forgive your daddy. I was involved with this woman, Norma, for awhile. Just recently she gave me the shaft. She was out for my money," he added, with dejection.

He looked so pathetic, she couldn't tell him what she really felt. Here he was being used—being made into a damn fool. He was a grown man, and should have learned his lesson by now—or he never would. Allyson wanted to tell him how angry she was at him for hurting Mama and her, but he had received what he deserved. The years were beginning to show on him too. Yet, despite the crow's feet around his eyes and the deep lines that creased his forehead, he was still as handsome as she remembered him.

"Dad, how did you find me?"

"I keep track of my little girl."

"Dad, I'm not your little girl anymore—I have a son. I'm a mother, and you're a grandfather."

"I've known about that for quite some time, but I was away...."

"Excuses. Everybody's got excuses. I needed you. Where were you, Dad?" she asked, with anger that turned into sobs, as tears coursed down her cheeks.

"The thought of losing my little girl and becoming a grandfather terrified me. I couldn't accept all this," he said with tears forming in his eyes.

It was the first time Allyson saw her dad show emotion. She never even saw a tear in his eye at her mother's funeral. She just assumed he was holding back his sorrow, and would release his loss in solitude. That's what she wanted to believe.

"But Dad, you were never in jeopardy of losing me. Your fears have only kept us apart."

She looked into his eyes. They were sincere, but she could feel no sympathy for him. At that brief moment, he reminded her of Kyle—a lost boy inside a man's body, with absolutely no means of turning into a man.

"I know. You're right...there's more. There's something I've got to tell you—you should know. I've kept this secret for too many years," he said looking into her eyes, searching for the right words.

"Go ahead, Dad. Don't stop now. I'm a big girl—I can handle it."

"I can see that—you've become very responsible and I—I just hope that what I have to say won't destroy any love you have left for me."

"Dad, please, just tell me."

"You have a brother," he said in a low voice, bowing his head in shame.

Oh, great! He got somebody pregnant, and now I have a baby brother somewhere. Probably about the same age as my son. How wonderful, she thought sardonically.

"Is this Norma's child?" she asked, hating him at that very moment, wondering how many other illegitimate kids he may have sired, through those many years of committing adultery.

"No, Ali. He's your older brother."

"What! You were having an affair before I was born?" she yelled, in disbelief.

"Your mother and I tried for a long time to have a child. And I thought...."

"Save it. I don't want to hear anymore," she said, covering her ears. "Why, Dad? Why?" she cried.

"I was wrong, honey—I admit it. Please don't hold this against me," he implored, as he fell to his knees and cried. "It was a long time ago—your mom and I were under a lot of stress."

"Dad, please get up. This is a lot to grasp at once," she said, feeling both disgust and anger. She was confused and deeply hurt. She was furious with him, but she knew she couldn't dwell on the past—it was over and done with. And there was nothing she could do to change that. She prayed that her mother had had no knowledge of his sinful acts—she knew nothing about this child born from his infidelity. He was her father and she was his child, yet here he was weeping at her feet, begging for her forgiveness.

As she looked down upon this weak man, she couldn't believe this was the same man who took away her fears and made her feel so secure, years before. The man she once thought to be so strong and wonderful.

"What you did in the past is irrelevant to me now. But I do want to know her name and where she lives."

"Why is this so important to you?" he asked, as she took his arm and led him to the sofa.

"The same reason this was so important for you to spill your heart out to me. He's my brother—I need to know more about him. Dad—he's your son too."

"I know. I've never told anyone. It's been eating at me for years. As time rolled on, I thought it would all go away. I've been so ashamed."

"Dad, this could never go away—he's a part of you. Just like I am. I'll find him, Dad," she said, hugging him generously, letting him know everything would be all right, and that she wasn't laying judgment on him. It could destroy him. She had to stand by him, and try to put aside all the bad feelings that were stirring up inside of her.

She could tell that tremendous pressure had been lifted from his heart, when she looked into his sorrowful eyes. This dark secret must have haunted him for years.

"I'm lucky to have you," he said with shaky hands, dropping his handkerchief to the floor.

When she bent down to retrieve it for him, she realized it was the hankie she had given him for Christmas when she was eighteen. She had hand stitched his initials. Her heart sank for a moment as she remembered that Christmas long ago. It had been with the three of them together. Her parents had made it special for her, because it was the first year she'd been away at college. They had given her a gold locket, engraved "To Ali, with love always, Mom and Dad."

"We're lucky to have each other, Dad," she said, returning the old hankie, now soiled with wetness from his tears. "Now, please, tell me my brother's name and his last known address," she said, grabbing a pen and a pad of paper from the desk.

"His mother's name is Catherine McCaffrey," he said, somewhat dreamily. "The last I knew—she lived in a small town outside of Los Angeles. Canton, I believe it was."

"You mean California!"

"Yup. A long ways from here," he said, looking down at his feet, calmer now. Exposing the truth to her after all these years had seemingly released him from all the bottled-up guilt he kept hidden so long.

"Another one of your business affairs," she mumbled. Evidently he didn't hear that comment, or he overlooked it, because he didn't respond to it.

She wondered if there was more. She prayed not. She had all she could ingest in one sitting.

❦   ❦   ❦

When Ben finally awoke from his nap, she introduced him to his grandfather. It was difficult for her dad to accept the fact that Benjamin was his grandchild, but he emulated his part as the grandfather quite well. Not that he wasn't happy for her, but she thought for him it was a sign he was getting older. Whatever her dad was feeling wasn't revealed through his interactions with Ben. He played nicely with him for a short while, and then he surprised her with a sealed white envelope.

"What's this?" she asked, slowly opening it.

"A little something for your son. My grandson," he said reservedly.

"Thank you, Dad. This is very generous of you," she said, embracing him. It was a five thousand dollar savings bond.

"It's the least I could do. I wasn't there for you when you needed me."

"You're here now. That's what counts. I hope we've closed the gap between us," she said smiling at him.

He smiled back. And there was silence for a long time afterward. Then she served him coffee and a piece of lemon pie. It was beginning to feel like old times. When he'd come home from a business trip—they'd sit and chat at the kitchen table, eating one of mother's delicious pies. She'd tell him what happened at school that week, and he'd listen. But this time, Allyson was doing most of the listening.

"It's getting late," Alexander said an hour later, after looking at his watch. "I really must be going."

He put on his coat. He looked great for a man of fifty, she thought. Alexander was tall, and his salt and pepper hair, made him distinguished. His body was still very lean, except for a little pudginess around the center. He had always been a sharp dresser—not too extravagant, but quite nice.

"Dad, how am I supposed to keep in contact with you?"

"Here's my beeper number," he said, handing her a business card. "I move around a lot, so this is the best way to reach me. After you dial my number, you'll hear three beeps—press in your phone number. It will read up on this gadget I have here," he said, showing her where the number appears on the small screen. "I'll return your call."

"Good-bye, Dad. I love you," she whispered, giving him a bear hug.

"I love you too. I'll be in touch—I swear. Take care of yourself and my—my handsome grandson." He kissed her on the forehead, and then he took Benjamin's little hand into his. "So long, little fella. You be good for your mommy. Grandpa will see you soon."

Even though Allyson knew his words were only figures of speech, she yearned to be close to him again. She watched him walk to his car, settle in, and drive away. It was a sad yet joyous reunion, but she couldn't dwell on the dark regions of it.

CHAPTER 22

After her dad left, all she could think about was finding her new brother. What did he look like? Was he tall like her father? What did he do for a living? Did he have a family? All these unanswered questions were flooding her mind. All she knew was—she had to find him. Allyson didn't want to waste any more time. Too many years had passed already.

She was ensconced in such heavy thoughts about her new brother that when the phone rang, she was so startled she sprang from her chair like a frightened frog taking an unexpected leap off a lily pad.

"Hello," she answered, out of breath

"Is someone sitting on the phone?" Marc asked humorously.

"Oh, Marc. Thank God it's you. I have so much to tell you. My dad stopped by. He—he told me I have a brother! A brother I never knew I had. We have to find him, Marc. I tried reaching his mother, but the operator said there's no listing for her."

"Slow down. Slow down, Ali. May I come over—we can talk about this?" he said calmly.

"Of course."

"Stay calm. I'm on my way."

In a matter of minutes, he was in her driveway. She hurried to the door to greet him.

"Thanks for coming right over," she said, taking his jacket. He walked her over to the kitchen table, where they sat down. "I had an unexpected visit from my dad today. I hadn't seen him in God knows when. Any way, he tells me—out of the blue—I have a brother!"

"A brother you knew nothing about?"

"Exactly. He had an affair—she got pregnant."

Then Allyson decided to fill Marc in about their family history. Even though she was ashamed, she had a gut feeling Marc would understand. At least, he would be sensitive to her feelings.

"Definitely a mind blower," he said, not saying whether he meant the bits and pieces of her life, or the news about her brother. But all of this, she was sure, was a shocker to him, too. "Do you want me to help you find him?"

"Yes. Yes! More than anything."

"Take two deep breaths and blow out slowly." She did. "Now that you're relaxed," he said, smiling at her, "let's begin. What do you have?"

"Just a name and a town," she said, showing him what she had scribbled down. "The operator said there's no listing for a Catherine McCaffrey," she said, panic starting to creep into her voice.

"We'll try again. Did you spell her name correctly—and the town?"

"I'm not sure. Maybe not. This is what he gave me," she said, dangling the paper in front of him. "He could be wrong about the town. It's been a long time. Maybe she doesn't live there anymore."

"McCaffrey can be spelled McCaffery too," he said, crossing his fingers. He dialed the long distant operator. She heard him say, "I see. How about the surrounding towns?" Then there was a long pause and he said, "Yeah. Yeah. What's that? Can you give me a street address? I understand. Thanks anyway," he said. He hung up the receiver, and right off she didn't like his look.

"Well? What'd she say?"

"She said there was a C. McCaffrey in Ashton. A town next door to Canton."

"That's it. That's got to be it! Why didn't you get the number?"

"It's unpublished."

"You could have told her it was an emergency."

"No. She wouldn't believe me. Anyone could call up and say that."

"What are we going to do?" she asked, hanging her head.

"Don't worry, Allyson, I know a private investigator—who owes me a favor. Don't give up," he said, lifting her chin. "Remember the old saying, 'where there is a will there is a way.' You've got the will, and I've got the way." Then he winked at her.

"It took this many years to find out I had a brother out there, somewhere. I guess I can wait a few more days to meet him."

"That's my girl. Now, let me go home and get working on this," he said, lifting his jacket from the sofa.

"Thanks, Marc. I appreciate this." She kissed him tenderly on the lips. "How can I ever repay you?"

"That was a good start. Go for a second round?" he asked, puckering his lips for another kiss.

"Later," she said, sealing them with her fingers.

"Does Felicia know about this?"

"No," she answered, searching his eyes for his reason for asking.

"I think it's best we keep this quiet for a while."

"Maybe you're right," she said, not knowing why. She wanted to let the whole world know she had a brother. "Until we find him—I guess this should be kept quiet."

After Marc left, she lay down on the sofa. She was so absorbed in her pleasant dreams about meeting her brother, she never heard Felicia come in.

"You all right?" Felicia inquired, looking at her peculiarly.

"Yeah. I'm fine," Allyson said sitting up. "I must have dozed for a minute. Umm, something smells good."

"I got a Pu Pu platter for two, some pork fried rice, and chicken chow mein too."

"Make my day."

The two of them ate like little piglets. The sudden turn of events had elevated Allyson's appetite.

CHAPTER 23

At 4:45 A.M., Allyson woke up feeling refreshed and renewed. She knew Ben and Felicia would be sleeping for at least another hour, so she quietly put on her jogging suit, and sneaked out to the beach.

As she jogged the white sands, she rehearsed over and over again the words spoken between her dad and her. He was the man she had put on a pedestal when she was a little girl. He was the man who once had taken away her fears and wiped away her tears. But she despised him for the person she now knew him to be—the man who made her mother cry all those lonely nights, when he was away on presumed business trips. Was he making love to various women? Now she had learned of an innocent child—the product of his unfaithfulness—a child who needlessly had suffered because her father couldn't keep his penis in his pants. And her dad didn't have the backbone to face up to the consequence of his iniquitous actions. He'd kept this dark secret buried all these years, whether to spare her mother from any more pain, or because he was so shameful himself.

As she ran, she visualized her brother in front of her. She was chasing after him. It was still dark, but the full moon illuminated the beach enough to follow the distorted shadow. As she ran, faster and faster, playfully trying to catch this imaginary figure, she could hear the waves crashing roughly against the jetty. Suddenly, a gust of cool wind blew sand into her face, blurring her eyes. Unable to see in front of her, she tripped and fell over a large piece of driftwood that had washed ashore.

Stunned, she sat there for a few seconds. But when she tried to rise, a throbbing pain shot through her left ankle. She sat back down, rubbing it, trying to soothe away the soreness. But the pain became more intense as the minutes passed. Her ankle began to swell immediately. She thought for sure that it was broken. The sand was saturated from the high tide and cool winds. Daybreak was at least another half-hour. Allyson wondered who would find her so far out, if anyone. Why had she neglected to leave a note for Felicia? She'd never anticipated anything like this. She knew once Felicia found her bed empty, she'd be calling all over creation looking for her.

She attempted to drag herself along the shoreline, but her clothes became more soaked and heavy. And each time her swollen ankle stumbled over a shell or some other hard object in the sand, it irritated it even more. It was throbbing so bad she wanted to scream. But what good would that do? She pulled up her pants and rolled down her sock to get a good look. The sun was barely peeking over the horizon, but she could see her ankle turning various shades of blue. She didn't dare lift off her sneaker, even though she wanted to get a better glimpse of the whole foot, because she might not be able to get it back on—not the way this ankle was swelling.

She had jogged at least a mile, or so, down the beach. Summer cottages stood in a row, high above her, overlooking the ocean. A few of them were occupied, but there were no signs of civilization. The owners or renters would stay up late at night and sleep late into the morning. This was their vacation privilege, and unfortunately for her, it was to her disadvantage.

Allyson hopped on her right foot for a little bit, taking a break every minute or two. She could detect that it was getting close to 7:00 A.M. Felicia had to be at work soon. She was probably frantic by now, wondering where she was.

She perched her bottom against a large boulder for a few minutes before continuing on. The pain kept shooting through her leg like a sharpshooter, not missing a single mark. Her eyes stung, as they filled with water. After awhile she couldn't feel the cold anymore; she had become numb to that. She only shivered from pain. The sun was gradually warming her hands, but not the rest of her. She wasn't prepared for any accident and, of course, she'd never dreamed something like this would happen.

If she hadn't been daydreaming about chasing her mysterious brother, maybe she would have seen that hunk of wood that she carelessly stumbled across. In spite of her mishap, she truly believed he was worth fantasizing about. And as Allyson hobbled along, the more she thought about finding him, the less she worried about her injury.

She imagined the different things they could do together. True, they had different mothers, yet they were still bonded by the same father. There was no reason they couldn't be friends.

She visualized her brother and her riding bikes, swimming together, and even sharing family dinners. It saddened her to think that so much time had passed; she had missed out being with a brother she so desperately wanted, and needed, in her growing and formative years.

Every now and then she let out a loud scream for help. If anyone were out there, someone would hear her. In the distance she could hear sirens. They sounded a million miles away. When she looked toward home she saw, what appeared to be, miniature people moving about. She continued hobbling along, and the little people became larger as they got closer. There were three of them.

Excitedly, she hopped faster, waving her arms high in the air, yelling, "Over here, over here."

When they got near enough, she could see it was Felicia, with a policeman and a paramedic. Once they realized it was her, they ran toward her, and she collapsed just as they reached her. Felicia and the hefty paramedic took hold of her, one on each side.

"I never thought I'd be this happy to see anyone. I never thought you'd find me."

"You've got to give me more credit than that, Allyson."

"Are you all right, Miss?" the young officer asked politely.

"Now I am," she said with a weak smile, just happy to see them. The paramedic wrapped her ankle with bandages.

"I don't think it's broken. Probably a good sprain," he said.

"Well, that's a relief—I think," she said in agony, as the second paramedic met them with the stretcher. "Thanks for knowing me so well, Felice," she said, as they carried her across the sand.

"At first, I thought you had sneaked out in the middle of the night," Felicia said smiling. "But after speaking to Marc," she said looking at her, "two heads can be better than one. We came to the conclusion that you'd be right here. We couldn't think of any other explanation—you didn't leave a note or anything...."

"I know. I hope you forgive me," she said. "That was really dumb of me."

"Marc is on his way over."

"You're kidding! I can't let him see me like this. I'm a mess."

"I don't think he cares. He's more worried about you."

By the time they reached the parking lot, Marc was parking his car. He told the guys in the ambulance that he'd drive Allyson to the hospital. They didn't argue. They released her to him, and he drove her to the outpatient section of Cape Cod Hospital.

CHAPTER 24

The waiting room was packed with people. If she had taken the ambulance, she would have had faster results, but since her injury wasn't life threatening, she had to wait hours before they'd even look at her foot, much less take x-rays. Eventually, a nurse strolled out with a pan full of cold water, to soak this grossly enlarged, bluish-purple hoof of hers. They waited for the results from the two pictures that had been taken of it.

She was glad Marc was the one who brought her to the hospital. Kyle was never around when she needed him, and he was less sympathetic than Marc. Marc was calm and soothing, and, oddly, she felt much more comfortable with him.

Finally, after sitting all morning in the emergency room, in throbbing pain, a doctor attended to her. He cheerfully informed her that there were no broken bones, and that the foot was just bruised badly from the sprain. He gave her a painkiller, rewrapped her foot in bandages, gave her crutches, and sent her on her way.

As tired as she was and as much as she wanted to leave that place right away, she asked Marc if he would mind if she visited an old friend. She told him about Emma, as they rode the elevator up to her floor. She told him how wonderful she was to her when she was in the hospital after having Ben. She'd promised Emma she would keep in touch, but time had passed so quickly—what with working and taking care of Ben, she never got the chance.

They stopped by the gift shop first, and she picked up an initial silver pin to give to her. Allyson couldn't wait to see her again. Just as they were about to enter her ward, a nurse stopped them, informing them there were no visitors allowed before 2:00 P.M. Allyson explained that they weren't there to visit a patient but to see Nurse Buck.

"Emma Buck?" she asked, staring at her awkwardly.

"Yes, that's her. Is she working today?"

"I'm sorry—I guess you haven't heard. Emma is no longer with us. She died two months ago…unexpectedly. She had a heart attack."

"Excuse me. That can't be. She was my nurse…my friend," Allyson said, devastated, as she turned and looked up at Marc, who was standing close to the wheelchair he had been pushing her in. "I didn't get to say good-bye," she said, with tears starting to sting her eyes. Marc bent down to comfort her, and she buried her head in his broad shoulders and wept for the woman who had once been so kind to her and Ben.

"How were you supposed to know, Ali? I'm sure she knew how much you cared," he said, handing her a tissue.

"Thanks for your help," she said to the nurse, as she wiped away her tears.

"I'm very sorry," she responded with sincerity.

"Me too," she said softly, as Marc turned the wheelchair around and wheeled her away.

By the time they got outside again, the sun had practically vanished as the clouds rolled in. The sky was as gray as her mood. The painkiller was wearing off, and she was ready for another. Tears from loss and pain were filling her eyes again. Felicia had taken Benjamin to Fairview Acres Day Care, and she said she'd retrieve him. Allyson was grateful to her for that.

When they got to Allyson's place, Marc helped her into bed. He said he would stay with her for the rest of the day, or at least until Felicia got home.

"Let me try to reach my PI friend, Shane, before you nod out on me."

"I won't go to sleep now," Allyson said with enthusiasm, sitting up straight, against the headboard. Although she was feeling drowsy from the medication, she suddenly became more aware. "Wouldn't it be nice…. Bring the phone in here; the cord will reach."

"If he can't find your brother, no one can. This guy's got connections in all the right places, including some police departments."

"I hope he's there," she said, crossing her fingers.

When Shane answered and Marc told him what he needed to find out, he raised his thumb to Allyson, letting her know it looked good.

"That's great. Thanks, Pal," he said and then hung up the phone.

"What did he say?" she asked anxiously.

"He said he had ways of finding out the phone number, and as soon as he had something he'd get back to us. In a day or so."

"It's sounds promising. It's the best news I've heard today, anyway. Thanks Marc. And thanks for being here with me."

"There's no other place I'd rather be," he said with a smile.

She smiled back, and they just stared amorously at each other. Then her eyes became heavy again.

"I need to lay down."

"Let's get you more comfortable." He fixed one pillow behind her head and another under her sprained foot, and then he covered her up. "Sleep well," she heard him say. She managed a small smile, before drifting off.

❧   ❧   ❧

A few hours later, the loud ringing of the telephone aroused her from her deep slumber. She leaped out of bed, briefly amnesiac, but when the dull pain shot through her foot, her memory was suddenly jolted. Groggy from the medication, she heard Marc's far-off voice.

"Much obliged, my friend," he said. Then she heard the receiver being placed on the hook.

"Who was that?" she called from the bedroom.

"I got good news," he said coming through the doorway, smiling widely at her.

"What? Tell me, what is it?" she asked with full awareness now.

"We got it! McCaffrey's phone number!"

"Help me up," she said instantly, forgetting her pain. She dragged her big foot to the trestle table and sat down. "Where is it?" she asked. However, when he handed it to her, she just stared at the number. What was she going to say to a woman who had borne her father's child? "What if she hangs up? Marc, what should I say?"

"Start with the truth. That always helps. She has no reason to be angry with you."

"Gee, this is much harder than I realized."

"You can do it," he said, as he handed her the receiver. "I have faith in you."

"Well, I'm glad somebody does," she replied, dialing the number slowly. Her hands trembled. "One ring…two…three…four. She's not home."

"Let it ring a few more times."

"Five," she said, holding up one hand. "Six, seven, no answer," she said, and hung up.

"All that worrying for nothing. Now you call her again…in an hour," he insisted.

"In an hour!"

"That's right. And no second thoughts."

"Not a chance," she said more confidently.

"Good girl. You're a woman of strong will."

"Thanks for the confidence," she said, smiling at Marc.

They never did get Catherine that day. In some ways, she was relieved. This one phone call could instigate anguish for both of them, but she still had this resolute wish to meet her brother. She couldn't stop now.

CHAPTER 25

Allyson hobbled around on the crutches pretty well and being her left foot, she was still able to drive. When she got to Cape Cod Realty, she received a standing ovation from the other employees. She stood there dumfounded.

"What is this?" she mouthed to Taylor.

She shrugged her shoulders and said, "They missed ya, I guess. How do you rate?"

"Beats me. Luck? I sure have a lot of that lately," she mumbled, glancing down at her foot.

"A little more than luck, I'd say," Taylor said with a touch of jealousy in her voice.

"What can I say? When you've got it, you've got it," she said jokingly, without conceit. "Okay guys, I give up. What's going on?"

"Mr. Steinberg called. He's looking to purchase something. He was very adamant about speaking with you, and no one else," Carl whined.

Carl was one of the youngest brokers in the office, anxious to succeed in life. His family had always been very poor, and he was determined not to live the life they had lived. But sometimes his approach was overbearing, turning people off—losing potential prospects.

"So—what's the big deal?"

"The big deal is, when Mr. Steinberg calls he doesn't pussyfoot around. He's an important man in town. He's got bucks. Lots. He's gonna buy something big. I can feel it. Million dollar range. Mark my words."

"How'd he get my name?"

"Who knows. Who cares? The point is, he got it."

Right away she called him back. He explained how he had met her at the Caldwell party a couple of years ago, and how he had spoken with Janice recently and had inquired about her. Janice had enlightened him as to where she was working. Evidently, she hadn't revealed anything else. Allyson remembered Steinberg vaguely; she had met so many people that night. Harold had introduced her to him, but they'd spoken only briefly.

"You dance beautifully, Miss Porteus."

"Thank you," she said, somewhat shocked that he still remembered. It was nearly two years ago now. Although, she could still recall it vividly, as though it was only yesterday. The way Kyle romantically held her, as they danced closely, to the music of *Will You Still Love Me Tomorrow*. And then their erotic movements to *Staying Alive*, captivating the attention of all those who attended the annual, end-of-the-summer bash at the Caldwell mansion.

"Getting down to business, there's some commercial buildings over at Cedar and Hill. I want them."

She was glad he didn't ramble on about that unforgettable night. A legend etched in an open book; a fairyland depraved by the tales of truth. She was stunned by his request. These were the ritziest buildings in town. They had a country effect, not a commercial impression. The lawns were impeccable and a deep green. The underground sprinklers helped maintain their blooming mien.

"I hear your request, Mr. Steinberg, sir. The asking price is 1.3 million," she divulged hesitantly.

"My dear, money is of no concern. Do what you have to do on your end, and I'll be over in an hour with a deposit."

She thanked him, and hung up the phone, more than a little elated. Everyone in the office was silently clustered around her desk, waiting to hear.

"Yes!" she yipped. Some gave her the thumbs up, others nodded in envy. So much was happening at once. She felt intoxicated as visions of dollar bills, floating in slow motion, occupied her head.

She sat at her desk mentally compiling her life's happenings into a sound sagacity.

"Allyson."

"Yes," she answered, in a fog. She was a million miles away.

"Telephone."

"Hello, Miss Porteus speaking," she said, more alert.

"How business like."

"Hello, Kyle. What's up?"

"You shouldn't ask that question."

"Funny...funny."

"Can we meet tonight?" Kyle asked.

"My time is valuable, as yours always seems to be. I have plans."

"With who, that lawyer friend of yours?"

"That's my business. Besides, you have a wife—or did you forget about that?" she asked, cuffing the phone, not wanting the others to hear. "I think I'm entitled to have a friend."

"Ali, why do we always fight? I don't like quarreling with you. I love you, and you love me, so why do you act like this?"

"Pick me up at eight," she said reluctantly, giving in, again.

"How about nine?"

"Always has to be your way, doesn't it? Good-bye," she said, slamming the phone down, forgetting momentarily where she was, making a complete spectacle of herself.

She twirled around in the desk chair a few times to let off steam; otherwise, she would have exploded. She ignored the few heads that popped up from what they were doing, and were now staring at her. She didn't care what her co-workers thought. She did her job, and she did it well. And her personal life was her business. Not theirs. And she refused to apologize to them for her childish behavior. She despised Kyle for causing her to act angrily, but she couldn't stop loving him, and she continued to let him manipulate her. She promised herself she wouldn't let this man rule her. That was a promise she had broken again and again.

The day was winding down. Mr. Steinberg didn't come by with a deposit as he had pledged. After two hours, she thought maybe he had changed his mind. Her dreams of all the things she was going to do with that money were slowly dissipating. Earlier she'd had plans of taking Benjamin to Disney World, stashing money away for his education, and investing in a new wardrobe for herself.

She should have learned from her past history that she should never count on something before it happens. Too many disappointments can arise. But just as she thought those reveries were shattered, Mr. Steinberg strutted in with a sweet smelling stogie suspended from his mouth. The short stubby, bald-headed man handed her a certified check, as a binding deposit for the sale of the luxurious commercial property at Cedar and Hill!

CHAPTER 26

Marc was waiting for her in his car when she got home. He jumped out when he saw her and hurried over to help her.

"Busy day today, Counselor?" she asked, smiling up at him.

"Never too busy for you, Miss Porteus." He picked Ben out of his car seat and carried him into the house, and then he trotted back out to assist her. She loved the attention he gave her.

"How was your day."

"No sales, at least nothing definite, but I can't complain."

"I see your managing quite well on those crutches."

"I get frustrated sometimes—when I can't move as fast as I'd like to."

"Just remember you won't be like that forever."

"I try."

"Slower can be nice, especially when one's admiring a beautiful young lady as yourself.

"Flattery can get you everywhere."

"I was hoping," he said, taking a deep breath, sporting a wide grin. "So, have you reached Catherine McCaffrey yet?"

"No. Not yet."

"Now is a good time to try. Don't you think?"

"Yeah, definitely. Why not," she said, feeling a bit of discomfort. She was afraid something might go wrong. They wouldn't find him or, worse yet, he wouldn't want to see her. She had been procrastinating, and Marc knew it. Marc was extremely perceptive. He knew what she was feeling, sometimes before she did.

Once Ben was content in his playpen, they sat down at the kitchen table to make the phone call, the one that could make a significant change in her life. Marc had the look of encouragement plastered all over his face. She picked up the piece of paper that had her number and carefully dialed. She heard a small soft voice, far away, say, "Hello." She couldn't speak at first. Mrs. McCaffrey repeated the greeting, "Hello."

"Uh…. Uh…,"she muttered.

"I say, is anyone there?" Catherine McCaffrey asked, a tad louder.

"Yes, Mrs. McCaffrey." She finally said in a squeaky voice.

"Who is this?" she demanded.

"You don't know me. My name is Allyson Porteus," she announced in a shaky but stronger voice. There was silence for a few moments.

"Alexander's daughter?"

"Yes, Ma'am."

"How dare you contact me. How did you get my number?" she asked clearly miffed now.

"Mrs. McCaffrey, please hear me out," she cried.

"This is nonsense. I don't need to listen to this."

"I'm sorry for any pain my dad may have caused you, but I'm not him. I have grown up without brothers and sisters. I was a very lonely child. My father recently confessed to me that I have a brother…your son. I just want to meet him."

"This is ludicrous."

"Please, Mrs. McCaffrey. Please tell me where he is. It would mean so much to me."

"He doesn't want to see you," she said bitterly.

"Let him tell me that."

"He can't. Don't call again," she said, wrathfully. Click! Down went the phone in her ear. Holding the receiver away from her, she looked at Marc, and he could see how profoundly disappointed she was.

"Don't give up, Ali. She's upset. That's understandable. Give her time to think things over. She'll come around," he said with great assurance in his tone.

"What if she doesn't?"

"When have you become a pessimist?"

"Right now."

"Can I cheer you up, by taking you and Ben for a spaghetti and meatball dinner, at Roseys?" he asked with a hopeful smile.

"Just one meatball?" she pouted.

"For the lady, all the meatballs she wants," he added.
"Then how can I refuse? It's a date," she said, smiling.

❋   ❋   ❋

The young waitress warmed Ben's milk; this old family restaurant catered to children. Marc showered Ben with attention, keeping him in good behavior. A customer stopped near their table, stooped down to pick up one of Ben's squeezable toys that had fallen on the floor, and remarked to Marc that he had a beautiful and well-behaved son. Marc beamed from ear to ear and thanked the elderly gentleman.

Allyson was having such a good time with Marc, she almost forgot about Kyle. She couldn't tell Marc she was meeting him at nine. She'd only being confusing him again. As they were finishing up dessert, she glanced at her watch. It was quarter to seven, close to Ben's bedtime. She was so afraid Kyle would arrive before Marc left. How was she was going to handle the situation if this happened? With Felicia being home, she could end this evening earlier than usual with Marc. She wished she had put Kyle on hold, but he still had an undeniable hook in her. Maybe because he was the father of her son, or because in many ways he reminded her of her dad.

She tucked Benjamin into bed, and the three of them sat down for a cup of coffee. They chatted awhile about the real-estate business, then about Felicia's teaching job, and finally about Marc's prestigious position as an attorney. She felt a little guilty knowing their relationship revolved around her, and she knew so little about Marc's personal life. Nevertheless, when the cuckoo clock on the wall in the hallway struck the half time at 8:30 P.M., she knew she had to break up this little social gathering.

"It's later than I thought," she said, yawning. Hint, hint. Felicia cleared the coffee cups from the table.

"I think it's time I leave. You girls look a little tired."

"Oh, no. I'm fine. Don't leave on account of me. I'll go to my bedroom." Allyson gave Felicia a swift kick under the table, and then gave her the pungent eye. "Ouch," she yipped, as she leaped from her seat. "I think something bit me. A yellow jacket flew in the other day, but I never caught him. He must still be around."

Allyson felt her face getting hot. He looked over at her. She couldn't avoid the dubious glimpse he was sending her. She knew he suspected something.

"I appreciate that, but I have a busy day tomorrow. Thanks anyway," he said, reaching for his jacket.

She started to get up to walk him to the door. "Don't get up," he said, bending over to kiss her on the forehead. "I can see my way out." She wasn't sure if he was being considerate of her condition, or if he was just incensed at what he may have surmised.

CHAPTER 27

Kyle arrived only minutes after Marc left. She was hoping they didn't pass each other, and if they did that they wouldn't take no notice, but that was doubtful in a small town—Kyle's shiny red convertible could hardly be missed.

"I don't believe this. You didn't tell me you were meeting Kyle tonight!" Felicia screamed upon seeing his car.

"I haven't had a chance. He called me at work today, and when I got home Marc was here."

"Wow, that was close."

"Too close."

"What a life! Should I be so lucky!"

"It's not as glamorous as you may think."

Kyle honked the horn when he pulled up. Felicia beckoned him to come to the door. But before he even made a move, Allyson hobbled past her on her crutches. Instead of rushing up to assist her when he saw her, he stopped midway, looking at her as if she had two heads.

"I only have a sprained foot. Don't worry, I'm not contagious."

"What happened?" he finally managed to ask.

"When I was running the other morning—before dawn, I stumbled over some driftwood. Nothing serious. I'll live."

"When is that thing going to come off?" he asked looking down at her bandages.

"Why? Does that make a difference to you?"

"No. Of course not," he answered indignantly. "Why should it?"

That was the start and end of their conversation, until they had their first nightcap in Hyannis.

"I passed your attorney friend on Beaver Dam on the way to your house."

"Did he see you?"

"I don't know. Is there something going on between you two?"

"Do you mean, am I making love to him?"

"Are you?"

"No. Should I be? Stupid me is hopelessly devoted to her married lover."

"Why do you act like this?" he asked, moving over to nibble on her ear. She could feel his warm breath, as he panted down behind her neck. Her body was already warm from the minty liqueur they had devoured. Smelling his cologne, he was even more desirable to her.

"Spend the night with me," he whispered in her ear.

"How?"

"She's away. She left tonight at eight. I helped pack her bags, and I drove her to the airport before I came to get you."

"For how long?"

"A few days. We can spend every night together."

"You mean the three of us? You, me, and Ben under the same roof?"

"You got it, babe."

"Fabulous."

She called Felicia to tell her what was happening. But when Allyson told Felicia she was spending the night with Kyle and that she'd be home in the morning, before Ben awoke, she told her to be careful. Allyson told her she would.

When they got to the guesthouse behind the Caldwell mansion, their secret hide-away, she fantasized she was a princess being carried by her prince into the palace. He dropped her gently on the bed, and slowly undressed her. Then she watched him undress himself under the dimmed wall lights. Then he placed his strong chiseled body next to hers. His large warm hands cupped her breasts. He fondled them playfully while kissing her lips. She closed her eyes as he worked his tongue slowly down her neck, across her chest, and over her stomach. She arched her back waiting fervently for his manly part to enter her. And when he finally hooded her body with his and she felt his hardness, she moaned and moaned with intense pleasure.

However, it seemed to be over much too quickly. They were alone. There was much too discuss with him. She wanted to talk about Ben. Them. She needed to know if there was a future for the three of them. But after she took a shower, he was out cold. She nudged him, but he didn't budge. He was already snoring.

She didn't get much sleep. Even though she and Marc had no real physical intimacy, somehow she felt closer to him than she did to Kyle.

The next few nights, Kyle showed up just in time to climb in bed with her. He never came early enough to talk about their life together. It was always postponed until another time, a time, which of course would never come. Kyle had an excuse for everything, and everything he said made sense, when he was around.

Janice was back from her trip before they had a chance to resolve their differences. They never did discuss them. Allyson wanted to know if there was a future for them, whether they'd ever be together as a family. Or was this the way it was always going to be—separate lives bound together by moments of shallow passion.

CHAPTER 28

Tourists were coming in droves from all over the country. The traffic was horrendous as usual, and every fast food restaurant, antique shop, and ice cream parlor on Cape Cod was booming with business. The beaches were crowded, but they were fortunate to have their own private beach. Ben's copper tan glittered in the sun as he played with his pail and shovel in the chalky sands and splashed in the small pools of tepid water, left behind from high tide.

Suddenly, a beach ball rolled past their blanket. Out of the corner of her eye, Allyson saw Ben stand up, take a couple of steps and try to chase the ball, but he tumbled. She nudged Felicia, who was lying next to her with her eyes closed.

"Did you see that?"

"See what?" she asked, sitting up, shading her eyes from the bright sun.

"Ben took two steps!" Allyson said excitedly.

"That's great," Felicia said lying back down. "He's due."

"I can't believe this."

"Before you know it, he'll be jogging right along beside you. They say kids grow up fast...."

It made Allyson think of the future filled with those many wonderful events—his first day at elementary school, when Ben would get on the big school bus. She visualized her son looking almost lost, so small, standing next to it.

"Hello. Earth to Allyson."

"Felicia, I was just thinking. Kyle will probably miss out on a lot of important events in Ben's life. I feel so bad for Ben."

"Don't feel bad. Lots of kids grow up without a father today. It's the eighties. It isn't like it was years ago. I remember the time when I was the only kid in the class whose parents were separated. Now half the students in my classroom come from broken homes. Kids adjust."

"Did you?" Allyson asked.

"No. But that was different. Times have changed."

"Maybe so, but people haven't. They still have all the same feelings we had, Felice."

"You're strong, Ali. And you and I can make up for Kyle not being around. I'll spoil him rotten. Ben will be just fine, you'll see."

"Won't he need more, being a boy and all? Every boy needs a father."

"That's an old wives' tale. You can give him just as much as Kyle could—and more. Believe me. It'll all work out. Stop worrying."

"If you say so. You know, Felice, I'm so happy we're friends."

"Yeah, me too."

Ben didn't take any more steps that day, but it was the beginning.

As Allyson watched her son play in the sand, wishing the best for him, she thought about her own life too. She had no luck in getting through to Catherine. Ms. McCaffrey got so fed up with her that she changed her number. "Unpublished," the operator told Allyson. She'd unintentionally stirred up a lot of old emotions in the woman. Just hearing her name was enough, she was sure. Catherine tearfully begged Allyson to leave her alone. Allyson could understand some of what she was feeling. She had no right to invade her privacy or to hurt her; her selfish and irresponsible father had already done that. Too many years had passed, and she couldn't even be sure if her brother would want to see her anyway.

Allyson was conversing with Marc on a regular basis, but he thought it was best to stay away for awhile, well aware of her confused state concerning Kyle. She couldn't blame him. He had no idea where he stood with her. She was certain he cared deeply for her, and she was not clarifying anything by having an ongoing affair with Kyle. Could it even be labeled that? She called it a hit or miss affinity. She was the bait, ready and willing, and she continued to allow him to chew her up and spit her out—whenever he wished.

CHAPTER 29

When Allyson and Felicia arrived home that afternoon, a silver Lincoln was parked directly in front of the house, with a chauffeur sitting inside. They looked at each other. A black gentleman stepped out of the car when he saw them approaching.

"Miss Allyson Porteus?"

"Yes?"

"For you, Madame," he said, handing her a sealed envelope, addressed to her in handwriting that was unfamiliar to her. She hesitated, then she opened it.

Dear Allyson,

I sent my chauffeur, Nathan, to invite you and your son to my place for a small tea party at 4:00 P.M. today. There are matters of importance that need to be discussed immediately. I hope you'll accept my invitation. I'll be waiting in the tea parlor.

Cordially, Janice Caldwell

She looked up at Nathan and asked him if he knew what this was all about, and he just shook his head. What prompted her to think a chauffeur would be informed of anything, especially Janice Caldwell's chauffeur? She looked at her watch. It was 3:45 P.M. and there was no time to change. She had her bathing suit on, covered with a black net smock. Her body was oily from the tanning lotion, and her hair was dry from the sun and salt. Ben was wiped out, and his diaper was drenched. She had a few minutes to freshen up. She hurried into the house with Ben and changed his diaper. She quickly dressed him in a clean, cool outfit. Then she ran a brush through her hair, putting it into a ponytail, and she slipped into lightweight cotton pants and a body shirt. In only five minutes, they were ready and en route to the Caldwell mansion.

The ride to the big old colonial was cool and relaxing, and the music was soothing to her ears. Due to the salt air and the hot sun earlier, then entering the air-conditioned Lincoln, Ben fell asleep instantly. In spite of the car's coolness, she was still perspiring from the heat of curiosity. She wondered what this meeting was all about. Had Janice Caldwell found out that Ben was Kyle's baby?

Maybe she asked him for a divorce, so that they could live together, finally, as a real family. Pipe dreams. She may just want to speak to her about Mr. Steinberg. Or maybe Mr. Steinberg raved about her so much that she now wants to purchase or sell some property through her. The suspense was driving her crazy. Why did she invite Ben? Was she just being polite? Maybe she should just have Nathan turn the car around and go home. The closer they got to the mansion, the more her stomach churned. She thought she'd be sick when the Lincoln finally glided to a smooth halt in front of the big sturdy white structure.

When Nathan opened the door to escort them out, her legs went completely rubber. She carefully unfastened Ben and picked him out of his car seat. He stayed asleep as she carried him in her arms to the front entrance of the huge mansion. Her legs were weak and trembling when she rang the bell. A short, middle-aged Chinese man opened the door.

"I'm Miss Porteus and this is my son, Benjamin," she said.

The man gawked at them oddly for a moment.

"We're expected, at 4:00 P.M., for tea," she said, trying to pull out the note she got from Janice to show him. "We're a few minutes late."

"Ah, come in. Yes, she's expecting you."

How convenient, she thought.

The little man led her through a maze of French doors and hallways. Between her agitated nerves and the heavy weight of Benjamin, she thought she'd collapse before she got there. When they finally reached the tea parlor, Janice was waiting to greet them. The room was as lovely as the rest of the house. The walls were subdued in a pale mauve and Monet paintings. The two eighteenth century Queen Anne chairs and the tall curio cabinet were carved elegantly in rich cherry wood. The glass casing was filled with bone china and sterling silver trays, cups, and bowls. The wood floors were protected with plush white carpeting, which her feet sank into as they crossed the room. Janice Caldwell ushered them over to a custom-made sofa, designed in a pastel floral print. Adjacent to the sofa was a matching love seat. She had everything she wished and hoped for, even the man she loved.

"Thank you for coming," Janice said graciously, extending her hand to her in the same way she did the night of her summer's end party.

"My pleasure," Allyson said, shaking her hand. Her eyes were intense and laid directly on her, while she completely avoided looking at Ben. As always, she looked lovely as ever. Her beautiful silvery blonde hair was swept off her neck and pinned up perfectly in a barrette, exposing shimmering diamond earrings. She wore a V-necked crepe black blouse, revealing a gold chain with a diamond pendant which hung nicely from her swan-like neck. A diamond-faced Rolex watch was anchored around her tiny wrist, and there was that big shiny rock on her left hand. Allyson observed her as she easily moved about in her pleated vanilla slacks, complimentary to her youthful figure.

"How've you been, my dear?" Janice inquired, looking at her intently, as she seemed to study her.

"We've been just fine. Excuse our appearance. We just got off the beach when we saw your chauffeur waiting for us." Allyson couldn't believe she was actually apologizing to Janice for their casual, less-than-opulent attire. If she could have, she would have kicked herself. But admiring her impeccable beauty prompted the words from her mouth. Maybe it was more than just money that attracted Kyle to this luxurious lifestyle.

"That's quite all right. It was short notice. I'm a very busy lady."

"I understand. My dad ran for town moderator when I was a kid," Allyson conveyed.

"Is that so," Janice remarked, staring with interest at her. "Is your father still running for a position?"

"Actually, that was a long time ago. I was very young, and I really don't remember much about it. I want to thank you for referring Mr. Steinberg to me," Allyson uttered, changing the subject, wishing she'd get to the source of this insignificant meeting.

At that moment, a stocky dark maid walked through the French doors carrying a silver tray that held a teapot and crumpets. She poured the hot tea into two bone china cups, and left. Janice handed her her cup, and she placed her average-sized hand onto the tiny ring to lift the delicate cup to her mouth.

Allyson suddenly felt uneasy. The small talk was getting boring. They talked about the weather, the tourists, and what stars were coming to the playhouse. Janice glanced at her diamond watch after a few more minutes of this ridiculous nonsense.

"I may as well get to the core of this little meeting of ours," she said.

At last, hallelujah, Allyson thought. The dreadful waiting would soon be over. At that split second, Ben awoke. Frightened by the strange atmosphere, he began to cry. Allyson kissed him and rocked him in her arms, until he quieted down. Janice's attention was drawn to Ben. Her concentration was only on him now. She seemed to be in a trance. Allyson became convinced at that very moment that she knew. Her face said it all. It was indisputable that Ben was Kyle's son.

As Ben became more active, squirming in her arms, Janice appeared to be getting uptight. She stood and started pacing. It was as if all of a sudden she lost her train of thought. She wasn't used to having children around. After all, it had been years since her children were that small.

Then she spoke. "I was taken off guard for a moment by the slight interruption. I might as well get to the point. The reason I requested your presence…I wanted to give you and your son…let's say…a gift—a quarter of a million dollars."

"Why that's very generous of you, Janice. May I call you Janice?"

"Sure, we're both adults."

"And what, may I ask, are you asking from me in return?" she inquired with great apprehension.

"Just a small favor, my dear," she said, smiling sweetly, treating her as if she were a child.

"And what is that small favor, may I ask?" Allyson said, smiling plastically back at her.

"There's no sense of beating around the bush. I want you and your baby to leave the Cape. Permanently. Forget who his father is," she replied, staring at Ben, and then back at her.

"That simple, huh?" Allyson said, staring at her bleakly, the anger starting to build up now.

She nodded. "There's no future for you here. You can accept the money and start a new life for you and your baby—somewhere else, where no one knows your situation."

"He has a name," Allyson said pointedly, speaking louder than her normal tone of voice. "His name is Benjamin."

"I didn't mean to upset you."

"No, I'm sure that wasn't your intention…. Does Kyle know about this?"

"I didn't see any reason to have to bring him into it. He'll never divorce me," she said with reliance. "And, nevertheless, in spite of his silly attraction for you, I have no cause to divorce him. As you can plainly see, he's still with me, so there's no reason for you to stay here. Besides, what kind of life would Ben have when he finds out his father is married to me? Have a little dignity, my dear. Hide your shame, and spare—your Benjamin, pain."

Allyson wanted to slap her face, but she had Ben in her arms, and she didn't want him to witness any physical violence, not that he'd remember, but she didn't want to belittle herself either. As she clenched her teeth, seething with anger, she could feel her blood pressure rising. Ready to explode.

"You can't put a price tag on people's lives. Who do you think you are lady? Kyle loves Ben, his only son!" Allyson emphasized, shouting at her. "I'll never leave this town!" she screamed, carrying Ben in her arms, stomping from the room.

"You'll regret this," Allyson heard Janice say distantly, as she hurried through the French doors, uncertain of her whereabouts but trying to find her way out of there as fast as she could. Her vision blurred from tears that had welled up. Ben felt her tension and began to cry, but she didn't stop to comfort him. She kept running until she ran straight into Sam, the butler. He saw her distraction and showed her to the main entrance, where she exited hastily.

Nathan was standing by the door of the Lincoln when Allyson came rushing out. He swiftly opened the rear door for her to enter. She scrambled inside with Ben snuggled in her arms. He was clinging to her tightly, sobbing. The poor kid had no clue as to what was happening. All he knew was that something had upset his mother, so on the ride home she consoled Ben, letting him know his mommy was okay. He must have felt reassured because he fell asleep rather quickly.

Allyson cried a river of tears. This woman had the audacity to surmise that the money she offered her would make her melt away. Although the more she thought about it, the more she believed Janice was right. What kind of life would Ben have seeing his father married to someone other than his mother? It would also be tough for him to face ridicule at school. If kids overheard gossiping parents, they might tease Ben about his daddy. It would break his heart, and this in turn, would break hers.

There were a lot of decisions to be made. It would be hard to leave the place she had always loved; this peaceful region Aunt Edith had helped her discover when she was only a child. Cape Cod had introduced her to a happiness when there was none.

Her life was suddenly in a complete turmoil—so much was happening at once. She still yearned to find her lost brother. Kyle was floating in and out of her life, while Marc remained on hold. She wasn't sure how much longer Marc would wait for her. She had not only her own life to consider, but Benjamin's life as well.

By the time the Lincoln pulled into her driveway, her tears had dried. She freshened up the best she could. She had to hide her feelings from Felicia. Janice's offer needed to be kept a secret. But as she had anticipated, Felicia was waiting apprehensively for them to return.

"Curious George, I'm going to keep you in suspense."

"Come on. How can you do this to me? Does she know?"

"Know what? That Ben is Kyle's?"

"Well—does she?"

"If she does, she didn't let on."

"Why'd she invite you then?"

"Didn't I tell you? She referred a wealthy gentleman to me. Who, by the way, is buying some commercial property valued at 1.3 million dollars," Allyson said, smiling. "She just wanted to know how I was doing with the deal. Looking for gratitude, I guess."

"That's it?" Felicia asked, the sound of disappointment clinging to her voice.

"That's all she said."

That night when Allyson went to bed, she reluctantly thought about the money Janice was offering. They could have a good life. She could buy a small farm in Kansas or Wisconsin, and have chickens, and cows, and a few horses. She could teach Ben how to ride. He would love it. She would always be there for him. She couldn't take the place of his father, but she'd surely give him enough love for two parents. On the other hand, she would miss the beach, and the smell of the salt air, and the ocean breeze blowing through her hair. However, she realized Janice had the ammo, "villainous saltpetre" to capsize their lives as long as they remained here on the Cape.

CHAPTER 30

Other than the winter months, summer was one of the slowest times of the year for the real-estate profession. Folks couldn't be bothered with buying or selling their property during these warm and favorable months.

Allyson had a sufficient amount of money to live carefully for a while, knowing it wouldn't be long before she'd be relishing a grand commission from that 1.3 million dollar sale. She hadn't even thought about calculating her fee yet, though. She wanted to be sure that Janice wasn't going to find a way to screw things up for her. She had the power to destroy her sale in a split second, even if it cost her a few grand in the process. For her to lose a few thousand, it would be painless, but to Ben and her, it was everything. It would mean survival.

For days she was haunted by the fear of not being able to provide for her son in the coming years; of not being able to give him all the nice things other little boys his age would have and enjoy as he grew toward manhood. The real-estate profession was great when homes and business property sold. But what if they had another recession. Then what?

She hadn't whispered anything about her meeting with Janice. It was something she would have to decipher by herself. At least she thought she could do it alone. Then it became a question of whom does she talk to first about the conditions of her outrageous proposal. And when? In a flash, she became apprehensive and worried that others wouldn't give her the answers she wanted to hear—or wanted to accept. She didn't want to be persuaded by whatever solution they thought, in their minds, was best for Ben and her. She needed to figure it out from her own soul. However, before she even got a chance to do all of that, she received a certified letter from Janice. It was even more disturbing than the Tea.

༨

"Dear Allyson,

After the last upset, I thought it would be best to address you in writing to avoid any further confrontation. Kyle and I have discussed Ben's welfare at great length. Since Kyle is obviously the father of your child, we feel it is wise that the boy reside with us. We're able to offer him so much more. We can send him to the finest schools. He'd be happy here. We don't expect an answer immediately. To make it worth your while, we're willing to sacrifice a handsome four million.

Sincerely,

Janice Caldwell"

Allyson couldn't believe what she was reading here. This woman thought money could do anything! She was trying to destroy her life, and Allyson knew she could do it if she really wanted to. Well, bull, she thought. She wasn't going to let this cruel and heartless bitch take control of their lives. Not now! Not ever! Tears coursed down her cheeks, but anger was the emotion that prevailed. She folded up the letter and stuffed it into her purse. She lifted Ben into her arms, hugged him, and told him she loved him. Then she swiftly carried him out to the car, buckled him in, and drove to the Caldwell mansion. When she reached the long driveway leading to the mansion, she glanced into the mirror to wipe away any remaining tears. She didn't want her hurt and pain to be interpreted as signs of fragility. Not that she should care about what Janice Caldwell thought, for Allyson knew she was born a combatant when the situation called for it. And it wouldn't be long before Janice would discover that her money couldn't—and wouldn't—buy her out.

Then, lost in her reveries and without any warning, there, right smack in front of her, was the silver Lincoln. She slammed on the brakes. Thank God, Ben was secured tightly in his car seat. She sat still and thought for a moment, her hands clenched to the wheel. Nathan, Janice's chauffeur, was by this time standing next to her window.

"Are you all right, Miss Porteus?" he asked with concern.

"We're fine, Nathan. Thank you."

"Mrs. Caldwell is not at home. She had an engagement."

"I'm really not here to see Janice. Is Kyle around?"

"No, Ma'am. He spun out of here on two wheels about an hour ago."

"Thanks Nathan."

He bowed politely and walked back to the Lincoln. She left and headed directly to the Sea Breeze Inn. She had always found it to be a cheery spot with a great deal of class—both an Inn and a country club. It was a place where Kyle liked to mingle with the beautiful people. He was a popular figure among the help, and also the clientele.

After getting herself in such a tizzy and aware of the fury that was seething just below the surface, she found that he wasn't there after all. In fact, nobody in the place had seen or heard from him that day. So they claimed. Next she swung by a couple of the other clubs where he hung out fairly regularly. These less classy spots were where they'd often meet and felt comfortable being who they were. As much as Kyle enjoyed the affluence of his lifestyle, he didn't completely fit in with Janice's clan. They were much older than him and sometimes far too sophisticated for Kyle's blood. At thirty-three he was just beginning to sow his oats, and Janice's friends were advancing toward, or had already passed, their fiftieth birthday.

After driving about for more than two hours trying to track Kyle down to give him a piece of her mind, somewhat calmer now, she ventured down a shelled road whose borders were alive with lush vegetation. Along with everything else that was a part of the Caldwell estate, there was a horse stable that sheltered six well-groomed horses, cared for by two retired jockeys. Janice had acquired many more of these beautiful beasts when her father was alive. And from what Allyson understood even some prized racing horses once occupied these now near empty stalls. Kyle told her that after his father-in-law passed on, eventually; one by one she sold the horses. All but these six remain.

Allyson trampled over the green grassy field filled with wild flowers, pondering the idea of Ben living with Janice and Kyle. Almost instantly she began to loathe this man. Every inch of him. She couldn't perceive how he could even contemplate the idea of taking Ben away from her. She was at her boiling point. She needed desperately to hear his version of the story, but maybe it was better that she couldn't locate him, because she was so enraged that she felt as though she could scratch his eyes out. She searched each stall frantically hoping to find him. A place he'd sometimes come when things weren't going the way he wanted them to. She wanted to find him right away, but he was nowhere to be found.

She sat alone weeping in the lofty field, while Ben ran freely about the open vastness, picking dandelions and daisies. And when he could hold no more in his small hands, he ran over and gave them to her. His smile was so big. Right then, she knew she would never let anyone, including Janice Caldwell, take Ben away from her. Not even his father. She would stand up to both of them, and do whatever she had to do to keep Ben with her, where he righteously and morally belonged. She took Ben's hand in hers and they walked back to the stables.

"Let's go see the horsies," she said, smiling down at him. Ben got very excited when he saw them. He pointed and she saw the gleam in his eyes. Her son wanted to ride, but there was no time for that now. "Another time, Mommy will take you for a ride," she said.

"No, now," he cried, shaking his head fiercely.

She knew there could be a lot of "no's" in the future, and the thought of not being able to give her child all that she wanted to give him, what he deserved, saddened her.

Unable to locate Kyle, she drove in the direction of Marc's house. She had to talk to somebody who'd understand, and at the same time she needed somebody who could be objective too. Mr. Kelsey was the perfect one for her to turn to.

❧   ❧   ❧

Marc opened the front door of his house, looking frazzled—like he had stuck himself in a light socket. His hair was disheveled, with his reading glasses roosting on top. His shirttail was dislodged from his pants.

"I hope I'm not interrupting anything. Do you have company?" she asked, peeking in, praying she was wrong.

Do you mean, do I have another woman here?"

"Yeah, something like that."

"I'm saving myself—for you," he said smiling genuinely. "Come in. I've been working on a case." He showed them inside. There were business papers scattered throughout the dining room table and others were crinkled up on the floor.

"Pretty heavy stuff, huh?"

"No, nothing I can't solve. Had I known you were coming, I would've cleaned up a bit. How ya doing, big guy?" Ben just smiled.

"Sorry for the intrusion. I needed to talk to someone."

"Well, here I am," he said, with his arms stretched open for her to enter them. She didn't hesitate; she ran straight to him and began sobbing.

"Now, now. It can't be all that bad," he said, with his arms gently around her.

"It's worse. Janice and Kyle want to take Ben away from me," she said, sobbing even harder.

"What? They can't do that! You're his mother. They have no right," he said, wiping her tears away with his hankie. "Start from the beginning," he insisted.

She reached into her pocketbook and handed him the note Janice had sent her. As he began reading her hurtful words, his eyes widened.

"There's more. Not long ago, she invited Ben and me over to the mansion for tea. She referred a wealthy client to me, so I thought this was what it was all about. But it wasn't," she said, still sobbing.

"Go on," he said, holding her hand, looking intently into her eyes while sitting across from her.

"She wanted to give me a quarter of a million dollars to leave the Cape, and to forget who Ben's father is."

"That's crazy. Who does this woman think she is?" He stood up and began pacing the floor. "She doesn't have a leg to stand on." Then he stopped pacing and thought for a moment. "Ben doesn't have his name, does he?"

"Why? Does that make a difference?"

"Just tell me."

"No."

"That's good," he said, with a sigh of relief.

"Yeah?"

"That's right. This makes a significant difference. They can't make any claims on him. Unless they want to go through a paternity suit first. Then the court would have to find you an unfit mother, and so on, and so on. It's such a long and drawn-out procedure. It could take a couple of years. The entire town would get wind of it. I don't think the prominent lady herself would want any scandals. It would scar her reputation and may hurt her political stature. God forbid should that happen," he said, grinning mischievously.

"But she can still make our lives miserable."

"Only if you let her."

"Maybe this is being selfish of me, but they can give him so much more than I can. Better schools…clothing…trips…cars."

"Do you hear yourself? What did you just describe?"

"I know. Material things are important to kids today. They fear they won't fit in, otherwise. Let's face it, it's a material world out there."

"It's not the real world, and you know it. Ben won't suffer from not having any of that stuff."

"But...."

"But nothing," he said, sitting down across from her, sealing her lips with his fingers. "Don't give it another thought."

Suddenly, she realized Ben wasn't in the same room as them. "Where's Ben?" she asked in a panic.

"He's in the den with Tricia and Kasey."

"Who?"

"My two Persian cats."

"He may have met Charlie too."

"Charlie?"

"My parakeet."

"Oh," she said.

They held Ben's interest while Marc and Allyson tried to make some sense out of Janice's depravity. Allyson felt Janice was trying to seek some kind of vengeance because of her affair with her husband. But she was being far too wicked.

Marc tried to console Allyson and did his best to convince her that Janice and Kyle couldn't take Ben away from her. She felt so rehabilitated just being with him, but she still feared losing Ben. Marc invited them to stay for supper, and she gratefully accepted. The old Cape had a big, sunny country kitchen with a good-sized pantry. She helped him prepare, while he barbecued some chicken breasts, boiled up some clams, and steamed several ears of corn.

"Can I use your phone. I wanna give Felicia a call to let her know where I am. She worries so...."

"Sure. Go ahead. You can use the phone in my bedroom upstairs to your left, or the one in the dining room."

"I can call from dining room. That's fine."

"I want to warn you, it's a bit disorderly in there," he said, as she walked in. "That's where I am the most. That's where I spread my wings, so to speak."

"Maybe I will use the phone upstairs."

"Turn left, first door on the right," he said.

She climbed the stairs and hooked a left, and an immediate right. His bedroom door was open when she walked in. She noticed everything was orderly, even in his open closet. But other than a double bed, with an ordinary bedspread and matching curtains, a larger dresser, and an old chest, there was little else in there. The room was clearly unadorned, but she saw possibilities.

"Your place is really nice. Would you mind if I took a look around?"

"Not at all. Don't mind the mess. I did have a housekeeper coming once a week. She moved out west somewhere. About a month ago. Her sister was sick. I never looked for anyone else."

"How old is this place?" she asked, as she dialed home to tell Felicia not to wait dinner for them.

"It was originally built in 1872, and then refurbished in the early 1900's by a man named Nickerson."

"It's really nice. Cozy."

"It needs a woman's touch," he smiled at her, holding barbecue utensils in his pot holder hands. He was headed outdoors to check on the chicken.

After the delicious meal, they played some ball with Ben, in Marc's nicely landscaped yard. Ben and Marc still seemed to get along quite well. Although, after a short while, Ben showed signs of being tired. It was time to leave. She didn't want to wreck what had turned out to be a really pleasant evening.

As she drove home, she tried to rationalize what was happening. Janice's hurtful letter, along with Kyle's participation in all this, would have crushed her entirely if Marc hadn't been there to explain the law to her.

CHAPTER 31

She was surprised to see Kyle's Porsche parked in her driveway. She gazed into the back seat at Ben. He was sound asleep. She prayed he would stay asleep, so that his father and her could have a talk. She quickly, but warily, retrieved Ben from his car seat and carried him to the house. But once she was inside, Felicia and Kyle weren't to be seen anywhere. Allyson became so flustered when she saw Kyle's car in the driveway, she forgot to see if Felicia's car was also there. She tiptoed inside with Ben, undressed him, put him in his pj's, and laid him in his bed. But as she was leaving his room, she thought she heard the slightest whisper of a sound coming from the vicinity of Felicia's bedroom.

"Felicia, is that you?" she asked quietly. But there was no response. Felicia's door was shut tight. Maybe she was sick or something. Allyson tapped lightly upon her door. Still no response. Her hand froze on the door latch. She couldn't get herself to lift it.

She swiftly released her hand and walked briskly through the rest of the small-canal of the cottage. The bathroom door was slightly ajar. She asked if anyone was in there. But nobody answered her. The light was off, so she opened the door fully. There were no signs of Kyle, or Felicia. Only the mystery that remained behind Felicia's sealed bedroom door. A puzzlement she wasn't ready to confront. She hurried to the window to see if Felicia's Volvo was out-side. It was. Then she heard what sounded like moans. And she could tell they definitely were moans of fervent passion. She had to face what she was afraid to see. What she had surmised was true. Her head began to whirl. Her body was trembling fiercely. But that didn't stop her. She tore into that bedroom like a mad woman. And there in front of her, was her best friend, and the man she loved, in bed together!

"You son of a bitch! You get the hell out of my house!" she screamed at the top of her lungs. Kyle jumped from the bed in a spasm of surprise, looking as if he were about to perform a jackknife dive at the Olympics. He hurried past her and went straight into the bathroom. Felicia stood there looking astonished, her naked body concealed under a bed sheet.

"I—I didn't think you'd be home," she said, stuttering.

"So that gives you the right to be with Kyle?" she screamed, seething with fury.

"I'm sorry. Please forgive me, Ali. I didn't mean to. It just happened," she said.

"And I just happened to come home at the wrong time, right? I would've never known about this if I hadn't caught you two bastards together!"

"Kyle and I were talking about you and I…."

"Save it! Pack up, and get the hell out!"

"Now?"

"Yeah now!"

"But I have nowhere to go," she cried.

"I have no mercy. I don't care if you sleep in the street. Just get out. You're no friend of mine."

"But Ali, I'm really your friend," she pleaded.

"Past tense," Allyson uttered, walking out of the room.

And as Allyson walked around the corner from the hallway, she collided with Kyle. He was exiting from the bathroom, fully dressed now, except his shirt wasn't completely buttoned.

"You bastard," she said, taking her fists and pounding them as hard as she could into his chest, weeping hysterically. "How could you do this to me?"

"You were with your attorney friend."

"So this justifies what you did?" He didn't answer. "For the record, I wasn't sleeping with him, you stupid jackass! I forget sometimes how you make a career of doing this."

"Stop it, Allyson. I told you I'm sorry. What more do you want? It was a mistake."

"A mistake!"

He took her in his arms, and she sobbed against him. His embrace, however, wasn't comforting. Suddenly, it didn't feel the same anymore. It felt different, foreign and alienated. She backed away from him. His perpetual charm wasn't working this time. She was still too enraged and overwhelmed with all that had happened.

She pulled the letter Janice sent her from her pocketbook, and flung the now raveled sheet.

"What the hell is this all about?" she asked, as he picked it up from the floor and began reading. Before he could answer, she shouted: "You'll never get my son!"

"I don't want to take your son from you," he said calmly. "He belongs with you. You're a great mother. It's just that…."

"What?"

"Well, Janice feels we can…well…she can give him…I mean we have the pool…tennis courts…horses. We have everything a little boy could ever want."

"And what about love? Can she give him that?"

He looked vacantly at her.

"No! She's as cold as ice. That's why you turned to me, don't you remember? I gave you the one thing she couldn't—until now. You proved to me tonight that even my love is worthless to you."

"I love my son, Allyson," he proclaimed.

"For some insane reason, I believe you do Kyle. But your words aren't enough."

"I don't know how to show him like you can."

"It really doesn't require much talent. But God only knows, your talent seems to lie only in one area."

"Forgive me, Ali—I was wrong."

"I'm glad you're man enough to admit it."

He turned and walked away from her.

"Hey, do me a favor," she said.

Kyle turned around to look at her. "Relay this message to your sweet wife for me. Tell her under no circumstances will I give up my son, or leave town with him. Tell her to take her money and shove it! Got that?"

"Yup. You drive a hard nail when you have to."

"It's called love. But you wouldn't know anything about that."

There was nothing more to be said. When she looked into his eyes, they were far away. They didn't mesmerize her the way they formerly had. Now they appeared cold and heartless. There were no warm good-byes.

After he left, Felicia slid sheepishly from her bedroom, with packed bags in her hands. Allyson gaped angrily at her, then abruptly turned away. Tears were already stinging her eyes. As Felicia walked past her, she mumbled she was sorry and that she didn't mean to hurt her. Allyson never looked her way. She stood motionless long after she was gone. Then she buried her head into her pillow and cried incessantly, until she could cry no more. She felt betrayed and profoundly hurt by the two people who once meant the world to her. She couldn't comprehend how her best friend and her lover, her son's father, could even think of doing this to her. The two people whom she cared about most had deeply wounded her, and she wasn't sure she'd ever recover.

She wanted to confide in Marc; he was the only friend she had left in the world that she could depend on. It wouldn't be fair to him though. She would only confuse him in her vulnerable state. He wanted to be more than just her patsy. And even though he'd never pushed himself on her, she knew how much he wanted to be with her intimately. Now she wasn't sure she could be that close to anyone again. Not ever.

She couldn't focus on TV, or a novel—or anything. She was too devastated...hurt and enraged. Now she knew how her mother felt all those lonely nights when her father was away having his affairs. She thought she was reliving her pain. She couldn't fathom how her mother found it in her heart to forgive him.

She watched the clock on her rickety night stand tick away, the hours slowly passing, as she lay in bed reviewing the worst day of her life. Again, she thought of Felicia, her childhood friend, whom she had trusted, with her deepest thoughts. To think, she had betrayed her! Allyson wasn't sure she'd ever trust again.

CHAPTER 32

The phone jingled loudly, near midnight, astounding her. She was loath to answer it, afraid that it might be Kyle or Felicia. She wasn't ready to speak to either of them. However, on the third ring, she lifted the receiver, and before she could even utter a mere sound, Marc's deep soothing voice penetrated her ears.

"I apologize for calling so late," he said. "But you forgot your sweater, and I just happened to notice it hanging on the back of one of the dining room chairs."

"How foolish of me," she said, smiling, with tears still in her eyes. He was her clairvoyant. He possessed a sixth sense, she swore. That's what she loved about him; he was so tuned onto her.

"I hope I didn't wake anyone."

"No. Ben's been sleeping like a log ever since I left your place." She couldn't believe he didn't hear all the commotion. Thank heaven for that. "Uh, Feli . . cia's not here," she said, feeling her eyes filling up again. Just saying her name was difficult for her.

"Ali, is everything all right?"

She knew he could detect just from her voice that she was upset about something. "No. Actually, I would like you to bring my sweater to me. Right now," she implored.

"Aye, aye. See you in about fifteen."

"Okay. Drive slow. Bye."

She pulled two peerless crystal goblets that had been collecting dust for years, from one of the smaller kitchen cabinets, which was brimming with odds and ends, and quickly rinsed them. Then she poured the white wine that

Kyle had inadvertently left behind. Afterwards, she hopped into the shower. She was combing out her wet hair when she heard a ruffle on the front steps, then a light rap on the screen door. She reached for her robe, which was hanging on a metal hook behind the bathroom door, slipped it on, and then scurried to let Marc in.

It was just marvelous seeing his cute freckled face right before her, her sweater dangling from his hand. Even though Marc wasn't handsome, he had something far more appealing beneath his surface. He was not only kind and caring, but he was sensitive, yet strong.

"Come in," she said, taking her sweater from him. "Thanks for coming."

"I'm always willing to assist a lady in distress."

"Did I sound that bad?" she asked, walking him over to the sofa. The glasses of wine and the bottle were sitting on the small pine coffee table.

"Never. I see the glasses are filled," he said as he sat down, then looked into her eyes.

She gulped down the wine and quickly replenished her glass. Once she was relaxed, her words began to flow freely, as did her tears. She informed Marc of her surprising discovery after returning home from his place.

"Felicia never expected me to be home so early. She thought she'd get away with this! Great friend, huh?"

"Wait a minute, Ali. I know how much you're hurting, but you shouldn't put all the blame on her. It takes two. Kyle's just as much at fault."

"It hurts so bad," she cried, lying against him.

"I know," he said with empathy, as he put his arms around her.

"You do? Really?" she said, sitting up, looking into his eyes.

"It happened to me too—long time ago now. I guess that's why I've been so cautious about getting involved. Relationships scared me for a while. I lost trust. You can't let that happen to you though. It only destroys a person."

"What happened?" she asked, very much intrigued at what hurt him at one time.

"It was about five years ago. I had been going out with this girl for about two years. I was going to ask her to marry me." He paused.

"Go on," she said.

"One night, when were supposed to go out, she called and said she wasn't feeling well. She said she wanted to be alone, so she could get some rest."

"Yeah."

"Later that evening, I decided to give her a call to see if she was feeling any better, but her line was busy. In fact, it was busy for more than two hours. So, I went to her apartment to check on her. I didn't want her to know how worried I was, so I brought her some soup and crackers. Anyhow, I had a key, so not to disturb her in case she was sleeping, I just let myself in. But when I called out to her and she didn't answer, I started to walk toward her bedroom.

All of a sudden, this skinny little runt flew out of her room right past me. Buck-naked! He ran out the front door like a scared rat…with his tail between his legs. His clothes over his arm."

"So, what'd ya do?"

"Nothing. I couldn't even speak to her. I left the groceries on the kitchen table and never saw her again. End of story," he said, bowing his head, beginning to laugh.

"What's so funny?" she asked, amused at his reaction.

"It wasn't funny at the time, but when I look back and think about that weasel…so frightened of me…If you had only seen this guy…" he said, laughing so hard his eyes were beginning to water.

She couldn't help but join in. It somehow struck a funny bone in her. "Maybe we could fix him up with Felicia. Is he still around?"

Facing him now, he stared at her. The laughter had gone and in its place was desire. She closed her eyes and felt his lips on hers. He kissed her lovingly and with tenderness—and suddenly she felt closer to him than ever before. They could no longer deny the existence of passion in their friendship. He gently slipped off her night robe, and it floated delicately to the floor. Still kissing her, he lifted her in his arms and carried her into the bedroom, where he made love to her. A lovemaking which left her with a deep sense of wholeness, unlike Kyle's lovemaking—which left her feeling shallow and alone. The dynamic chemistry that they once experienced was now slowly dissipating, just as the threatening cumulonimbus retreats after a brutal storm. Holding her stingily, he peered gravely and profoundly into her eyes. She knew what he was feeling; she felt it too. Then he spoke the words she was destined to hear.

"I love you, Allyson Porteus."

"I love you, too," she said, but she knew by looking into his eyes that he didn't believe her. She felt a strong admiration for him. She wasn't sure if it was love, or just a yearning in her, but it was a stalwart sentiment she couldn't dispose of.

"Tell me again tomorrow." He made her promise. "Wine can sometimes make a damsel say things she may not ordinarily say."

"I don't think that is the case."

"We'll see."

She didn't want tomorrow to come. She just wanted to stay secure in his arms, and make the night stay dark for a long, long time.

CHAPTER 33

Allyson went out in the yard to get the newspaper and found it to be a beautiful Indian summer morning. Then she went back into the house to make some coffee and sat down at the table. It seemed strange without Felicia. She tried to recant some of the hostility she was feeling towards her—and Kyle, from her mind, but she wasn't successful.

"Will ya look at this," she said aloud, responding to an article that intrigued her. But when she glanced up from reading the Cape Cod Times, she found that she was alone. Nobody was listening. How odd it felt. She was already missing Felicia's company, her curiosity and her corny remarks. But at the same time, the pain was still too fresh. And she knew she couldn't live with her ever again. She told Ben Felicia had to go away—on a long trip. He loved her, and she loved him; it will be tough for both of them for a while.

Marc phoned and lit up her moment. He always seemed to call or be there at the right time—when she needed him. Although it wasn't so much need anymore, it was want. And she wanted to be with him, more and more.

"Hello."

"What'd ya doing?"

"Nothing. Just reading the paper."

"Beautiful day for a picnic? I'll even make the sandwiches," he suggested.

"Sounds great. I'll bring the chips and drinks, and whatever else I can find around here. Any particular place in mind?

"Nickerson? I figure we could pedal around for awhile, see the sites. We can rent the bikes right there."

"Perfect. How about if we pick you up, oh, say around 10:30?"

"I'll be ready."

"Bye, Marc."

When she told Ben about the picnic, he was excited. He couldn't wait to go. He helped her pack up the food, and the Tupperware plates and cups. He remembered the water bottles and asked his mother if she'd fill them with his favorite drink, orange soda.

"We don't want to bring too much, Ben. We have to be able to fit this stuff in the basket on the bike."

"Just orange soda, please?"

"Okay," she said, giving in. Are we ready now? Did you bring a sweatshirt, in case it gets chilly?"

"Yup."

"Okay, I guess we're off."

They loaded the car and were on their way. She told Marc she would pick him up.

❦   ❦   ❦

They rented two ten speed bicycles at the park. Marc's bike had a child's seat attached for Benjamin. They biked around the park for hours enjoying the warm weather and the beautiful foliage, until they were starved. The fresh air and exercise had made them hungry.

Finally, they stopped in front of a large picnic table. Allyson took the red and white plastic tablecloth from the wooden basket on her bike, and spread it across the newly stained wood. Then, she brought out the pickles, the chips, and some homemade oatmeal cookies, she and Ben had made the night before. She pulled out the plastic dishes and displayed the food on them. Ben was pre-occupied with killing some early ants.

Marc made wonderful deli sandwiches. They were stuffed so full, she could barely get her mouth around the one he handed her. She watched Ben with his, as he decided to take the sandwich apart and eat only the meat.

She realized Marc was watching her watch him. And when she looked at him, he just shrugged and smiled. "This is fun," Ben said.

"It sure is," Marc said, unzipping his backpack, fumbling through it, and withdrawing three plastic cups. Then he proceeded to fill them with what she thought to be champagne.

"What are you doing?" she asked, suspiciously.

"A drink for each of us. Ben included," he said, handing Ben his cup.

"Thank you," Ben said, with a smile, taking it from him, as he looked at his mother, as if in defiance.

"What is it? He can't have alcohol."

"Don't be so alarmed, my dear. If you read the label," he said, showing her the small print on the bottle. "I'm just filling the cups with a sparkling grape juice."

"This is amazing. A bubbly grape juice that looks like champagne. This even looks like a champagne bottle," she said, handling it. "You're too much," she said smiling.

She watched Ben and Marc scamper about, collecting colorful fallen leaves. They gathered up huge piles and began throwing them at each other. Marc walked over to Ben and whispered something in his ear. Seconds later, she became their victim. Marc picked her up and carried her over to a huge piling of dried leaves and plunked her down on them. Allyson screamed as they covered her with them. And after they had her completely buried, except for her head, Ben leaped on top of her, laughing hysterically. She closed her eyes and lay quiet. Ben stood mystified for a moment. Then, without warning, she jumped up, scaring him momentarily, and afterward he laughed even harder.

Marc stood aside watching them, cackling too. I'll fix him, Allyson thought. When she asked him to pull her out of the big pile of bright leaves, she yanked him down with them. The three of them rolled around in the leaves, laughing, and having a magnificent time.

Before the sun went down, they bicycled over to the park's biggest pond, and perched together on a big flat rock on the gravel. There they sat in silence, staring across the calm mirrored water at the beautiful foliage, drinking in the phenomenon of nature and its lull. While they were digesting the handsome vista, somewhat awed by the flaming hues, she got out the camera and took some pictures, so that she could keep this colorful image forever, as a permanent reminder of the wonderful time the three of them shared that day. These memorable prints would eventually be pasted in her scrapbook, right beside the very last photographs she had taken of Felicia, Ben, and her.

The warmth from the sun brought back happy memories of this past summer with Felicia on the beach. She brushed those thoughts away quickly and decided to take one day at a time. She would not let the pain of yesterday, or the uncertainty of tomorrow, darken the shadows that seemed to continually follow her footsteps.

CHAPTER 34

When they got home that day, she checked the answering machine. Taylor called wanting to know about a closing. Aunt Edith phoned too. She said she hadn't heard from her in a while and wanted to be sure that everything was okay with them. The last message was from a man who said he had information about her brother's whereabouts.

"Play that back," Marc insisted.

"I know where your brother is. I'll call back again."

"Do you think it's for real?" she asked, holding her breath. She was about to burst with joy.

"I would assume so. It's my old PI buddy, Shane Sweeney. I recognized that voice right away. But let's wait to be sure."

"Oh, I hope so," she said, crossing her fingers and closing her eyes.

Marc embraced her. "I know how much this means to you."

"He's my brother," she cried. They were the lost tears of yesterday, for all those years without him. She sat tensely waiting for this Shane Sweeney to supply her with the necessary information she needed to find her brother.

The phone rang at 6:15 P.M. She nearly jumped out of her skin, never mind the chair.

"Something wrong, honey?" Aunt Edith asked, when she heard the anxiety in her voice.

"No. I'm sorry, Auntie. I should have called you back, I've been waiting for an important call." Marc had been giving her the hand signal to end her conversation.

"It must be a big sale."

"Auntie, can I call you back later?"

"Yeah, sure. No problem, honey."

"Thanks. Talk to you soon."

Allyson was afraid the private investigator would give up, if he found her line busy. Marc did say even though he was good in his field, he was a very impatient man. And when she placed the receiver on the hook, the phone resounded almost immediately. She quickly picked it up. It was he. Shane Sweeney. She nodded to Marc, and he quickly slapped a pen and a memo pad in front of her. She jotted down the California address the detective gave her, and asked him to repeat it, but he had already hung up, leaving her with just a dial tone. 1873 Howard St. NE, San Francisco, she kept repeating to herself.

"California here we come!"

She was so nervous, she was afraid she might have transposed the street number. When she stood up, she was trembling she was so inexorably ecstatic. Marc joined in her ecstasy. They were like two children on Christmas day, who had been waiting anxiously for the gift they'd dreamed about all year long, and, at last, they had received it. If it hadn't been for Marc, she wouldn't have continued searching for her brother. Marc had all the right connections, and somehow through them, this PI had given her the tip she needed to unite with a sibling who not so long ago she never knew existed.

"When do you want to leave?" Marc asked her.

"Is tomorrow too soon?" Allyson asked eagerly.

"Tomorrow it is."

"Really?"

"Yup. I'll make the reservations for San Francisco right away."

"You are wonderful! The best. Thank you, Marc. Thank you so much," she said, giving him a hug."

"My pleasure. You're very welcome," he said, smiling.

CHAPTER 35

That night she packed up just about everything that was in their drawers to pack. When she finally got three suitcases closed, after sitting on them, it looked as though they were planning a long stay. She figured that once they got settled in their motel room, she could pick and choose what she and Ben should wear, when they did go meet him. The strangest thing was, she didn't even know his name.

Marc went home early, so that he could get ready for the early morning flight. Allyson tossed and turned all night, wondering what her brother looked like and whether or not there would be a resemblance between them. What she feared mostly though, was that he would reject her. How should she act when they first meet? Should she run into his arms, or should she simply shake his hand? Will he treat her like a stranger, or will he want to know all about her?

She awoke at 5:00 A.M. Everything was dark and quiet. She showered, and then she sat at the kitchen table with a cup of coffee. Everything was serene, but her head was pounding and her heart was racing. This was an important day in her life. Allyson was as happy and excited as anyone could be, but at the same time scared out of her wit. Marc picked them up at quarter to seven. They had a 9:00 A.M. flight from Logan Airport.

They left right on schedule, but the morning traffic into Boston quickly came to a standstill. People were honking their horns and yelling out of their car windows. Some were already out of their cars shouting and cursing, wandering aimlessly about.

"Is it always like this?" she asked Marc.

"Usually. But it seems to be much worse today. Maybe there's an accident up ahead."

She looked at her watch. It was ten minutes before eight. They had been sitting for a good fifteen minutes. She was becoming more nervous with each passing minute, but she tried not to show it. There was nothing Marc could do. They had to sit and wait it out, just like everybody else.

Nevertheless, Marc seemed to be more agitated than she was. She knew how much he wanted to help fulfill her dream, and she adored him for that. Rapidly losing patience, he rolled down his window and yelled to a passer-by.

"What's going on here? We have to get to the airport."

"Well, buddy, I have to get to work. I hear a tractor trailer overturned. Spilled gallons of oil. Could be tied up for hours."

"Damn. We won't make it."

"We got to, Marc," she cried. "Can't we seek an alternate route?"

"And how do you suppose we do that in this mess?"

"There must be something we can do."

"Yeah, pray we make it on time."

Ben fell asleep with a bottle in his mouth. Allyson stared out the window. Like the fading sun behind the clouds, dreams of meeting her brother were slowly dissipating. There were already two strikes against her. Beginning with the fruitless phone calls to his mother. Mrs. McCaffrey was so distraught just from hearing her name, she quickly changed her number. Unlisted. And now, a freak accident up ahead is preventing them from reaching the airport on time. Was someone up there trying to tell her something? This prodded her into wanting to find her brother all the more. Conclude the mission. Her life wouldn't be complete unless she did.

Suddenly, trumpeting horns roused them from their dazed state. Marc flashed open his eyes and raised his head from the headrest. She became more alert too. She sat up straighter.

"Yes! We're moving! It's 8:25 A.M. Will we make it?" she asked.

"I think we will. If there's no more delays. We're going to have to fly. So buckle up again, honey."

She kept her fingers crossed. They were only minutes away from reaching the airport. When they finally got there, Marc dropped her off out in front, so that she could run in and get the reserved tickets while he found a place to park. The lobby was bombarded with all sorts of people standing about, either waiting to get their tickets or saying good-bye, or welcoming home friends or loved ones. Some were waiting patiently to retrieve their luggage, while still others were searching frantically for their lost belongings. Taxis and buses were idling in a serpentine line along a curb, waiting to transport travelers to their destinations.

Allyson never felt more relieved when they, at last, boarded the plane. They flew first class in a Delta 747.

She sat next to the window, nearest the wing, with Ben on her lap. He sat quietly, curiously eyeing the people and objects around him. He had seen life-like pictures of planes in his little Golden Books, but Allyson wasn't sure if he actually knew he was on one. She pointed out the wings to him. He smiled and pointed to them too, as he gibbered in playful baby language. He became frustrated and frowned because he couldn't say the word 'plane.' Marc and Allyson looked at each other, trying not to laugh and upset him even more.

"That's right, honey, plane. Big plane," she said, and he gave her a big grin.

It was a five-and-a-half-hour flight. Non-stop. They watched a couple of old flicks, while Ben amused himself with a musical screen-boxed TV, which viewed and played riddles and rhymes, over and over again. When he became tired, she rocked him to sleep.

Marc ordered two glasses of Chablis so that they could relax a bit. The stewardess contributed some crackers and cheese for them to munch on until the main course was prepared.

It was fascinating, watching the clouds float all about them, as the wings of the plane were descending, and then elevating. When they dipped below the clouds, Allyson could see the various towns and cities. They resembled miniature Lego's in a faraway landscape. Allyson imagined she was a giant, in control and on top of the world, stepping across acres and acres of vast countryside. But when the solid earth disappeared and became a reservoir of deep blue, her great giant faded into a vaporous mist.

Marc shook her out of her reverie, to let her know lunch was being served. She shared her plate with Ben. The flight was quite pleasurable, until they flew into a snow squall. The plane took a huge dip when it encountered an air pocket. A woman in the back of the 747 let out a screech so loud that everyone turned and looked in her direction at once. Allyson's heart flip-flopped and nose-dived right to her feet. Suddenly, they were on a very rocky ride. An announcement flashed above: "Stay in your seats—Fasten your seat belts." The attendants paraded up and down the aisles checking everyone. An elderly lady stopped a flight attendant and asked what she was afraid to.

"Are we in any danger, Miss."

Allyson held her breath.

"No. It's just routine for your safety. They have some good pilots up front," explained the stewardess, smiling.

After what seemed an indefinite time, the disturbance at last subsided. The lights above went out. A few of the passengers got out of their seats. They'd finally passed through the storm and were out of danger!

"Were you scared?" Marc asked, smiling at her, while still holding her hand. He must have felt her tension release.

"Who me?" she asked, her eyes and head glancing any which way, acting as if she didn't know he was actually referring to her. "Not a chance."

"Is that why your knees are still knocking?"

She looked down, thinking they were. "Smart guy. All right, I'll admit, I was a tiny bit scared," she said, showing him a measurement of air with her thumb and forefinger. He eyed her in disbelief. "All right, a whole bunch scared. Are you happy now?"

"I'm always happy when I'm with you," he said, leaning over to give her a kiss.

He always said the right thing, at the right moment. It was reassuring, feeling his warm lips on hers. And his playful comments were always spontaneous. He never gave her any reason to doubt him.

"You're drifting away from me," Marc whispered.

"Nah, I was just thinking how lucky I am to have you."

"Well, in that case, I won't take you away from those invigorating thoughts," he said, taking her hand in his. It was so warm. "I love you, Ali."

"And I love you, Marc Kelsey," she said, looking into his big brown eyes. And this time, those precious words of hers were real, so genuine.

At that instant, a flight attendant approached and instructed them to fasten their seat belts. They were getting ready to land. The three of them sat excitedly as they watched the wing take a dip downward. She felt her stomach flipping as they descended, down, down, down, until at last the plane's wheels met the earth with a big thump, throttling across the air field until it came to a screeching halt.

After disembarking and retrieving their luggage, they hailed a taxi from the airport to the Holiday Inn, in the heart of San Francisco. Many of the streets were old and on steep hills, and most of the buildings had an air of antiquity about them. The homes and apartments were closely wedged.

After unpacking, they settled down on reasonably comfortable beds. What more could be expected from a motel room? The three-hour-time difference between the east and west coasts was having a big effect on them, so they turned in early.

CHAPTER 36

The following morning they were much rested and totally renewed. Marc showered first. And while he was getting dressed, Allyson bathed Benjamin and got him dressed in his most handsome outfit, a three-piece suit. His little red vest made a colorful contrast to his navy blue pants and jacket. Underneath, he wore a blue-and-white striped shirt with a navy bow tie under his collar. When his blue-and-white saddle shoes were tied, Ben looked like a million-dollar-kid.

When she stepped out of the shower, she was amazed to see that Marc was dressed in a suit quite similar to Ben's. The navy colors and fabric were the same, except that Marc's shirt was in a red-and-white stripe instead of a blue-and-white. They looked like a father and son. It gave her a warm feeling inside just to see the two of them looking so clean and so complimentary.

Allyson slipped into an olive skirt and jacket, but when she realized how much she clashed with the two of them, she changed quickly into a deep red, high collar, jersey dress. Plain but not too shabby, she thought.

They three, the portrait of a family, waited patiently in a long line to be seated in the Holiday Inn's large restaurant. They were absolutely famished after that lengthy flight, so they forfeited the free continental breakfast, which was included with their stay, and had the hungry man's special. Eggs, pancakes, sausage, bacon, and home fries. What a banquet!

After breakfast, Marc picked up a map of the city. They sat in the lobby trying to dissect it. They traced Howard Street, but there were many of them. Howard Street N, Howard Street S, Howard Street West, et cetera.

"Here it is," she said excitedly, pointing to it, while hovering over his shoulder. "Howard Street, NE"

"It looks like it's about three miles from here."

"Great. Let's go," she said excitedly.

"Wait. Don't you think we should call first? Make sure he's there?"

"Nope. This way he can't give us excuses for not wanting to see us. Besides, I'm sure his mother has forewarned him about me. And he may have an unlisted number too."

"Maybe you're right. I'll call a taxi."

"There's no need. There's a chain of them out there," she said, smiling.

"For a split second there, I forgot we were in the city."

While Ben and Allyson waited on the sidewalk for Marc to hail a taxi, she made an abrupt decision to go alone. As much as Marc wanted to be a part of her life, this was something she needed to do on her own. And when she turned and looked at him, he already knew what she was thinking.

"Would you mind terribly if I went alone?" she asked warily, searching his eyes for some kind of understanding, on a decision that had already been sub-consciously seeded. Now she needed him to concur.

"Of course not," he said, lovingly. "I'll take care of Ben. Go ahead. We'll be fine."

"Are you sure?" she asked hesitantly.

"Yes, you go. Ben and I will visit a toy store I noticed as we came last night. You take all the time you need," he said, kissing her tenderly, before closing the door to the cab.

"Thanks. I love you both," she said, through the glass window, as she waved good-bye.

CHAPTER 37

Some of the hills on the streets were tremendous. The sun kept playing hide-and-seek with the puffy white clouds, which were floating dreamily across the azure sky. The taxi driver kept glancing in his rear-view mirror at her, attempting to make conversation.

"Where are you from, Miss?" he asked.

She didn't hear him at first. Her thoughts were drifting with the clouds. She wondered how her dad could have ignored his flesh and blood. She worried about what feelings her brother would have towards her, and whether he would hate her for being his father's daughter. She would have to make him understand she wasn't her dad, and not even close. Allyson wanted so much to be a part of his life. She wondered if he had a family, and she wondered what he did for a living. She couldn't keep her fidgety hands that were resting on her lap still. She didn't smoke, but she sure wished she had a cigarette.

"Um, I'm sorry, what'd you say?"

"Where you from Miss?"

"Massachusetts. Cape Cod," she said, with pride.

"You're a long way from home," said the middle-aged driver, whose hair was thinning at the top.

"Yes, sir," she said, not contributing anymore than she had to.

They passed through an older section of the town. It was a bumpy ride. The potholes in the road were unavoidable; there were too many of them. The second story houses were badly run down. One could reach out from an open window with a yardstick and virtually tap on a neighbor's pane. Clothes were pinned up on ropes, which were strewn amid the housing. Old women with their hair in bobby pins and rollers huddled together on their front steps prattling. She saw winos and early-morning derelicts scrunched in corners of porches in various states of oblivion. Young children played in the street getting their ragged clothes dirty.

As sad as it made her feel, they appeared very content, matter-of-factly. Why shouldn't they? They didn't know any other life. It suddenly made her appreciate the beauty and pristine loveliness of the Cape. The freedom of space and fresh air. She hoped she could share her good fortune with her brother one day soon—even with just an occasional visit from him now and then.

It never occurred to her that her brother could be living in these dreary parts. She knew absolutely nothing about him. But just the thought of him, or anyone for that matter, living like this made her shudder. She prayed, as she closed her eyes, that the taxi wouldn't stop in front of any of these shabby looking buildings.

They turned down another street and the ride became smoother. When she opened her eyes again, she sat up more tall, and she looked around in amazement. It was as though God heard her request, and her prayer was answered. The buildings here were new and the streets were freshly paved. Flower boxes were hanging from many of the windowsills. A herd of businessmen scampered across the immaculate sidewalks, unified by some common pursuit.

She dared not breathe as the driver slowed to scan the brass numeral stuccoes above the main entrances of each high-rise. When they at last stopped in front of a brick complex showing 1873, she let the air exhale from her lungs.

She told the driver not to wait if she was later than five minutes. Although, she gave him more than enough money to linger much longer than that.

She strolled past a nice looking guy, about her brother's age, coming out of the 1873 building. He smiled and said hello while checking her out. And she was busy observing him too. He had her color hair. It could be him, she thought. "Say something," a little voice inside her kept repeating, "before he gets away."

"Mr. McCaffrey?" she asked timidly.

"Sorry. Wrong guy," he said, as he walked away, looking slightly disappointed.

When she got inside the main foyer, she was overwhelmed by the list of names inscribed on each mailbox, but she didn't see the name McCaffrey. However, there were apartment numbers engraved on the boxes. Not that that did her any good. His apartment number was never mentioned.

Just then, the mailman sauntered in with a stack of mail in his hand. Without thinking, she blurted out, "Anything for McCaffrey?"

"Let me see," he said, thumbing through his huge pile of envelopes. "Nope. Wait. Here's one," he said, handing it to her. "And one more," he added, without looking at her. Allyson now had two cream-colored envelopes in her possession.

She was afraid the mailman would be curious as to who she was, but he didn't seem to care.

The first envelope she carefully examined had no apartment number; it was simply addressed to Stephanie McCaffrey. Whoever she was? His wife? His daughter? The piece of mail beneath it happened to be an electric bill, addressed to G. McCaffrey, Apt. #22, 1873 Howard Street, NE. "Bingo! #22, Yes!" It was one of the unidentified mailboxes.

The mailman timed it just right. If he hadn't walked through that door when he did, she might not have ever discovered which apartment number belonged to her brother.

She finally got the courage to press the buzzer, which rang in his apartment. She waited nervously for someone to answer. Nothing happened. She pushed the black button again. Relentlessly this time. "Who is it?" a woman's voice echoed. Startled, she fell backward then caught herself. She peered up, and discovered an intercom system right above her. "Is anyone there?" someone asked again.

"Uh, Uh…yes, Mrs. McCaffrey." Assuming she was right and it wasn't a girlfriend—but instead his wife. "My name is Allyson. I'm your husband's half sister. I was wondering if I could have a word with you?" This wasn't even rehearsed.

"What? Half sister? He's never mentioned you."

"Well, I'm not sure he even knew about me. May I come in?"

"Go away, or I'll call the police."

"Mrs. McCaffrey…." There was no answer. Maybe Catherine had said something about her. Tears stung her eyes. Maybe she came all this way for nothing. She needed to speak with her brother and explain to him why she hadn't tried to contact him sooner. He couldn't hate her for just wanting to meet him, could he? All she wanted was to be his friend.

Suddenly, an elderly lady appeared with more bundles in her arms than she could manage. Allyson quickly pretended to be looking for her supposedly lost keys. She politely offered to help the woman, and she was grateful. With her thick bifocals, Allyson wondered how she could see anything. She slowly unlocked the security door, and Allyson quickly followed behind her, carrying her shopping bags for her. The lady gibbered the whole time as though they knew each other. She briefly mentioned her deceased husband, Mr. Green.

"How are the girls doing?"

"Fine, they're fine." Allyson surprisingly answered her without thought.

"I used to see them from time to time. They're probably busy with school and all."

"They are. I barely see them anymore myself."

Mrs. Green obviously had confused her with someone else, and she didn't have the heart to tell her differently. Allyson gathered she was just happy to have someone to chat with. They rode the elevator to the third floor, where they got off and walked down a long carpeted hallway until they reached her apartment, #8l.

"Thank you, Stephanie. Say hello to the girls for me."

"I will."

Mrs. Green thanked her, addressing her as Stephanie, the same name on the envelope...Stephanie McCaffrey. What's going on here? She wondered. How would this sweet old woman know anything? And why did she call her Stephanie? Was it a coincidence or something more?

Her brother had to be on the first floor of this towering skyscraper, according to the number sequence, so she rode the elevator back down. As she walked warily down the well-lit corridor scanning each apartment number, she kept wondering why Mrs. Green perceived her as Stephanie.

One side of the hallway consisted of even numbers upon each door, while the other side had the odd numbers. Numbers 16, 18, 20, and finally #22. She stopped dead in front of it. She curled her right hand into a fist. But just as she was about to knock upon the door, the one that could make such a significant difference in her life, she found herself lowering her arm to her side. The palms of her hands were sweating profusely. She thought her heart would pound straight through her chest. And when she got brave enough to raise her arm once again to knock, two young girls came strolling down the long hallway, giggling. She turned quickly and walked the other way, hoping they wouldn't notice her. When they were out of sight, she went back to apartment #22, bolder this time. Without hesitating, she knocked firmly upon the metal door.

There was a small peephole in the door. She heard three locks unfasten. Then the door stood ajar as far as the length of the short chain allowed. A small platinum blond in braids with big ice blue eyes peered up at her.

"Is your daddy home?" she asked. Immediately the little girl, who looked between six and seven, began to cry.

She heard a woman's voice ask, "What's the matter?" Then she came to the door. Allyson was astonished at what she saw. It was as though she was looking into a mirror at herself. This woman who stood before her had her auburn hair. She was even built like her—with long thin legs. The woman gasped too when she saw the resemblance. Except for the color of her eyes, she could have been her clone. The similarity was frightening, but there was something comforting about it too. No wonder the old lady in apartment #81 had confused them. It was rather odd that her brother should happen to marry a woman who possessed so many of her physical attributes, she thought.

"I'm sorry to barge in on you. My name is…."

"Allyson, I know. I'm not going to ask you how you got in."

"The mailman…uh, here's your mail, Stephanie," she said, handing her the two pieces of mail, hoping she had greeted her with the correct name.

"What's this all about?"

"It's a long story. I don't know where to begin. Your husband is my brother," she said candidly with a deep sigh. "I know this may sound bizarre, but it's true. I don't know what he's told you, if anything. I'm not even sure he knows I exist. I knew nothing about him either, until recently," she admitted dolefully.

"Come in, please. Sit down." Stephanie directed her to a contemporary sofa. The modern furniture appeared fairly new, and the white walls smelled freshly of paint. Two other beautiful little girls were sitting on a matching love seat, watching cartoons. They could have been twins they were so close in size, or maybe a year apart, around five-years-old. Their hair was more of a mousy brown, and they had dark eyes.

Their mother asked them to go into their rooms, so that they could talk. The two youngest ones whined, but reluctantly took each other's hand and moved slowly off the couch into a room adjacent to the kitchen. The oldest child had already disappeared into another room.

"You have well-behaved children. I 'm sorry if I upset your daughter," Allyson apologized, staring at her, still not believing what she was seeing. The resemblance was remarkable.

"It's been hard on her…being the oldest and all."

Allyson looked at her, bewildered. "Am I missing something?"

"Oh, you don't know, do you?"

"Know what?" she asked.

"Gerry died…a year ago. In the line of duty."

"Who's Gerry? Line of duty?"

"Your brother…Gerry. He was a police officer."

Allyson was stunned for a moment. Did she hear her right? Yes, the words couldn't have been plainer. "No!" she screeched, shaking her head. "He can't be dead! He can't be," she cried. "I didn't get to meet him. I wanted to tell him how much I loved him." Wide streams of tears rushed down her face.

All her dreams of them being together were suddenly ripped from her. "I wanted to tell him I was sorry for not coming sooner, and now—I'm too late." Stephanie put her arm around her trembling shoulders, and she continued to sob. "I'm sorry," she said, looking up at her. "His name was Gerry?" she asked between sobs. Stephanie nodded.

"Gerald Arthur McCaffrey. His friends and I called him Gerry," she said, smiling, remembering his sweet memory.

"What was he like?" Allyson asked. "Do you have any photographs?"

"Ah," Stephanie said with a sigh. "He was a great husband...and a wonderful father. The kids adored him. Other than his work, we were his life, and vice versa. He always put us first. He cared about people," she explained, with tears building in her own eyes.

"I'm so sorry to have burdened you again," Allyson said to her, as she walked away into another room. Allyson sat trying to collect her thoughts; she was still in shock. A few minutes later, Stephanie returned with a fairly recent photo of Gerry in his police uniform, standing tall beside Stephanie and the girls. She blinked numerous times. Gerry had looked very much like her father when he was young. He was very handsome.

"This was taken two months before he died."

Allyson sat just staring at his face. Her fingers lightly caressing the pane of glass, protecting his image. She still cried and then she became furious with her dad. Who else was she to blame? His child—his only son was dead! And he wasn't even there to bury him. It was as though Gerry had never existed for him. She felt a cold chill race down her spine. She wasn't sure if she knew her dad at all anymore.

"Is there anything I can do?" Stephanie asked.

"You've done enough already. Even though my brother had a short life, it's obvious he had a happy one with you and the children."

"I know he would have loved you too. Even though he never mentioned anything to me, there had to be some deja vu there. I'm a carbon copy of you," she said, with a smile.

"Thanks," Allyson said, solemnly, even though it made her feel worse, knowing her brother may have somehow known he had a sister, whom he longed to be with.

Stephanie disappeared into the bedroom again and returned with another photo of Gerry, unframed this time. It was a smaller version of the first, but without his family beside him. He stood tall and stern and alone in his blue uniform. There were merit badges affixed to his broad chest. Stephanie said he was a dedicated policeman for seven years, honored and remembered by all those who knew him and worked beside him. His dark eyes seemed to be peering straight at her, as though they were trying to tell her something.

"Please take this. He'd want you to have it." Stephanie gave her a loving squeeze. It was easy to understand why her brother picked her; she was kind and gentle, and much more. She had been a perfect match for her brother.

CHAPTER 38

❁

After Ben had torn open the Lego boxes Marc had bought him and played for awhile, he wandered over to Allyson's bedside. He was more curious as to what Marc and his mother were so intrigued with.

"Your brother has a kind face."

"Yeah, he does. Peaceful looking," she said pensively.

"Do your nieces look like him?"

"Actually, they do. And he looks an awful lot like my father when he was his age. I wish I had known him," she murmured.

"I know," Marc said gently.

"Look, Ben. This is your Uncle Gerry. Short for Gerald Arthur McCaffrey. He sounds pretty important, huh?" she asked.

Ben just smiled and pointed to the stranger in the picture. Soon after, he decided he was totally uninterested and strolled off to play with his new toys. He was too young to understand. Someday she would tell him more.

The trip back home seemed so much faster. There was little talk; Ben and Marc slept most of the way home. There was no turbulence this time, a smooth ride. If only her life could have been this smooth, she thought. But the cards weren't dealt that way. She sat by the window again, daydreaming. The enormous puffy cotton balls appeared undisrupted. She despised her father for what he had done. He'd disposed of his son, not even staying in contact with his firstborn. She wondered if her dad's love for her was ever real?

CHAPTER 39

On Monday when she went to retrieve Benjamin from Fairview Acres, she was casually informed by one of the teachers that he'd already left for the day.

"What do you mean he's gone? With who? When!" she barked at the young woman.

"Please Ms. Porteus, don't get upset. I'm sure there's a logical explanation for this. Let me speak with Marion before we panic," she said. She hustled over to interrupt a decorously dressed, white-haired woman who was conversing with another apparently concerned parent. As the young woman was speaking to her, she saw the elderly schoolmaster nod her head a few times and then glance over at her.

"Where's Karen?" she asked the young woman when she returned. Karen was Ben's assigned instructor, and Allyson had much faith in her.

"She wasn't feeling well. She left early today. Ms. Hobbs said she'd speak to you in a moment." Marion Hobbs was her advisor and the owner of Fairview Acres.

"This wouldn't have happened if Karen was here."

"I'm sorry, Ms. Porteus. Marion said that Kimberly was in charge of Karen's kids, and she believed that Benjamin had left with his mother."

"That's ridiculous, I'm his mother! What sort of operation are you running here?" Allyson asked, rather loudly and excitedly. At that second, Marion Hobbs, seeing her distress and not wanting to draw attention from any other parent there, hurried to her side.

"I apologize for any inconvenience this has caused you. Kimberly is our newest and youngest teacher's aide. She's only been with us a week. She's a very bright girl—I've been teaching her the procedures. But unfortunately, she hasn't been here long enough to remember whose child belongs to which parent; this takes time. It was purely an innocent error on her part," Marion Hobbs said, protecting her newest member.

"And a major disaster on mine."

"Do you think maybe a family member, or a friend, picked Ben up for you? To help you out? A favor?"

"No," Allyson said, shaking her head vehemently.

"Let's go inside. I'll try to reach Kimberly at home. I'm sure she can give us more insight on what exactly happened here. At least a description of the person who came and got your son."

"Fine," Allyson said, bewildered, as they walked hastily toward the entrance of the old school house, built in the late 1930's, still standing on three acres of hilly land, full of trees and tall grass.

Ms. Hobbs marched assuredly to her private office, and she trailed hastily behind her, practically nipping the back of her ugly black shoes. On top of a maple desk was a roller deck file with names of children who had been registered with the center, since it had been in operation. But evidently the hired help wasn't in that dossier because she ignored those cards, and pulled out a key from under her desk calendar and proceeded to unlock a side drawer. She removed a crammed black book, where she kept a list of all the employees' phone numbers and addresses, dated as far back as the 1970's.

Allyson paced the freshly waxed floors, almost slipping once or twice, as she waited anxiously for Ms. Hobbs to find the young aide's number.

"I need my other set of glasses," she said, squinting, looking around for them. "I have them here somewhere."

"Let me help," Allyson said eagerly. "I can dial the number for you."

"Oh no, dear. I can't let you do that. These numbers are confidential."

"This is my son's life we're talking about," she cried.

Just as she spewed those words at her, she looked up and saw the schoolmaster's wire-rimmed frames on a bookshelf, not far above her head, in front of some dusty old books, untouched in years, except for the empty space where a book had evidently been removed recently.

"There they are," Allyson shouted, as she pointed to where they lay.

"How forgetful of me," she said, fetching them from the dusty shelf. She slowly took off the pair she was wearing, and replaced them with her nearsighted rims. But finding them laden with dust particles, she reached into her top drawer and pulled out a small bottle of cleaning solution. She squirted the stuff on the lenses and then stretched over the top of the desk for the tissue box.

How could this woman be so calm when her son was missing?

She languidly moved her finger down each page. "Here it is," she said, finally, in a composed manner.

"Please, Ms. Hobbs, just dial the number," Allyson implored mercifully. Then her borderline flurry of nerves erupted into a brimful fit of delirium when she realized the young girl wasn't going to answer. Her whole body began to quiver, like a volcano getting ready to blow. To keep her sanity, she began pacing faster and faster.

"Ms. Porteus, sit down," she ordered. Mrs. Hobbs helped her into a hard chair, with a soft cushion. "You look pale. We'll keep trying. Have a little faith, my dear. There's never been a kidnapping in all the years that I've been here."

"Kidnapping?" Allyson asked, timorously.

"Well, I'm sure it's not that. We've never had any quandaries of such nature. I'm sure it was just a misunderstanding. I don't think any harm was intended. Ben'll probably turn up at any moment," she said sagely.

Wishful thinking. The waiting, not knowing if and when he'd show up, was torturous. Unable to wait any longer for Ben's safe return, Allyson telephoned Marc.

"Hold on, darling. I'll be right there," he said.

But she couldn't sit still. She felt desperate. She knew the longer they delayed the less of a chance she had of finding him. Her mind was coiled with Janice's previous threats of taking Ben away from her. The quarter of a million she so generously offered her at first, wanting Ben and her to become extinct by making a permanent long-distance move, and for her to become perpetually amnesiac regarding Ben's father. Then her later offer of four million dollars, if she was willing to turn her son over to her and Kyle. She thought Janice must have been terribly irritated when she flatly refused her colossal generosity—as if money was the cure for all.

She phoned Kyle but when he wasn't available, she reluctantly spoke to Janice, informing her of Benjamin's disappearance.

"This better not be one of your cruel pranks," Allyson said bravely, not worrying about Janice's threats or her power any longer. Her son was worth more than any harm she could do to her. "Do you have Ben?" she blurted coldly. "Tell me now," she demanded, with desperation.

"Oh, you poor child. No. Of course not. I don't have time for such nonsense," she said callously.

"You better not be toying with me. I haven't forgotten your threats. The police will know about them too."

"There's no need to get the police involved, my dear. I'm sure he'll turn up soon. Keep me posted," she said sweetly. "I'll track down Kyle and inform him of your dilemma."

"I bet you will," Allyson mumbled in a low voice, after she hung up.

Marc had arrived during the middle of her conversation with Janice. Everybody had left the school except for Marion, herself, and now Marc. Marion left them alone so that they could have some privacy.

"What's the latest?" he asked, with deep concern.

"Janice claims she knows nothing about Ben's disappearance. She said she'd tell Kyle about Ben being missing."

"Do you think she's behind this?" Marc asked.

"I don't know what to think. I wouldn't put it past her. Who else would do this? She's threatened me. Maybe it's her way of getting revenge."

"Call the police. We'll put an end to this fast. I don't care how much money she has. She can't get away with this."

"Benjamin's probably scared to death, and wondering why I'm not with him," she cried.

"I know how you feel, and I swear to you we'll get him back—safe and sound," he said earnestly, seeming to believe his own words.

She wanted to cling to that belief, but with each passing minute his promise seemed doubtful. The police got to the school quickly with blue lights flashing, but no sirens.

The school and Allyson gave them all the pieces of information they had, so they could try to solve the puzzle of Ben's mysterious vanishing. They suggested she go home, just in case Ben was returned, and wait by the telephone to see if there was a ransom. She couldn't believe what she was hearing.

"Do you think this could be a kidnapping?" she asked, stunned.

"Could be. Don't know, Ma'am. We have to take every precaution for the safe return of your child. We may need to tap your phones just in case. In the meantime, I have sent one of our men out to try to locate Kimberly Harper. She can give him a description of the suspect," said the lean, plain-clothes detective, who appeared to be somewhere in his thirties.

Marc cradled her in his arms, and Allyson clung to him as if he was the only person she had left in this world. Why was God giving her the cross to bear once more? Had she been so awful to deserve this? As much as she loved Marc and felt pretty secure in their relationship, the thought of losing her own son was beyond her imagination.

Each time the phone jingled her heart fell to her feet, and her stomach churned. And in spite of her hands being unsteady, her voice remained balanced and her thoughts clear. The first call was from Taylor, the secretary at work. The word had already spread like wildfire about Ben being missing. She was deeply concerned, and Allyson told her she would let her know when she had some news.

The second ring was from Aunt Edith. Allyson broke down when she heard her voice. Aunt Edith told her she'd pack up and leave right away. But Allyson suggested that she wait, she was sure Ben would be home any minute. Even though she wasn't feeling too assured, she tried to convince her Aunt that her son would be home soon. She promised to call her as soon as she heard anything, anything at all. But knowing Aunt Edith as she did, she knew she wouldn't wait long, if at all. She loved Ben too much to sit at home, so far away, and not be able to help.

With all the commotion in and outside of the house, Allyson didn't realize Kyle was now amongst the growing crowd of spectators clustered in and around her front yard, until she heard one of the officers commenting on the red Porsche.

She watched him from the bay window. He was thriving on the attention the crowd was giving him. They were encircling him as if he was the apogee of affinity. This fascination seemed more important to him than the disappearance of his son. He took no notice of her feelings. However, he knew Marc was there for her, and maybe he didn't want to intrude. They hadn't been on speaking terms since she'd unearthed him with Felicia.

As she was walking outside to speak with Kyle about Ben, the media suddenly appeared. Kyle loved every reporter and photographer. He lunged in front of the camera, pretending to be the concerned loving father he wasn't. He begged the perpetrator, who allegedly abducted his son, to bring him back home. He smoothly offered a million dollars of Janice's money for the safe return of him. His puny liberality repelled her. With clenched teeth, she doubled the offer. She thought she saw Kyle wince at the proposal, but he outwardly seemed unaffected, as they both pleaded mercifully for their son to be returned safely.

"This publicity could ruin Janice's highly respected reputation," she whispered to him.

"He's my son. That's more important," he said, peering at her through eyes that appeared distressed. "I know you don't think so, but I do love my son."

"Maybe you do, Kyle. Maybe you do at that," she said, with tears burning her eyes. "It's sad though that it took an awful thing like this for you to show it."

"I'm not perfect."

"Nobody said you had to be perfect."

"My priorities have been screwed up. At least I admit it," he said.

She couldn't be bothered with what he was trying to get across to her.

"Let's just concentrate on getting our son home," she said coolly.

The neighbors, along with more observers and newscasters dressed in winter coats and hats, were about in the front yard, voicing their opinions on Ben's whereabouts. Other concerned parents and onlookers gathered in the street, their warm breath lingering in the night air, as they grouped on this chilly evening to pray for the safe return of Ben. There was something endearing and innocent about a child that joined all of them together in the time of need.

And although these wonderful people gave her the support she needed, Marc was her strength. And that's what she needed most. He was the force that kept her together. The grudges she had had against Felicia, Kyle, her father, and Janice were now immaterial. All those things that hurt so much seemed petty now. Nothing else seemed to matter, except finding Benjamin.

The cars were stationed midway down the road. Suddenly, the crowd began shifting, moving swiftly toward the pavement. Two officers guided Kyle and her through the confusion to the end of the stone driveway. One officer babbled profusely into his walkie-talkie. She wondered what all the fuss was about. Had they found Benjamin? She didn't know what the codes meant that the policemen were using. She didn't want to know. Why were they being hustled through the crowd? Everything seemed to be happening so quickly. The cops were now restraining people from entering the street, as a pathway was being cleared just for them.

She blinked her eyes several times for in her vision, coming leisurely down the road, was Felicia, with Benjamin by her side. Ben was smiling blissfully, holding onto Felicia's hand. His happy round face was plastered with chocolate. Felicia appeared confused. Tears ran down Allyson's face when she saw them. She was speechless. She hurried to him, lifted him in her arms, and held him tightly, afraid to let go.

"Is this your boy?" asked one officer.

"Yes! Yes!" she cried. "Where have you been? You had Mommy so scared," she said, kissing and holding on to him for dear life. Kyle was beside her, smiling with relief, as a tear slid down his cheek.

"Where ya been small fry?" Kyle asked, holding Ben's little hand in his.

Marc stood nearby. She wanted to let him know that he was a meaningful part of this burgeoning family, but all she could do was concentrate on Benjamin.

"I'm sorry, Allyson. I missed Benjamin so much," Felicia confessed with tears.

"Who are you, Ma'am?" the detective inquired.

"Felicia Olson, sir. I…."

Before she could finish what she was going to say, the officer handcuffed her. "I'm placing you under arrest for the kidnapping of Benjamin Porteus."

"Please, Allyson. No one will understand. I could lose my job. I would have asked your permission, but I was afraid you wouldn't let me see him. I love him and I missed him so much."

"Why did you stay away so long? You had us worried sick."

"I guess I got carried away. Time just slipped by," she said, begging on her knees. Ben, seeing Felicia so upset, ran to her side, put his little arms around her neck, and began to cry. He didn't have a clue as to what was happening. He saw only that the people he loved were upset.

Allyson was so elated to get Ben back that she mellowed when she saw how broken-hearted Felicia was. She resembled the same scared and sad young girl she had met on the beach, ten years earlier. She was always sincere, and Allyson knew the feelings she had for Ben were genuine. She loved Ben as if he were her own, and this had always been quite evident with the constant fuss she always made over him. And, like Ben, she missed her too. How could she press charges? It would destroy both of them. She'd been a good friend for a very long time, until that night when she found Kyle and her together. How could she hold a grudge forever? Felicia was as human as she.

"Officer, please release her. She's my friend."

"I thought you said…."

"Never mind what I said. Please take those handcuffs off her," Allyson appealed to him softly. "I'm not pressing charges." He reluctantly set Felicia free, shook his head, and walked away.

The two of them held each other for a few moments, and it felt so good. Tears of repent were honorably mixed with tears of a blissful reunion. Then all of them walked slowly toward the house. Smiling faces were everywhere, congratulating Ben's safe arrival. They ignored the reporters, concealing their faces from the cameras, being flashed all around them. Marc and Kyle did their best to dodge the cameramen as well.

Kyle threatened the reporters. Money had seemed to give him such a sense of power. Control. He recommended strongly that they not print any of this. There was too much at risk for all of them. Felicia's teaching position could be jeopardized from all this coverage, and Janice's reputation could turn to mud. And now, her child would be on public display from all the publicity of a mysterious disappearance, and hours later a miraculous return. But whether they liked it or not, their lives would soon become an open book. The skeletons would no longer be hidden, and Janice could be the one to suffer the most. She had more to lose than any of them. She was the pillar of the community. People respected her. Allyson was not a vengeful person, and she wasn't out to ruin her life.

The loyal crowd was gradually dissipating, thinning out. Millions of stars shimmered in the stillness of the crisp evening, and the man in the moon seemed to be smiling down upon them, celebrating in this victorious ending. And when she tucked Ben in that night, she thanked those lucky stars for bringing him back home to her.

CHAPTER 40

The sun's beams were filtering through the worn shades. She smelled the strong aroma of coffee brewing and heard the sizzling sound of bacon frying. She put on her robe and walked into the living room, where Ben was preoccupied with his toys.

"Good morning, sleepyhead," Marc said, smiling broadly, while tending to breakfast.

"What's all this?" she asked, yawning.

"I thought since I don't have any clients lined up till tomorrow, why not make the most of it."

"This is really nice, but you're burning the toast," she said, sniffing.

"Do you have to come out and spoil everything?"

"I didn't mean to. I just hate burnt toast," she said wryly.

"Give me a break, will ya."

"I'm only kidding. This is really wonderful. A real nice surprise. All the amenities of a restaurant but much finer. And best of all…no tipping."

"I was hoping we could negotiate on that," he said, with a wide grin.

"It depends on what the trade-off is."

"Well, I was thinking, being a beautiful day and all…."

"Yeah?"

"How about taking a drive to the western part of the state?"

"To see your folks?"

He smiled and nodded. "What about your closings?"

"Well, I do have someone who will cover for me."

"Sounds great."

After breakfast, Allyson combed her closet for the outfit that would be most appropriate for the occasion. She knew absolutely nothing about his folks. He had kept his personal life private. This was the first time he'd asked her to go with him to visit them, and she was delighted. She really wanted to know more about Marc's background. Both his parents were living. She knew Marc had three sisters, two older and one younger, but he never discussed them. She knew he loved them, and he visited them as often as he could.

Marc stood by her bedroom door watching her as she paraded back and forth in her underwear from the closet to the bed, laying out a variety of suits. She could feel his roving eyes keenly inspecting her.

"Don't fuss. They'll love you just the way you are."

"In these?" she questioned, looking down at her black silk underwear. "You're just prejudiced, that's all."

"Let that be my privilege," he said, approaching her, wrapping his big strong arms around her small waist. He kissed her gently on the lips. And as he moved closer, she could feel that he was aching for her, as she was him.

"I'll let that one pass," she said, giving him the eye, as she removed a navy blue, polyester pantsuit from the closet, making it her choice. She found a white body suit in the bottom drawer of her dresser to wear underneath. Then she pulled her hair back, fastening it tightly in a large barrette, clothed with a red bow. She complemented the apparel with her small gold hoop earrings and a plain gold chain around her neck. Then she slipped into a pair of red pumps. She looked very patriotic with her red, white, and blue. She dressed Benjamin in his three-piece suit, the same one he had worn in California. It was a tad big then and barely fit now, yet it still looked good.

The ride was relaxing, and the sun beaming on the windshield made it warm and pleasant in the car. Traffic on the highway was light, and Allyson attributed that to the holiday season. Being the beginning of the week, people were either working or Christmas shopping, she'd gathered.

She worried about whether or not his parents would approve of her. What will they think when they discover that their son is involved with a woman who had a child? To complicate things—by a married man? What will their feelings be towards him then? She wondered if they were as open and as flexible as their son was. Her situation would certainly not be acceptable to them otherwise. The more she thought about it and the nearer they got to their home, the more nervous she became.

"They're gonna love ya," Marc said, taking hold of her hand and squeezing it gently.

"How can you be so sure?"

"I do."

"That's you. That's entirely different."

"Not really. I'm their son. If I love you, they'll love you too."

She really hoped that his parents would like her. It would make things so much easier.

After about two and half-hours on the highway, they finally veered when they reached their exit. They drove another five miles until they came to a very lovely neighborhood. Taking a few more turns, they stopped in front of a painted wooden sign, which read, "Private Way." They proceeded down a winding shelled lane that eventually led to a smooth pavement and a tall locked gate. Marc leaned over her to open the glove compartment. He extracted a square black opener. Then he punched in a code that caused this fancy, black wrought-iron entrance to slowly swing open.

Driving through, she was totally mystified by the ambiance. The grounds were immaculate, and there were beautiful gardens everywhere. It was mid December and, amazingly, the grass was still quite green and lush. The landscaping was a topiary splendor. Hedges were neatly carved into different animal shapes of various sizes, and there, straight ahead, was the biggest brick mansion ever. It resembled a castle. She felt as though she was accidentally whisked up in the midst of some fabulous fairy tale.

"Wow! You never told me about this!"

"What...and have you love me for my money? I had to be sure that you cared for me first before I brought you here."

"You never had to worry about that. I can't believe this. Shake me. I must be dreaming."

"It's real. All of it," he said. "This was my granddaddy's. He used to represent quite a few Hollywood stars in his time."

"Really."

She was utterly flabbergasted. Marc had never clued her in about his affluent upbringing. But why should he have? He was such a down-to-earth type of guy, she would never have guessed. He never flaunted or used his wealth to foster himself in his profession or his personal life. And money obviously wasn't the link that made him the wonderful and caring person he was.

"Is there anything else I should be aware of?"

"Yeah, Jarod...our one and only butler for many years. My dear, you are about to meet him."

She brushed out the crease in her pants, as she got out of the car. Marc retrieved Benjamin, and the three of them proceeded up the brick walkway to the front steps. Just as they approached the top step, the heavy oak door opened slowly. A tall, thin, dark man greeted Marc warmly, with an amiable and vigorous handshake.

"Good to see you again, Mr. Kelsey."

"And you too, Jarod. It's good to be back. I'd like you to meet my friend, Allyson Porteus and her son, Benjamin."

"Please to meet you both," he said, bowing.

"Thank you, likewise."

At that moment, a heavy set Jamaican woman, in her late fifties or early sixties, appeared in the huge foyer. Her eyes were glowing as they fastened on Marc.

"My dear boy, it's been awhile. This place hasn't danced since your feet left here."

"I missed you too, Carmen," he said, putting his arms around her, squeezing her shoulders. "I want you to meet the two most important people in my life. Besides you, of course. This is Allyson and her son, Benjamin."

"Greetings and happy holidays to both of you. You fetched yourself a fine young man. Don't let him slip through your fingers, young lady. There's few of this blood left."

"I know," Allyson mouthed softly, nodding her head, agreeing with her. "And I have no intentions of letting him go," she avowed, with a smile.

"Come along. Your mother is waiting for you in the library."

"Why the library?"

"I'm not certain. I think she has something to say to you in private."

Marc looked worried. He ushered Ben and Allyson into one of the parlors. The room was large, cool and airy, with crown molding trimmed elegantly in gold. The furniture was exquisite. The walls were wallpapered in an ancient print from the early nineteen hundreds. Paintings of famous people over the centuries were hung in gold frames about the room. This was an interesting showplace to admire.

Ben was getting restless. To keep him occupied she played the card game, Old Maid, with him until they met Marc's parents. She carried the pack of cards in her pocketbook for times like this. First impressions were usually lasting impressions, in spite of what the state of affairs tend to be. Marc's parents weren't accustomed to having little ones around. Their kids were all grown. And from the smidgen Marc yielded to her about his family, his mother and father had no grandchildren, as of yet. She tried to keep Ben's spirits high, at least until they got through this initial meeting. When Marc and his mother at last arrived, she composed herself and rose promptly to greet them.

"Mother, this is Allyson and her son, Benjamin," Marc said with great admiration.

"Hello, Mrs. Kelsey," she said, extending her hand. Aimee Kelsey's handshake was gentle and soft, as were her brown eyes.

"At last we meet, my dear. Marcus has told me so much about you and your son," she said smiling. "What a handsome boy you have. He has your bright eyes and your endearing smile. I'm glad the two of you could join us today."

"Thank you for inviting us. You have a lovely home."

"We're happy here. We do our best. We love when Marcus comes to visit. He livens up this place. We don't see him as often as we'd like to," she said pensively.

"Oh, mother. Are you trying to make me feel guilty?" Marc asked.

"No, son. It's just not the same around here anymore. Everyone is getting older—including me. This house needs some youth," she said, with a smile, fixing her eyes on Ben.

"Mother, don't embarrass me. I know what you're hinting. And no, I cannot come back here to live."

"I didn't mean to imply anything by it. Now, all of you, go and enjoy yourselves. Maybe Allyson would enjoy a tour of the gardens. Your father will be back soon. Dinner will be served at three," she said, and left the room.

Aimee Kelsey was a very gentlewoman, with hazel-brown eyes and short chestnut hair. Her smile appeared authentic, but in her eyes was a faraway sadness. And in spite of all her wealth, she had an air of simplicity about her. One that made Allyson feel right at home. She could see much of Mrs. Kelsey in Marc, and it was plain to recognize that he had inherited many of his mother's finer qualities.

"Come on, Marcus, show me around. I want to know what else you're hiding from me!"

"Ten wives and twenty-five kids," he said, wide-eyed, grinning.

"Wow! You are a secretive man and very promiscuous, to say the least. I had no idea. Where did you find the time to fit me in?"

"It's difficult," he said as they marched down the halls, stopping here and there so that she could admire the intricate details and beauty carved into each invincible chamber of this magnificent mansion.

The old nursery, which hadn't been used in years, was as bright and cheerful as if children had played it in only yesterday. Rainbows were painted on the walls. Mobile dolls and animals, stars and moons dangled from ribbons and fine string, that were affixed to the mural ceiling. The built-in cabinets and counter tops were brimming with trains, fire trucks, cars, and more. The colorful nursery was festooned with glitter and gadgetry filled with child-like mirth.

They left Ben in the care of Carmen, while Marc and she strolled about the aesthetic estate. It was more beautiful than the Caldwell place. Even though most of the trees were bare and the ground was becoming solid, the scenery was breathtaking. They strolled across acres and acres of land that belonged to the beautiful manor, until they came to a rustic barn, recently restored, and well hidden amongst the rolling hills. Inside were two beautiful horses. Marc knew how much she enjoyed riding, so he saddled them up, and they trotted about the estate and further on.

As they galloped over the fields, she had the sense of being free once again. A brisk wind was blowing her hair relentlessly, dampening her eyes. It was a freedom she treasured, a place where no evil could enter. She rode with the clouds as they floated swiftly and lightheartedly across the vast azure sky.

After an hour of exploring the enormous estate, crossing rivers, marshes, and both highlands and lowlands, they halted so that the tired horses could rest. They were getting old and hadn't really been ridden all that much.

They rested beneath an old apple tree, high on a hill, overlooking the quiet and composed countryside. She wasn't cold, in spite of the wintry chill hovering in the air. The ride had invigorated her.

"I feel like I'm on top of the world," she bellowed, as she rose from the solid ground, and swung herself around.

"I love to see you happy," Marc gleamed.

"It's you who brought me happiness."

"I can't take credit for that. You discovered it all by yourself."

"With your help," she said.

Nestled under the tree like two very young lovers, they kissed and hugged. Marc got up, removed a small jackknife from his pant pocket and carved their initials into the huge trunk. She took her red bow out of her hair and stuck it on the tree, in remembrance of their immortal love. It wasn't the traditional yellow ribbon, but this wasn't any ordinary love either. Their love had opened up an inspiration within her far more spectacular than any love she'd ever had.

It was almost time for dinner. They galloped the horses back to the barn. It seemed good being with the man she loved, alone, without the interference from the continuous demands of motherhood. And she didn't realize how much free time Felicia had actually given her, until after she'd moved out.

When they returned to the nursery, they found Ben absorbed in a world of his own. He was so preoccupied with the vintage train set, he didn't even know they had returned. He seemed to be having the time of his life. They didn't disturb him right away. Instead, they observed him quietly for awhile. Carmen was wonderful with him. She was assisting him in connecting the boxcars.

"A typical boy," Marc whispered in her ear.

"I guess it comes natural, huh?" she whispered back.

"I hate to break up this circle of *Babes in Toyland*, but it's close to three, and we're expected in the dining room soon," Marc said, giving Carmen a wry smile.

We didn't hear you come in, did we Benjamin?" Ben only shook his head and continued playing with the train.

"This is a beautiful set. It's really old," Allyson said, examining it. "Look at some of these pieces," she marveled, picking up the caboose, admiring the great craftsmanship that went into it.

"This was Marcus's train set when he was just a youngun. Not much older than your boy when his Granddaddy fetched it for him."

"It's original," Marc added.

"Like you," Allyson said quietly. "Something you want to hang on to for a long time," she added, smiling.

"Are you trying to make my face grow red in front of Carmen?"

"Why honey child, I used to change your diapers. I know what's original, and there ain't a boy in this county whose got a heart like yours."

"Bless your soul, Carmen. You'll always be my favorite," he said, placing his arm around her shoulders, as they walked toward the dining room.

The antiquated mahogany dining set could easily seat twenty-four, but was much more suitable and comfortable for twelve guests. Above, in the center of the oblong table, a chandelier with candlestick lights illuminated the room. The creamy beige walls were artistically stenciled with assorted fruits.

Maids carried in the food. Since there was only five of them for dinner, they clustered at one end of the banquet table. The turkey and dumplings were brought in first. Steam was billowing from all ends of the deeply roasted bird. Hands were distributing mashed potatoes and gravy, yams, and a mixture of green veggies. And last, came a loaf of piping hot, homemade raisin bread.

Allyson placed Ben's linen napkin over his shirt, tucking it in at his neck. His eyes widened at the sight of the big turkey. He was hungry and naturally impatient, eager and ready to eat. But since he wasn't able to, he started to act up. Making a scene. He took his spoon and helped himself, enthusiastically dipping into the mashed potatoes. She was thankful Marc's parents hadn't joined them yet, because he went into a complete temper tantrum when she spanked his hand.

"It's long past the lunch hour. He's hungry, Ali. Make him up a plate. My parents will understand," Marc said calmly.

"What if they don't?" she asked apprehensively.

"I'll deal with them, honey, don't worry," he said, with a smile.

Ben remained quiet as he dug into the food with his fingers, filtering through it. She had showed him over and over again how to use the utensils, but Ben's a stubborn child, quite insistent on doing things his way. Aimee and Marcus Kelsey walked into the room just as she was disciplining Ben. Marcus was a tall and dignified man, with a full head of white hair. His dark eyes were obscured somewhat behind a pair of tinted granny glasses. She rose when Marc introduced her to his father.

"Sit, sit," he said, motioning with his hand.

"I'm sorry we're late. Something pertinent…your father and I had to tend to," said Aimee Kelsey.

Only a few words were swapped during dinner. Everyone ate heartily. Once or twice, she noticed Mr. Kelsey observing Ben. Occasionally his eyes wandered over at her. It was hard to know what he was thinking. The dormant atmosphere was becoming vastly overcast. She wished that somebody would break the silence.

Suddenly, Ben sneezed. He had a mouth full of peas when he did. The peas shot across the table like pellets being shot from a pistol, aimed directly at Mr. Kelsey. Allyson was mortified. Her face grew hot, and she thought she'd die from humiliation. She wanted to duck under the table after seeing Mr. Kelsey's eyes widen in horror.

Just as she was about to apologize for Ben's outburst, Mr. Kelsey's frown was erased and his lips curved upward. A small cackle emerged and his body shook jovially. Almost spontaneously, Aimee Kelsey's concealed smirk burst into an open chuckle, and before long they all converged in a gale of full-fledged laughter. This broke the silence and when the dessert was served, she was much more at ease with his family. They obviously were not uptight with Ben's unpredictable behavior. They were real people, and not the product of an artificial substance, such as she had noticed existed with the Caldwell clan.

After dinner, Marc escorted them into the living room. It was surrounded with long, wide windows, letting every ray of sunlight penetrate through, making it bright and cheerful. In the center of the room stood the largest and fullest Christmas tree she had ever seen. It must have stood ten feet tall, and every limb was decorated with unique and sparkling ornaments. Santa and his helpers immediately captured Ben's attention. Miniature, shiny packages and angels, made of blown glass, no doubt, dangled poignantly from the thick branches. The tree was resplendent, as was everything about this place.

Ben was captivated just by the mere sight of this enormous wonder—as was she—but soon his interest dissolved and the words "choo choo" were spat at them. It was obvious where he wanted to be. They reluctantly gave in to him and headed towards the nursery when they ran into Carmen who insisted on relieving her parental duty. She adored kids and found taking care of Ben to be a joyful assignment.

"Is this tree real?" she asked Marc when they were alone.

"No, Ma'am. Genuinely fake. But made in the USA"

"It's gorgeous!"

"So are you. They love you, Ali," he said, with an endearing smile.

"How do you know?"

"They're my parents. Who would know them better than me?"

"I tried," she said, "till the incident with the peas."

"I haven't seen my father laugh like that in years. You and Ben were a hit! You brought laughter back into this house," he said, with a smile, and a glumness she hadn't noticed before. Then a trace of moisture filled his somber brown eyes.

"Is there something you want to talk about?" she asked warily, searching his eyes for a response.

"It's a beautiful day," he said. "You look so happy."

"Happier than I have ever been," she said. "But this relationship is two-sided, remember. Your happiness is just as important to me."

Before she could finish what she wanted to say, his folks made an untimely entrance. There were some peculiar eye signals going on, some private code amongst the three of them, she gathered.

"There's something I need to take care of. Excuse me for a minute," Marc said, and left her stranded in the room with Aimee and Marcus.

His mother sat next to her on the sofa, with her hands folded neatly on her lap. His father sat quietly in the corner of the room, reading a newspaper and puffing away on a pipe. Every once in awhile he'd glance up and contribute a word or two, just enough to be sociable. The atmosphere was getting heavy again with silence.

"So, my dear, how did you and Marcus come to meet?"

"We met at the registry of deeds. In Barnstable. I'm a real-estate broker."

"That's right. Now I recall Marcus telling me you were in real estate," she said, smiling.

Allyson prayed she wouldn't get too personal.

"Were you born and raised in Massachusetts?"

"No, Ma'am. In New York."

"Upper state?"

"Yes. In a small town named Burlington. Close to the Vermont line."

"I see. Is this where you knew your husband?"

"Actually, no. We met on the Cape. He was from Connecticut."

"It's a shame it didn't work out between the two of you. Ben is a lovely child."

"Well, he was killed tragically…in an automobile accident—Ben was only a few months old. Ben doesn't really remember him," she said, trying to continue the story line.

She had Kyle dead and buried, and she couldn't retract those shameful declarations. Not to mention the fact that she failed to correct Aimee when she addressed Kyle as her husband. And she had to cast more fabrications just to close up this less-than-truthful discussion.

"We're terribly sorry, Allyson, for your loss. Aren't we, Marcus?" she looked toward her husband for support. He nodded. "It must be difficult for you bringing up your son alone."

"I manage. When you love someone as much as I love Ben, it's an enjoyment rather than a burden," she said with a slight smile. She believed she had made a positive impression with that comment, for they were using their eye signals again—this time with a smile, which appeared to her, as one of approval.

She hated herself for being dishonest with them. But at the same time, she wanted to perpetuate the sweet image they had of her. And they were so proud of their son; she especially didn't want them to be disappointed in him.

At that moment, Marc entered the room with a young woman wearing a baseball cap, work boots, and Wranglers. The focus instantly turned onto them.

"Sorry I'm late," said the young woman.

"Allyson, I'd like you to meet my sister, Lou Ann."

"Louie," she said pointedly, gazing at her brother, with these big brown eyes.

"Hi, Louie," Allyson spoke immediately, extending her hand.

"Nice to meet you," Louie said graciously, with a smile. Then she swiftly turned her attention toward Benjamin. "I've heard a lot of good things about you, Ben."

Ben gave her a puzzled look.

"Do you like baseball?" she asked reaching her hand into her back pocket.

He nodded enthusiastically.

"Great. These are for you," she said, handing him some baseball cards. "You promise to take good care of them?"

He nodded.

"They'll be valuable someday. Look here, we got Nolan Ryan. Oh, here's an oldie, Mickey Mantle," she said, handing them over.

"Thank you," his voice squeaked.

"You've missed dinner, darling," Aimee Kelsey cited.

"I'm sorry it couldn't be helped. I'll just grab a sandwich from the kitchen, if it's okay."

"Of course," Mrs. Kelsey said.

"I'm roofing today."

Aimee shook her head. "I wish you'd stick to the paper work."

"I can't stand being cooped up inside too long."

"It's dangerous for you to be up so high. What if you fall?"

"Then I may be out of work for a while."

"It doesn't become you to be sarcastic."

"I'm sorry. But, Mom, you know life is a gamble. I could get hurt or killed just walking across the street."

"Don't speak to your mother in that manner. She doesn't want anything to happen to you kids," Marcus Kelsey intervened, defending his wife.

"Lou Ann is going to school to be an architect," Aimee was proudly telling Allyson.

"So, do you two have any plans for the future?" Louie asked, giving her brother a wink.

Marc and Allyson stared momentarily at each other, with love dancing in their eyes.

"Possibly," Marc answered.

"Wow! You mean I may have a sister-in-law soon?"

"Don't put them into an awkward situation," Aimee Kelsey uttered to her daughter.

"It's getting late. We really must be leaving. It's a long drive, and Ben's getting tired. And the weather has been so unpredictable," Marc said.

"Time seems to fly when you're here, darling."

"We'll be back again—real soon, Mom."

"I'm glad I finally got the chance to meet you, Louie."

"Me too."

There were warm good-byes, and then they were on the road again, headed home. Allyson felt so much a part of Marc's family. Although she hadn't met the other two sisters, there was already a strong sense of belonging.

Driving home, he reached out for her hand, and held it in his.

"I was hoping everybody could have been here today to meet you," Marc said.

"Well that couldn't be helped."

His oldest sister Alexander, a flower child of the sixties, who never married, was in Italy buying merchandise for a chain of discount stores. Maureen, the middle child, was home with a stomach virus. The family was hoping she was pregnant. Mr. & Mrs. Kelsey were longing for a grandchild, although it was unlikely. Maureen found studying criminal law more intriguing.

"There'll be another time," Allyson said.

"You're right."

"What was that sadness I saw in your eyes today? I thought you were about to tell me, when your mother and father came into the room."

"It's nothing," he said, his eyes averting hers—keeping them on the road.

"I have a feeling it is. I'm not going to leave you alone until you tell me."

"You have enough to worry about."

"I want to know. It's obvious it's something that bothers you very much. Please tell me."

"Okay. I had a brother who died," he said pensively.

"I'm so sorry. What happened?"

"He had spinal meningitis. He had such a short life."

"How old was he?" she asked.

"He was only five."

"Oh, that's awful. I'm so sorry. It must have been hard on your folks—on all of you," she said, remembering that far away sadness she saw in Mrs. Kelsey's eyes, which obviously still affected Marc, especially when he was around her. That explained why the nursery looked so bright and fresh. Aimee Kelsey couldn't let go. She was still living her pain—her loss. Allyson immediately felt sorry for her. Having a child of her own she understood.

"My mother wouldn't let me out of her sight for a moment. She was so afraid she'd lose me too, I guess. I was only three at the time. My sisters would tease me—call me, 'Mama's boy.' I think they resented me. I got all the attention. They were older—but they needed her too."

"I'm sure they don't blame you. Not now. It's been a long time."

"I wonder sometimes," he said.

"If it bothers you that much, talk to them about it. Tell them how you feel."

"Good advice."

Although he had good intentions of doing so, Allyson doubted he would, especially since he hadn't had a heart to heart with them about this, much earlier.

Surprisingly, it wasn't long afterwards, after a great deal of coaxing, a special family gathering was arranged. During that time he found out, as she suspected, the girls had never held any grudges—or any resentment towards him; it was his own mind that had tortured him with this needless distress, all these years. That slate was wiped clean that day and, thenceforth, there seemed to be even more closeness between all of them.

His sisters were all very distinct but delightful, and she felt very comfortable being around them whenever she visited. In spite of how different they all were, Allyson loved each one in her own way.

CHAPTER 41

One frigid evening, they bundled up warm and went prowling the woods for a Christmas tree. The dark clouds were sprinkling fluffy white flakes all about them. The crisp air was quite still, and over yonder they could hear church bells ringing and carolers chanting hymns. It was a peaceful time of year, and Allyson allowed that peace to seep through her, while the three of them strolled happily across the fields, letting their boots scuff the virgin snow.

She could hardly believe three years had passed since Ben was born. So much had happened during those years, and she had been exposed to enough misfortune to last a lifetime. She was sure she had paid her dues. She still had mixed emotions about her dad. She detested what he had done to her...to her mom...and to Gerry. The man she once idolized had vandalized all her hopes and dreams. Nevertheless, she loved him for he was her father. Learning of her estranged brother's death, the brother she never had the pleasure of meeting, was another devastation. A huge one. The final straw—but hardly the least, was finding her best friend in bed with the man, she thought, she loved. Allyson knew she couldn't turn back the pages and rewrite what had already been engraved; she could only look toward the future and hope for better passages.

Nevertheless, out of all of this misfortune, something good had come. She was blessed with Ben—and she found Marc, and she was very thankful for both of them. So many who had touched her heart, had left her wounded, and she feared that loving too much, would only bring more suffering to her at a later date. She gave all of her love to her son, knowing a child wouldn't inten- tionally take that love from her, and turn it into something lesser. She loved Marc, but deep down a voice warned her to be careful, and not to give all of herself to one man, who may someday transform her devotion into a confining purgatory.

The snow was falling heavily now, as they floundered through the wilderness, hunting for a tree. Marc launched the first snowball, unintentionally hitting her directly in the face. She knew he thought he hurt her at first, but when he saw her lick the wet snow with a vindictive grin, he began rolling them faster. She got him back, but not quick enough. She was mercilessly being snowballed to death. Ben, seeing her as an easy target, excitedly joined Marc, throwing the white balls at her, as fast as he could roll them.

As they wrestled in a snowy brawl, she accidentally slipped and tumbled down a hill, like a log falling precariously from an over stacked pile. When, at last, she landed at the bottom. Protected by heavy layers of clothing and soft snow, she was uninjured. When she looked up—she saw the perfect tree, right before her—the one that would become their Christmas tree.

"Are you all right, Allyson," Marc bellowed nervously, as he dashed down the cliff, sliding most of the way.

"I'm fine," she said, sitting up, shielding her face with her arm from the brightness of the flashlight he had with him. "Marc, hand me the flashlight," she insisted. And when he did, she shined it on the snow-covered pine.

"That's nice, Mommy."

"It sure is, honey. I think we've found our tree."

Ben and Allyson stood at the top of the hill, while Marc harvested this piece of perfection at its trunk, using an ax he had brought.

Marc dragged the seven-footer back to his place. Before they stepped inside, he shook the snow from its branches. There were a few bare areas and a couple of broken limbs, but all considered—it was in decent shape. Next, he built a toasty fire in the hearth so that they could thaw out. They rubbed their frozen hands over the roaring flames, and hung their soaked hats and gloves over the mantel to dry. Then, he put the tree in a stand, and they waited for the branches to dry before decorating it.

Marc swathed the pine with an abundance of white lights. Allyson draped its branches with shiny, silver garland. And then, they let Ben put on a few ornaments, before giving it the ultimate touch—the angel. Marc got out a ladder, placed it near the tree, climbed to the top, and delicately crowned the pine with the divine figure.

Allyson curled up on the sofa and gazed triumphantly at the beautiful sight that was standing not far from the pretty decorated fireplace, where flames were rocketing from an intense inferno. She laid her head on Marc and lapsed into a peaceful state. Ben curled up beneath the tree's branches and fell asleep.

Later on, Marc made some hot chocolate while she wrapped presents. She knew this Christmas would be the best ever, because she had Ben—and she had Marc. What more could she ask for? Suddenly, she wanted to scratch out all the ugliness and just take comfort in the actual present. And at that instant she was happier than she'd ever been, and she thought Marc sensed what she was feeling. He raised her head toward his and his lips lingered sweetly on hers for a long time. Beneath a blanket, in case Ben should awake, they disrobed and let their bodies intertwine. And something very extraordinary emerged from inside. It was as though two souls were trying to converge into one.

CHAPTER 42

The next morning when Allyson and Ben returned home, there was a note stuck between the screen door and the main door. She hesitated at first, wondering whether to get rid of it. She didn't know if Janice was delegating her venomous threats again. But curiosity drove her to delve into the contents.

Dear Ali,

I have some presents for Ben. I'll stop by later.

It was unsigned, but she recognized the handwriting immediately. Kyle, she believed, really did love Ben in his own way. He surely hadn't enriched Ben's life with emotional support, but he was providing for him financially. Even though it wasn't nearly enough, it did help in many ways. Especially since Kyle was almost illiterate when it came to expressing his love for his child. Or to anyone. Instead, he expressed his deep affection for Ben by showering him with gifts, the same bandwagon his father used to demonstrate his love for him.

To no surprise, Kyle never stopped by later. In fact, it wasn't until two days after, Christmas Eve, when he staggered over with a bundle of presents for Ben. There had been a party at the mansion, and Kyle had had more than his share to drink. She was grateful that Ben had already gone to bed for the night. She didn't want him to see his father intoxicated. Kyle stumbled through the door wearing a Santa's hat, carrying an armful of presents. He practically fell on his face he was so drunk. And his words were slurred badly.

Forget the drunken sailor, I got me a drunken Santa, she thought. After being so thoughtful and in the state that he was, she couldn't just throw him out; she was afraid he might hurt himself, worse yet someone else. So she decided to let him stay until she was able to sober him up enough so that he could get home safely.

Marc had departed only an hour earlier, so that they could catch a good night's sleep before the big day. Furthermore, they both had last minute gifts to wrap, and phone calls to make. He wanted to call his family, and she wanted to wish Aunt Edith and Uncle Steven a merry Christmas. Marc said he'd be over early in the morning to see Ben open his presents, and later that day they were planning to go to his house for dinner.

Kyle attempted to become intimate with her while she was trying to force black coffee into him. After casting aside his wobbly advances and ignoring his babbling nonsense, he passed out on her couch. She covered him with a blanket and left him there. Then she went to bed.

Allyson phoned Marc before retiring to make sure he didn't have any surprises in store for her, such as an unexpected visit or phone call, which might stir Kyle just enough to cause her a problem. She didn't need anyone to ruin her Christmas with Marc. If Marc even suspected Kyle was over, he'd oust her in a flash, as he did the last girl he was involved with. She couldn't jeopardize losing something so wonderful. Something that might never come again.

"Is everything okay?" he asked.

"Uh, huh. Ben went right to sleep, and I've been stuffing the stockings with last minute goodies."

"I really wish we could be together tonight."

"Me too. But in just a few hours, we will be."

"Maybe old Saint Nick will sneak down your chimney a little later for some milk and cookies."

"No," she blurted. "No, please Marc. I really need a good night's sleep."

"Ali, are you sure everything is okay?"

"Yeah. I just need this time alone. It's a sensitive time for me...being without my family. You understand, don't you?"

"Of course I do. How selfish of me. Sometimes we do need that time alone."

"Thanks. I appreciate your understanding. See ya for breakfast?"

"You bet. Ali...I love you," he said.

"Me too," she said modestly, holding the receiver close to her body before hanging up, feeling a bit guilty because Kyle was in the next room. She wasn't lying when she said she loved him. And she was being honest with him when she told him she was thinking about her family. It's just that she happened to omit the present situation, unknown to him, thank goodness.

Allyson had been reminiscing about the happy times she used to have with her family during this special holiday and how much she missed all of that—them. With her mom gone now and her dad in and out of her life, Christmas with the both of them would never be again. And she knew that. Nothing could be the same.

Christmastime for her dad, once immensely meaningful, appeared to be just a tradition to him. But it was just as special to her as it had always been, and she had a new family to think about and to celebrate with. Which certainly didn't include Kyle.

It wasn't all that long ago when she wept night after night for Kyle to be by her side, to share in the joy of their baby growing inside of her and to participate in his birth. Kyle missed out on all that mattered because to him money was of greater importance. The man she once fantasized about as being her Julius Caesar, the supreme ruler of her empire, was now only a phantom of her past. That once profound sensation had long since vanished. He had atomized all the infatuations she ever possessed for him with his arrogance, his selfishness, and his foolish priorities. Furthermore, he had squelched any love she had leftover for him on the night he slept with Felicia. But would Marc be convinced of that, if he found out that Kyle was now occupying her couch? She didn't think she would understand if the situation were reversed, especially considering all past circumstances.

Therefore, he shouldn't be told.

Allyson set her alarm clock for 1:00 A.M., so that she could get Kyle up and out before he was discovered. She didn't need Kyle to be seen by Benjamin in the morning; it would only confuse him. However, she wanted to be sure Kyle was sober enough to drive. Fortunately, when she awoke him, he left peacefully.

CHAPTER 43

It was the morning their Savior was born. A joyous beginning awaited to be celebrated.

When Ben opened the presents that Kyle had left for him, she saw him light up like the Christmas tree. Kyle had given him a big red fire truck, making Marc's and her gifts appear small and unattractive. The truck had every gadget imaginable attached, including a remote control that moved it in all directions, and a loud siren that gave her a pounding headache.

Allyson watched Marc open the small package she gave him, containing a pair of eighteen-karat gold cuff links that she bought him when they were in San Francisco. His delightful expression indicated to her that he was more than pleased with her choice. Forthwith, he asked her to help him into the French cuffs of his shirt. He beamed as he looked at them. Then he whirled her around in delight. Afterward, he sat her down on the ottoman and handed her her gift from him. The box was about the size in which a pin or a necklace might fit. She paused before opening it.

"Give me a hint?" she asked, smiling. He shook his head. Then she slowly lifted the cover, and the white cotton inside. "Oh my God! It's beautiful," she said, smiling through her joyful tears. It was a pear-shaped diamond ring!

"It's a carat and a half. I hope you like it."

"Like it…I love it! But I can't accept this," she said, weeping with happiness.

"I don't want to push you into anything you're not ready for. Let it be a token of our friendship for now. I can wait," he said with a smile.

"This is much too expensive to accept as a friendship ring."

"I know I'm jumping ahead of things, and I know that nothing definite has been discussed for our future…. But you are the most remarkable woman I have ever known. And someday I hope you'll want to be my wife."

"Oh, Marc," she cried happily, holding out her right hand so that he could slip the ring on, "I love you."

"I love you too, Allyson Porteus. Please accept this ring in remembrance of my love for you."

"I will. And when I look at it, no matter where I am, I'll think only of you. For our love will prevail. And our souls will strengthen with this everlasting emotion," she said, looking deeply into his eyes.

PART II

SUMMER—1985

CHAPTER 44

Ben was sprouting like the weeds. And his appetite was growing as much as his feet were. It was hard for her to believe he was five years old already. Time had just slipped away so quickly.

The real-estate business was slowly declining and becoming more and more competitive. It had just about reached its peak, and the sales of homes were leveling off. Money was getting tight, and she refused to accept any of Marc's generous offers. He was not Ben's father, although he'd made a wonderful one. Each day Allyson became more and more angry as she thought about how Kyle shrugged off his financial responsibilities as a father.

She and Marc bumped into him at the Sea Breeze Inn. He was obnoxiously drunk, and he told Marc they slept together on Christmas Eve.

"Umm, is she good in the sack," Kyle said, smirking, as he staggered about. "I bet you and her aren't as good as we were," he said, slurring his words. "Did she tell ya about Christmas Eve? Ah, was she good that night," Kyle bragged, raising his empty glass in mid air, swaying back and forth.

Marc didn't say a word. He walked over to him and, without warning, he decked him. He slugged him so hard in the face that Kyle fell to the floor and never got up. What a punch! Allyson was flabbergasted. Everybody scrambled about, and many went to assist Kyle. Marc just took her hand and led her to the car.

Marc started the motor and sped down the road in utter silence. Suddenly he squealed to a forceful stop, frightening her. She'd never seen him this upset.

"What happened Christmas Eve?" he asked, biting his bottom lip, while his eyes glared intensely at her.

"Nothing. He's drunk. He doesn't know what he's saying."

"Allyson, I'm not playing games with you. What went on that night? Did you make love to him or not?"

"No. No! Of course not. He came over with some presents for Ben. He was really drunk. I let him sleep it off on the sofa. That's it. I swear to you," she cried, with tears streaming down her face and onto her jacket.

"Why didn't you tell me?"

"I was afraid you wouldn't believe me."

"How can you think like that?"

"After all that's happened between him and me. I was afraid…I don't know. I didn't want our first Christmas together to be ruined, and I didn't want him to get killed or hurt someone else either."

"You could have told me."

"It was Christmas and I wanted everything to be perfect. I'm sorry," she said.

She was surprised at how quickly he mellowed. He believed her that's why, she thought.

"I didn't mean to jump at you like that. Hey, let's put it behind us," he said, with a long sigh taking her hand in his.

"That was one incredible slug," she said with a smile.

"I don't want anyone to ever hurt you," he said soberly.

"Nobody will again."

She would not let them. And she knew that as long as she had Marc she didn't have to worry. He wound never hurt her.

Would he?

❦   ❦   ❦

There had been no contact with Kyle since their last confrontation when Marc decked him. Mouths had been flapping everywhere about that night, but she hadn't heard any rumors since.

Marc began visiting his parents as often as he could. During those times, Ben would ask about dads in general. Many fathers, those with children in kindergarten, came to pick up their kids for their working spouses.

One afternoon, Ben surprised Allyson with a question, which she wasn't prepared to answer.

"How come my daddy never picks me up from school?" he asked.

"Well, your daddy is a very busy man, honey. I'm sure if he had the time he would."

"Oh," he said, crinkling up his face, as he walked into his room.

Allyson diluted the truth somewhat. Maybe a whole lot. What was she going to tell him? That his father's priorities were mixed up…that he was too busy filling his own needs. And she had no idea how occupied he really was, until she drove with some reluctance to the mansion one night to discuss Ben's welfare with Kyle. Marc was visiting with his family for the weekend, and she got wind that Janice was away on a political voyage, so it made it convenient for her.

As she drove through the gate, she realized those anxious feelings had vanished. It's funny, that even though she had gone from love to hate, to repugnance, and recently back to loathing again, she now felt a complete numbness. She had experienced all these mixed emotions for this one human being, whom she will never be able to completely rid from her life because of one important tie—Benjamin. And because of him, Kyle and she will be in tandem, bound together, in some way for a long time to come.

When she looked back, she couldn't believe how foolish she was to let her emotions rule her. Her only concern now was for her son, and he needed to know where he stood with his father. She was shameful for choosing a man not worthy enough to be the father of her son. Nonetheless, Kyle was Ben's father and she couldn't change that fact. She wondered if her mother had felt the way she did, about selecting the wrong mate to be the father of her child.

It was a calm summer night, but extremely warm and humid. A good night for a swim. She heard voices coming from the pool area. As she walked closer, for a split second she thought about turning back. She figured he was having a rendezvous with another woman, and she was about to spoil his fun. But she didn't care; she gloated at the thought. Those one-time deep and intimate feelings she had had for him were so far buried they could never be retrieved. It was as if they never existed to begin with.

When Allyson finally reached the fence surrounding the pool and opened the gate door, she stood still in profound shock. There was Kyle's naked body in the pool with an old friend of his from Provincetown, Stuart Hanson. They were feverishly caught up in a romantic kiss. She couldn't believe what she was seeing. Kyle was actually kissing a man! Immediately, she became disoriented and nearly toppled over a lounge chair.

"Allyson, you okay?" Kyle asked, quickly getting out of the pool.

"What do you think?" she asked sarcastically, watching him grab a towel, and wrap it around him.

"You remember my friend, Stuart?" he asked, handing Stuart a towel—so that he could cover his manly part.

"No," she said, even though he had a face she would hardly forget. He was gorgeous with his blond hair, almond eyes, and muscular body. He was something women of all ages would die for. And apparently men too. Kyle had introduced him to her at the Caldwell party.

Who would have guessed?

"Can I talk to you—alone?" she asked sternly, giving him a harsh eye.

"I'll just mosey on into the kitchen and get something for us to snack on. Okay, darling?" Stuart asked, winking at Kyle.

Allyson felt sick to her stomach. She was still in awe at what she had witnessed only a few minutes earlier, and now with what she was hearing.

"You take all the time you need," Stuart said, as he strutted into the house.

"Okay, Darling? Are you for real? Who are you?" She demanded to know.

"Stuart is my love. Plain and simple. I'm sorry you had to find out this way."

"You're a married man for God sakes."

Kyle just shrugged his shoulders.

"You're my son's father! How can you do this to him? You can hate me, but don't hurt Ben," she cried.

"I'm not trying to hurt anyone. Stuart understands me. He knows where I'm coming from."

"Get off it."

"I think I was about thirteen when I knew. Maybe twelve. I tried—for my parents—for society. I did start liking women more. Then Janice proposed—well…you know the rest."

"No. I loved you. And I will always love my son. But it's different with Stuart—I wish you could understand."

She just looked at him and shook her head.

"What do you want me to say?"

"How can you love your son and disgrace him like that? How do you think he's going to feel when he's in school and kids make fun of him because his daddy's gay—or bi-sexual?" she asked, seething with anger.

"We've got a few years yet. I'm sure you'll think of something," he said, rather nonchalantly.

"Me?" Allyson put her hands up in disgust. If she were a horse, she would have kicked him with her hind legs—to kingdom come.

Stuart came strutting out onto the patio. "I hope I didn't interrupt anything. Would you like some?" he asked her, as he held a tray of shrimp and sauce in front of her.

"No. Thank you. I gotta go," she said abruptly, walking away. The thought of being in the company of those two was inconceivable right now. She got in her car and sped out of there.

And as soon as she got home she began packing her suitcase. She immediately called Marc and told him she needed to get away for awhile. She didn't tell him why, and he didn't press her for an explanation.

CHAPTER 45

The three-hour drive to her Aunt Edith's home in New Hampshire was long and lonesome. Benjamin slept most of the way. Each time Allyson looked at him, visions of Kyle and his lover flooded her with bleak thoughts. The mere thought of Ben becoming gay, being different, put chills down her spine. This is what she feared most now. A mother's ultimate nightmare. Ashamed and saddened by not being able to see her son walk down the aisle with a woman. Or never having grandchildren. The sky was dismal; it was filled with gray clouds. There were threats of rain everywhere. But the only drops she felt were the ones upon her cheeks.

Once she reached the long dirt road which led to the old farmhouse, she felt an immediate sense of belonging. Aunt Edith was waiting on the porch when they arrived. She was smiling happily as she stood up from the old wicker rocker with open arms. She was wearing a blue denim dress with denim sneakers. They looked great against her rosy complexion and soft wavy blonde hair. Allyson knew she was home again, her home away from home.

When Uncle Steven heard her car pull up, he came out to greet them also, along with Damsel, their ten-year-old collie. Uncle Steven was tall and lean, and he had a built-in smile that was irresistible. And even though he was twelve years older than Aunt Edith, one would never know it. He was as pleasant as she was, and Allyson felt just as comfortable around him as she did with Aunt Edith. He was an intelligent man but quiet, a computer whiz. Although he often traveled in his profession as a computer consultant, he kept to himself. He never wanted to interfere with them women and "their girlish talk," he often said.

After they unpacked and got settled, Auntie served them lunch. She had prepared her homemade chili, Allyson's favorite, and she made chicken salad sandwiches. The rest of the afternoon they spent outside enjoying the sun, which was now shining brightly.

They had a huge back yard, where Aunt Edith cultivated a vegetable garden. While she pulled some weeds out of it, Allyson lay back in the hammock, soaking up the rays. She offered to help, but Aunt Edith wouldn't permit it.

"You didn't come to New Hampshire, Ali, to work. This is your vacation. Enjoy it."

A few minutes later, Allyson rose from the hammock and walked into the garden and knelt down on all fours to join her. "I wanna help. This is enjoyable to me," she said to her aunt with a smile. Her Aunt Edith smiled back and nodded her head.

Ben was amusing himself with Damsel. Allyson deliberately evaded discussing with her what she had learned about Kyle, even though it was troubling her immensely. She didn't want to spoil a perfect day. They reminisced and laughed about the good old times. The times when she was a youngster, free of the unthinkable. Free of the hardships she had since unearthed.

"It seems like only yesterday Damsel was a puppy," Allyson said, smiling as she watched Ben and Damsel frolic together on the lawn.

"Yup. I think you were around sixteen when we first got her."

"And I thought life was tough then," she chuckled.

"Life is full of ups and downs. We have to take the bad with the good. As long as we grow from the rougher ones, we can keep moving forward."

"I wish I could inscribe that philosophy onto my brain."

"After forty, you'll mellow out. Things that mean a great deal to you now will seem trivial when you reach my age," she said, with a smile.

"Thanks. You mean I have to wait that long?" she said wryly. Aunt Edith nodded and they both laughed.

Surprisingly, she slept peacefully that night, until Ben came bouncing in, Damsel tagging along behind him, wagging her tail. Ben was all excited. He took her hand and tried pulling her from the bed. Allyson jumped up wearily, put on her slippers and her robe, and scurried behind them. Her son wanted to go outside and play with the collie, so she walked out onto the porch into the cool morning air, to watch the two of them frolic around on the thick blanket of grass.

They simply adored each other. Damsel was as gentle as she could be with Ben. Ben pulled her tail and even tried to ride her, but Damsel remained nonchalant about it. She just seemed happy to have Ben there, enjoying his company.

It was another gorgeous day. The sun was shining brightly through the cloudless cerulean skies. As Allyson stood captivated by the view, Aunt Edith walked out onto the deck, and put her arm around her waist.

"How you feeling today?" she asked.

"Great. Look at them. Jovial and content. It makes you feel good just watching them."

"It sure does," she said, taking a deep breath. "Where there are children, there's joy. You can feel it all around you," she said, smiling, with just a trace of sorrow in her eyes. Allyson felt sad for her, knowing how much Aunt Edith loved children but was unable to get pregnant. She wondered why she never adopted. She had had her around a lot. Maybe at the time that was enough for her.

"So—what's on the agenda for today, Auntie?"

"I thought maybe we'd go blueberry picking since this is the season. They're nice and plump about now."

"Sounds good to me. You wouldn't have any plans of making blueberry pie, would you?"

"We'll see," she said, with a smile and a twinkle in her eyes.

CHAPTER 46

The bushes were plentiful and filled with ripened berries, plump and juicy, just like Aunt Edith said they would be. They brought small baskets to carry them in. Ben relished picking them. He devoured more than he picked. His face, all blue, along with his hands and his clothing, was confirmation of all that. They laughed when they saw him. Damsel was licking his face. Allyson wished she had brought the camera.

When the baskets were filled, they strolled back to the house, enjoying what was left of the sunshine. The days were getting shorter already as it neared closer to another autumn.

Auntie washed the blueberries and prepared them for baking while she cleaned up Ben. Then she put him down for a nap. They baked the rest of the afternoon. They had picked enough blueberries for two twelve-inch pies, a few turnovers, and a batch of blueberry muffins. It was a fun day. Aunt Edith always tried to make it pleasant for them.

Instead of dwelling on Kyle and worrying about something Allyson couldn't change, she let her thoughts drift to Marc. She missed him very much. Ben even asked about him when they first arrived. Marc was such a big part of their lives now that Ben couldn't understand why he didn't come with them. She needed this time alone. She had to try and sort out her feelings about Kyle and…Marc. But most importantly, she had to try and get to know herself, and find out in what direction her life was headed.

"Auntie, you do good work. Look at these pies! They're perfect!"

"With your help. I couldn't have done it without ya."

"Come on, Auntie. I can't take any credit. I can't cook."

"Sure you can. I remember when you were yea high," she said, gesturing with her hand from the floor to about four feet, "we baked all sorts of pastries. Don't you remember those chocolate chip cookies?"

"How can I forget. I would dream of them. I think I had a third of the batter eaten before they'd even made it to the oven," Allyson said, laughing. "You always let me lick the bowl, and I'd lick it clean."

That evening they had a nice roast for dinner. For dessert, they each had a big slice of the scrumptious blueberry pie, topped with vanilla ice cream.

After Allyson got Ben settled in for the night, they sat out on the porch. It was a warm summer evening and the stars were shimmering brightly. Allyson rocked in the large wicker chair and closed her eyes. She could hear the sounds of crickets singing and the owls hooting. She thought about Marc and their future together, and then her mind drifted to Kyle and his lover. She became restless in her chair, rocking faster and faster as the haunting memory of seeing Kyle and Stuart naked in the pool kissing, intimately. Somehow, she would have to save Ben from this repulsiveness. If she never went to the mansion, she would have never stumbled upon this amazing discovery. But if she was the last to know, how could she find a solution in time to alleviate the pain her son will endure when he discovers that his daddy is different from other fathers?

She wished she had taken the money Janice had offered her, to leave town and forget who Benjamin's father was. This would have been the perfect solution, and maybe it still could be the ideal means for escaping this horror show. They could run far away where no one would ever find them. They could begin a new life together.

But the more she thought about it, she knew she couldn't leave Marc. He had been too kind and too wonderful to them, and she would miss him terribly. She looked down at her hand, at the beautiful pear-shaped diamond he gave her last Christmas. They both knew at the time that she was not ready for any commitments. She was still vulnerable from her relationship with Kyle.

Understanding how she felt, instead of this ring representing a symbol of the traditional engagement, he had placed it on her hand as an acknowledgment of their lasting friendship. And as she gently rubbed the ring he gave her, she could feel the warmth from this deep connection immersing through her. She knew then how much she loved him, and knew she could never be apart from him forever.

Marc had been her inspiration from the minute she met him, at the registry of deeds. He had shown her an authentic love with his kindness and his deep compassion. His honesty had her realize how fortunate she was to have him as a special friend. And through him she learned that money wasn't everything and it didn't have to monopolize their lives.

"Are you coming in, Ali?" Aunt Edith asked.

"Oh gee, what time is it?" she asked, looking up at her. Allyson noticed she was knitting a sweater for Benjamin. And it was almost complete. "I guess I lost all track of time," she said, smiling at her.

"I guess you did. You seemed to be in heavy thoughts. It's almost eleven. I thought maybe you'd want to see the news."

"Oh, yeah," she said, yawning. "It's a beautiful night. Maybe I'll sleep out here."

"You can if you like. But I don't think you'll find it very comfortable. You'll probably end up with a stiff neck."

"Nah," Allyson muttered, stretching, as she stood. "Let's see what the weather's going to be like tomorrow," she said, walking in behind her.

Aunt Edith turned on the set, while she went into the kitchen to fix them a late snack. Uncle Steven had already turned in for the night. He had to be up early.

Their home was like her own. She had no reason to feel uncomfortable helping herself to anything. They hung out in the kitchen most of the time. It was bright and warm with a drop-leaf table and bow-back chairs, and country curtains on the windows. It vented a very cheerful and cozy atmosphere. One that just drew her in. She poured two glasses of milk, and just as she was about to warm the blueberry turnovers in the microwave, Aunt Edith quietly called out.

"Ali, come quick. There's something on TV you might want to see."

Allyson ran into the living room with the milk and turnovers and sat down beside her. They were showing a terrible automobile accident at the Sagamore Bridge. There were fire trucks and state police all around the area. It looked to be at least a five-car pile up. All the cars, which had been traveling at an average speed of forty miles per hour as they went over the bridge, had suddenly come to a deadly stop. The newsman said one man apparently had suffered a heart attack and crossed the double lines, plowing head on into another car. Cameras flashed the vehicles at close range for a few seconds, but it was hard to distinguish all of the cars' models. Some were badly crushed from the impact. Her eyes were glued to the set. She was sitting on the edge of the couch waiting for the newscasters to announce the names of the victims who were injured.

The newsman said the man who had suffered the heart attack died. He was alone in the car. He was driving a Ford Escort, and the two people who were critically injured were driving a Buick LeSabre, while a third person, who was in stable condition, drove a black BMW. The rest of the people had scratches or complained of neck and back injuries and had fender benders.

Then it struck her. Marc drove a BMW. He drove over the bridge often for business, and he visited his family frequently. Allyson began to panic. She was biting her nails, as she listened intently to the news. She hoped she didn't know any of the people who were involved in this dreadful scene, but there was always that possibility.

There were many tourists crossing the bridge. She prayed she wouldn't recognize the names of the victims about to be disclosed. What would she do if something happened to Marc? Her hands clutched the end of the sofa, as she waited anxiously to hear. Just as they were about to announce the names of the people involved in the crash, another reporter interrupted. He stated they had to hold off with the identification, because they weren't able to contact one of the victim's family. They hoped to release names before the eleven o'clock news concluded.

During the commercial, she rushed to the phone to call Marc. There was no answer. Maybe he was sleeping, or didn't want to be bothered. She let the phone ring and ring until, at last, she heard a click.

"Marc is that you?" she asked zealously. But it was only his answering machine coming on. Auntie was calling her, so she decided to hang up before leaving a message.

She hustled back to the couch. Her eyes fixed upon the TV, as they heard the forecaster predict the weather for the following five days. Allyson saw pictures of sun and rain, but it didn't register. She wasn't sure what days were supposed to be sunny, or what days when it would rain. Suddenly, none of that mattered. She only wanted to know if Marc was all right. Then she saw the sportscaster, but never heard a word he uttered. This was the longest news program in history. She waited feverishly to hear who was driving that BMW, but she was afraid she wasn't going to find out that night.

Just as she thought she would have to wonder all night, a newsman interrupted and said he had an update on the accident at the Sagamore Bridge. They had fortunately located the last victim's family during the broadcast and were ready to reveal the names of the people who were involved in this remarkable chain reaction.

Aunt Edith held her hand as they waited for this crucial moment. The man who was driving the Escort and died was from Mansfield. He had had a known heart condition and was eighty years old. The man and woman, who were in the Buick and now listed in critical condition, were a married couple in their thirties, from Connecticut. So far, she didn't know anybody. Now the one and last name, the person who was driving the BMW, who was reported to be in stable condition, was…Janice Caldwell from Chatham!

"She doesn't drive a BMW. She drives a Mercedes," Allyson said excitedly. "They must have made a mistake."

"Don't they look alike?" Aunt Edith asked, knowing very little about cars.

"No. Not at all. Although, she has so many cars, maybe one's in the shop and that was a rental."

It was a blessing not to hear Marc's name, but it was somewhat of a blow to hear Janice's. Allyson couldn't move. It was a shock to hear a name, which was so familiar to her. Evidently, they couldn't reach Kyle, at first, to inform him of his wife's bad fortune. Most likely he was off with his lover somewhere, she thought.

"Can you believe this, Auntie?" she asked, squeezing her hand. "Thank God it wasn't Marc. I truly hope Kyle helps her through this ordeal. There's no love between them, and he's skittish towards physical injuries. He actually fainted one time—after witnessing his own blood. And he's as sympathetic as a cow."

"She'll recover. That's the main thing. Now let's relax and enjoy our snack. Oh, looks like the turnovers have cooled down," she said picking up the plates. "I'll put them back in the microwave to warm them," Aunt Edith said, as she walked away.

Allyson knew she wouldn't relax that night. As much as she was glad Marc was okay, the wheel inside her head were beginning to rotate. She couldn't believe all that had taken place within the last seventy-two hours. The shock of finding Kyle intimate with a man, and now Janice, his wife, hospitalized because of this tragic accident.

The phone rang and she jumped two feet. "Are you expecting to hear from anyone?" she asked Aunt Edith, as she came walking through with steaming turnovers.

"Not at this hour. It must be for you."

And it was. It was Marc. He heard the news also. And when someone didn't leave a message on the machine, he thought it might be her.

"Are you okay?" Marc asked.

"Yeah. Boy that was a shock. Umm, it sounds like she'll be all right, huh?" Allyson asked.

"She'll be laid up for awhile. According to the news, she's in stable condition. That's all we know at this point."

"That's really too bad. I don't wish Janice any harm.... In fact, I actually pity her."

"I know that. Ali...I miss you," he said quietly.

"I miss you too. More than you know," she confessed. "We'll be home before long."

"I'll be waiting. Good-bye, Ali. I love you."

"Me too. See ya."

It felt good to her, just hearing his voice. It always comforted her when she was upset.

She sat up reading for awhile until she became sleepy. Then she dozed off into a peaceful sleep, but was awakened by the sound of Ben's cry. She hopped up and scurried to his room. He was sobbing, and his little arms reached out for her.

"Did you have a bad dream?" she asked. He nodded. "Well don't worry, Mommy's right here. I won't let anything hurt you," she assured him, as she kissed him on his forehead and gently removed a wisp of fine hair from his wet face.

His small body shook in her arms, as he pointed to the shadows upon the wall. Allyson told him that they were only shadows of the different things that were in the room, and she explained how the moon played a big part in leaving these unfamiliar silhouettes. She sang him a lullaby like her mom did for her, whenever she was frightened of something. Her mother's soft and soothing voice made her forget all about her fears. That was when she was much stronger, before she weakened from all the heartache her father imposed upon her.

With the racket they caused, they awakened Aunt Edith. Allyson could smell the coffee brewing. Uncle Steven slept like a log. The only thing he ever heard was his alarm clock.

After Ben floated back to sleep, she tucked him in bed and raised the sides of the child safety bars so that he wouldn't fall out. Aunt Edith went out and bought all the securities of home as soon as Ben was born, knowing they could visit without any worries.

When she walked into the kitchen, her Auntie was wearing her white ruffled apron and pouring the coffee. She smiled sweetly at her. It was 3:00 A.M., and she was bright and cheerful, as though it were seven in the morning. Aunt Edith rarely got angry or upset, and never spoke harshly about anyone. She was a forgiving and very loving individual. "Everybody has problems, some more than others," she would say.

"Sorry about all this," Allyson said, smiling back at her.

"This is part of the course, and kids have a knack for making it interesting. Now sit down and have your coffee, before it gets cold."

Allyson was suddenly feeling sad for her aunt again. She could feel her emptiness from not being able to have children. There had been a big void in her own life before Benjamin came along. Her aunt would have made a wonderful mother if only she could have conceived. She had so much love and tremendous patience to offer.

While sitting quietly at the kitchen table having their coffee, Allyson broke down and told Auntie about Kyle and his new lover.

"You poor child," she said, with tears welling up in her eyes, "you have suffered enough for a young woman."

"Auntie, what am I going to do? How am I going to explain this to my son?" she cried into her bosom.

"I know it's a tremendous shock right now, but everything will work out. You have to take one step at a time, honey. One step at a time," she murmured.

Feeling perpetually secure in her arms, Allyson unloaded all the ruffled feelings that had amplified inside her. She told her about the quarter of a million dollars Janice had offered her to leave town and forget who the father of her baby was, and then about the second proposal of four million, if she agreed to release Ben into their custody. Aunt Edith seemed more than astounded as she listened warily to every word she was saying.

Lastly, she unveiled to her her determination of wanting to take the money and flee, to harbor her son from any unjustified pain. But then the mere thought of losing Marc was more than she could abide. Ben and Marc meant everything to her, but she wanted to spare them from any scandal, which would stay with them throughout their lives. Even though she knew it wasn't her fault, she felt responsible for subjecting them to these continuous nightmares.

"Auntie, I need your guidance. Help me do what's right."

"Oh, honey, I can't tell you what to do with your life. You're a grown woman. I know it's hard right now, but running away isn't the answer. Knowing how much you love Marc and love the Cape...I know you'll do the right thing. In the meantime, go back to bed and get some rest. The sun will be rising soon, and we've got another full day ahead of us."

CHAPTER 47

They went shopping, and Auntie insisted on buying Ben a delightful cowboy outfit that was on display in a store window. Ben was so excited he couldn't wait to try it on. After he put on the boots and hat, he looked so much the quintessential young cowboy that Allyson agreed to let him have it. She couldn't, however, let her pay for it; she had done enough for them already. But still, her Aunt Edith insisted on paying half the bill.

On his first pony adventure that afternoon Ben was propped up in the saddle like an authentic cattle king. Lofty and noble, as he was led slowly around the coral.

For a mere instant, she imagined Kyle when she studied Ben. A smaller version. Allyson could easily see why his mother pampered him as she did. From the pictures she had seen, he had been a beautiful child—as was Ben.

Damsel followed the horse around, not letting Ben out of her sight for a moment. Ben had become her sole companion while they were there. Aunt Edith had the video camera in motion the entire time. With all the shattering tales she had bombarded her with since their stay, Allyson was glad she was enjoying their little outing.

Ben was far from satisfied with only two rounds of riding the pony. He pleaded for more. They gave in, and he was granted two more rounds.

Afterwards, they had lunch at a nearby Friendly's restaurant. Ben loved that idea because hot dog and fries were on the children's menu. While they waited for their sandwiches, the waitress supplied Ben with a small box of crayons and a picture for him to color. And while he entertained himself, Allyson chatted with Aunt Edith about all the blissful wonders that had filled the day. There was no mention of the previous night's discussion. They both wanted to keep their short time together happy. Furthermore, Ben wasn't as infantile as he used to be, and he was much too wise as to what was happening around him.

Each day at Aunt Edith's was as delightful and fulfilling as the day before. She kept her very busy, leaving no time for her to brood over things she couldn't change. And Allyson was too exhausted at night to dwell on what couldn't be modified. And when she dreamt now, it was always sweet dreams of Marc. The longer she stayed away from the Cape, the more she missed him, his love, his face, and his touch.

The two weeks with Aunt Edith and Uncle Steven had flown by. They'd had so much fun that they hated to leave. Ben and Damsel had become good pals, and she and Aunt Edith had become closer than ever before. It was hard saying good-bye, but Allyson was ready to go home. She couldn't wait to see Marc. She wanted to rush into his arms and tell him how much she loved him.

She and Aunt Edith kissed and hugged as though there were no tomorrow. Ben fought her every inch of the way; he didn't want to leave Damsel. The dog lapped Ben's face and whined as she tore Ben away from her. Growing attached to the old lovable collie, he was heartbroken when he found out that Damsel wasn't coming home with them.

"I love you, Auntie," she shouted, as they drove away. "Give Uncle Steven a big kiss for me."

"I will," she hollered, as she waved good-bye, keeping her smile bright. Damsel chased their car until her legs tired.

CHAPTER 48

The house seemed different to her somehow when they got back. Although nothing had really changed, and everything appeared to be in the order in which she had left it. Maybe it was just her. After she put Ben down for a nap, she unpacked their things. It felt good to be home. Strangely, the house seemed brighter, more cheerful. And it didn't take long to adjust to the quietness. She sat down on the couch and soon dozed off.

She was abruptly removed from her sound repose by the ringing of the phone, but by the time she got to it, whoever it was had already hung up. That's when she noticed that the answering machine was full of messages.

Two calls were from a client, another three were from Felicia, and one was from a woman who didn't identify herself but left a phone number. She claimed it was urgent and in reference to her father.

Immediately Allyson became concerned and hastily replayed the tape. Ordinarily, she would have left a number where she could be reached in case of an emergency, but when she had departed, her mind was so boggled with confusion about Kyle that she really wasn't thinking too clearly.

As she dialed the number that was left on her machine, she hoped the call wasn't about anything serious. As much as her dad had betrayed her in the past, he was still her father. Not only did she love him, she cared about him deeply and wouldn't want anything bad to happen to him.

The phone rang and rang on the other end but nobody answered. Was someone trying to scare her? She pushed the button on the phone to get a dial tone and then she re-dialed, but still no one picked up. Then she remembered her father had a beeper. She scrambled hastily through the desk drawers and found the piece of paper where she had scribbled the instructions for beeping him. She immediately dialed his number, waited for the three beeps, and then punched in her number, which would appear on the small screen of his beeper, and waited for him to return her call. He never did. Evidently, as she had foreseen, he moved and no longer had the same number.

Who was this woman who knew her father anyhow? And why didn't she say what was wrong with him? She prayed he wasn't lying in a hospital somewhere all alone. He really didn't have anyone but her; his family was all gone. But all Allyson could do at this point was to wait a while to see if she called back, and if not, she'd just keep trying the number she left.

CHAPTER 49

Allyson was spellbound as soon as she saw Marc coming through her front door. She was extremely happy to see him, and both she and Ben showed him how much he was missed by showering him with an array of hugs and kisses. Marc invited Ben and her to his place for a welcoming home meal. He wanted to prepare something special for them, this being their first night back. But she didn't want to leave the house, knowing she could miss an important call concerning her dad.

Marc understood completely and went down the street to one of the fast-food restaurants and brought back fried clams for himself and her and a burger for Ben. He also brought a basket of curly fries, and a tub of cole slaw for them all. The food looked really good, but she couldn't eat anything. Even though she was very happy to see Marc, a growing concern for her dad had taken hold of her. And each time the phone resounded, her heart skipped a beat. Aunt Edith rang, checking to see if they arrived home safely, and her friend Felicia phoned again, wondering where they had gone this time. She was curious as well as concerned.

After many attempts to reach someone at this number, finally at 10:30 P.M. a female who sounded pretty young and quite inebriated slurred an indecipherable sound into the receiver.

"Hello. This is Allyson Porteus. Someone there called and left a message on my answering machine, saying it was urgent that I call back. It had something to do with my father." She could hear laughter in the background as she waited for a response.

"Who is this again?" asked the woman, garbling her words.

"Allyson Porteus. Alexander Porteus's daughter," she announced louder. "Is my father all right? Is he there?" she shouted.

"Yeah sure, he's here," she said, and put the receiver down. "The no good, useless…. Too drunk to get it up…." Allyson heard her mumble in the background.

Minutes later her dad answered. He didn't seem nearly as intoxicated as the unseen floozy, whose company he was sharing.

"Ali honey, is that you?" he asked, in a pleasant tone.

"Yes, Dad, it's me. I got a call, mentioning it was urgent that I get in touch with you. What's happening?"

"It wasn't a hoax. Your daddy was hospitalized for a few days for an angina attack. But I'm fine now…I was lucky."

"Dad, I'm really sorry to hear that. I'm glad you're all right though. I know it's none of my business, but…drinking can make matters worse."

"Don't lecture me, Ali. I just had a few drinks to relax. Knowing I almost had a heart attack can be nerve-racking, you know."

"I sympathize…. Who's the woman? She doesn't seem to have much class. I think she's using you, Dad."

"You have no right, Allyson, butting into my business, making accusations you know nothing about."

"Maybe not. But I have a right to speak my mind. You are still my dad, and I care about what happens to you, even if you don't. Chasing wild woman and drinking will give you a heart attack for sure!"

"I don't want to argue with my little girl. By the way, how's my grandson?" he asked, more quietly, quickly changing the subject. "He must be getting big."

"Yeah, Dad, he is. He's a toddler now. He talks. He runs. He even rides ponies," she said sadly, knowing he was missing out in all of this.

"Give him my love," he said, earnestly.

"Yeah, I will. Take care of yourself, Dad."

Ben didn't even know his grandfather. Alexander Porteus wasn't in his life long enough to be remembered. Her dad had taken very little interest in his grandson, much like his Lilliputian regard for his own son. She had wanted to scream at him, informing him his son, Gerry, was dead! What good would it do though? Her father's health was going downhill. Just because she couldn't find evidence he was harboring any guilt for deserting his own flesh and blood didn't necessarily mean that there wasn't any. And if he was carrying this ever-lasting debt somewhere inside his soul, then this sad news could initiate another attack, or, worse yet, his own death. As much as it gnawed at her, she didn't have the heart to tell him that his son had died.

"You take care of yourself too, my precious doll. I love you, Ali," he said quietly.

"I love you, Dad. See you soon," she replied.

CHAPTER 50

Allyson dropped Ben off at a friend's house to play, and then she drove to Provincetown. It had been years since she was last there, and she felt the need to visit again. Her father had taken her there once or twice, when she was too young to appreciate it, and he had shown her where he was stationed, at one time, when he was in the coast guard. It was an extraordinary town—quaint, with narrow streets, full of unique shops and restaurants. Home for many talented artists and writers, who were enticed with its beauty and historical sites. It was also a place where people freely expressed their sexuality, without any repercussions.

Her first stop was the old coast guard station, nestled amongst the beach sands, where she tried to imagine—for the first time, what it was really like for her father back then, when he served for his country.

Afterward, she climbed the steps to the top of the Provincetown Monument. As she viewed the landscapes below her, she thought of how different the world seemed, from up high....

High or low, how different we all are.

Strolling down Commercial Street and observing others was a sudden insight of that. And accepting that could be a gift in itself. Hot and thirsty, she finally stopped in an ice cream shop and got an ice cream soda. Then she sat down on a bench outside, slowly drinking it, while watching passers-by. Her main focus was on the gay couples. To her, they seemed much more happy and attentive to each other than the heterosexuals, Why was that?

The site of Kyle and Stuart was still living in her mind, but she knew she had to overcome it. The initial shock and anger seemed to have assuaged, but it wasn't enough. Being able to accept Kyle's sexuality was the only way she'd be able to get passed what she was feeling. She didn't hate Kyle for his choice; she only worried now about what it would do to Ben. She needed to accept who he was, so that she could help Ben with his feelings toward it, knowing others' reactions, to his father being gay—would be more of an impact. And keeping Ben away from his father was not going to solve anything. She finished her drink, threw the cup in a basket next to her, and then she strolled leisurely back down Commercial Street, lightly brushing against loners and 'happy couples' in the crowd. The visit to Provincetown gave her just enough of a feel to refresh her senses.

CHAPTER 51

Allyson slept like a log, nestled in Marc's arms, till the timbre of rain beating relentlessly upon the roof stirred her. She extended her arms, reaching for him, but he wasn't there. She opened one eye, and saw that it was still dark outside. As she stretched her arms high above her head, from the corner of her eye she saw a note lying on the night table. She sat up and switched on the lamp. It was from him.

"Dear Ali,

As much as I wanted to make love to you, I couldn't disturb you. You were sleeping so peacefully, like sleeping beauty. I have an early morning court appearance. I'll call you later.

Love Marc."

Allyson placed the letter close to her heart and closed her eyes, smiling happily, while feeling his love channel all through her.

While Ben was still sleeping, she took a shower and got dressed. When he still didn't stir, she felt his forehead, but he was cool. She figured he was just relaxing in the comfort of his own bed and in his own surroundings. He was recovering from an enjoyable but a very tiresome two-week retreat at Aunt Edith's.

Allyson had to get things back into perspective. She had phone calls to return, the house to clean, and she had to make plans for returning to work.

Ben missed his playmates. He chatted about them often. And, ironically, she missed socializing with her friends at Cape Cod Realty, especially Taylor. With Ben in preschool and her back to work, resuming their schedules would help get their lives in order.

While she was vacuuming, she heard a loud rap. It was Felicia banging on the front door. She shut off the vacuum. After she let her in, it was plain to detect Felicia had something interesting on her mind. Her face said it all. Felicia immediately embraced her, and then ran over to Ben and gave him a big squeeze. They had missed her too.

"I've been calling you for days," Felicia said.

"We just got back last night. We went to visit Aunt Edith for a couple of weeks."

"You didn't say a word. I was worried sick, and when you didn't return my calls, I came right over. And when I found everything dark and locked up tight, I didn't know what to think."

"I'm really sorry. I should have called you. But, as you can see, we're fine. I'm glad that somebody cares though. Now tell me, what's on your mind. I can tell, Felice, when those wheels of yours are in motion," she said, smiling.

"Gee whiz, I can't hide anything from you. Okay. First of all, you must have heard about Janice's accident?" Felicia asked her.

"Yes, that was horrible. Go on, I can see you have more to tell me."

"There are rumors. Maybe they're just rumors but…."

"But what!" Allyson asked anxiously. "Don't do this to me."

"Janice and Kyle are getting divorced! Nobody seems to know why."

"Are you sure of this? That's probably just what it is, a rumor. Where did you hear this?" Allyson asked, intrigued.

"I've got my sources," she said cunningly.

"But are they reliable?"

"You win. I overheard two of Chatham's gossip hounds yapping when I walked into Marsha's Boutique to buy a new dress for the autumn concert. At first they didn't see me, but as soon as they did, they hushed up real quick. I did hear them say that Janice was filing for a divorce. That was clear as a bell."

"How do you know they meant Janice Caldwell?"

"Well, how many Janice's on the Cape have been in a major car accident recently?" she sneered.

"Oh. Well, that's interesting," Allyson said quietly. She was glad that's all Felicia had zoomed in on.

"'That's interesting.' That's all you have to say?" Felicia asked, dismayed. "What do you want me to do, jump up and down in joy? At one time, Felicia, I would have. This would have meant everything to me, but not anymore.

"Was it because of me?" she asked, sullenly.

"Oh, no, Felicia. If anything, finding you two together helped me. That was merely one isolated incident from a multiple of flaws I have since found in him."

"But things haven't been the same between us. We're not as close as we used to be. Is it because you'll never trust me again?"

"I know you well enough to know that you'll never make a mistake like that again. You're human like all of us. We weren't made not to mess up from time to time. I know I have. I'm sorry if you feel our relationship isn't quite the same. Nothing can stay exactly as it was before. You are still my best friend, and I hope we stay this way—always," Allyson said hugging her, with water building up in her eyes.

"Ali," she said, soberly, "there will always be a place in my heart for the two of you."

"I know, and the same goes here," she said handing her a tissue she happened to have in her pocket. Ben ran into the bathroom and brought them the box of Kleenex.

"What are we going to do, sit around and cry all day?" Allyson asked.

"Nah. Let's go to the mall and have lunch. I'll treat," Felicia said, a big smile lighting up her face.

"We can't say no to that, can we, Ben?"

"Nope," he said and shook his little head.

"Let's go guys. The housework can wait. Especially when you're buying," she said to Felice with a grin.

It wasn't until she got home and began to unwind, did she think about Janice divorcing Kyle. Although word of the divorce initially shocked her, she was afraid that if she reacted Felicia would get the wrong message. Felicia had no inkling obviously, as of yet anyway, about Kyle and his lover. If she had, she would have questioned her for hours.

To her amazement, Allyson actually felt kind of sorry for Janice Caldwell. Here lay this incapacitated woman in bed, and sadly she learns her husband not only still cheats on her, but with a man this time. And in spite of all her money, true love still couldn't be bought. So—between the two of them, Kyle rejectees, she knew she was the more fortunate because she wasn't married to him.

Allyson was lost in meditation when someone knocked on her door. She peered out the window and saw a decorative van in the driveway. She quickly opened the door to a deliveryman who was patiently standing on her doorstep holding a package.

"Are you Allyson Porteus?"

"Yes I am."

"These are for you," he said, handing her this long narrow box. She peeked inside and found beautiful long stem, red roses.

"Who they from?" she asked excitedly.

"Don't know, Ma'am. Card is in there," he said, waiting for her to tip him. She scrounged up a dollar in change. He thanked her halfheartedly and departed.

The roses smelled heavenly, and she couldn't stop taking in big whiffs of the sweet scent. It must have cost someone a fortune, she thought. Roses were not in season. And as she had suspected, they were from Marc. The card said, 'I love you. Forever, Marc.'

Allyson was very appreciative of his thoughtful and loving gesture. It meant so much. Kyle could never have measured up to him. Sending flowers just for the sake of sending them, out of love, would just never have occurred to him. Marc had far more sentiment. He was the true Valentine.

CHAPTER 52

Rosey's had become a familiar dining spot for them. Since it was early, there were many vacant tables to choose from. The hostess pointed them to a nice booth in the center of the room. It was such a delightful atmosphere, even with Ben with them. Allyson ordered veal, Marc ordered lasagna, and Ben asked for his favorite, spaghetti and meatballs. He couldn't pronounce spaghetti properly. He called it "sketti." They tried not to grin because he seldom had to struggle with the pronunciation of words and it frustrated him terribly. They thought it was sort of cute, convincing them he hadn't completely left babyhood.

While they were enjoying their meal, somebody dimmed the lights, making the ambiance very romantic. Ben quietly indulged his fondness for spaghetti and never made another peep. A small group of gentlemen dressed in old Italian troubadour attire and playing violins serenaded up and down the aisles and over to their table, chanting sweetheart melodies. Allyson blushed. Love was dancing in Marc's eyes, and Ben began clapping feverishly to the tunes. Every table was practically filled now, and couples and families were gazing pleasantly at these gentlemen who had been singing around their table. When the gentlemen closed with their last love song, 'Tonight I Celebrate My Love' Marc thanked them. There was a short silence. Then Marc stood up in front of everyone and proposed to her.

"I love you, Allyson Porteus, and I want the whole world to know…I would like you to be my wife."

"Well," Allyson said softly, "this isn't quite the whole world," she said, extending her arms somewhat with the palms of her hands showing, making an exaggerated belief of disappointment. She hesitated for half a second and then yipped…. "Yes!" she said it so loud, she was sure the whole world did know now. "I would be honored to be your wife." Hearing her emotionally heartfelt reply, the entire restaurant, including the chef and the rest of the help who had come out from the kitchen by now, cheered. Clapping and whistling. When things quieted down, the music began again, and the men paraded off to other tables.

"What are you thinking about?" Marc asked. "I hope I didn't embarrass you too much?"

"What would make you think that, Counselor? Just because you couldn't see my face turn various shades of red under these lights is no excuse for what you did," she said. "Actually," she said softly, I was daydreaming about becoming Mrs. Allyson Kelsey. It's got a nice ring to it, don't you think?" she asked, smiling pensively at him.

"It couldn't sound nicer," he said, holding her hand, gazing lovingly into her eyes. Then he glanced over at Ben. "What do you think, champ?" he asked, ruffling his hair.

"Okay, I guess," Ben said, and kept eating.

"I wish I had waited on giving you the ring," he said, regretfully.

"Ah, don't be silly. Here," she said, giving him her hand, "take it off, and put it on my other hand. This will make it official," she said, smiling at him. "Won't it, Ben?" He nodded again. He didn't seem to care what the grown-ups decided. He was too engrossed with the big juicy meatballs he was enthusiastically attacking.

And when she looked back at Marc, his eyes revealed so much love for her that she wanted to cry. It was a love she had been yearning for all of her life. And she couldn't hold back the happy tears that were beginning to fall from her eyes as he placed the diamond ring on her finger. She was the happiest woman alive. She had the perfect man and a beautiful son. Life was splendid!

At that moment, she reached across the table and pecked him lightly on the lips. He kissed her back with a much larger smooch, making a loud smacking noise that started Ben giggling. So, spontaneously, they slapped kisses on each side of his cheek. He wiped them off saying, "Yuck."

When they got home and tucked Ben into bed, Allyson and Marc sat by the fire and talked about everything that was important to them. He opened her eyes to what really mattered in life, and showed her that the finer things can be reaped extravagantly from the inside.

"I wish Ben was yours," she said. "If only things could have been different."

"Shhh," he said, gently tracing her lips with his finger. "You can't think like that, Ali. Ben is like mine in many ways already."

"It's funny, here we were strangers in the night, and then, poof, there you were."

"Meeting you at the registry of deeds was the best day of my life," he said, with a perpetual smile.

"Mine too. It's funny how things work out, huh?"

"Yeah, especially when it turns out for the best."

"I have to agree with that totally."

When Marc made love to her that night, it was as though their hearts shared one soul and their flesh intertwined as Romeo and Juliet's must have once. Marc always made her feel like a goddess, and he respected every inch of her being, physically as well as emotionally. And she knew his love for her would live on in her heart forever.

She fell asleep in his arms and dreamt about their wedding day. It was absolutely beautiful. How handsome Marc looked in his tux, she thought. Her dad was walking her down the aisle. He appeared extremely proud. She saw tears in his eyes. He really didn't want to give up his little girl. Her mother was sitting in the first pew, smiling. She looked so lovely in her stunning pale pink suit, hat, and matching shoes.

Then she saw Aunt Edith next to her with tears in her eyes. Felicia was sitting among family members, looking a bit envious. Poor Felicia, she thought. She never really found anyone special. And then she saw the light of her life—Ben. He was their ring bearer. He looked awfully handsome in his little white tux. His delightful smile and sparkling eyes lit up his adorable little face. All heads were turned when he marched assuredly down the aisle, carrying the satin white pillow, which held their wedding bands.

Then she awoke to a soft kiss that Marc had planted on her lips. She smiled.

"It must have been good dream. You were smiling from ear to ear," he said, kissing her on the neck, making her giggle like a schoolgirl.

"It was," she said, smiling, stretching her arms up high in the air, taking deep exhilarating breaths as she recalled the dream. "You disrupted me right in the middle of our wedding ceremony."

"Oh," he said, quite enthused, "already dreaming of becoming Mrs. Marc Kelsey? Does that mean I get to take advantage of you more?" he asked, with a wide grin.

"Not until we're married," she said, teasing him. "Wait a minute. What do you mean take advantage of me more?"

"Oh, you just caught that, huh?" he asked, grinning devilishly, tickling her on the hip, where she was most sensitive.

"I hope you don't change after we're married. Some people do, you know," she said, soberly.

"And jeopardize what I got? Are you crazy!" he said, without a smile this time. "I might be a little cushy, but I'm not foolish, my dear. I know what I have, and I want to keep it," he said.

"That was a stupid thing to say. I'm sorry. Will you ever forgive me?" she said, with a wistful look.

"How could I not," he whispered lovingly.

CHAPTER 53

Allyson was a very lucky woman. Marc was the nicest and the most understanding guy in the universe…and he chose her to be his wife! What could be more exhilarating?

Ben could feel her joy, and he smiled broadly at her. After he washed up, he let her comb his dark wavy hair. In his blue jeans and light blue Izod shirt, he was a knockout! In a few years the girls would be calling on him, although she wasn't looking forward to that.

Just as they were headed out the door, the phone jingled. It was Kyle. He sounded upset. He said he needed to talk with her right away. She told him she was on her way out to drop Ben off at the Fairview, and then she was headed to work. But he insisted it was important, and it couldn't wait. Reluctantly, she agreed to meet him. She told him she would drop Ben off first, and then they could meet somewhere between the school and Cape Cod Realty. They settled on a location they both knew well.

She traveled down an unpaved road until she reached a deserted cranberry bog. The only other thing nearby was an old run-down shack. Kyle was already there in his Porsche waiting for her. She pulled up along beside him. He jumped quickly out of his car, came around to the passenger's side of hers and hopped inside.

"What's going on?" she asked him.

"You gotta help me, Ali. Janice found out about Stuart and wants a divorce."

"Yeah, I know. Word gets out fast," she said coolly.

"What am I going to do? She's leaving me penniless," he said, practically in tears.

At first, she felt like rejoicing and telling him he got what he deserved, but after seeing how pathetic he looked, she kept quiet. He looked like a little boy who had just discovered his favorite toy was broken. And repairing it would be next to impossible.

"Money isn't everything, Kyle. You can survive without it."

"I know you're right, but I never had to. I'm really scared, Ali. Maybe you can talk to her for me," he implored.

It seemed kind of funny to her sitting there listening to Kyle beg mercifully for her help, when not too long ago, although it seemed like ages ago now, she was sitting in this exact same spot, staring dreamily at the stars while he held her in his arms. They had no cares then. She used to think that the sun rose and set in him. They were young, and so much in love that nothing else seemed to matter. The future was a long ways off. He never had to worry then about Janice divorcing him, because he felt secure.

"Boy have times changed. When I look back on all that's happened…."

"I know. I know. Don't start on me. Please. I've been wrong about a lot of things and I regret it, but I can't change what's happened."

"No, but you can begin by making changes in your life now, Kyle. It's never too late, you know. What's really important to you anyhow? And what about your son?

"Allyson, Ben is everything to me. I do love him—more than you'll ever know. I was really afraid I'd never have kids. And when Janice proposed marriage even though there was no love between us, I couldn't pass it up. I had hoped this marriage would stop my constant desires for men. So as much as I wanted to have a kid of my own, I was sort of relieved when I found out she was too old to have any. I knew it wasn't right or fair to have a kid knowing I felt the way I did.

And when I met you…you were the only one I thought about. You made me feel good about myself. There was no one else I wanted. I believed I was cured from whatever cursed me. You brought me hope, and every day I looked forward to being with you. And when you got pregnant even though I was scared as hell I wouldn't get anymore money if Janice found out, I was so happy to know I was going to have a child I could call my own. I never thought it would be possible. I know I had a weird way of showing it, but I 've always been grateful to you for giving me a son.

I told Janice I'd give up Stuart, even though I didn't mean it, so that I could keep her allowance. But she wouldn't go for it. She said I had humiliated her enough and that this was the end," he concluded, with a long deep sigh.

This was the most he had ever opened up to her. Their problem was always lack of communication. If he could have opened up to her before the way he expressed himself now, he could have spared both of them a lot of pain. It was too late though now to matter. Time moved forward, and the future brought new beginnings. New hope. And looking back wasn't resourceful or wise.

"I don't know what I can do to help. I don't think she'd appreciate seeing me."

"Don't be so sure. She conceals a lot, but she's also revealed a lot to me when she was under the weather.... She's really very jealous of you, Ali."

"Oh, stop. Jealous of what?"

"We did have something special once, you have to admit that...and she couldn't compete with what we had, and she realized it."

"This is what I was trying to get across to you when I became pregnant. Love is far more powerful than money, or anything," she said, looking straight into his eyes, wondering when he finally realized all of this.

"You're so right. And I want another chance to love my son—the right way. If you let me? I don't want to give up Stuart either though, to be able to do that. He understands me in a way that nobody else could," he said.

And in many ways to her Kyle was like an overgrown kid. She gave in and told him if he got his life in order and didn't expose Ben to any of his intimate relations that he could see him on a regular basis, but only under her terms.

"If you hurt him in any way, whatsoever, the deal's off. You got that?"

He nodded..." Will you speak to Janice for me?" he pleaded again.

"I can't believe you. Has anything sunk into that noggin of yours?"

"Everything did. Really. But I'd feel much better knowing I could give my son nice things."

"I give up with you. I have to go to work. Some people have to work for a living, you know."

"Thanks, Ali. I owe ya one."

"Yeah, sure," she said, in disgust.

Allyson tore out of there on two wheels, leaving billows of dust behind. He had suckered her in, but if his intentions of seeing Ben were sincere, then she'd do it for her son. She wasn't sure he'd follow through on what he had proposed. Was he sincere about wanting to be with Benjamin or was he only worried about losing his weekly allowance from Janice? She knew it would be hard for any one who had lived with that kind of money to wake up one day and discover it's no longer at his fingertips. After witnessing Kyle's destitution, she was glad that she didn't get the opportunity to know the world of great wealth on intimate terms.

The only way for her to find out if Kyle meant what he said, was to have that woman-to-woman chat with Janice. She wasn't sure she could make a difference. She was probably the last person on earth she'd want to see. If she flatly refused to give him any finances, she wasn't going to dispute her decision. This was his problem, not hers. She was only doing him a favor. Why? She knew it was to help her son.

CHAPTER 54

Allyson was sort of stunned when Janice agreed to see her. She really never expected to see the inside of that mansion again. The last time she was there was when Janice offered her a quarter of a million dollars to leave town and forget Ben's father. That memory would stay with her forever. The money was tempting on one level, but the thought of dividing a father-and-son's love was even more shattering.

Janice was still very weak from the accident. She moved about slowly, but she was still as graceful as ever. She greeted her warmly this time, with a pleasant smile and a brief embrace, as though they had been old cronies from way back.

She had changed somehow though. Not so much physically, but she was softer, supple, as if she had come down from her high horse. She had plenty of time to think about her life, being laid up in bed all those weeks, recuperating from the car accident.

She had broken ribs, and she wore a brace around her neck. She also had obtained some cuts and bruises that would take some time to heal. In spite of her mishap, she looked lovely, with her silver blonde hair in a chignon. When the sunlight hit at the right angle, her dangling diamond earrings sparkled pristinely against her peachy complexion. Her one-piece black jumpsuit fit perfectly over her slim body. She was very attractive for a middle-aged woman. No wonder Kyle had accepted her proposal. Not only was she rich, she was beautiful too.

The maid served them tea and finger sandwiches. This gathering was much more relaxing than their last encounter. Ben was at Fairview this time, so they didn't have to worry about him distracting them. Their conversation centered mainly on Kyle. They were actually communicating on the same level for once. Something they weren't able to do before.

She was a nobody to Janice, until she got involved with her husband. And then, she was just another one of his affairs, and now she was willing to be her friend. Janice had no one else to talk to about this devastating discovery.

"Where did I go wrong?" Janice asked, rather coolly.

"Don't blame yourself. Kyle had had these feelings inside of him long before he knew you. We just never knew about them."

"I gave him everything. Money…freedom…and this is what I get in return? What will my friends think?"

Allyson felt sorry for her for an instant. Her main worry was what her friends would think. How sad, she thought.

"I'm sure Kyle appreciates all that you've done for him. Are you still going to divorce him?"

"He's humiliated me in every way possible," she said, in a voice clearly distraught. "First it was the affair with you…the child…and now this. What choice has he given me?"

Allyson wanted to retaliate, but she was right, and she had been wrong. She had borrowed what belonged to her, and she had no right. Janice put her hand to head as though she might faint from all of this. Her peachy skin suddenly turned pale. Allyson rushed to her side and sat her down in a nearby chair.

"Is there anything I can get you?" Allyson asked her, feeling as though this whole thing was her fault, and she owed her something.

"No. No," she said, waving her hand. She regained her composure rather quickly. "I'm all right. I'm just a little weak from the accident."

"Maybe this isn't a good time. I can come back when you're feeling better," Allyson said warmly. This still unfolding discovery about Kyle was more than Janice could endure.

"No, my dear. I'm fine. I need to get this off my chest before it does me in. I gather Kyle has spoken to you about him not receiving any financial resources from me after the divorce. I had stipulated this in the prenuptial agreement right from the beginning. He was well aware of it."

"Frankly…yes, I do know. And I don't blame you. This is crushing. This is beyond our comprehension. But we both know Kyle will be lost without your support. Let's face it, between you and his mother, he's been spoiled to the core. He's much like a little boy; he's not capable of making it on his own. He's depended on you for so long now, I don't know what will become of him if you cut him off entirely."

Here she was spilling her guts for Kyle. Sticking up for him when he didn't deserve it. He had given her nothing but grief and heartache. Nonetheless, Kyle was Ben's father, and she felt committed to defend him and help him in some way.

"I don't know. I'll have to think about it. I really owe him nothing."

"You're absolutely right. I couldn't agree with you more. He's been nothing but a heartbreaker from day one."

"What do you gain from all this, coming over here, trying to persuade me to continue to accommodate Kyle?"

"Personally, I don't gain anything. But he's my son's father and in that way I do care. I know this divorce could destroy him. Beneath that strong and debonair exterior lies a very incompetent man."

"You have a lot of compassion in you, my dear. That's a quality I admire."

"Sometimes too much."

"Don't be hard on yourself. Sometimes it pays off," she said, with a smile that seemed genuine for once.

Allyson knew she had won. Won what? A contribution to Kyle's dependency. She felt confident Janice Caldwell would consider an allowance for Kyle after the divorce, although somehow she didn't feel happy about what she had just done.

Not at all.

He had become used to being spoiled, constantly showered with the best of everything…including Janice's sweet charity. It was like a second nature to him. He had no real skills that she was aware of. Womanizing, at one time…A bit of good that did him. If he had to begin from scratch, it was unlikely he'd succeed. He had too many years of easy living. Without Janice's help, he'd be finished. And Ben shouldn't see how inadequate his father really was.

They parted as good friends, or at least sociable acquaintances. Allyson was amazed when she invited her to come again. They were able to communicate woman-to-woman, without being defined by a caste system. She knew Janice would be lonely once Kyle and her separated. Kyle had said once that she never really had any close friendships. He was the only one in whom she could confide. She had her family, of course, but they were very glacial and reserved.

CHAPTER 55

Kyle and Stuart eventually moved in together. They rented a luxurious penthouse in Harwichport. Since Ben was too young to understand, Kyle told him that Stuart was just a roommate. Kyle had promised her that he would never flaunt his love for Stuart in front of their child. There wasn't any reason for animosity amongst any of them anymore. They were all living the lives that they had truly wanted to live.

Allyson kept busy preparing for her and Marc's wedding day. They had planned a May wedding. She couldn't wait to be Mrs. Marc Kelsey. And Ben thought he was pretty special having a dad and a soon-to-be stepfather, both of whom loved him very much. Without Marc's understanding, none of this would have been possible.

Felicia was spending more and more time with them as her wedding day got nearer. She was to be one of her bridesmaids. Aunt Edith was going to be her maid of honor. It was a tough decision, and Felicia was a tad disappointed at first, but she knew how much her aunt had meant to her. Allyson had also asked Taylor Hart, whom she was greatly fond of, and Marc's two older sisters to be in their wedding party, and they were delighted. She hated to leave out Louie, but she had told Marc getting all dolled up wasn't her thing. She preferred to be just a guest. And Allyson and Marc were okay with that.

Marc's parents were very adamant about them having the reception on their estate. She had no reason to contest their request. In fact, she loved the idea. It would be the perfect setting for any wedding. And May was the time of the year when every tree and flower would be in blossom, making the surroundings colorful and majestical.

"Just imagine it, Felicia," she said dreamily. "A fairy tale wedding comes alive as the bride…me," she said gesturing to herself. "And the groom…Marc walk separately through the beautiful rose arbor way into the breathtaking garden where we say our vows to one another, kiss, and then leave arm and arm down the green-filled pathway to a glorious and wonderful beginning as husband and wife."

"Very melodramatic but utterly dreamy. If only I could be so fortunate," she said wistfully. "You've got the perfect man and the perfect child. What more could one ask for?" Felicia eyed her, with a touch of green.

"Not a thing. I am very lucky and very grateful."

"And you deserve the good fortune that's come to you. I just wish you'd throw some my way," Felicia said, with a grin.

"What about that sweet guy you've been seeing recently?"

"Oh, Jimmy. Sweet, that's about it. He's just a good friend."

"Sometimes it's better to begin with a friendship. Getting to know a person can really help. Take it from one who knows."

They both chuckled. Her past was of no secret to Felicia, and if anyone could learn from her mistakes, she could. And she had long since forgiven her for falling into Kyle's ambush. She totally understood her frustrations and desires and her desperate need to be loved. None of the past mattered anymore. Nevertheless, it was obvious to her that Felicia still went out of her way to make up for her past mistakes.

They had found the perfect bridesmaid gowns when they were shopping one afternoon. The cotton dresses had a white background covered with a small flowery print. The dominant color in the dresses was violet, which flattered Felicia immensely. The gowns were coordinated with big floppy lilac hats that were old-fashioned, yet beautiful.

Felicia and Allyson had the best time together. They pranced happily around the bridal shop like two schoolgirls getting ready to go to the prom. Afterward, they stopped by the flower shop, and selected the flower bouquets, filled with lots of daisies and roses. The ushers were to wear a single white carnation in their lapel, but she didn't have to be concerned about them because Marc was taking care of the guys. Allyson even remembered the guest book and the white satin pillow, which would hold their wedding bands, like the one she saw in her dream the night Marc proposed to her. Ben would be carrying it, as he sauntered slowly down the pathway of the beautiful estate.

Mr. and Mrs. Kelsey were hiring the band, the catering service, the huge tent, and the open bar. It wasn't their responsibility, but they were very resolute about taking care of everything. She supposed they wanted the best for their son, and she couldn't blame them. He was the best! She was grateful to them in so many ways, especially since she surely couldn't rely on her dad to make this exceptional day in her life worry free.

She wasn't sure she could count on her dad anymore for anything. He had always floated in and out of her life. She wanted him to walk her down the aisle and proudly give her away, but it had been months since she had heard from him, so it was unlikely that would happen. He obviously was on the road again. He had promised to be there for her, but she was afraid he'd disappoint her, and he'd miss seeing her marry the man who had long since taken his place, giving her a chance for real happiness.

As their wedding day neared, Marc was as excited as she was. She had never seen him so nervous. They both had the matrimonial jitters. There were last minute preparations that had to be taken care of. Marc had ordered the tuxes, and then there were the rehearsals in the church. It just seemed endless and nerve-racking but at the same time exciting and fun.

One calmer afternoon, they went to Marc's parents so that she could address the wedding invitations with his mother. Aimee Kelsey had a long list of relatives and friends. Her list was short in comparison. Not that she needed to compare.

Allyson never realized how much work was involved in preparing for a wedding. She prayed for a beautiful day since the reception was to take place in the beautiful gardens at the Kelsey's. She had planned to wear her mother's wedding gown, which was securely packed away in her hope chest. The simplistic, high-collared, Victorian style gown was sequined with tiny pearls throughout and down to its long and elegant chapel train. It was gorgeous!

She had promised her mother if she could fit into it when the time came, that she would wear it. Her mother was quite petite when she married her dad. And when Allyson tried it on, she could just barely squeeze into it. She knew she had to lose a few pounds to be comfortable, and so she did. It saddened her knowing her mother wouldn't be there to watch her walk those slow and endearing steps to a new beginning. Yet even though her mom couldn't be by her side, her sister would be, and she would be glad she had someone as dear to her as Aunt Edith to take her place.

CHAPTER 56

Marc convinced Felicia to baby-sit, when she had a prior engagement, and he dined Allyson at the Chatham Bell, where they indulged their palates in a five-course repast. Marc ordered white wine to start. Then they had shrimp cocktail. Fruit-salad compote and more hors d'oeuvres followed this. The home-made turkey soup was superb. The main course consisted of their choice of meat. It was a very relaxing evening, just the two of them.

They behaved like two children as they sampled each other's dessert. Allyson tried the strawberry cheesecake and he chose a mud pie. Marc leaned over to put a spoonful of his mud pie into her mouth and his hand slipped. He spilled the mushy combo of ice cream, brownie, and fudge down her chin and onto her spotless, white blouse.

She immediately began to feel warm from embarrassment. Everything and everyone was prim and proper in this fine establishment. She wanted to duck out of there quick, but when she looked at Marc and saw how hard he was trying to hold up that sophisticated demeanor, she began to giggle and couldn't stop. She wanted to stick her cloth napkin in the water glass and try to remove the stain right there, but opted instead for the ladies room. She felt all eyes upon her stain as she took long strides away from the table. She told Marc to be ready to leave when she got back.

"Allyson, we can't leave just yet," he said, smiling up at her when she returned.

"What do you mean? I have to get out of here," she said in a low voice from across the table. "Look at this blouse. I can't stay, people are gawking at this!"

"Don't be paranoid. Nobody cares. Really. Forget it's even there."

"Yeah, right. You don't have to worry. You're not wearing it."

"I have a surprise for you."

"Can it wait?"

"No. See, I…made reservations for us to stay here for the night."

"Here! You can't be serious," she said, astonished, as she watched him nod his head "But I have nothing to wear."

"Yes you do. I had Felicia pack a bag for you."

"Why didn't you tell me?"

"Because I wanted to surprise you. Plus I like to see you squirm. Wait till you see these rooms. They're absolutely elegant."

"Is this supposed to be a sneak preview of what our honeymoon's going to be like?" she asked, smiling mischievously at him.

"I want to make sure everything checks out," he said grinning. Actually, I was hoping it would take the edge off, so that you wouldn't chicken out on me."

"Are you calling me a chicken?"

He shrugged his shoulders with a smirk.

"Well, you're going to have a tough time wrestling with this chick," she said, staring into his big brown eyes that were now gazing lovingly into hers.

The rooms were as elegant as Marc pledged them to be. Being the versatile man he was, Marc rented a contemporary suite. The living area was decorated in black and white, with plush wall-to-wall carpeting. And the unique honeymoon attraction—a large heart-shaped hot tub, in a chamber that was beautifully tiled and wallpapered in black and white.

After they got settled, they couldn't wait to try out the tub. She quickly undressed while Marc turned on the faucets. And while it was filling, he deposited an entire bottle of bubble bath into the running water, creating millions of bubbles. Before he stepped into the heated reservoir, he untied his silk robe and let it drop to the floor. She couldn't help but stare at his young-looking physique. She couldn't help thinking that he had the nicest buttocks. He was very sexy to her. Once he got the temperature regulated and got in, he put his hand out for her to grasp hold of it. His smile was so big and inviting, she couldn't wait to climb in beside him. Even though she skittishly took hold of his hand and sunk sheepishly into the boiling water, she adapted real fast.

Marc pulled out a bottle of champagne from a bucket of ice that had been sitting on the ledge at the far end of the tub. She held the plastic goblets that had been placed beside the bucket, while he poured the sparkling beverage into them. They drank slowly from each other's cup, delighting in the exotic ambiance of the sensuous bath. And not only were their bodies warm and relaxed from the heat of the water and the alcohol, but from the love they declared for one another. Animating that sentiment even more were hundreds of floating orbed rainbows. Marc kissed her lovingly on the lips, and as with many of the soap bubbles, she was bursting too—with passion. Allyson was his and only his, now and forever. Her breasts lay firmly against his chest and when his thighs brushed against hers, she could feel his stiffness near her opening. Not able to hold off any longer because she wanted to feel him, all of him, so badly, she slowly guided him into her damp canal and let his love penetrate through and through until, at last, they climaxed together. Afterwards, they toasted their love and then began exploring each other all over again, and they did this until the champagne bottle was depleted and so were they. She imagined she was on a pontoon moving slowly down a river, floating carefree with all the bubbles. Between the heat of the water and their fervent desire for one another, they became almost inert. And she lay completely content on the bed that night, wrapped in Marc's tender embrace, feeling indefinitely safe and eternally happy.

CHAPTER 57

The next morning, she was in such a deep sleep Allyson felt like she'd been sedated. Marc was shaking her gently, trying to dislodge her from this heavy repose.

"What's the matter? What time is it?" she asked sleepily.

"It's eight o'clock. It's your dad, Ali," he said soberly.

"Tell him I'll call him back later," she said, still not quite awake.

"He's not on the phone, Ali." She looked at him with her lids partially open, and his puppy face was looking sadly down at her.

"What?" she asked, sitting up, more aware. "What about my dad?" She felt her calmness instantly turn to panic. "Is he all right?" She knew the news was tragic, Marc's expression confirmed that. She didn't want to hear anymore. She covered her ears and began to sob, and she couldn't stop.

"I'm so sorry, Ali. He had a heart attack in the middle of the night. He didn't suffer. He was asleep," he said, lifting her into his arms.

"No. No. No!" she sobbed profusely, laying her head on him.

All sorts of emotions were stirring inside of her. She was angry and hurt. She was mad at him for leaving her way too soon, before the most important event of her life. Allyson had wanted him to walk her down the aisle, feeling proud. Proud because she was his daughter and he was giving her away. It didn't seem real that she had just lost him. She was hoping they would resolve their differences and develop a brand new bond, bringing them close to each other once again. She was hoping a close relationship between Ben and him would emerge too, just as it did with Kyle and Ben. Allyson had hoped things would get better between them when he saw his little girl on her wedding day.

But now that was only a dream that could never come true. None of that could take place. Not ever.

Knowing she would never see, or even hug, her father again made her feel isolated and totally alone. Even though they hadn't been together that much lately, he was still a great part of her. He was always in her heart, even if she didn't understand his ways. Not being able to tell him good-bye left her numb. There were so many questions left unanswered. Why did he desert his only son? Why did he have the affairs? Did he love her mother? Did he really love her like he proclaimed? And if he did, why did he continue to hurt them? She knew she would try and search for those answers for the rest of her life, but she would never be able to learn any of the answers from him.

CHAPTER 58

The April morning sun came pouring in when she pulled up the shades. She stood for a long moment with her eyes closed, letting the warmth from the rays soak into her pores, as she envisioned her wedding day. The last few weeks were hectic with last minute preparations. Nevertheless, it kept her busy, so she didn't dwell on the loss of her dad. Every time his memory surfaced, she focused only on the fun times they had together. She wanted to remember the better times, and in time she knew she would find some solace.

Marc was so wonderful. He couldn't wait for her to become his bride. His wife. And she couldn't wait for him to belong to her. To be her husband. He showered her with so much love and affection there wasn't time to be sad. He worked diligently, every day, to make their day to come, special.

Saturday morning Benjamin woke up earlier than usual for him. The sun wasn't up yet, but he couldn't go back to sleep because he was going camping with his dad, and he was so excited that's all he could think about. He'd been daydreaming about this trip ever since Kyle had mentioned it to him, two weeks earlier.

This was the weekend he normally visited with Kyle, but this was going to be a very special weekend for the two of them. Ben was so excited about this little adventure that he packed his duffel bag, along with his sleeping bag and extra warm clothing, a week before they were to leave.

Ben waited patiently on the doorstep with all his gear, ready to go as soon as his dad pulled up. This was a new experience for Ben. He was about to get his first lesson in learning to survive in the wilderness, and he was ecstatic about it. She thought he was a little too young for this, but Kyle assured her he'd be safe. Ben had been babbling about this little outing in every other sentence ever since he knew he was going. Very few people camped out this time of year, so they'd basically be by themselves. She was a bit apprehensive about that fact, but Kyle had become so involved and responsible in the care of his son during the last few months that she had to agree to let Ben go with him. How could she say no? There wasn't a doubt in her mind that Kyle loved his son and would take good care of him. Nevertheless, she lectured Kyle about watching him closely and told him not to let Ben out of his sight for even a second. He said she sounded like a mother hen, an overly protective mother, but he promised her he wouldn't abandon Ben for any length of time.

When Kyle didn't show up promptly at 9:00 A.M., in front of the house, she didn't get too concerned. In the past he had a reputation for being perpetually late, but since he'd been seeing Ben, he'd been pretty good about being on time.

Allyson watched Ben from the kitchen window. He was sitting big and tall, looking very grown up. Kyle could have had the decency to call, she thought. But maybe he wasn't near a phone—giving him the benefit of the doubt. She was becoming more and more angry with him as the minutes passed. This wasn't any ordinary weekend! This was a trip Ben had been looking forward to, and his small world would topple if his dad didn't come to pick him up like he promised.

After an hour had passed, she knew it was time to place a call to Kyle. But there was no answer at his home. To her, it meant one of two things, he was either on his way or he had totally forgotten his obligation, his promise to his son. And she preferred not to think of the latter.

Ben's bright and smiling face was slowly fading as the clock ticked away. The longer he waited, the more upset he seemed to become, and the madder she got at Kyle for doing this to him. After waiting another half-hour outside, Ben strolled back into the house, with his head down, scraping his little feet. He dragged his small body to the kitchen table and plunked down.

"Daddy's not coming," he said, with tears sliding slowly down his precious, still baby-like face. His eyes were sad and filled with disappointment. Allyson went over to him and bent down to talk to him.

"Daddy will come. I'm sure," she said, hoping to reassure him. However, she had her own reservations too. She didn't think he would consciously disappoint his own child by forgetting something so important.

"Any minute Daddy will be here." Allyson couldn't believe what she was claiming. This poor kid had already waited long enough. "How about a bowl of cereal and a glass of juice while you're waiting?"

He nodded.

She had never seen him look so down. He put his elbow on the table and held up one side of his head with his hand and slowly spooned the cereal into his mouth with the other.

She continued to try and reach Kyle while he ate his breakfast, but there was still no answer. Just as they both thought he wouldn't arrive, they heard the tooting of a horn coming down the road. Ben shot up from his seat like a rocket taking off. His smile returned instantly, and he ran outside to greet his dad. She found it amazing to see him bounce back so quickly.

Ben couldn't get his stuff into the car fast enough. He had waited so long for his dad, and now he wanted to be sure that nothing was going to prevent him from leaving with him. Kyle apologized profusely for being late, but he gave no explanation of what had detained him. She was furious with him, but she wasn't going to get into an ugly confrontation knowing Ben was just delighted that his dad had come.

Kyle looked like he had a rough night. He was pale and he had dark circles under his eyes. He wasn't his frothy old self either, and he had a nasty, persistent cough.

"Are you sure you're up to going?" she asked him, in between coughs.

"Oh yeah. I'm fine. I'm just getting a little cold. But that won't keep me down, right son?" he said, as he turned and smiled at Ben, who was sitting next to him, with his seat belt on.

"Yup." Ben was illuminated just being by his dad's side.

"Take care, sweetie, and have a good time," she said, blowing him kisses.

"I will, Mommy," he said, blowing kisses back.

"And remember…I love you," she said.

"I love you too, Mommy," he said, waving good-bye.

"You and Daddy have fun," she hollered, waving ceaselessly, as they drove away. In her mind, she could still see Ben's bright smile long after they disappeared.

CHAPTER 59

Since she was going to be alone, she decided to stay at Marc's for the night. He had arranged a candlelight dinner, and they took a long walk on the beach, hand in hand.

On Sunday morning they went out for breakfast at a local coffee shop. It was great having him all to herself. They really hadn't had all that much time together, with both of them so busy at work and then preparing for the wedding.

After breakfast they drove to her place so that she could get a change of clothing. Being a beautiful spring day, they decided to go horseback riding, a sport they both loved but never had enough time for. They planned on spending a full day together and since Ben wasn't expected back home from his camping trip until Monday morning, they rented the horses for the entire afternoon. They galloped the seashore for miles, smiling radiantly at each other. She felt free as a bird as the wind blew coolly across her face and dropped sprinkles of ocean water over her. She found it very refreshing. She only wished her horse had wings.

"I love you, Allyson Porteus," Marc yelled as they galloped along.

"What? I can't hear you," she yelled back, even though she heard perfectly what he had declared.

"I love you. I love you. I love you!" he said, louder and louder.

"And I love you, Marc Kelsey," she hollered back.

At last, they slowed the horses to a trot. Then they eventually got off and walked them far down the beach where there was no one and tied them to a sign which read "Private Beach." Many of the summer homes were still boarded up after the long winter. That would all change in a few short weeks when the kids had their spring vacation. But until then they owned the beach. The only sign of civilization was a plane-encircling overhead. Marc chased her into the dunes and kissed her playfully. His lips were moist and salty, and tantalizing. She returned his kiss and before long they were rolling in the sand, fondling each other like two young sweethearts. Then she knew he wanted her as much as she wanted him. So, without words, they blanketed themselves beneath the multi-colored sands and made love.

He held her hand in his as they drove home later that afternoon. She had another happy memory to store away with the man who continued to fill her dreams with a genteel love. Pure and wholesome. The day was winding down to a successful end. At least that's what she thought, until they reached her driveway and saw a police car stationed there. A policeman was sitting inside. As soon as he spotted them, he abruptly got out of his cruiser and hustled over to them. Her heart stopped in mid beat. Something has happened to Ben, was her immediate thought. What else could it be? Everybody in her immediate family was gone. Panic set in instantly, and she could hardly move as she watched the policeman coming towards them.

"Miss Porteus?" he asked, bending over to look straight into the open window at her. She couldn't answer him at first. She was afraid to. She looked at him but she couldn't speak. She just nodded. Allyson held her breath as she saw his mouth in motion, but she couldn't rationalize, at first, what he was saying.

"We have your son, Ben, down at the station. His father became very ill and had to be hospitalized.

"Is Ben all right?" Marc asked.

"He's fine. He's a grand little boy. He's entertaining the rest of the department as we speak. He's quite a kid. He's very concerned about his dad though," the police officer said gravely.

"Did you hear what the officer said, Ali? Ben's fine," Marc said, looking into her eyes, while holding her hand securely.

"Yeah. I'm sorry," she said sighing, releasing some of the tension that had built up so quickly, from imagining the worst when she saw the police cruiser in front of the house. Once she was convinced Ben was really safe, she was able to think more clearly. The officer's phrases had unraveled, and he was making much more sense to her now.

"What happened?" she asked, more composed.

"Your son was very brave. It seems that your ex collapsed from fever."

She let the insinuation pass.

"When the paramedics arrived, he was unconscious. Your boy contacted the authorities by using the pay phone nearby and dialing 911. He saved his father's life. He's an incredible child," he praised.

"Indeed he is," Marc spoke up before she had a chance. "And we're all very proud of him. Aren't we, darling?"

"Yes," she said, nodding. "Can we go and see him now?" she asked anxiously.

"Oh, of course. Would you folks like to ride with me?"

"No. Thank you. If you don't mind, we'll drive our own car. If you just escort us over there, we'd appreciate it," Marc said.

"No problem. Stay behind me."

The town's people gawked as they drove through the center of town, following closely behind the police car. Cars were pulling off the road left and right to let them through. Some stopped dead in their tracks to observe the excitement. She was too immersed in her own thoughts to even care. She kept wondering if Ben was scared, and what he must have felt when he found his dad in an unresponsive way. She tried to put herself in Ben's place, trying to figure out what she would have done in the same situation. She really didn't think she would have handled it as well as he did. He must have been terribly frightened being in the forest all alone with no one to turn to. Ben had to be strong and do what he knew how to do to get help for his dad. And by watching the emergency show 911 on TV every night, Ben had saved Kyle's life.

Suddenly her little boy was growing up, but too fast, and becoming responsible too soon. Allyson couldn't wait to tell him how brave he was, and how proud she was of him for taking good care of his daddy.

When they pulled up in front of the police station, tears began filling her eyes. She tried to hold them back because she didn't want Ben to see her all upset after he had been so brave. But Marc saw it coming and handed her his hankie. As they walked hurriedly through the brick building with high ceilings and wheat-tiled floors, the policeman, who had escorted them, exchanged a friendly greeting with an officer standing behind a big metal desk. Sitting on a bench near him, secured in handcuffs, were two scraggly looking guys with long hair, and tattoos plastered all down their bare arms. They even smelled dirty as they strolled by them. One of them flashed a comment. "Hey, Baby."

Allyson ignored it. And them. Marc turned and gave them a stern look. The mere thought of her son being near people of this sort, made her cringe.

"Come with me, please. They put your son in a private room, so that he wouldn't be frightened by the riffraff that traffic in and out of here."

"Thank you." She was very grateful to the department for that. Her young Ben had gone through enough for one day. He needn't be frightened anymore.

She peered through every glass cubbyhole in the place, as they trailed behind the obliging officer. There were piles and piles of paperwork on each desk. These dedicated patrons of law either had their heads stuck in a file, or were on the phone, or staring into a computer.

When the officer turned the knob to the door where Ben was being held in safe custody, she didn't know what to expect. But there he was, sitting in a chair like a big guy, chatting with a woman officer, holding a can of soda in one hand and a cookie in the other. Allyson felt her tears welling up again, and as soon as he spotted her, he quickly got up out of the chair and raced into her arms. She hugged him tightly.

"Mommy, why are you crying? Is Daddy okay?"

"Mommy's just happy to see you. That's all. I missed you," she said, wiping away the tears that were streaming down her face.

"Can we go see Daddy, Mommy?" he implored with wide eyes.

"Sure," she said, regaining her composure. Once Ben knew he was going to see his dad, he acknowledged Marc right away, giving him a big hug. Marc ruffled Ben's hair and shook his hand. Allyson thanked all the officers, including the matron who had taken care of Ben, for their assistance.

By the time they reached the entrance of Cape Cod Hospital, Ben was almost asleep, but as soon as Marc shut off the engine, he sat up straight. As young as he was, he was brilliantly conscious of what was going on, and he remembered about seeing his dad. Distractions were only temporary with him. Even though she felt he had gone through enough for one day, not to mention how tired he now was, she knew he wouldn't be satisfied until he saw Kyle and knew that he was going to be all right.

CHAPTER 60

The hospital's information booth was closed that night. Ben's eyes were pleading with her to find out the whereabouts of his dad. His eyes, which were always so big and bright, were now small and sad, and they tore at her. As angry as Allyson was at Kyle for taking Ben in the first place when he knew how lousy he felt, she couldn't stay angry with him. She was concerned about him too.

She stopped a nurse who was strolling by and asked her if she could tell her in what room Kyle Riker was, but she just referred her to the head nurse on duty.

"Are you relatives?" she asked, looking strangely at them.

"Ah…no. I mean…yes. Well, he is," Allyson said, looking down at Ben, who was now clinging to her.

"He's too young. He can't go in," the nurse said, staring at Ben awkwardly.

"Oh, please. This is his son," Allyson pleaded. "He really needs to see his dad. He was the one who found him and called 911. Ben saved his dad's life. He just wants to see him for a minute, to make sure he's all right."

She seemed moved by Ben's heroism, but then she stiffened and stood by the rules. She looked down at Ben. Tears were launching upon his cheeks.

"Rules are rules and there are no exceptions. You're a good boy for helping your dad. He must be real proud of you," she said, with a smile that was so slight, it could barely be detected. "If you two are relatives," which she knew they weren't, "you can see him. One at a time. But only for a few minutes. He's in our intensive care unit. On the third floor. Room 302," she said, as she was called away.

"What's wrong? Is he going to be all right?" Allyson bellowed, but the nurse never turned around. Evidently, she didn't hear her.

They took the elevator to the third floor where they got off and scurried the halls until they came to a set of swinging doors. On the other side of those ICU doors was a long counter. And behind that counter many nurses were clustered about, reading charts and filling medications. A couple of nurses were speaking intensely with a doctor while another young nurse was on the phone. It was really a mad house, but they appeared to be well organized and very much in control. Allyson was quite impressed with their confidence and good nature.

"May I help you?" asked a sweet woman, who looked to be in her early thirties, with a nice smile.

"Yes. We're here to see Kyle Riker, room #302."

"Are you family?" she asked, looking down at Ben.

"Yes. Yes we are. And this is his son, Benjamin. Ben smiled at the friendly nurse.

"Oh, yes. I heard all about you, Benjamin. When your dad was feeling better, all he talked about was you. He was very worried about you. He kept saying he'd left you at the park. We thought he was just delirious from fever. I guess you weren't left at the park, after all. I heard that you were the one who saved your dad by calling the rescue squad. Is that true, young man?" she asked, smiling down at him.

"Yes, Ma'am," he said modestly, wiping away his tears with his sleeve. "Can I see my dad?" he asked timidly.

"You know son, I could get in big trouble for this. But under the circumstances you being your dad's hero and all, I'm going to let you go in this time. If you promise not to tell."

Ben nodded.

"Besides, he's in a private room and I don't see what harm it can do. I think your dad will be just fine once he knows you're here."

One by one, they singled-filed down the hallway to his room. Marc waited outside while Ben and Allyson went in. Kyle was hooked up to an intravenous bag and an oxygen tank. His eyes were shut. His face was ashen and drawn. It seemed scary for a young boy to see. It amazed Allyson, how fast people's appearance can change when they become sick. She didn't get the chance to ask, but he had to have pneumonia. He had all the signs. It was really eerie for her to see him like that. The entire time she had known Kyle he had never been sick, not even a sniffle. Now here he lay practically dying because he was too stubborn to give in to the signals his body was giving him, and being outdoors only made him worse.

She watched Ben as he slowly walked over to Kyle. The machines intimidated him and he stepped back after hearing a weird noise, but then he looked on curiously.

"Don't be afraid. Those machines are just helping your daddy get better faster. That big one is helping him breathe easier, and the tube that runs to his arm is feeding him until he's able to eat on his own."

"But will it keep his belly full, Mom?" he asked. His cunning query made her smile.

"Yeah, it will. Your daddy wouldn't want any more to eat. Once he gets some rest, he'll be his old self again. I promise," she said.

Her eyes filled as she watched Ben nestle as close as he could to Kyle's bedside, examining everything very carefully. And then, unpredictably, she saw him cautiously lean over Kyle's bed and whisper something into his ear, while sticking a cookie, he must have saved especially for him, into his hand.

She saw Kyle's eyes flutter and his hands move slightly as though he knew Ben was there. Then he started to cough. Kyle was coughing so hard, he seemed to be choking. Allyson raced out of the room to get the nurse, who was standing in the hall, speaking to Marc. She didn't seem too alarmed. She said this was normal, he was expelling all the phlegm that had built up in his lungs. She confirmed that he had pneumonia.

When the nurse came back into the hallway and told them they could go back into the room to see him, they found him to be more settled and this time his eyes were partially open and he was somewhat alert. He seemed to be smiling despite the fact he was heavily medicated, and the tube in his mouth prevented him from responding to Ben. Allyson was sure he was much aware of their presence. Ben was chatting freely to him as though Kyle comprehended every word he was saying, and quite possibly he did.

When their time was up, she had to practically drag Ben away from his dad. He didn't want to leave him. Then he begged her for a couple more minutes. Somehow, Allyson thought Ben felt responsible for his dad being there. He kissed Kyle on the cheek and in his ear he whispered, "I love you." She could read Ben's lips. And then with tears in his eyes he walked over to her, and the two of them walked out of the room.

Marc was reading the newspaper and looked up when he saw them. No words were exchanged as the three of them walked down the corridor to the elevator. Ben was rubbing his eyes and dragging his feet. Marc picked him up and carried him from the hospital. Ben put his small arms around his neck, and laid his head against Marc's chest and was asleep even before they reached the car.

At home, Marc carried Ben into his bedroom and slipped off his shoes and jacket, and tucked him into bed. Then he gave Allyson a goodnight kiss.

"Get a good night's sleep, hon. I'll call you in the morning. I love you," he said, in his deep masculine voice.

"I love you too. Thanks for everything, Marc. I really appreciate it."

"I know you do."

When Allyson got under the sheets that night, she tossed and turned half the night, rehashing the bizarre episode, which should have never occurred that day.

Ben had been very brave and she was so very proud of him, but anything could have happened to him, and the thoughts of losing him brought tears to her eyes. She couldn't imagine her life without Ben. He brought her so much joy and happiness that words couldn't define the exuberant thrill his mere existence continued to bring to her. And after witnessing the deep concern and love Ben displayed for his father, she prayed Kyle would never hurt him.

How different their lives would have been if she had chosen the money that Janice had satanically tempted her with and fled. They would not be with the people they loved and who loved them back. Their wondrous circle of endearment would never have come to be. She was really pleased that Kyle played a major part in Ben's life now. Seeing those two together in the hospital room and watching Ben express his love for Kyle by whispering words of love in his ear brought back sad memories of the unsettled alliance she had had with her own father. She wished she could have been by his bedside before he died, telling him how much she loved him.

Ben got to say good-bye to his dad when he left the hospital room, but at least it wasn't a final good-bye. Ben had nothing to fear. Kyle only had pneumonia and he was still young and would recover completely. But her dad was gone forever and even though she felt good about his memory, knowing they did reconcile their differences somewhat, she still wished she had had those last moments with him to perfect some of those sentiments.

CHAPTER 61

Ben and Allyson overslept. The persistent ringing of the telephone aroused them. By the time she got to it, there was only a dial tone. Oh, well, if it was important, they'll call back, she thought. She raced around fixing a light breakfast for the two of them. Ben was still tired from all the excitement of the day before. He was ornery from all the rushing around, and he didn't want to wear the clothing she had picked out for him to wear to school. He wanted to wear jeans and a sweatshirt, inappropriate for Fairview. But after she mentioned about seeing his dad later on, after school, he was much more cooperative.

He ended up wearing trousers, a shirt with a crew neck sweater, and his Dockers. He looked quite preppy and utterly handsome. He had certainly inherited his dad's good looks. With all the heartache Kyle had instilled upon her in the past, Benjamin was the one confirmed joy he fortuitously gave her, a product of their lustful desires, which could never be taken away from her. Through their sinful and selfish deeds, something beautiful and good was created—their Ben, whom Kyle himself could not be more delighted with; he had admitted that to her not too long ago.

She dropped Ben off at Fairview, and he seemed elated to be back with his peers. As soon as his friends spotted him, they rushed over to greet him. One cute little girl with pigtails and freckles gave him a quick peck on the cheek. And a little boy with a huge pout on his face began tugging on Ben's sweater, trying to get Ben to pay attention to him. As he walked away with them, he turned around and looked up at her. She gave him her approval with a warm smile and a nod, and he scrambled contentedly onto the playground with the rest of the kids.

Marc called her at work to see how she was doing, and at 12:00 noon she received a call from the hospital. A secretary said that Kyle's doctor wished to speak with her, which she thought was odd. As she waited for the doctor to come to the phone, Allyson felt a growing apprehension, but then she thought she was getting herself all worked up over nothing. After all, Kyle only had pneumonia.

"Is there anything wrong, doctor. Kyle's all right, isn't he?" she heard herself chirp.

"We'll discuss his prognosis when I see you. When will you be able to get here?" He didn't give her a chance to answer him. "My schedule is quite full today. I can arrange to see you in an hour, in my office," he said in a rushed but controlled tone.

"I'm sorry, Doctor, I didn't catch your name."

"Calvin Travis. Can I expect to see you then, Ms. Porteus?"

"Yes, sir. I'll be there."

He hung up abruptly without saying good-bye. "What a rude son-of-a-gun," she said aloud, holding the receiver.

Thank goodness no one at Cape Cod Realty heard her. She didn't need to draw attention to the fact she was leaving because Kyle's doctor requested to see her. None of her office colleagues would fully understand her concern. Kyle had done a number on her, and a few of them thought he was a complete jerk. To keep any rumors from starting, Allyson told them that Ben wasn't feeling well, and she was going to pick him up, so that the other kids wouldn't catch whatever it was he had. They seemed to believe her tale, without being suspicious.

When she got to the small building near the hospital, she was ten minutes early. She certainly didn't want to miss him. Evidently he had something important he wanted to discuss with her, because this doctor seemed to be too busy for trivial matters. But when she got inside the waiting room, the receptionist told her he was still making his rounds at the hospital, but that he should be arriving shortly.

"Have a seat and relax," the receptionist said, munching away on some potato chips.

"Thanks."

Allyson was the only one sitting in the waiting room. Easy listening music was piped in and there were comfortable leather chairs to sit in, with magazines scattered about on a large table. She skimmed through a couple of articles in the *People* magazine, then she glanced at her watch. It was 1:17 P.M.

What was taking this guy so long? He wanted her to be on time, but he wasn't. Allyson eyed the heavyset woman who was sitting behind the desk. She smiled, and Allyson smiled back. Then she skimmed through a few more magazines and did the word power quiz in the *Reader's Digest*. She glanced at her watch again; it was 1:45 P.M. There was still no sign of the doctor. This is ridiculous, she thought. Allyson finally got up and walked over to the secretary.

"Excuse me. Could you tell me how much longer I'll have to wait?"

"Your name?"

"Allyson Porteus. I had a one o'clock appointment. It's now close to two."

"He should be in soon. Let me give him a jingle at the hospital. Let's see," she mumbled, as she peered down at her appointment book. "I don't have you down here."

"The doctor called me only an hour ago."

"Oh, I see. I'm sure he wanted you to meet him at the hospital then."

"No. He specifically told me to come here. I'm sure of it."

"If he called you, then I'm sure it's important that he speak with you. Why don't you go on over there, and I'll give him a call and tell him you're on your way."

Allyson thanked her and barreled out of there, cussing the two of them under her breath. She had wasted all this time waiting for him, and she was about to wait even longer. She didn't like this man already. She had no idea what he was going to tell her, except maybe that Kyle had pneumonia, and that she already knew.

When she got to the hospital, they were expecting her. She was directed to the second floor to the doctor's lounge. She knocked lightly on the door, but no one answered. She tapped louder, but still nobody came to the door. A nurse strolled by and saw her standing there and asked if she could be of any help. She explained to her how she was to meet with Dr. Travis. She told her that he'd be tied up for a while longer. Allyson took a seat in the hallway near the lounge, so that she wouldn't miss him. Twenty minutes went by and still no signs of Dr. Travis. Then she spotted a gentleman in a white coat headed for the lounge. She jumped up and scooted over to him.

"Doctor Travis?" she asked hopefully.

"No. But can I help you, Ma'am?"

"If you can. I have an appointment with Dr. Travis, and I'm supposed to be meeting him here. But somehow we got our signals crossed and I waited in his office for over an hour and then I was told to come here."

"I'm sure he hasn't forgotten. But just to be sure, I'll have him paged so that he'll know you're here waiting for him. Give me your name…. Oh, here he is now."

Allyson came into eye-to-eye contact with this mysterious doctor, who had dark blond hair and a full beard. His dark green eyes glared emotionlessly at her. Beneath his hardened exterior, she could detect a warmth trying to escape. She figured this shell, he concealed himself under, was to protect him from the dispirited job he had of revealing sorrow-stricken data to families, concerning their loved ones. But she knew she had nothing to worry about. Kyle only had pneumonia. It was just that she hadn't been informed officially yet of his condition. The nurses had mentioned pneumonia, but didn't have the authority to breathe any privileged information without the doctor's consent.

They sat in two chairs across from each other at the far end of the room, to give them complete privacy if anyone should enter. There was a coffee table leaded with magazines, and there was a coffeepot on a counter near a sink. There was a studio couch and two end tables, with a lamp on each. It was a quiet place where the doctors could eat their lunch and relax, or could use this room for any professional purpose, such as revealing to her what was wrong with Kyle. The doctor's shifty eyes made her feel uneasy.

"Can I get you a cup of coffee?" he asked. She thought it was his way of apologizing for being so late.

"No. Thank you. I'm fine."

"There's no easy way of putting this." He looked at her again, and from his puzzling green eyes she could see something, but she wasn't sure what it was. "Kyle wanted me to tell you about his diagnosis. It was difficult for him."

"What do you mean? He's got pneumonia, right? Doesn't he?"

"Yes. He does."

Something in those eyes of his told her there was more to come.

"Ms. Porteus, after all of the blood tests were in, we found Kyle's white cells vastly defeated his red cells."

"Well, that makes sense. Isn't that what happens when you have a virus like pneumonia?"

"Yes. That's true." He paused for a moment. "But Kyle has the Acquired Immune Deficiency Syndrome."

"What does that mean?"

"Have you ever heard the term AIDS?" he asked.

She nodded.

"It's a virus that attacks particular cells in the immune system. Kyle has contracted the AIDS virus, and will eventually die from it." His bluntness hit her like a brick.

"Oh, no," she said quietly, as she felt her body slump in the chair. She suddenly felt light-headed as if her head would spin off her shoulders.

"Ms. Porteus, are you all right?" She heard his voice as though it was far away. Her head pounded like thunder and then she blacked out.

When she came to, she was stretched out on the sofa, with a wet cloth over her forehead. Dr. Travis was kneeling beside her with smelling salts. His eyes looked much softer than before. He held her hand, and told her to rest for as long as she needed to. The shock of Kyle having AIDS was too much for her system. As she lay there thinking about Ben and what it was going to do to him, tears rolled down her cheeks. Dr. Travis handed her a tissue.

"I strongly suggest that you and your son get tested—just to be sure."

She nodded.

"I'm sorry. I'm going to have to leave you now. Are you going to be all right?"

"Yeah." What else was she going to say?

However, the physician's blunt, no-nonsense words echoed repeatedly in her head. "Kyle has the AIDS virus and will eventually die from it." Allyson shivered from disbelief. A virus which has no cure, and Kyle will one day die from it. Eventually, we're all going to die. So what he is saying? Kyle was too young to leave this world. He was her son's father.

She was so distraught, she almost forgot about Ben. But when she rose, she became dizzy again. She took two deep breaths and let them out slowly. Allyson regained her composure and strolled tediously out of the lounge and down the hallway to the elevator. She most likely appeared drugged or intoxicated to passers-by, but she couldn't be concerned about what they thought. The only thing she concerned herself with was pulling herself together enough for Ben. She'd recently lost her dad, and now Ben will be losing his.

No sooner would she be picking him up from Fairview and he'd be expecting her to keep her promise, and bring him back up there to visit with his father. And she wasn't ready to face Kyle so soon. She just couldn't.

Before leaving, she stopped in the ladies' room, and when she peered into the mirror, the person staring back at her was unrecognizable. Her hair was disheveled and black mascara was smudged under her eyes and halfway down her cheeks. She splashed cold water on her face to bring back some color, and then she renewed her make-up. At least she was presentable now. Allyson had ten minutes to get to the school, and it was at least a twenty-minute ride. But she made it on time, with two minutes to spare. She used that extra time to try and relax. She closed her eyes and took some slow deep breaths. She didn't want Ben to suspect anything.

Parents were arriving in droves now to retrieve their youngsters. Many of them acknowledged her and waved. She gave them an abrupt wave back and turned her head. She lingered in her car until they got their kids and left. Then she rushed in to retrieve Ben. One of the more talkative teachers spotted her and smiled, but she was in no mood for a conversation, and her abrupt attitude gave her the message, for the woman only said hello and went about her business. Usually Ben would dillydally before leaving, but when she mentioned about seeing his father, he grasped her hand and practically pulled her out of his classroom. Ben had a strong grip and a strong mind; he never ceased to amaze her.

"Hi, honey. Did you have a nice day?" she asked, forcing a smile.

"Yup. We going to see Daddy, Mommy?" Ben asked excitedly.

"Yeah. But he's sleeping right now. I thought maybe we could go tonight. Right after supper."

Ben pouted.

"I thought maybe we go for pizza first? Would you like that?" she asked, hoping he'd concur. Allyson needed the break before seeing Kyle, so she could gather her thoughts, whatever they were, more collectively.

"Can we bring Daddy some pizza?" he asked with such innocence that it brought tears to her eyes. How was she going to tell this little guy his daddy was dying; he didn't know what death was.

"Sure, why not," she said, squeezing his hand gently, as they drove home.

She checked the answering machine when they got in. Doctor Travis had called early, in the morning, but evidently when he couldn't get her at home, he called her at work. So even though that call was history, their later discussion wasn't; it couldn't be permanently erased for it was etched in her mind and in her soul. She was hoping that Doctor Travis had made a terrible mistake and she'd wake from this exponential nightmare and find out it was only that, and that Kyle never really had AIDS to begin with.

Felicia and Marc had phoned too. She called Felicia back hoping she was home. Allyson wasn't ready to tell Marc what she had learned about Kyle. She needed another female to talk to, and she and Felicia had become real close again during the last few months. Allyson knew she could confide in her, the way she used to, before everything happened. Besides, she couldn't express her deep concern over Kyle to Marc. And she didn't want him to see her being woeful about the fate of the father of her child.

"Come on, come on. Please be there," she said aloud, waiting for Felicia to answer her phone. And on the fourth ring, she picked up. "Felicia, what are you doing? I hope you're free tonight."

"Now that's an idiotic question. My life is so ostentatious as you know. Full of gorgeous hunks…all sorts of excitement. What makes you think I'd be free?" she asked with a slight snicker.

"You're a doll."

"If that was true, they'd be breaking down my door. So…what's up?"

"Ben and I are going for pizza. Would you like to join us?"

"Sure. Besides, it doesn't look like I'm going to get a better offer tonight."

"Great. I'll pick you up at five."

"Five o'clock? How come so early?"

"Well, you see, Ben would like to make another stop afterwards…to the hospital…to see his dad. Maybe you've heard? Kyle has pneumonia."

"Oh, my God! Is he going to be all right?"

"Yes and no. That's what I want to talk to you about," Allyson said getting all choked up.

"I'm here for you. If you want to come over sooner, that's fine too."

"Thanks. I thought we could talk when Ben's in visiting with Kyle."

"Sure. See ya then."

Allyson called Marc but he wasn't home. She left a message on his machine, letting him know that she was going out for supper with Ben and Felicia, and then they were headed to the hospital so that Ben could visit with Kyle. This way she could avoid Marc for the evening and discuss her feelings about Kyle's illness with Felicia. Felicia would know what she was feeling, and she wouldn't feel guilty about expressing her anger and her sadness over this horrible disease, which Kyle had unfortunately contracted.

CHAPTER 62

They had a pleasant time at Pizza Hut, as expected. Allyson did her best to make everything seem normal—as normal goes. As far as Ben knew, his daddy was going to be okay. Neither Ben nor Felicia had any idea of how sick Kyle really was. And dwelling on his illness was tearing her up so much, she was beginning to feel sick to her stomach. Felicia knew Allyson was bothered by something—so to relieve her, she kept Ben entertained to spare her nerves. And although Felicia didn't ask her what was going on, she did glance at her watch every so often, letting her know she was still as curious as ever. And as miserable as Allyson was feeling, Felicia's warm spiritedness actually amused her.

Allyson thought about Janice on the way to the hospital. She wondered if she knew of Kyle's condition, and, if she did, whether or not she cared. Janice was just a memory from his past. Stuart and Ben filled and completed his life now. From what Kyle had revealed to her, he didn't really have that much contact with Janice anymore. He was, however, still receiving a check in the mail from her each week, which she had generously concurred to give him for one year following their divorce. He had heard from somewhere that she was dating someone older. A mature gentleman, as Janice sarcastically had put it to Kyle.

With death continually knocking upon Allyson's door, it was as if she had lived two lifetimes already. In four short years, Emma, a nurse who reminded her of her grandmother and helped her with Ben after he was born, died before she got a chance to continue to express her gratitude to her for all that she had done to make their stay at the hospital more comfortable. And then she found out she had a brother she didn't know existed, and when she thought she had at last found him, she discovered he's already left them, died a year earlier. And her most recent loss was her dad, to a heart attack. And now she finds out Kyle is terminally ill, and would be leaving this world far too soon, and there wasn't a single thing she could do to stop it.

Ben saved two slices of pizza for Kyle. And when they got inside the hospital, he insisted that they stop by the gift shop to pick out something nice for his father. After Ben carefully looked over all the nice gifts, he picked a teddy bear. The plush animal was dolled up in trousers and a vest, and he had big glass eyes that looked real.

"This is so he won't get lonely, Mommy," he said with a small smile, displaying the bear on the counter, before it was wrapped. Felicia and Allyson looked at each other and smiled. He was such a loving and caring child, the kind of kid every parent desires. Her heart fluttered, contemplating the pain he would soon endure witnessing his dad fade right before his eyes. The pizza began rumbling around in her stomach, and she thought from the stress of it all she'd surely heave at any given moment.

Allyson peeked around the corner when they got to Kyle's room to see if he was awake, before leaving Benjamin there alone with him. He noticed her standing in the doorway and signaled for her to come in. Kyle had just finished his dinner; the empty tray was sitting on the portable table. He was much more alert. He was sitting upright against a pillow. The breathing tubes had been removed from his mouth, and the intravenous needle was gone from his arm. He looked pretty good to her. A heck of a lot better than he did the day before. She tried to act casual, but she had a hard time even looking at him, knowing the agonizing reality.

Kyle said that Stuart was in earlier that day to see him, and that he would be back later on. He said he was feeling better than formerly, and he looked much better. Maybe a miracle was in the works after all, and this devastating disease was going to vanish without a trace.

Allyson finally left Ben with Kyle, and she led Felicia down the corridor into the nearest solarium. It was bright and warm in there, even though it was darkening outside. A television set, stationed high above in the room, was being watched by two young children who had their necks cranked up like ostriches and their bodies slouched low in the chairs.

A couple of grandmothers were sitting in the smoking section, puffing away. A cloud of smoke encircled them as they boasted loudly about their new grandchildren. They were boy and girl twins, from what she couldn't help but overhear. One lady was hard of hearing, and the other one was totally frustrated because her friend wasn't grasping everything she was telling her. If Allyson wasn't so distraught herself, she would have found them quite comical, but under the circumstances, she found them annoying.

She and Felicia sat down on chairs far away from everyone. A few stragglers strolled in from time to time, but they didn't stay long.

As soon as Felicia looked into her eyes, Allyson burst into tears. She needed to tell someone other than Marc how she felt. She had already burdened Marc with too many of her problems. Felicia was a woman and a friend. She would understand what she was feeling before anyone. Felicia had had a mad crush on Kyle once; they had even made love. Something that Felicia can always relive, especially since her love life hadn't ever been spectacular. Although their love had long ago diminished, they had Ben to keep those memories available—and somewhat alive.

"Spill it. I'm all ears. It's just you and me now," she said, grasping both of her hands.

"Kyle's got AIDS!" Allyson blurted.

"What! AIDS? I've heard about that. It started over in Africa, I believe."

"He's going to die, Felice," she said, looking at her.

"Never happen. That gorgeous hunk of man is too mean to die," she said.

"This is not a joke, Felicia. His doctor informed me only a few hours ago of his poor condition," she said.

Felicia became quite still as tears rolled down her face. She sat quietly for a few minutes, the longest Allyson had ever seen her sit still, and then she spoke gravely, revealing intimate info, which Allyson had kind of surmised all along.

"I love him, Ali. I always have. I knew it would never be mutual, but I had accepted that. Just watching him from a distance was good enough for me. I know I hurt you badly, and I tried desperately to forget him, but I just couldn't."

"I know, Felice," she said softly, squeezing her hands firmly.

From the moment when Felicia, at last, divulged her true and deep feelings for Kyle, she immediately felt closer to her. She had admitted what Allyson had believed all along, she was just waiting for her friend to tell her. They now had each other to lean on, to help survive through this painful encumbrance of losing a man who'd meant so much to them. But more heartbreaking, Kyle was being taken away from Ben—his little boy. The boy who loved and worshipped the earth he walked on.

"What do we do now, Ali?" she asked, dabbing her eyes.

"There's really not much we can do, except give him all the support we can. He's got to take care of himself. Kyle's not a strong person. One thing I'm certain of…he loves Ben. Kyle will do whatever it takes to keep himself well. We have to be strong for Ben's sake, as well as for Kyle's."

"Does anybody know besides us?" Felicia asked.

"His lover."

"His lover!"

"You honestly didn't know, did you?" she questioned, looking at her peculiarly. "Felice, I didn't' think anything got by you."

"Well, this one did."

"His name is Stuart Hanson. He's from Provincetown," Allyson said, witnessing Felicia's face turn a ghostly white.

"He's really gay?" she asked, her mouth pouting circle of incredulity. She looked monstrously bewildered.

"For Ben's sake, please keep this quiet."

"Ali, you know I wouldn't hurt Ben for the world."

"I know. You'll have to forgive me. I'm just not myself these days."

"No wonder. You've gone through so much," she said with a deep sigh.

More than Allyson could fathom sometimes, but she wasn't going to get into it. Besides, the mental and physical suffering Kyle would endure in the months to come would far exceed anything she could ever encounter. She only wished she could redo what shouldn't have happened. But how would she have ever known that AIDS would taint the earth.

"Listen, you got to promise not to mention Kyle's condition to Marc. He knows he's got pneumonia, but he has no idea that he has AIDS. I think it's best we keep it between us until I can sort out things."

"Okay, whatever you say. But if Marc finds out before you tell him…."

"He won't. I just need a few days to put things into perspective," she said, looking at the clock on the wall. "Visiting hours are almost over. Let's go get Ben."

When they got there a nurse was coming out of Kyle's room with Ben by her side. He was smiling and chatting up a storm with her.

"Hi, Mom," he said when he saw her. He seemed much happier than the day before. "Dad's getting better. He's going home soon. Right?" he asked the pretty young nurse, who was smiling down at him.

"He sure is," she promised. She barely looked twenty. A babe from the cradle, who probably knew very little about life—and the hurdles that can accompany it. Nevertheless, she was lavishing Ben with positive commentary.

When they got outside of the hospital it was pouring. And on the way home the rain was so heavy, Allyson had to pull over until it let up. By the time they got to Felicia's place, the car had already stalled twice.

Felicia insisted that they spend the night, she didn't want them to get stuck somewhere. She had a small apartment, but she assured Allyson she could accommodate them. There was a twin bed in her room, and the couch opened up to a full-size bed.

Ben became all excited. "Can we stay, Mom? Please?"

Allyson was too exhausted to argue with the two of them. It would probably be hours before the car would start up again. And Ben really enjoyed the idea of being with Felicia, especially for the whole night. It was like old times, and Allyson needed to be with her as much as she needed to be with them.

"Sure. Why not."

She called Marc to let him know where she was. She knew he'd be worried when he called the house and found no one there.

"I'm really glad that you and Felicia are getting along again."

"Me too."

"Well, you have a good time, sweetheart, and stay warm."

"We will."

"You know where I am if you need me.

"Yeah. Thanks."

"I love you, Ali."

"I love you too," she said.

Just hearing him say that made her eyes watery. He was always so comforting and understanding. But could he be so considerate, when he found out she was carrying on over Kyle?

Felicia tucked Ben into bed, and he never made another peep. Then she pulled the cushions off the couch and unfolded a full-size bed for the two of them. And while Allyson was trying to get comfortable on the flimsy mattress, Felicia went to get some popcorn and soda. Meanwhile, she turned on the TV and went flicking through the channels. They both agreed on a Peter Falk mystery.

"This is really fun," Felicia said, during a commercial break. "Sometimes it gets a little lonely. I'm glad you're here."

"Me too."

And twenty minutes into the movie, Felicia was snoring. Neither one of them brought up the subject of Kyle, which was a relief to Allyson.

Nevertheless, when Allyson finally dozed off, around two, she had a disturbing sleep. She dreamed that Kyle died on her wedding day, and Ben was extremely upset with her for not being by his dad's side when it happened. Every time she looked at Ben he looked back at her with unforgiving eyes. Her once blissful little boy never appeared happy before her—again. No matter what she said, or did, made a difference; he had made up his mind, and he just wouldn't forgive her—for deserting his father, in his final moments.

Felicia snapped her out of her dismal fright. "Are you okay? You were whining in your sleep. Look at you," she said sympathetically. "You're a mess. What were you dreaming about? You kept calling out Ben's name."

"Oh, Felicia…I can't get married, not just yet anyway." Allyson said, sitting upright now against the back of the couch.

"What are you talking about, lady? You must be delirious or something. You've been planning this wedding for months. You can't back out now. Does any of this have to do with Kyle?"

"Yes and no. I kinda feel responsible for him."

"In what way? This wasn't your fault. You aren't still in love with him too, are you?"

"No. No," she said shaking her head. "He was such a part of my life once, even if it was for a short time. We had a son. And that's like a lifetime. I think it's best I postpone my wedding at least until Kyle…." She couldn't say the word. "I owe him that much."

Death seemed to be following her, and it was beginning to be more than she could cope with. Tears were flowing freely. Allyson and Felicia embraced and they rocked back and forth on the bed as their bodies trembled with sorrow.

"It could be months before Kyle leaves us. Maybe years. Only God knows how long he really has. Are you willing to sacrifice your happiness—the one that has been long overdue, until that happens?"

"I have to, Felice…for Ben. He would never forgive me if I didn't."

"Well, it looks as though you're not going to be at peace with yourself if you don't. But what about Marc? Will he wait? I know this might seem cruel, but is Kyle worth risking the rest of your life for?"

"I won't be totally content with myself, or with Marc, if I don't do this for Kyle. I know that Marc will be hurt, but I have to do what I think is right. What feels right in my heart. Can you understand that, Felicia?"

"I think I do. I don't have a kid of my own, but I'm sure I'd do the same," she said with a sympathetic grin. "But then again, I don't have anyone who loves me like Marc loves you—so I can't really answer that. All I can say is that you're a damn good mother to be able to forfeit your happiness for him. You must be some kind of saint."

"I wouldn't go that far. Sometimes you tend to exaggerate, Felice—but I love ya just the same."

"Me too. Now—can we get some rest, so that we're not complete zombies in the morning?" Felicia asked, reaching over the side of the bed to shut off the light. She was snoring in a matter of minutes.

Allyson lay awake wondering how she was going to divulge the dreadful tidings to Marc. There was no time to waste; their wedding day was getting closer and closer. And Marc wouldn't be the only one furious with her, his family would be too, and they'd probably never forgive her. They'd all hate her.

Mrs. Kelsey had already given a retainer for the band, the tent, and the caterer. She was insane to even think of pulling a stunt as outrageous as this. But she felt she had no choice. She had to postpone their wedding no matter how much upset it caused.

Felicia was getting up, the bed covers were shifting. Allyson figured it was about six thirty. She detected that by where the sun's rays were spilling in.

"Get up, sleepyhead," Felicia growled, throwing her pillow on top of Allyson's head.

Allyson moaned.

Felicia immediately went into the kitchen and switched on the coffee maker. Allyson waited until it was perking, and then she got up and managed to get herself to the kitchen table. Felicia was as balmy as the sun, which was now beaming in through the skylights of her small kitchen.

"What makes you so jolly this morning?" Allyson asked.

"Just look outside. It's so beautiful out there. I can't go to school with a long puss. What would the kids think? It would hamper my self-image."

"You're right. I just wish I had some of your spunk."

"This is totally unlike you, Ali. You usually have the world in the palm of your hands. You never used to let anything keep you down for long."

"Yeah, but this one's too much."

"You'll pull through. Once you dump the bomb on Marc's lap and ride out the aftermath, things will start getting back to normal. You have a lot to cope with right now. It's a lot for anyone, but I know you'll be okay."

Allyson wondered how she could predict that things would be okay again? And if Felicia loved Kyle as much as she proclaimed to, how come his illness wasn't affecting her more? Or was it? How could she constrain what she was really feeling?

The pitter-patter of Ben's small feet scampered across the linoleum floor. He had his receiving blanket from birth, which now closely resembled an old rag, in one hand, and a tattered stuffed monkey, which belonged to Felicia, in the other.

Allyson couldn't help but smile when she saw him. His long and fine tousled hair was whisked about his precious face, and his grin was as wide as the Grand Canyon. His eyes twinkled, reflecting the beginning of a new day, and she began to feel revived just looking at him. She had to be strong for him. He would need her strength after he found out about his daddy. He would be depending on her to make things all better when his father regressed into a helpless…. She quickly gave that morbid thought a swift death, and acknowledged Ben and the beautiful morning.

The Saab started right up, the wires were dry. Allyson dropped Ben off at Fairview and drove to work. As she was driving, her mind began overworking again. She didn't know how she was going to tell Marc about Kyle. Where would she begin? Every muscle in her tightened from just the mere thought of it.

Cape Cod Realty was so busy that day, she didn't have time to think about anything else, and the day ended sooner than she really wanted for she knew that in a matter of hours, it could be the end of what could have been a wondrous beginning. She figured that once she told Marc, the man who has shown her more love than she had ever known, of her decision about delaying their marriage because of Kyle's illness, he would soon be gone from her, from Ben, from their lives—forever. Someone like him only comes along once in a lifetime, and here she was recklessly about to challenge all that they had built together—because she felt obligated to Kyle, not due to their past romance, but from what came out of that romance—Ben

CHAPTER 63

Marc phoned before coming by. And during their short conversation, he chatted excitedly about their wedding day. He rattled on about picking up his tux early in the week, and said that only a few of the guests hadn't responded yet to their invitations. The anticipation of phoning these guests and informing them that the whole thing was off, that there was no wedding and may never be, made her fell horrible, but she knew it had to be this way. There was no other way. And she was sure that many of these guests wouldn't be satisfied with just the simple fact that the wedding was cancelled. What was she going to tell them? That her son's father was dying of AIDS, and she had to be there for him? Maybe she should advertise in the Cape Cod Times, and maybe then she would be spared from the immeasurable onslaught of questions. All this was tumbling around in her head, giving her a massive headache, while Marc continued to jabber excessively about their wedding. She couldn't spoil his exhilarated expectations of that day, yet. It would be best if she told him in person rather than over the phone. It was the only proper thing to do. If nullifying their wedding could be considered proper.

Marc, however, being the perceptive person he was, quickly noticed how quiet she was and easily surmised, as he always did, that something was bothering her.

"Ali, is anything wrong? You don't seem your self."

"I'm just a little tired. That's all."

"I'm not going to be able to see you tonight; I have a board meeting with the yuppies, and it sounds as though you need a good night's sleep. Knowing you and Felicia, you probably stayed up half the night talking."

"You gotta come," she said, sounding almost desperate.

"Why, do you miss me?"

"I do. And I need to discuss something with you."

"Okay. I'll see ya at ten."

The headlights of Marc's BMW glared through the front window of the living room at exactly 10:05 P.M. She opened the front door for him. He looked utterly handsome in his pinstriped suit. His shirt was unbuttoned at the neck, where his tie had been removed. He was glowing. He was as happy as any man could be, nearing the final steps to matrimony. He kissed her and whirled her about as soon as he saw her.

"I missed my bride...to be," he said beaming, looking deeply into her eyes.

"I missed you too," she said, smiling back at him. She had a hard time pretending that everything was fine. How was she going to tell him she couldn't marry him, at least not yet? Seeing him so happy, the heartbreaking dialogue she was about to utter got stranded, left high and dry somewhere in her throat, and nothing came out.

How could she hurt him? He'd been so wonderful to Ben and her. It tore her apart just visualizing what it would do to him when she informed him she couldn't marry him just yet. At this point, Ben was her main concern, and he would definitely need her more than Marc would.

"Okay, Allyson," he said, once they were on the couch, "what's wrong? Are you getting premarital blues?"

"Maybe." This annoying little voice inside of her kept urging her on, "tell him now." But she couldn't. His long tender fingers etched her face and he peered lovingly into her eyes. Then he covered his sweet lips over hers, and she closed her eyes and forgot about everything. He swept her up into his arms and carried her as though he was carrying her over the threshold. He put her down on the bed and blew softly into her ears, whispering intimate sounds. Allyson belonged only to him at that moment, and she made that known to him by making love to him as though it was for the last time, giving all of herself to him, as she had given herself to no other man. She wanted him to remember this night always, and she assured him that she would love him just as in the vows— "till death do them part." Yet here she was about to break that pledge.

After they made love, they lay there for a long time just holding each other. Then she showered, and while he was in the shower she poured them a glass of red wine. They lay next to each other in bed with only their robes on, sipping the wine. Marc looked so content and relaxed, she hated to spring her sad news upon him. He would despise her for making such an abrupt and preposterous decision, just as he despised his last love when he caught her with another man. And now she was about to hurt him all over again.

"Marc...."

"Yes, my darling. What got into you tonight? You were fantastic, just wonderful. I love you so much, Allyson...Mrs. Kelsey," he said, gently stroking her hair. "You know, I kinda like that. You make me the happiest man on earth," he said, staring blissfully at her with loving eyes.

"Marc, I love you. More than you'll ever know" she said, with tears beginning to fall.

"Stop, honey. Don't cry," he said, holding her tenderly in his arms. "I know you love me. You don't have to prove it to me. That's one of many reasons I want you to be my wife. I know what I have, and I'm not going to give it up for anything. And the sooner we're married the better."

"That's what I got to talk to you about," she said, shedding monstrous tears that were steadily flowing like a fierce rainstorm. "I can't marry you yet."

"What are you talking about? You're not making any sense, Ali, honey. You just told me you loved me. So what's the matter? Oh, wait a minute, I got it. Are you getting cold feet on me?"

She shook her head.

"I know what it is, crowds bother you?" He was grasping at straws.

"No. No," she said, shaking her head to all of his conjectures. "None of that. It's...Kyle," she finally managed to say between sobs.

"Excuse me. Did I hear you right? There must be a bad connection here somewhere."

"Kyle's dying, Marc. He's got AIDS!"

"I'm sorry to hear that. I really am. But what does his dying have to do with our marriage?" he asked, stupefied.

"Everything. Don't you see that? He's Benjamin's father. And if Ben sees us married and happy while his father's lying there dying, he'll never forgive me."

"What are you saying? The marriage is off?"

"Just temporarily. Until Kyle..." she said, looking into his stunned eyes, now clouding with anger, making her feel sick inside.

"I can't believe this. A dying man is ruling our lives. You owe him nothing, Allyson," he said.

"True. But I owe my son. He's too young to understand. Ben has only seen the good side of Kyle; he adores him. I have to be there for him. Please try and understand, Marc."

"What am I going to tell my parents? They have put so much time and effort into trying to make our day perfect. Not to mention the money they have already spent for the band, the tent, the caterer, and the flowers. And my God…what about the guests! What do we tell them? There's well over a hundred people coming. Have you gone mad, Allyson?"

"You really can't understand, can you? You don't have a child."

"Don't tell me I don't understand. I understand plenty. But I don't think this has anything to do with Ben. He's young; he'll get over it. So, it looks like this is it. It's over?"

He was spouting out such venom, with cold and pitiless tones. But she knew he was hurting, and she didn't want to become angry with him. She really had no right. She was destroying everything they had planned together. Their future together was literally being thrown away, and all because of her. She had no right to dispute his anger.

"Of course, it's not over. I don't ever want it to be over between you and me. I just need to wait a while before we get married. Till things are right."

"Till when? When the heavens fall in and hell freezes over? For God sakes, Allyson, Kyle may never die. Only the One above knows when our time is up. I don't give a damn what the doctors say," he said, enraged with anger. "So, am I supposed to wait forever? Is this some sort of game you're playing? Are you still in love with him, is that it, Allyson?" he asked icily, as he buckled his pants and slipped into his loafers.

"No! Of course not. I love you and only you. Please try and understand, Marc," she pleaded.

"I can't, Allyson. Not this time. I gotta go," he said, looking at her as though it was for the last time. His eyes appeared distant, and cold, and deeply hurt. Then he turned away from her and headed for the bedroom door. Suddenly, he wasn't the Marc she knew and loved. He had become obstinate and callous. "Take care," he said coldly, without looking back at her.

"Wait!" she cried helplessly, as she sat up on the bed, her arms stretched out for him to enter them, but he just kept on walking. She listened for a minute and waited anxiously for him to return and whisk her into his arms and tell her everything would be all right, but she knew those blundering steps of his were a walk of no return. She heard the front door close, and soon after his BMW sped away.

She buried herself under the blankets. His very last words to her, "take care," lingered heavily. As she lay there thinking about Marc and what had just happened, not believing her happiness could come to an end so abruptly, she suddenly felt like a chunk of flattened dough that had been rolled over by a rolling pin, an infinite amount of times. Allyson knew all too well that it was the colossal closure of what started out to be a beautiful beginning.

How was she going to cope with losing the man who taught her so much, about life, about love, about who she was? Allyson cried herself to sleep. All her happy memories with him surfaced simultaneously, and they floated around in her head like a moving merry-go-round. Round and round these jumbled thoughts circled until there was a portrait of a man she hardly recognized. It was definitely Marc's face she was seeing, but it appeared old and worn. Deep lines creased his forehead, revealing years of unforgivable anger and hurt. She wanted to get off of the carousel, but it kept whirling. She became frightened and felt totally alone. Allyson cried out, but nobody was there to hear her cries—only this one, estranged Marc, who began to laugh and laugh haughtily until he became utterly obnoxious as his face grew larger and larger, and closer and closer to hers. She jumped from fright, and found Ben at her bedside.

"Mommy, you having a bad dream? You were screaming. You woke me up," he said, rubbing his eyes.

"I'm sorry, honey. Wanna come in bed with me for a while?"

"Okay," he said, holding on to his bear, climbing in next to her. He snuggled up close to her, and she kissed the top of his head. He was growing up fast, but he was still her baby, and she intended to protect him from this vicious world.

Allyson looked at Ben as he slept. His features were perfect and his round face was so sweet and chock-full of innocence. He was still untouched by the impurities that inhabited, and slowly destroyed, their great earth. Their hearts. Their souls. And pretty soon the protective haven in which she had harbored him in would be shattered and there would be nothing she could do to spare him from the pain he would soon endure.

CHAPTER 64

At once, she began reading up on all the literature she could get her hands on, regarding AIDS. There had been little research done. At this time they had no cure. It seemed to be spreading dominantly amongst the homosexual community. There were even reports of heterosexuals contracting the infection. There were essentially three means of transmission: through unprotected sexual intercourse, by sharing a contaminated hypodermic needle, or a pregnant woman, who was infected with the virus, might transmit it to her unborn child.

One afternoon, she sat down at the kitchen table and began reading a well-written pamphlet that she had picked up at the library earlier that morning. It said that a person infected with HIV might have no visible symptoms of the disease. It could take several years before any symptoms appeared. Then it concluded with: "Always use condoms."

Suddenly it dawned on her. Allyson remembered. It was after she had passed out and come to—Dr. Travis said they should get tested. Have I been in denial? She wondered. My God, what if I had it? Worse yet, what if Ben had it? She didn't know how long Kyle had had it in his system. He had told her how he had had an interest in males since he was very young. He could have carried this virus in his body for years. All at once, she began to panic. Big time. All those times they made love before Ben was born they used nothing, no protection. She had been more careful after she got pregnant, but obviously that wouldn't help her now. The damage could already be there. Was he involved with Stuart then? Or any man? This can't be happening, she kept telling herself. Will this nightmare ever end? Ben without a father. Now Ben without a mother? "No. No. No!" she cried aloud, and pounded the table with her fists.

"I hate you, Kyle Riker. I hate you," she bellowed, with rivulets of tears streaming down her face.

After what seemed like hours of sobbing, in fear of all of them losing their lives because Kyle may have infected them with this deadly virus, she reluctantly phoned Dr. Travis to set up an appointment to get herself tested. His secretary answered and said the doctor wasn't in. As was his routine, he was making rounds at the hospital. Allyson was a little embarrassed about asking her to set up an appointment for her to have an AIDS test, so she told her to have the doctor get in touch with her. A.S.A.P. The secretary made it quite clear that she couldn't guarantee that or that he'd be back in the office before she was ready to leave for the day. But either way, she said she'd make sure he got the message. Allyson thanked her politely and told her she'd sit by the phone until she heard from him.

He returned her call far sooner than she thought he would. About an hour later.

"Ms. Porteus, Dr. Travis here. How can I help you?"

"Thank you for calling back so soon. She hesitated for a second, but not any longer because he was a busy man, and his time was valuable. "I think I should have an AIDS test. I'd like to keep this confidential."

"I don't see a problem. How about next Thursday?"

"Next Thursday?" she echoed with disappointment. "Can I get in any sooner?" she asked. A week of worrying about whether or not she had AIDS would seem like an eternity.

"Fine," he said with a deep sigh. Is today at four okay?"

"Yes. Thank you. Thank you so much," she said, with even a bigger sigh. Allyson knew she was putting him out, but this was her life they were talking about.

Allyson strolled sheepishly into Dr. Travis's office exactly at four. There wasn't a soul there, not one patient in the sitting room. Evidently he took time off from his rounds, to cater to her, and she was more than grateful to him for doing so. The receptionist was nowhere to be seen either. The music could scarcely be heard. She just sat down when a door from one of the examining rooms suddenly opened. Dr. Travis stepped out with his white coat on. He did a double take when he saw her sitting there.

"Ms. Porteus, I didn't hear you come in. You're awfully quiet today."

I wonder why, she thought, sarcastically.

"My secretary left early today. Why don't you come right in. I'm just finishing up with someone." He motioned to her to enter the first door on the left, and told her he'd be right back. Then he walked into an adjacent room. Oh, evidently some other poor soul needed him as desperately as she did. They were receiving special attention during the hours when he was supposed to be making his rounds at the hospital. And lucky them, they get to hear their futures in private.

She sat in a straight chair next to the long, cold, metal table, twiddling her thumbs. The room was small with a framed print of a Cape Cod landscape, and a few sterile doctors' instruments, hanging just above the black-cushioned examining table.

Allyson just wanted this whole crazy thing to be over with. If she had the bloody virus, she wanted to know now, and if she didn't, there was no need for panic. She didn't want her visit with Dr. Travis to be like their last meeting, when she found out that Kyle had AIDS and fainted on the spot. The shocking news had overwhelmed her and her psyche wasn't prepared for such a holocaust.

Sure, she was frightened for herself, but more so for Ben. Who would take care of him when Kyle and her were gone? Who would be there for him when he was afraid? Hurt? Lonely? Who would love him the way she did? There was more than a slight possibility that she could be infected with the virus—she was fully conscious of that and, unfortunately, awfully aware of what it would mean. But she knew she couldn't fall apart before she heard the results from Dr. Travis. And she also knew she wouldn't be able to wait. She'd have to have the facts right away. Allyson didn't want to waste another day, or even another hour, not knowing if she was going to be around to see her son grow up.

Dr. Travis strolled in a few minutes later and peered at her with those ambiguous green eyes of his. He still maintained his full, reddish-blond beard, which made him look older and worldly-wise.

"How we doing today?" asked the doctor, with a mere smile.

"Okay, until I started reading about the basic facts of HIV and AIDS."

"A simple blood test can determine that," he said, having her roll up her sleeve. Then he wrapped her arm with a thick rubber band and had her make a fist. "Ah, we've got some good veins here," he said. She turned her head when he withdrew the blood. She hated needles. He filled a couple of tubes, and when he finished he said, "There, that wasn't so bad, was it?"

She nodded.

"What about my son, should he be tested too?"

"Let's check you first," he said, turning his back, to mark the tubes.

Allyson wondered if Ben would be okay, even if she wasn't. Dr. Travis was volunteering little, and she really wasn't ready to listen to anything he was knowledgeable of; she could only deal with one thing at a time.

"We'll have the results for you in about a week," he said casually.

"A week? I can't wait a week!"

"Well, see, after I draw the blood, I have to send it out to a lab to be evaluated. We don't do it here. When the analysis comes back, I'll give you a call."

"You mean I have to wait a week to know whether or not I might die from this damn virus?" she said in anguish and tears.

"Sometimes it's sooner, but not usually. But I'll call you as soon as I have the test results in my hands. It's the best I can do for now. I'm sorry," he said rather coolly.

Dr. Travis definitely had ice running through his veins, and only a splinter of compassion passed through from time to time.

"Thank you, Doctor Travis. I'll be waiting to hear from you."

It was the longest week of her life. She kept herself busy at the office, and at night, she read story after story to Benjamin. And when he nodded off, she watched TV until her eyelids drooped.

There was so much she wanted to do with Ben if she had the infection, and even if she didn't, there were a few minor adjustments she wanted to complete.

Allyson knew she was less materialistic than she was a few years earlier. New clothes and fancy cars, homes and furs were of minimal importance now.

Love was of the greatest.

And if Marc were in her life, she'd feel more complete.

She missed him terribly, and she still didn't know if she'd ever see him again. When he left that night he was deeply hurt. She wasn't sure if he'd ever recover from the shock of her postponing their wedding, only a couple of weeks before they were to be united as one.

Marc's parents would wonder what sort of girl Marc had gotten himself involved with. Maybe after finding out the truth about her, they'd be glad there was no wedding. And by now, they would've known that Ben's father really wasn't dead, he didn't die in a car crash after all, but was about to die from AIDS. And maybe Ben's mother would too. But she couldn't think of that yet. She had to put that possibility behind her. It wasn't a reality for sure, and she prayed every night that it would never come to be.

As much as Allyson missed Marc and dreamed of being with him again, Kyle still took precedence. He wasn't going to be around to see his son's first baseball game, or be there for him on his prom night, or even be able to attend his wedding. At least Marc's life will go on, and he'll recover from the pain she unintentionally caused him. And maybe someday he'd find it in his heart to forgive her, the way she'd forgiven Kyle, for all the wrong he had done her.

But what if her life was suddenly shortened, as was Kyle's? Who would take care of their Ben? Would he ever recover from losing two parents? All these uncertainties were whirling about in her head as she waited anxiously for the results of a blood test; a simple test that could change everything.

Then one rainy evening, four days after the blood was drawn, Dr. Travis phoned to inform her of the report. One thing about this doctor, he didn't beat around the bush. He told her candidly that she was clean! There were no signs of the virus! None whatsoever.

"Unless you've been exposed recently, there's no reason to be tested again."

"How recently?" she asked, holding her breath.

"In the last few months?"

It had been a lot longer than that since she was with Kyle. She was safe! Home free! It felt like a big weight had been lifted off her. Allyson was laughing and crying at the same time. She had kept these mixed feelings concealed for days, as she waited anxiously to hear what she feared to be the worst.

"Thank you, Dr. Travis. Thank you so much," she cried in great relief.

Allyson was free, and she was safe, and she thanked God for sparing her, giving her more time to be with her son. She was so happy to be alive! She wanted to screech out her happiness and share it with all those around her. She never told anyone what she did. There was no reason to until she knew for sure if she had been infected. But she was free from the disease, and she was given another chance, and this time she promised herself—and God, that she'd do better.

CHAPTER 65

Allyson felt fairly confident that since she didn't have the AIDS virus in her system that Ben wouldn't either. Still, it was a major concern. And she knew he had to be tested.

Dr. Travis set his small frame on the examining table and talked to him before withdrawing the blood. The doctor was so wonderful with him; she was sure he had children of his own. She sat in a chair, across from them.

"We're going to see how healthy you are—by taking a little blood. See if you're taking your vitamins."

"I am. See, I'm healthy doctor," he said, flexing his muscle with the opposite arm.

Seeing him sitting cooperatively and bravely as the doctor prepared him, made her eyes watery, so she instantly distracted herself, by rifling through her pocketbook, for a stick of gum. There was no reason to get upset. It was just the idea of seeing her son being subjected to something like this, but it had to be done—to be sure he was all right.

"Just a little prick—then you can watch the blood go in the tube."

"Cool," he said smiling. Then he looked at his mother.

Allyson smiled back and nodded.

"Remember, you can't move," Dr. Travis said.

"I won't," Benjamin promised him.

Allyson watched his eyes widen as he observed the blood entering the tube.

"Wow, my blood is bright red! This is so cool."

Allyson and Dr. Travis laughed.

"There," he said sealing the tube. "Now, let's stick on a cool Band-Aid,"

"It's got a happy face, Mom."

"That's for being good."

"Great boy," Dr. Travis said to Allyson, as they were leaving the examining room.

"Yes he is," she said smiling.

"I'll give you call."

She nodded. She knew it would probably be a week, or less, before she'd hear from him.

"Thank you," Allyson said, shaking his hand.

"Thanks, doctor."

"Thank you, Benjamin," he said, patting his shoulder.

Dr. Travis called her on Friday. Allyson stayed calm all week, but after hearing his voice, a tang of anxiousness suddenly ran through her. What she had convinced herself of, still weren't the facts. And she was about to hear them now. Nevertheless, Dr. Travis did confirm that Ben showed no signs of having the virus. And once Again, she counted her blessings—thanking the One above.

CHAPTER 66

Allyson mustered up the nerve to phone and inform her friends and family about the cancellation of their wedding plans. She surmised that Marc, knowing the kind person he was, would take care of his side. It was only fair for her to be the one to let them know she recklessly and foolishly had changed her mind. She could have tried the insanity plea, for she definitely had to be insane for not marrying Marc as originally planned. Surprisingly, only a few guests asked for an explanation. She concocted a plot by telling the more inquisitive ones that a very close relative of hers was dying of a rare illness, and she needed to be by his side. It was only a stone's throw from the truth because Kyle was a relative of Ben's—and a close one at that.

She hadn't heard a word from Marc. But then again, he certainly wasn't going to come running back into her arms, forgiving her for something he could never quite understand in the first place. She had pierced his heart, and she hoped it would mend. She, indeed, had delivered a double puncture wound that night. The second one into her own heart. But she couldn't abandon her son, or Kyle, at this trying time.

Kyle was eventually released from the hospital. His pneumonia had cleared up. But he was more in danger of sustaining viruses outside of the hospital. His doctor advised him to stay away from crowds. Although he was too outgoing and loved being around people. Even though his immune system was being run down, she knew it would be hard for him to remain isolated for long.

Ben was relieved that Kyle was better. He repeatedly told his dad that he better never go back to the hospital again. He told Kyle again and again that if they hadn't gone camping, he never would have ended up in the hospital. And no matter how much Kyle and Allyson tried to convince him that camping had nothing to do with his dad getting sick, it didn't sink in.

He wanted to be with his dad more and more, and Kyle wanted to be with him too. He knew his days were limited and being with his son made him happy. And it was quite obvious just by witnessing them, how much they meant to each other.

Allyson thought Kyle was beginning to realize how much he missed out on in the beginning, when money and love were miles apart. Money and power had priority then and love was scarcely in existence. But at the time Kyle was far from ready to become a father. He lacked maturity and life was just one big circus to him. It wasn't until these last few months during Ben's weekend stays with him that Kyle realized what fatherhood was all about, what it stood for. He and Ben had grown close and a father-and-son covenant was instituted. Something Kyle never had with his own dad.

Kyle mentioned to her once that seeing Ben made him relive different things when he was the same age, and it frequently instigated old feelings of neglect. And he didn't want Ben to suffer the way he had. Although Kyle's mom was loving and spoiled him rotten, his dad had hurt him greatly, because he was never there for him for one, and the few times that he was, he never showed him any affection.

This is why he thought he never wanted children in the beginning. He feared he would do to his own child what his dad had done to him. And Ben would feel ignored and unloved. And for sometime there, Kyle was repeating history until he, at last, broke the lousy pattern and began showing interest in his son. And all the love he gave to him was graciously reciprocated that day at the campsite when Ben became Kyle's ultimate hero. Ben bravely took on the responsibility of caring for his father by phoning the paramedics. A day in which Kyle would always be grateful to his son.

And apart from the fact that Ben had inherited much of Kyle's physical characteristics, he had far more compassion than his father ever had. Ben really cared about people and it showed. Unfortunately, Kyle was just learning about these wonderful traits, but almost a little too late. It had taken a terminal illness to make him aware of the pain he had caused others. She could never tell Ben that his daddy deserted them once, had been the husband of the prominent lady in Chatham, had made love to Felicia when he was supposed to be in love with her, and lastly had fallen in love with a man! And, finally, when Kyle tries to make amends for all the hurt he instilled upon those who cared about him, he contracts the AIDS virus! Allyson intended to keep the awful past hidden from Ben for as long as she could. Disregarding all the hurt Kyle had imbued on her, on many, she would still be there for him—for as long as necessary.

CHAPTER 67

The days were rapidly turning into weeks, and the weeks into months. Allyson wanted them to go by more slowly for Kyle's sake, but the more she longed for them to slow down, the faster they seemed to speed up. She wanted to preserve every available moment for him. She let Ben be with him as much as he wanted to be, rightfully knowing all along that in the end, it would be devastating for him. But if she denied Ben that opportunity, he might hate her for not letting him be with his dad, especially when he was well.

Allyson missed Marc something fierce, but she knew she had no right to bother him. She had broken the engagement and his heart at the same time. And she prayed that someday he would understand why she had to do what she did, and he would forgive her. But she also knew that the longer he stayed away, the less of a chance of them being together again.

One busy afternoon, while she was finishing up some paper work at the real-estate office, Kyle phoned her. He was very upset about something and wanted her to come right over. He had always been demanding. That part of his personality would never change. If he hadn't been so ill, she would have told him to get lost, take a hike, but he knew her better.

When she got to the penthouse, she knocked upon his door. When nobody answered, she took a spare key that he kept hidden under a shingle and let herself in. She went through the house calling for him. Then she thought she heard him crying. She rushed in quickly to see if he was ill, and found him sitting in a chair near a window in a puddle of tears, sobbing uncontrollably, while staring outside. The blustery winds were splattering large raindrops harshly against the panes. He was so engrossed in his own gloom, and with the rains and winds, he never heard her come in. She tiptoed quietly out of the room and closed the door. Then she tapped lightly from the outside.

"Just a minute," he called out. Allyson could hear rumbling around in there. No doubt, he was trying to regain his composure. When she first met Kyle, she thought of him as being fearless, afraid of nothing. And as she got to know him, she thought of him to be tearless too. His smile was deeply etched, and he was always lighthearted and cheerful. It was hard for her to see him in this state.

"Come in," he said sternly, covering up his unhappiness.

"Hi, Kyle. I came as fast as I could. I told them at work that a client wanted to see a house. You took me away from a job that makes me oodles of money, you know," she said, smiling down at him, as he rocked dolefully in his chair.

This made him smile because he knew at the rate in which the real estate was progressing these days, she'd never be rich, much less be comfortable. Even though sales had dropped quite significantly, especially during the colder months, Allyson had been the top seller for the last umpteen months, giving her more contacts than ever before. She had decided that since she had plenty of time on her hands, especially with Marc gone from her life, and Kyle well enough to be on his own, she'd accelerate herself. She wanted to make as much money as she could before Kyle became too ill to care for himself—should it come to that.

"Thanks for coming. I need a friend about now. Stuart walked out on me. He just packed up and left. He left this note," he said, handing her a sheet of wet, lined paper, saturated from his tears, leaving it barely readable. His hands were shaking and tears welled up in his eyes again.

The note read, "I have to leave. Please don't look for me. You take care of yourself. Love you always, Stu."

"Well, this doesn't tell you a whole lot, does it?" she said, trying to keep him amused. Allyson knew what he was feeling…what he was going through. She knew it all too well. "Maybe, he just got scared." She threw in, trying to sound optimistic, but it was difficult; she didn't want to give him any false hope.

"Scared of what?" he asked her, whimpering and carrying on like a child. She wanted to comfort him, but something held her back. He wasn't a child and shouldn't be treated like one, in spite of his illness.

"I don't know. Maybe he loved you so much that the pain of losing you someday was just too much for him."

"I don't understand," he bellowed.

"Well, love can hurt so much that sometimes we have to run from it." Allyson remembered the way she once felt when Kyle had deserted Ben and her, but there was no sense in bringing up something that was meaningless now. "It's clear to see he loves you. He states that right here," she said, pointing out the words, "Love you always, Stu."

"He's all I got."

"What do you mean, he's all you got? Did you forget about your son—Benjamin? He loves you very much."

Benjamin would never desert his father. Sick or otherwise. Although he didn't actually know his father was dying, Allyson thought he suspected that something was wrong. Kyle hadn't been all that perky since he was released from the hospital, and she thought he might have picked up on that. And Kyle's color had faded somewhat, but whenever he saw Ben, his eyes sparkled, and blood seemed to rush through his body and up to his face, giving him lots of brilliance. Kyle never regained the weight he lost in the hospital. His clothes hung loosely on him. And he wasn't as brawny as he always was, and, ruefully, she realized he'd never be that agile or strong again.

"I love him too. He's my boy. Ben and I are going away on a real camping trip next summer—up in the mountains," he said smiling, daydreaming of that adventure. She didn't want to disappoint him and tell him that that might never happen, and that dreams were only an illusion of what could never really be.

"That's wonderful. He'll enjoy that. In the meantime though, would you like to see your son tonight? How about the three of us having Kentucky Fried Chicken, right here? And I'll even rent us a movie. How does that sound to you?"

"Terrific. I just couldn't bear to be alone tonight," he said, wiping his eyes.

His words rang a familiar bell. How well she remembered those lonely nights when she waited to hear from him and heard nothing…when she sat by the phone night after night fruitlessly hoping it would ring.

Ben was absolutely ecstatic when she told him they were going to his father's for supper. Allyson let Ben choose the movie for that evening. And, of course, it was a Walt Disney film. It was a moving story about a young boy and his valuable show dog. The kid's golden retriever was stolen by a couple of thieves and was taken over the state line into a neighboring state. And when the dog couldn't be found right away, the boy stopped eating and couldn't sleep at night, wondering what happened to his best friend. Eventually the young boy got so sick from not eating or sleeping, he had to be hospitalized. But even though it was sad in the middle of the story, the movie had a happy ending. The dog escaped from his kidnappers and found its way home. The lovable mutt sneaked into the hospital, dodging doctors and nurses and other personnel as he made his way to the child's bedside, wagging its tail and licking the boy's face. The child instantly recovered, and they lived happily ever after.

It brought tears to her eyes watching it, because she knew a similar situation would occur—not far down the road. But it wouldn't be about a boy and his dog; it would be a story about a boy and his dad. Although, this story wouldn't have a happy ending. Allyson tried not to show any emotion but the tears started coming.

"Mom, you don't have to cry. The doggie came back. It's all right," he said, as he jumped in her lap and hugged her.

"Oh son, your mom has always been the sensitive type," Kyle remarked.

"Your dad's right. I have to get a little tougher," she said, smiling at Ben. "Okay guys, where's the popcorn?"

"Mom, it's all gone."

"It is! You mean I missed out?"

"Yup," he said, shaking his head, showing her the empty bowl.

"Oh, well, better luck next time. Okay, big guy, it's time to go home. You have school in the morning."

"Oh, Mom, do we have to?"

"We had a good time. Give your dad a kiss, then get your jacket."

"Okay, Mommy," he said glumly. He ran into Kyle's arms, nearly knocking him over, giving him the biggest kiss and hugging him so long that Kyle had to pry him away.

"Hey, little man," he said, ruffling Ben's hair, "your dad's not going anywhere. You'll be back before you know it."

Ben reluctantly put on his jacket and gave his father one last kiss.

That night, when Allyson lay in bed, she wondered if Kyle would be all right alone. He was in so much emotional discomfort that afternoon, she knew he would begin to feel it all over again once they left. She thought Stuart was a coward in so many ways. She couldn't help feeling sorry for Kyle.

However, when she finally fell asleep there were no more worries about Kyle. Allyson dreamed she was lying on the beach with Marc, on a warm summer night. A million luminous stars were looking down upon them. His big brown eyes were full of love and understanding. As he held her close, she felt safe and warm. It was the way it always was.

The next morning when she awoke, she was extremely disappointed to discover it was only a dream. It had seemed so real. Allyson missed Marc more than he knew, but there was nothing she could do. She couldn't call him; he left on his own accord. Albeit with good reason. And his last words daunted her, "I gotta go. Take Care." Farewell words. Allyson had never intended for their love to be over. She needed time, and he wasn't willing to give that to her. Starting out a new marriage by taking care of her former lover would never have worked. It would have ruined everything.

CHAPTER 68

The next six months she hustled at Cape Cod Realty, showing a lot of big homes on the north side of town. Allyson also spent much of her spare time with Benjamin, and when he was with his father, Felicia and she visited. Summers were usually a very leisurely time for Felicia, but this year she decided to work and grab every penny she could. Whenever she was free, the three of them would spend hours relaxing on the beach. Kyle joined them sometimes, but the heat seemed to bother him, some days more than others.

Kyle remained healthy through the winter months and sailed safely through the warmer months. Daily, Allyson prepared a wholesome diet for him, filled with summer's fresh fruits and often vegetables straight from Aunt Edith's garden. And Kyle looked better than she had seen him look in quite some time. She really believed that the sun's rays and the good food he consumed made all the difference with him.

He actually tanned and was beginning to look and act like his old self again, which kind of scared her. Knowing Kyle the way she did, if he felt too good he would go back to some of his old habits of drinking and wild socializing, or maybe just exert himself with late evenings of heavy entertaining. It was in his blood. It was the life he knew and had always enjoyed, and now with Stuart out of the picture, Kyle would be more vulnerable than ever. Kyle was still good looking, and he drew beautiful women to him. Even though women weren't his first choice, he still loved the attention he got from them.

Even though Allyson had lectured Kyle repeatedly about taking care of himself, he rarely listened. He was sneaking out of the house, like a bad boy, and partying until the wee hours of the morning. He would leave his answering machine on, or else he'd leave 'Do Not Disturb' signs on his front door.

If Allyson hadn't spent so much time and energy worrying about his well being, she'd have found his behavior rather amusing, but under the circumstances she was ready to kill him herself. It was totally stupid and irresponsible of him to behave this way when it could be so harmful to him. She only wished he could see what he was doing to himself. He didn't take into consideration all those who could be hurt by his inane actions, and such behavior could prove very costly to him.

"Why are you doing this, Kyle?" she asked him calmly, not to upset him.

"I gotta live, Allyson. Being stuck in this house day in and day out is no life for me. It's like being dead already!"

"I wish for once you'd stop thinking about yourself and think about what this will do to Ben if you get sick again."

"Ben's a kid. He's got his whole life ahead of him. What do I have? A few weeks—a few months, and maybe, if I'm lucky—a year or so? You can't try and keep me in a fish bowl forever, Allyson."

"Ben loves you more than anything in this world, and you can only think of Kyle! I can't believe this."

"I love him too. You know that. But I can't sit around here day after day, week after week, waiting to die. I do have some life left in me, you know."

"So what does that mean—you throw it all away with all this destructive activity?"

"Look at it any way you want. I call it living! It's not interfering with my time with my son, so why don't you get off my case!" he said angrily.

Allyson was burning up inside, but instead of saying something she may regret later, she stomped on out of there, slamming the door behind her. He knew how she felt and if he wasn't willing to take her advice, there was nothing she could do about it.

Slowly but inevitably the word got out that Kyle had AIDS. In a community this small something as serious as AIDS couldn't be kept a secret for long, no matter how hard one tried to hold on to his privacy. With the town not knowing that much about the disease, everyone feared it—and Kyle. They wanted no contact with him whatsoever. Women weren't flocking around him anymore. Even strangers quickly shied away from him. People were afraid that just by touching him they'd get the disease. Many of the clubs and restaurants, where he hung out regularly, posted notices for their employees about his illness. And some of the proprietors even drew a composite of Kyle, hoping news of this would discourage him from entering their establishments.

He eventually became the symbol of evil, and soon the gossip spread throughout the county like wildfire. Kyle was the first publicized known case of AIDS in Chatham. Newspaper reporters trailed him for weeks hoping for an exclusive interview. In spite of the humiliation he received from the stunned town, he harvested the attention he got from the media.

Overnight he became a celebrity, and his face was known to others across the country, and especially remembered by those who suffered from AIDS. Instead of making this ugly mess into a grieving memory of how beautiful life had been, Kyle mesmerized his television audience with a meaningful speech, making mothers and their daughters weep—giving fathers and their sons a special bond.

Kyle spoke briefly about his childhood years, and how badly he had felt for not getting any love or attention from his father, and because of that he felt he never really had any fortitude, and that this had harmful effects on the rest of his life. Then he mentioned how he had deserted his own son in the beginning, and how he regretted it deeply, since he wouldn't be around long enough to be the father his own father should have been to him. He said that he had learned a lesson in life that couldn't be learned just by someone telling him about it.

He said, "We sometimes take things and people for granted and don't appreciate them until we don't have them any longer. We don't realize how valuable our lives really are until we become sick, so sick that we're informed we're going to die. And one thing I've learned is that without love, life has no real meaning."

His words throttled her. Her eyes became saturated. Allyson couldn't believe her ears. Was this the Kyle Riker she had always known? He continued on.

"And I have one person in particular to thank—a friend—a real friend, one who has stood by me, and taught me all about the finer qualities—life so generously has to offer, which I was so vastly blinded to. I don't have to mention any names, she knows who she is. Without her support, I'd be alone. And I want to take this time to thank her—from the bottom of my heart."

Allyson sat on the couch immobilized, with tears rolling down her own cheeks, from the impact of his heart-warming address, which had not only touched her, but millions of Americans, many of whom could relate in a personal way with him.

The phone began ringing immediately following his speech. Felicia was the first to get through, followed by Aunt Edith, and then Taylor. They were all moved by his tantalizing speech. The phone was not only ringing at her place, but at the television station as well. It got to be more than they could handle. Everyone was asking to speak to Kyle, and he was more than delighted to talk to him or her.

Fan mail from all over the country began pouring in to the television station for weeks following his appearance. The station was overwhelmed with letters and postcards from all races—people who had either contracted the virus, or knew someone who had. Some even enclosed pictures of their loved ones. These devastated people were unable to open up and talk about their feelings concerning this horrible illness, until Kyle bravely unveiled what they themselves had been deathly afraid of.

The network asked Kyle if he'd be interested in helping sort out the abundance of mail addressed to him, which was stacking up all over their mailroom. He was excited and happy to do so, and Allyson gladly volunteered to help him. Together they opened, read, and literally responded graciously to thousands of letters. Some people were despondent, while others were tremendously relieved after seeing Kyle on TV. It was amazing, finding out how many people had been exposed to AIDS. Overnight Kyle had become someone whom so many people admired and highly regarded—and valued as a human being, whereas only a few weeks earlier, people in his own community had shunned him, treating him like an infected animal.

After Ben saw Kyle's face on TV and heard his words, he believed his daddy had suddenly become a star, but he didn't know why exactly. Unaware that there would be negative responses at his school amongst his teachers and his peers, Ben boasted excitedly about the man on television being his father. He bragged so much that the kids teased him cruelly, saying that his daddy was gay and very sick.

He retaliated, one day, when Allyson came to pick him up, by saying, "My daddy isn't sick. He's a movie star," he said firmly, holding his head up high. "If he was sick, he wouldn't be on TV," he shouted, marching away. Then he came over and took his mother's hand; they walked briskly to the car and drove home.

Ben sat pensively staring out the window. In spite of all the positive feedback from people all around the United States, there was still a lot of controversy—and much of it was in their own community. Cape Cod was still very provincial. Many were afraid to move forward—afraid of something new and different, afraid of a challenge, and they still weren't ready to accept Kyle's illness—if ever. Ben loved his dad, and she proposed to keep Ben's and Kyle's relationship snug, even if she had to shield him from the rest of the villains.

"Mom, why do the kids say mean things about Daddy?"

"Maybe they're just jealous because their fathers weren't on TV," she said.

"Yeah, maybe," he said, with a puzzled look on his face, pretending to understand.

"Listen, I wouldn't worry about it, sweetheart. You know your daddy is special—no matter what. And nobody can take that away from you—right?"

"Yup," he said, nodding his head in agreement, but still not looking completely satisfied with her explanation.

"Now, how about if we go outside and get some fresh air?"

It was a beautiful fall day, and the leaves on the trees were just beginning to turn. Allyson could estimate, just by the mood that Ben was in, that a simple walk wouldn't enthuse him. So—she decided to spice up her proposal, with an ice cream cone. The stern look that stayed on Ben's little face most of the afternoon suddenly vanished, and his eyes quickly brightened, while a great big smile replaced that somberness, indicating to her that he was more than just a little interested in her suggestion.

CHAPTER 69

After a few weeks of Kyle being the main focus of speculation, gossip and interest, with the media, reporters, and patrons—everything stopped. Seemingly, everyone forgot who Kyle Riker was, except for some of the local residents in their town, who were still paranoid at the mere sight of him. Kyle tried to stay out of the public eye. He was getting tired of being ridiculed, and feared by so many. He took long drives up north, into the mountains, and stayed for days. It was a place where he could stand tall, breathe deeply and watch the sun dip into the valley.

Ben was attending school with no more cross-examinations concerning his father. After that particular day when Ben received so much negative feedback after boasting about his father being on TV, he decided never to bring up his father's fame again, at least not in school.

As the fall months metamorphosed rather swiftly into the wintry frost, Ben visited Kyle more and more often. And as the bareness of the long and dreary winter came upon them, Allyson began to feel desolate and lonely, as the abandoned Cape always looked during these bitter months.

She was most lonesome at night after tucking Ben in, or when Ben was at Kyle's for the weekend. Leaving her with too much time to think. And during all those remote times, she thought mostly about Marc. Sometimes she thought she could smell his cologne in her pillow, but when she reached for him, she found the section of the bed, where he had always slept next to her, empty. With all the closings he surely had had at the registry of deeds, in Barnstable, not once did they run into each other, which she found rather odd. He was a real-estate attorney and represented numerous banks in the area.

At midnight, the bewitching hour, Allyson leaned over the bed, picked up the phone, and dialed Marc's number. He answered on the second ring. He sounded wide-awake. Just hearing his deep, confident voice made her feel close to him again. She let him repeat hello a few times until he became perturbed and hung up. As much as she wanted to talk to him, to tell him she was sorry, and that she loved him as much as she always had, she couldn't speak. It had been months since they saw each other last; Allyson was sure he would have found someone by now. She remembered him telling her once, how long it took him to get the courage up to even ask someone out on a date, after his last finance had burned him. Allyson had never cheated on him, although perhaps he felt this was some form of deception.

She lay in her bed angry with herself for not opening her mouth, because she didn't have the nerve to call him back. She just couldn't handle it if he turned her away. She had always hoped that they'd be back together one day, but what if he had found someone new? Or simply had no interest in her anymore?

Suddenly, the phone jingled, startling her, removing her abruptly from her trance. Allyson wasn't expecting any calls. She had spoken to Kyle and Ben earlier. They were fine. Ben was already in bed, and Kyle was retiring soon after. Maybe Marc knew it was her? She was afraid to lift the receiver, but she had to in case it was an emergency—she'd never forgive herself.

"Hel…lo," she said sheepishly.

"Excuse me, Ma'am, did you dial the wrong number a few minutes ago by any chance?" Marc said, in a tone that sounded to her as if he was hoping it was she. He made her smile.

"That could be a possibility. But I decline to accept any punishment that I may receive due to the slip of my finger."

"The only punishment I see fit is…," He paused. "To offer my love to you. I hope that reprimand isn't too steep?"

"No, sir," she said smiling, as if she were answering to a judge. Happy tears were filling her eyes. "I've missed you so much, Marc Kelsey."

"I've been such a fool. I was so caught up in thoughts of you becoming my wife, I couldn't see beyond that."

"Hey, forget it. Let's start fresh."

They chatted for nearly an hour, about work, and she filled him in superficially about what Felicia and Ben had been doing.

"How's Kyle doing?" he asked earnestly.

"Ah, he's holding his own. Considering all that he's been through, he's doing fairly well. Of course, you've seen all the publicity he's created."

"Yeah. That was really something. That secretive someone he was referring to during his speech wouldn't be you would it?" he asked.

"Yeah. I was really touched by his words. They surprised me."

"People can change. It was courageous of him to go on TV in front of millions of people."

"Yeah, and maybe someday when Ben's old enough to understand, he'll be proud of his father for coming forth and standing up for what he believed in."

"I hope so, Ali. I miss the little guy. How's he doing in school?"

"Great. He's a smart boy. He asks about you all the time. He asked me if we had a fight."

"What'd ya tell him?"

"The truth."

"You didn't?"

"No. I couldn't hurt him. I just told him you were busy at work and that you were taking a long trip, far away."

"You did the right thing. He doesn't need to know more, right now."

There was a long pause. Suddenly, they were both at a loss for words. Allyson just wanted him lying next to her. She wanted to touch him again, and feel his strong arms around her. She wanted his warm lips upon hers.

"Would you like some company?" he stuttered, and she almost laughed. He sounded like a teenager.

"I thought you'd never ask," she said softly.

"I can't wait to hold you in my arms again," he said, sounding wistful.

It seemed like a century ago when they last engaged in anything romantic, or even held each other. Allyson was as nervous as he sounded on the phone. After they hung up, she changed the bed linens and folded them down neatly. Then she hopped in the shower.

As she stood in the front of the mirror, over the vanity, combing her silky auburn hair, she saw a reflection of her mother. She had inherited many of her fine features. Allyson was looking more and more like her as she grew older.

Her mother was an attractive woman who was very modest and never flaunted her beauty, yet even her beauty couldn't keep her father from straying. Being the reserved Catholic she was, she cried alone at home trying hopelessly to drown her sorrow. However, the reflection she saw in the mirror now wasn't sad; the woman appeared quite content, and she seemed to radiate a New Hope.

Marc's headlights flashed through her bedroom window, and soon after she heard his rap on the front door. Butterflies were cached in her stomach, and her heart had been fluttering from the moment she first heard his voice on the phone. Now she felt like the young teen that was about to go out on her first real date—with someone very special.

Marc looked more appealing than she remembered. He had on blue jeans and a sports jacket. Underneath the jacket he wore a polo shirt buttoned a third of the way down. He only had a few curly hairs protruding, but enough to make him look sexy.

"Hi, Ali. You look beautiful," he said yearningly, as she watched his eyes widen with passion while surveying her. She wore a pink negligee and matching slippers. It was something Allyson was drawn to when Felicia and her walked into Victoria's Secret one day while shopping at the mall. They were so silky and soft—and beautiful, so they became part of her trousseau. Allyson had hoped that some day Marc would see her wearing them.

"You don't look so bad yourself," she said, smiling wistfully.

They sat down on the couch, and she poured them a drink. They clinked their glasses together and then drank from each other's cup. When their eyes met, there was no need for words. Their eyes revealed what their hearts already knew. He gracefully lifted her into his arms, and instantly her fears of renewing their love—diminished. When their lips touched, it was as though they had never been apart—and spontaneously their bodies and minds reacted in unison. She was convinced at that moment that nothing could destroy what was real.

"Our love is stronger and richer than any force that ever existed in my life, Marc," she said softly.

"That's true for me also, Allyson. I love you with all my heart."

Allyson closed her eyes and laid her head upon his chest and soon drifted off. She had never felt more safe, or more happy—or more loved.

CHAPTER 70

The holidays were approaching once again, and Allyson was glad she had reconciled with Marc before the most joyous time of the season. Their days were filled with the hustle and flurry of Christmas activities—baking and shopping, and parties. At night when she and Ben were alone, they wrapped gifts and sang Christmas songs. Being Kyle's first Christmas alone, she knew it had to be difficult for him. That's why she allowed Ben to stay with him more often than usual. Marc knew she would be spending a lot of time with him, and he seemed to accept that, which made things easier all around.

With everything going on, time had just slipped by and they nearly forgot about a tree. So—the eve of Christmas, when it was spitting snow, they went down town and found a merchant who was selling them. There were still plenty of them to choose from. They found a full balsam. Marc paid the attendant, and the man tied it tightly to the top of the car. On the way home, Marc slipped a Christmas cassette into the tape deck. Ben knew the lyrics by heart, and they all joined in.

When they got home, Allyson made them some hot apple cider, and they ate cookies that Aunt Edith had baked, and sent to them. Afterward, they decorated the tree. While they were putting on some of the old decorations, Marc surprised Ben with some ornaments he had bought—especially for him. They were Ben's favorite Disney characters, dressed up in holiday outfits. As Ben unwrapped the wooden figures, his face beamed with joy, and his eyes twinkled with delight.

"Thank you, Marc," his voice chirruped with excitement.

"You're welcome," Marc said, looking into Ben's eyes. Allyson could see much love between them. A love she prayed would one day be equivalent, or come close to, the love Kyle and Ben now had together.

"Come on, big guy, let's hang Mickey and his friends on the branches before there's no more room," Marc said, winking at him, and then looking over at her.

Ben spent most of Christmas day with Kyle. Normally, Allyson wouldn't approve of that, because she preferred Ben to be home—especially in the morning, so that she could see his face first thing, but they really didn't know if Kyle would see another Christmas.

When Ben got home late that afternoon, he was bubbling over with joy. He rambled on endlessly about his delightful day with his father. He was spoiled to the limit—with all kinds of toys, games, and puzzles. Knowing that Kyle had ordered him every popular item available on the market, for his age group, Marc and Allyson had decided on one gift, and one gift only—and it was parked under the tree.

Ben was excited when he saw the Jeep. And he became more ecstatic when he found out he was able to drive it himself—he wanted to get right in it and take off. Marc was all for it; he had been waiting anxiously all afternoon for Ben to come home. So—there was no stopping them now.

"Well...," Allyson said, waiting.

"I think your mom wants a hug," she heard Marc say to Ben.

He ran over to her and embraced her briefly. "Thanks, Mom. It's awesome." Then, Marc and Ben—and the jeep, were out the door.

She watched them from the bay window. Ben hopped right in and had the miniature replica in full speed, almost instantly. Marc ran along beside him, directing him, trying to avoid trees, street signs, or anything else—in their not-so-straight path.

At seven o'clock that evening they sat down for a ham dinner. Allyson was simmering cinnamon applesauce from an old recipe she'd kept from when her mother was alive. The delightful aroma had wafted in the house throughout the day.

Ben didn't have much of an appetite. He was still excited about all that had transpired that day. And besides, he did have an early dinner at Kyle's, plus he had been nibbling on sweets, and crackers and dip, on and off. Marc, on the other hand, was famished; he cleaned up his plate and helped himself to seconds. Ben scrambled his vegetables from one side of the dish to the other. But when the ice cream roll came out of the freezer, Ben's droopy eyes quickly widened with craving.

"Mom, can I have some?" he asked, a tinge of wonderment in his voice. Allyson looked at Marc, and they both glanced at his plate that was hardly touched.

"I don't know. What do you think, Marc?"

"Hmmm, I guess this time we can make an exception, being Christmas and all," Marc said, with benevolence in his tone. "But only this once, young man. You need good food to grow big and strong," he said sternly, flexing his arms. "Feel this," Marc said flaunting his muscles. Ben tried to put his hand around the bulging flesh but couldn't quite make it around, without using both his hands.

"Now, I didn't get these just from eating desserts. Understand what I'm saying, Champ?"

Ben nodded. "My daddy used to have big muscles before he got sick."

Marc and Allyson just looked at each other. And before they could think about responding….

"Now can I have some ice cream cake?" Ben asked, after waiting patiently for the pep talk to be over with. Marc and Allyson both smiled, as she handed a slice to him.

Later that evening, after the dishes were cleared and put away, they all sat down on the sofa and watched an old Christmas treasure, "Miracle on 34th Street." A wonderful Christmas day was winding down, coming to an end. Ben had had a wonderful day—as had they all, and chatted about it endlessly during the beginning of the movie. He got more presents from the three of them than most boys or girls his age would get, but they all enjoyed spoiling him. Finally, Ben's tired little head dropped against Marc's shoulder.

Before Marc got up from the couch to put him to bed, Allyson kissed Ben, and he smiled slightly. Marc took her hand in his and they stared at Ben for a few moments, watching him as he slept.

"I love this little guy," Marc said, admiring the child he held, and then he looked into her eyes. "I love his mother too."

"I love you more, Marc," Allyson said joyfully.

"I can't see how that's possible, but thank you."

And after he put Ben into his bed, he pulled her from the couch and stood her under the mistletoe. He kissed her long and tenderly. Then they walked quietly into the bedroom and shut the door.

"Merry Christmas, darling."
"Merry Christmas, Marc."

CHAPTER 71

The months to follow were cold and raw. There had been a few dustings of snow but nothing major. Kyle was losing more weight, and he had a difficult time swallowing solid foods and what he managed to get down, he vomited. He eventually became so thin and weak he had to be confined to a wheelchair. A full-time nurse cared for him around the clock. She was very attentive to him, in spite of his demanding disposition. Allyson and Ben spent the better half of their days with Kyle. They wanted to try and keep his spirits elevated. She put off telling Ben how sick his daddy really was. She knew, however, that it was getting near the time where she would have to disclose to Ben the seriousness of his father's illness, before Kyle got any worse—before it was too late. Kyle seemed to be failing fast. And this time it didn't seem as though there was much of a chance of him improving. The colds were coming more frequently, and each one seemed to linger longer than the one before.

One afternoon, when she was alone with Ben at home, she sat him down on the couch and tried to explain to him the seriousness of Kyle's illness, without revealing too much about the disease itself. But every time she looked into that untainted face of his, she'd clam up. A face that was always protected with love, and shielded from a world full of deceit and corruption, pain and suffering. Allyson wanted to spare her little boy from all of that, but after he heard what she was about to tell him, he would no longer be saved. And even though she thought it was totally unfair for Ben to have to face this horrible tragedy at such a very young age, she felt she had no choice but to tell him the blatant and painful truth, for she knew that Ben would never forgive her if he found out from someone else.

"Ben, honey, you know your daddy is real sick," Allyson said delicately.

"I know, Mom. But he'll get better," he said, with a doubtful look, paining his eyes. "Won't he?"

"No, sweetie, your daddy's not going to get better this time," she said, stroking the top of his head.

"Yes he is, Mom," he hollered in anger. "He was sick before and got better," he said, with a deep frown, and tears in his eyes.

"Not this time, Ben. Remember when I told you your Grandpa went to heaven to be with the angels?" He shook his head up and down. "Well, darling, your daddy is going to visit Grandpa soon," she said with tears welling up in her own eyes now.

"Mom, you mean he's never coming back? We'll never see him again?" he asked, as tears streamed down his cheeks. Allyson took him in her arms and began rocking him. The way she did when he was a baby. Every inch of her being, ached for him. And as she held her Ben close to her, she was crying inside for him. Children weren't supposed to suffer yet so many have and will and, sadly, her boy was about to become one of those unfortunates.

"We have to be strong for Daddy," she said, wiping the tears from his precious doleful face. "We can't let him know how sad we really are. We want him to be happy. If he sees us unhappy, then he'll be sad too. Do you understand what Mommy's trying to tell you?"

He nodded sadly but indubitably.

"I won't make him sad, Mommy. I promise," he said so sweetly.

"I know you won't, honey."

"Mom, but why did God make him sick?"

"We can't blame God for Daddy's illness. Sometimes people get sick and we don't know why, but it's not God's fault. He loves us all."

Ben accepted her reasoning in stride and didn't ask her any more questions concerning Kyle, the rest of the day. He was just too young to understand everything about AIDS.

And as she sat on the couch watching Ben sitting stiffly in his rocking chair, she wanted so much to run over to him and take away his sadness, safely returning him to the way he was, before she told him that Kyle would die.

Not saying another word, Allyson went into his bedroom and got his pajamas and his slippers and brought them out into the living room, and placed them on the floor next to where he was sitting. He didn't budge. She didn't even think he noticed her at first, but when he shook his head vehemently, she knew he had. It was obvious he didn't want to put them on.

"It's getting late, sweetheart. It's going to be chilly tonight. And you know how warm and cozy they make you feel," she said.

"No, Mom. I want to wear my T-shirt and underpants to bed. Just like Daddy," he said, with a stern look.

"It's raw out, honey. You'll catch a cold."

"Will I go to heaven with Daddy?" he asked, almost hopefully, wrenching her heart.

"Oh my goodness, no darling," she said, scrunching down, touching his hand. "Mommy needs you right here with her. You're the man of the house. I love you," she cried.

"I love you too, Mommy," he said, putting his little arms around her neck and holding them there. And when he released them, he asked, "Can we see Daddy tomorrow?" imploring her with his big and tearful eyes.

"Every day, sweetie, if you want."

Allyson smiled at him, and he finally surrendered his sorrow and gave her a weak smile.

She sat on the edge of Ben's bed, like she did every night, and read a book to him from his collection of Golden books. Then, out of the blue, in the middle of the story, he asked not about what was going on, in one of the scenes, like he often did, but what was evidently bothering him since she told him about his dad.

"Mom, you'll never go away, will you?" he asked with a sad face.

"No, never. I'll never leave you. And that's a promise," she said with a smile.

He put his arms around her, holding on to her for a long time. And in the middle of the night when she was in bed, not really asleep, Ben came into her room and very quietly, not to disturb her, got under the covers and snuggled up to her. Allyson put her arm around him and kept him close to her the rest of the night.

CHAPTER 72

She never discussed Kyle's illness with Ben again and life went on as usual. The whole world wasn't going to cry with them. They had to be strong, and they had to learn to accept the inevitable. Marc, Felicia and Allyson all tried to maintain a normal schedule for Ben, so that he wouldn't feel totally disheartened. Allyson continued working, and Ben kept himself industrious with various activities, in and outside of school, when he wasn't with his father.

And Fairview had been one investment that seemed to have paid off. Attending the school helped Ben grow socially, and emotionally as well. The lessons even helped him develop his more creative talents. His passion was drawing. He loved creating cartoon characters and was becoming a great little artist.

At the end of the day, however, when Allyson went to pick him up, seeing her only reminded him, all too vividly, about the pain he was still feeling for his dad. He didn't have to say anything, because it was clearly shown in his little face. Allyson knew it was hard for him, especially being an only child. Ben had mentioned to her, more than once, before all of this happened, that he wished she'd have a baby. But then, as presently, it was still a big commitment—to even consider.

Kyle looked forward to seeing them each day. His memory was beginning to slip, like an old man's often did. Ben would become agitated with his father when he forgot memorable events, which only the two of them would be able to recall. To make things less complicated, and not to disappoint Ben, whenever Kyle forgot something that meant a lot to him, he'd use reverse psychology, a Freudian-type strategy, so that Ben would think that Kyle remembered these special events, and in essence it was really Ben who remembered. Since

Kyle was practically confined to his bed, or to a chair, Ben and he played numerous board and card games. They were together constantly, and it broke her heart knowing that one day they'd be separated.

CHAPTER 73

April fools day was a beautiful sixty-five degrees. The sun was beaming brightly in the cloudless cobalt sky. With Kyle being confined to the house most of the winter, Ben insisted that they get his father out for a stroll. He said his dad needed fresh air and sunshine to make him feel better—and Allyson believed it would do Kyle good too, especially after months of being cooped up in his apartment all winter.

So, they got Kyle dressed and into his wheelchair. Then they wheeled him outside. And as weak as Kyle was, he smiled blissfully, savoring the sun's rays, taking slow deep breaths, inhaling all of life's incalculable rebirths around him. The trees and flowers were sprouting new buds and birds were chirping loudly. A bushy-tailed squirrel scurried across the road in front of them. All around them strands of deep green blades of grass were peaking through partially thawed lawns.

The white mask that had daubed Kyle's face all winter seemed to dissipate instantly, and a golden glow replaced it as his eyes lit up in awe, relishing in these wondrous treasures.

"Take me to the beach, Ali," Kyle demanded.

"It will be too cold down there. Very windy. Sand will get in your eyes," she said, trying to discourage him, afraid such a trip would prove dangerous for him.

"Who cares about all that. I miss it, and I want to see it. God knows, I might not get another chance. Please, Ali?" he asked.

"Please, Mom?" Ben started in on her too, with a big pout on his little face.

"Okay. Okay. I can't fight city hall. How do you suppose we get you onto the beach in this wheel chair?"

"Just get me down that old wooden ramp that leads to the beach."

"What happens if we get stuck in the sand?"

"That's the least of my worries."

There was no sense in arguing with the two of them. Worrying about something before it happened was utterly asinine, in Kyle's point of view.

It was much warmer at the beach than they anticipated. The waves were calm and it was low tide. Hundreds of seagulls inhabited the sky, the water, and sand. It was a meritorious spot for those who appreciated the ocean and its beaches. Allyson pushed the wheelchair down the dilapidated wooden ramp and the back wheels got stuck in a large hole. She pushed and pushed with every bit of strength she had until the wheel seemed to jump out of the hole and move rapidly away from her. It flew down to the bottom of the ramp and off into the sand, tipping Kyle and the chair completely over.

"Oh, my God!" she said, panicking, as she and Ben ran down to help Kyle. "Are you all right?" she yelled nervously, after seeing him lying in the sand, with the chair practically on top of him.

"I've never been better," he laughed. "In fact, it felt rather good. Almost reminded me of a carnival ride I took when I was about Ben's age," he chuckled.

Ben began to laugh once he knew his father was okay. Kyle was in such an awkward but entertaining position, she couldn't help but laugh herself. Ben lay down in the sand next to Kyle, but the sand was cold and damp, yet was providing the most fun he'd had in a long time. Besides, he was bundled up warmly in a goose down jacket and pants, and he wore a woolen hat and insulated gloves. And with the warm sun beating down upon him, he was well protected.

Somehow, Allyson managed to get Kyle back into his wheel chair. He had lost so much weight that he needed her help getting back up. So with his determination to rise and her adrenaline pumping, she had no trouble getting him into a standing position. She was amazed at how buoyant he'd become. It made her somber seeing a man who once carried her like a doll, was now unable to carry his own self about. A man, who was once inflated with vitality and had taken full advantage of all life's offerings, was soon to die needlessly. Kyle used his cane to steady himself, and she guided him through the sand onto the platform. He walked slowly like an old man, taking one step at a time. Ben stood by, sadly watching, as Kyle maneuvered warily, and slowly got back into his chair. Dampness stung her eyes watching him.

CHAPTER 74

It had been a very grueling day. Felicia watched Ben, while Allyson and Marc went out to dinner. Allyson really needed to get away from everything.

Marc never once pressured her into telling him why she felt so obligated to a man who had given her nothing but heartache, since the moment she met him. Instead, Marc respected her decisions—and never questioned her beliefs, or tried to lure her into something she found to be unsavory.

The seafood restaurant rested against a wharf down by the Barnstable harbor, and it had just reopened for another bustling season. Marc requested a table with a view of the bay. Except for a few singles and one family at the opposite end of the dining room, they basically had the place to themselves. The pine tables in there were lacquered in a shiny finish, and each one had a nautical lamp on top. Fishermen's nets and buoys, sharks, and a large whale covered the knotty-pine walls—and paintings of old sea captains and beautiful seascapes. Marc ordered a bottle of Chardonnay to start, while they perused the menu. In the end, they both decided on the boiled lobster special.

While sipping the wine, she gazed out the bay window at the panoramic view. Suddenly, as her thoughts drifted back to the precarious afternoon with Kyle and Ben, a cool draft swept over her. She shivered for a moment but continued to stare out at the large whitecaps beating relentlessly against the dock. The big reddish-orange sun, now low in the sky, was fading timelessly into the choppy waters, still frigid from the long, cold winter.

"You seem to be far away."

"I'm sorry. I was just admiring the power of Mother Nature. It's astounding how sometimes the waters are so serene, and other times—so violent."

"She can be very temperamental at times."

"Much like us, huh?" she commented, and smiled at him.

"So true. We're only human, Ali."

"Yeah, human…beings living on this planet—for a short time. What is our purpose here anyhow?"

"I think we're here to learn…feel…experience…love."

"It could have happened to any one of us."

"Yes, it could have, Ali—but it didn't."

"It's a crazy world we live in."

"It can be. It's what we make out of it though."

"Yeah. I guess you're right."

The Chardonnay warmed her up, inside out. The meal was delicious and Marc's witty and humorous side was superb, as always.

"I still want you to be my wife, Ali," he said. His eyes were so big and brown and loving—she found him irresistible, or maybe she felt this because she loved him too. And she wanted him to be her husband, as much as he wanted her to be his wife.

"And I want you to be my husband. More than anything," she said, smiling up at him, with tears of joy starting to fall. She couldn't have been happier with any other man.

"Allyson," he said, turning her around and lifting her chin to speak into her eyes, "You mean so much to me. I'm so lucky to have you."

"No, it's the other way around. I'm the lucky one."

"Let's just say we both got lucky."

"We sure have," she said.

"And then there's those other fine qualities of yours."

"And what may they be?" she asked.

"You're smart. You're witty. You're talented…."

"Talented?"

"You've captivated me, haven't you?"

"Really?" she said mischievously.

"Yup. And I have to admit—I do find you rather sexy."

"Is that so. Then let's get out of here and go home—where I can really get your motor purring."

"Hold that thought, darling," he said, smiling broadly, holding her hand, leading her out of the restaurant.

CHAPTER 75

Spring was delivering fresh animation to their earth's new existence. Flowers were blossoming and trees were sprouting new leaves everywhere. Seemingly, overnight, brown yards across the Cape were converging into beautiful green blankets. Animals that had been hibernating all winter were now emerging from their furrows, and birds were no longer migrating south. They were all here to stay for another divine and amicable season.

And although most of them felt rejuvenated just by the mere thought of summer docking again, poor Kyle wasn't doing well at all. Unfortunately the warmth and brightness of the new season wouldn't have any positive effect on him. He was deteriorating much faster than she had expected he would. Kyle's fatigued and frail body was covered with skin rashes and some had even turned into nasty purple sores. He also had the fungal infection of the mouth known as thrush.

It sure wasn't like a year ago, when the warm rays from the sun made Kyle feel alive and healthy. Even though the sunlight and its warmth along with their planet's beautiful creatures were encircling him with the renewal of life, Kyle wasn't responding anymore to the seasonal changes. Surviving through another day was all that he could think about. Each time he saw his son, he wondered if this time could be his last. It tore her apart witnessing Kyle become weaker and weaker and not being able to help him.

But he was in God's hands now. There wasn't anything Allyson could do, except to try and keep him as comfortable as possible. At times, she thought of bailing out because it was just too much seeing him like this, but he really didn't have anyone else, and she did care very much for him as a human being.

She'd bathe Kyle twice a day, a sponge bath, and she'd spoon-feed him his lunch and dinner. And in the afternoons, during his wakening hours, she'd read to him. Mostly humorous articles, to try and keep his spirits up. It would break the intense silence, which sometimes seemed to take anchor right before death.

She hired a nurse to sit with him through the nights, and each morning she was there at 9:30 A.M., after dropping Ben off at Fairview. Allyson had saved up enough money during Kyle's better days so that she could take off from work and be with him near the end.

Benjamin was adamant about still wanting to be with his father, but Allyson refused to let him see Kyle in the latter stages of his illness. She wanted Ben to remember him the way he was when he was well, as well as could be imagined at this stage of his illness. Ben cried and cried when she told him he couldn't visit with his dad anymore. Everyday he pleaded with her to change her mind. She was totally mystified. Allyson had let Ben be with his father for a time during his illness, and now she was cutting him off short.

And as much as Kyle wanted to be with Ben, he felt the way she did. Witnessing something beyond his comprehension could introduce Ben to nightmares for many years. He wasn't old enough to realize or fully understand what exactly accompanied the sometimes awful and painful road to death. He was just learning about life.

Any free time from caring for Kyle, Allyson spent with Benjamin and Marc. She was drained emotionally, but she wore a happy face whenever she was with them. They needn't to be burdened with what she was going through. Marc tried his damnedest to make every moment they had together cheerful. And he took care of the everyday affairs to alleviate some of the strain for her.

After seeing the toll it took on her taking care of Kyle every day, Marc arranged a weekend get-a-away for the two of them and hired someone to care for Kyle while they were gone. He made reservations at the Marriott Hotel in Boston. They had a beautiful view of the harbor. And Marc had surprised her with two tickets to the Shubert theater to see, "Cats."

Marc complimented her on her black cocktail dress. She wore a diamond pendant that her father had given to her mother when they first met. But the diamond that had any real value to her right now was the one she was wearing on her finger. The one that Marc had given her.

"You look lovely tonight," he said, looking her over, smiling broadly.

"Thank you, and so do you, Mr. Kelsey. Handsome that is…very handsome," she said blushing.

They never seemed to get tired of one another. Each date was like a fresh start, and the excitement and enthusiasm she experienced whenever she was with him was measureless—meaningfully so.

On Saturday they toured the big city, and they visited Fanueil Hall. An annual spring flower show was in progress. A beautiful display of hundreds of flowers. It was breathtaking. After a couple of hours there, they moved on to Boston Museum of Fine Arts. She was quite impressed with Marc's knowledge of famous artists. Then they dined in the heart of Boston in a small but very exquisite Italian cabaret. The food was delicious and the ambiance was so delightful, she felt as though she was visiting Italy.

Their weekend together was such a welcome diversion after being with Kyle all week. Yet she did feel somewhat guilty for not being with him. She was so afraid that he would leave them when she wasn't there. Allyson promised him she'd be there for him till the end, but watching Kyle die was overwhelming, and she needed to be away from him, now and then. This was Marc's and her time together, and she was fixed on not burdening him with her gloom. Unfortunately, it ended all too quickly, and she was back at Kyle's bedside waiting on him hand and foot, with absolutely no regrets.

CHAPTER 76

Alyson was showing Kyle some pictures that Benjamin had drawn for him. He motioned for her to come closer to him. Kyle was practically all bones now, and his face was very drawn. He resembled an old man, ready to be taken. His skin was wrinkled from losing so much weight, and jaundice had set in, turning the whites of his eyes a yellowish hue. Seeing him fade away into a skeleton made her more sure she was doing the right thing by keeping Benjamin from seeing him. In spite of the fact that Kyle was the same person he always was, he was also a very sick young man, aging quickly beyond his years.

"Yes, Kyle?" she said, leaning over his bed to hear what he had to say.

"Ben...ja...min. Tell him I love him," he said, barely audible.

"He knows you do. And he loves you too," she said, trying to fight back the tears that were welling up in her eyes.

Kyle smiled faintly, as he slowly skimmed over the colorful picture Ben had drawn for him, with his crayons. It was a sketch of Kyle and himself on the beach, flying a kite. The sun was shining brightly above them, and there were big smiles upon their faces. And Ben had even made the two people glow by coloring their cheeks in bright red. There wasn't a hint of sickness portrayed in his drawing. And when Kyle gazed at what his son had made for him, his eyes seemed to sparkle even through their dullness.

"Say good-bye to Benjamin for me, and tell him...." he said, without finishing. Then he closed his eyes. She saw his lips moving, but no sounds emanated from them. Suddenly his hand relaxed from hers, and his arms went limp. The machine he was hooked up to began buzzing. The alarm indicated that Kyle's body had stopped functioning. Allyson stood staring at him for a long time, not believing this was the end.

"I'll tell Ben that you love him, Kyle," she said, with tears coursing down her cheeks and onto the bed where he lay. She cried for him. She cried for Ben. A senseless loss gone forever.

CHAPTER 77

The following days were gloomy and hectic with the preparations for the funeral, and with the decision of whether or not she should let Ben go.

"Honey, come here. Sit down next to Mommy. There's something I got to tell you." He walked bravely over to the couch and sat down next to her.

"Is it about Daddy?"

"Yeah," she said softly, looking into his eyes that were now welling with water. "Your daddy's left us. He's gone to heaven with the angels."

"Why, Mamma? Why did God do that? Was Daddy bad?" he asked sadly, with a tiny tear trickling down his precious face.

"Oh, no, honey," she said, stroking his tousled hair with her hand. "Your daddy was sick. That's all," she explained, trying to hold back her own tears.

"Will he be happy, Mommy?" he asked.

"Very happy, darling. I promise you." She wanted to take away all his sadness and restore it with everlasting happiness, but that couldn't happen now. His once protected world was invaded and it broke her in two, knowing how hard she tried to keep it safe for him. But there was nothing she could have done to have spared him from this inevitable ending.

"I'm gonna miss him," he sobbed.

"And he'll miss you. He told me to tell you he loved you very much," she said, holding him close to her. He clutched her tightly around the waist, sobbing for a man who had been his world.

That night Allyson let Ben sleep with her. He was too upset and too afraid to be alone. Every time she turned over or sniffled he jumped up to see if she was all right. He was so afraid that if she got a cold, she would die too. After hours of tossing and turning, he finally reached a deep slumber with one arm around her and the other around his teddy bear. Allyson cried for him that night as well as for Kyle. She laid awake wondering and worrying about Ben's future.

CHAPTER 78

Kyle's wake was held for one night only, and the funeral was two days later. Kyle requested a closed casket weeks before he passed on. Above his casket was a nice picture of him taken when he was married to Janice. Benjamin was a duplicate of him as far as his looks were concerned. Allyson was determined not to let his good looks govern his life, the way they had governed Kyle's.

Out of respect for Benjamin and her, Aunt Edith came up from New Hampshire to attend the wake and the funeral, and to give them some support in their very sad and troubled time. Allyson knew she wasn't too fond of Kyle, even though she never said as much. Aunt Edith had known the misery Allyson had endured when she was with him, and when she was away from him as well.

When Allyson and Ben entered the funeral parlor, the funeral director and his ushers greeted them. They handed her a pen so that she could sign the guest book. The place was very warm and Allyson could smell the fresh scent from all the bouquets. Benjamin stayed very close to her and held on to her hand. He walked timidly through the plush lilac-scented room to where Kyle lay. Ben looked very grown-up in his new three-piece suit she had bought him, especially for the occasion. The ushers were standing by to seat each mourner.

They were the first to arrive and were seated in the front row to the right, nearest the casket. Ben sat quietly next to her, still holding her hand firmly, as he stared straight ahead at the box where Kyle was laid to rest. He was soon distracted, however, by Aunt Edith's entrance, followed by Felicia and Marc. Allyson was extremely surprised when Stuart entered. He was escorted to the back row, behind them, far away from all of them. Then she saw Taylor and a few other co-workers from the office, along with some distant relatives of Kyle's, and a few friends of his from college. People were quietly chatting as they looked around.

The reverend appeared and all was silent. He introduced himself and then proceeded with a heart-warming speech, which touched all of them. He condensed all of Kyle's better qualities into the area of fatherhood. He mentioned Benjamin and how much Kyle loved him and the good father that he was. The minister's strong and steady voice triggered a lot of emotion, especially in those who really cared for Kyle during his short lifetime. This man of God had a way with words, and sniffling and weeping could be heard from all those who were moved by his flattering sermon.

Ben beamed every time he heard his father's name being mentioned by this mysterious man, who looked pretty important to him in his long black robe. But when he glanced around and realized that nobody was amused, he instantly wiped his grin off and replaced it with a puzzled look.

When the sermon ended a single file was formed, and one-by-one mourners went up to pay their respects. Some passed briefly by the casket while still others knelt before it, praying quietly. After the last person walked away from saying good-bye to Kyle, Ben tugged on her hand, pulling her toward the long box that contained his father.

"Mommy, is Daddy in there?" he asked pointing. "There's his picture," he said excitedly.

"Yes, honey."

"Why can't we see him, Mommy? Please, Mommy," he pleaded, his eyes filling up with tears.

"I'm sorry, baby. Daddy wanted you to remember him like that. That's why his picture is sitting up there. So that people will remember him the way he was. Understand, honey?" He nodded his head up and down, as tears trickled down his bright pink cheeks.

"I want my daddy," he cried, holding on to the casket, spreading his small arms widely across it, as he laid his head upon it.

"I know you do, darling," she sobbed. "But you know what?"

He lifted his small head from the casket and looked up at her, the tears flooding his face now. "What?" he asked sadly.

"Your daddy will always be with you. Right here," she said, pointing to her heart and then his, "in your heart. And you can keep him there always." At that moment, he buried himself in her skirt. "Everything will be all right," she said, holding him close to her. "Dry those pretty eyes my precious one. The morning will bring a new day and soon these drops of sadness will be tears of yester-day," she whispered.

CHAPTER 79

The clouds were moving swiftly across the gray sky. It was the kind of day that coincided with a funeral. Ben was still sleeping soundly when she went into his room to get him up. The service for Kyle was to begin at 9:30 A.M. at the Chatham Union Church. And it was now quarter past seven. She hated to disturb him from the peace he finally managed to find. She stood over him for a few moments, admiring the beautiful child Kyle had given her. She had to fight back tears. Life hadn't been fair to either one of them. She stroked Ben gently trying to arouse him, without frightening him. His eyelids fluttered as he tried opening them.

"It looks like the sandman stopped by last night," she said softly, smiling down at him. He opened those big blue eyes of his widely and smiled brightly at her. For half a second, he forgot what day it was. Allyson hadn't seen that beautiful smile of his for days. It lightened her heart, hoping that one day soon his smile would shed some light for a brighter future. She hated to be the one who had to remind him where they had to be on this grim day. Ben sauntered sleepily around his room, preparing himself, the best he knew how, for another sorrowful day. This was the day they'd say their final good-byes to Kyle. A man who was once a son. Husband. Lover. Father. A man who had once influenced so many of their lives was now in a better place.

Allyson and Ben sat down at the kitchen table to have some breakfast. She had fixed them hot oatmeal and some toast with jelly. As she set it down on the table, Ben's face, so sad and distant, looked up at her.

"Mom, do I have to go today?"

Allyson was so stunned by his query she nearly tipped her bowl over.

"Ah…no. Not if you don't want to, honey," she said, not believing what he just asked. "It's entirely up to you."

"I think I'll stay home. Then he paused and looked puzzled. "You don't think Daddy will be mad at me, do you?"

"Oh, no, darling. Your daddy could never be mad at you," she said, looking at him. The way he placed his elbow on the table—with his hand holding up one side of his head, as he was spooning in his cereal with the other—vividly reminded her of how sad he looked, the time he was waiting for Kyle to pick him up, for their weekend camping trip at Nickerson. The trip that turned out to be an ongoing disaster. They both thought that Kyle wouldn't arrive and then suddenly his horn could he heard for miles. Benjamin bounced back that day. His mirthless little face instantly lit up like a lighted Christmas tree after seeing Kyle coming down the road. But this time she wondered if he'd ever be happy again, knowing his daddy wasn't coming back. Not ever.

Since everyone she trusted to care for Ben was going to be at the funeral, she telephoned a young girl who happened to be home on spring break from college. She had met her once when she was at the grocery store with Felicia, and she took a liking to her immediately. Brittany only lived a few streets away, so it wouldn't take too long to fetch her if she was available.

She was sleeping when Allyson called, but she said she'd be ready when they got there. Ben was eyeing her approvingly when she was in the car. Dressed neatly in blue jeans and a sweatshirt and sneakers, she spoke with a heavy Australian accent.

"Thank you, Brittany. Sorry it was such short notice."

"No problem. Glad I can be of help."

She was a sweet girl with a good reputation; Allyson felt safe in leaving Benjamin with her. Before dropping them off at home, she explained to Brittany briefly what had happened, and that it was Ben's decision not to go to his father's funeral. Then she kissed her son good-bye and left.

Allyson was pressed for time. She was supposed to be one of the firsts to arrive. After all, she and Ben were the closest Kyle had to having a family. His mother and father had passed on years before, and he had no siblings.

She was surprised to see the church parking lot full. Maybe there was something else going on besides Kyle's service. Allyson couldn't be bothered with wondering about that. She raced up the long narrow flight of stairs to the entrance of the church. She could hear the organ playing as she got closer. And when she got inside an usher greeted her and escorted her down the middle aisle of the holy sanctum. Both sides of the room were filled with old friends and acquaintances of Kyle's. So many had come to say farewell.

As she strolled down the long aisle, awed at the mere sight of so many of the townspeople in the pews, she caught Janice Caldwell's eye. She was sitting at the end of the pew, in the second row from the front, directly behind her. Her face was shielded with a black veil. She nodded when she saw her. It was nice that all these people came forth, showing they cared. But why now, when it was too late? Kyle had needed them while he was alive. Where had they been then?

The preacher conducted a resonant worship, and before he ended the sermon he asked Stuart if he was ready to come forward. Everyone turned and watched as the handsome young man rose from his seat, walked down the aisle and up to the podium. There was utter silence. Stuart brought a sheet of paper to the mike with him. He was nervous; Allyson could see the paper shaking in his hands. But surprisingly his voice was distinct and steady.

"Hello. My name is Stuart Hanson. I'm gay. I was Kyle's lover.

No, I do not have AIDS, but I did fear it, as you all did. And I'm sorry now that I did. I was too angry and hurt to look beyond—into the facts. Then, too much time had passed, and now…well," he looked up, *"I'm so sorry, my friend,"* he said, and paused, putting his head back down, wiping a tear from his eye. Then he lifted his head and continued on.

Kyle could sometimes be a difficult man, as we all can be, but there was also another side to him. A warm side. A sunny side. He was funny, and caring. And loving. He revealed much about himself to me. He explained that he found it almost impossible to show this to the women he knew. He felt bad about that. After a long friendship, Kyle and I fell in love.

I'm not here to justify his mistakes or mine. I'm here to try and make you understand that you can't get AIDS by touching someone, kissing someone, or even using the same toilet as they use. AIDS is a sexually transmitted disease, usually found in homosexuals, like myself. It can also be transmitted by using a contaminated device, usually a needle."

He took a break, a breather, and the minister handed him a cup of water. The notes from the sheet of paper he had begun from had been set down, and he proceeded more confidently, seemingly aware that he had captured everyone's attention.

"All of us here, myself being no exception, deserted Kyle when he needed us more than ever—to stand by him. To be his friend. To understand what he was going through. But fear stood in our paths. Instead of educating ourselves about AIDS, we got angry with Kyle and abandoned him. Because we were afraid," he

stressed emphatically. "*Afraid for ourselves. Our children. For all those we love. I'm ashamed to say that even I walked out on him when he counted on me to stand by him through this awful ordeal. He had to face those difficult months ahead—virtually alone.*

Let me retract that last statement. He wasn't alone at all. There were two people who were stronger than all of us here put together, who cared for him, loved him and tried to make his final days on this earth as comfortable as possible."

Allyson's tears were flowing freely now as Stuart was nearing the conclusion of what she thought was the most courageous eulogy ever expressed by someone who recently was as cowardly as the lion in the Wizard of Oz. Marc was sitting next to her, holding her hand; he squeezed it gently.

"*And I want Allyson and Ben to know that Kyle repeatedly expressed how special they both were to him. He loved his son very deeply. Ben meant the world to him, and I believe strongly it was because of him that Kyle hung in there as long as he did.*"

There was complete silence when he finished. One person in the far back of the church rose from his seat and began to clap. Then another person rose and started clapping, and another. Soon the entire assembly rose and was applauding Stuart for his honesty and his courage to stand before them, spilling his heart out in complimentary praise for Kyle.

When everyone was seated again, the minister announced that the ceremony had ended.

"Let us go in peace and harmony to say our last good-byes to a man who will leave us with a lasting effect, touching the lives of all of us here today. Open your hearts and let faith be your guide. Go in peace, my fellow friends."

CHAPTER 80

With each new day, Ben became less saddened by the loss of his dad. Marc was there for him but never crowded him. He wanted to give the boy the space he needed to heal. He wasn't trying to take the place of his father because Marc knew that nobody could do that, but he wanted Ben to know that he loved him like another father—and that he was his friend, as well.

One evening in May, Marc came with Allyson to Ben's school to watch him perform in a play. Ben played the big bad wolf in "Little Red Riding Hood." Marc had an important meeting to attend that night, but he postponed it so that he could be with them. He wanted Ben to know that he took a deep interest in everything that was important to him.

Ben smiled broadly when he spotted Marc and his mother sitting in the front row. He was a terrific little actor; they were amazed. Unexpectedly, in the middle of one of the scenes, the little girl who played Little Red Riding Hood surprised them by kissing the wolf, their Ben, on the tip of his nose.

"He doesn't scare me," said the brazen little girl.

The audience roared. Stunned, Ben wasn't quite sure how to handle the situation. He began to stutter and nearly forgot his lines. It was a good thing he had his face hidden under that mask, because Allyson was sure it was a beet red. When everyone settled down, Ben recited his lines more smoothly—without anymore interruptions. And when the play was over, Little Red Riding Hood—and the Wolf, received the most whistles and claps of all. Marc congratulated Ben on being the scariest wolf he had ever come in contact with, not to mention the most desirable one.

"Maybe I should be a wolf?" Marc said with a pout, looking at Allyson as they walked out of the school.

"Forget it. You get plenty of kisses," she said.
"Yeah," Ben remarked and laughed.
"What are you laughing about, Mr. big bad wolf?"
Ben shook his head and kept walking.

❀   ❀   ❀

Whenever Marc was free from his attorney duties, he insisted on bringing Ben to his tee-ball practice. It just so happened Allyson was doing nothing one particular day, so she tagged along. And poor Ben had the worst time; he couldn't hit the ball for the life of him. She winced each time he missed it. The other kids began making fun of him. He was a year younger than most of the little guys in his group, but they didn't take that into consideration. They were being downright cruel. She could never understand why kids had to be so mean especially when it was uncalled for. This was supposed to be a fun time. Ben's pride was pulverized. He ran into Marc's arms crying profusely, pounding him with his fists, as if to blame him because he wasn't doing that well.

"I want my daddy," he cried unhappily.

"I'm here for you, son," Marc said, letting Ben take all of his frustrations out on him. Marc grasped hold of Ben's forearms and held them tightly so that Ben couldn't move. Ben kicked Marc in the leg to retaliate. "Okay, that's it, young man," Marc said, lifting him high in the air with one hand. Letting him dangle like an ornament from a tree branch. "What are you going to do now?"

Ben's legs were swinging in all directions and this went on until he could fight no longer. Marc let him down cautiously and Ben lay on the ground exhausted. "Listen to me. How about you and I coming here tomorrow? We'll practice hitting the ball until you can hit it to the moon."

Ben shrugged his shoulders and then nodded. "I guess so."

Together they walked off the ball field with Allyson right behind them.

Marc worked with Ben the next day and every chance he could. When Ben went to his next practice, the coach and his peers were awestruck at what he could do. He did better than any of them there. He hit the ball every time, and he hit it far too. His teammates instantly became his chums and hovered around him, patting him on the back. Ben turned to look at Marc, and Marc gave him the thumbs up sign. From that day forth, Marc became his best buddy, and eventually Ben was able to accept Marc's love and to love him in return.

CHAPTER 81

On June 19th, Marc and Allyson took the big step they had long anticipated. They got married, and they decided to make those everlasting vows to one another on the beach, on horseback. The ceremony was unplanned, so that no hurdles could deter their chosen path. The Justice of the Peace was available upon request, and fortunately they picked a perfect day. The air was warm and still, the water was extremely calm, the sun seemed exceptionally bright and the cirrus clouds were scattered.

A quiet celebration at the Winchester Inn in Barnstable was to follow afterwards. They'd planned to spend the night there and continue on with their honeymoon in Hawaii. It was their first choice, but anywhere with Marc would have been just as satisfying for Allyson. Aunt Edith was going to remain at the Cape and care for Ben while they were away, and Felicia said she'd also help whenever she could.

Allyson thought about what it would be like to have her mother or father there for her on this special day, but she cast that thought aside rather quickly. This is one of the reasons why they were trying to keep it simple; the more elaborate, the more she'd longed for them to be there. They wanted their wedding to be unadorned, but at the same time unique. Something they both could cherish for a very long time.

What did sadden her, though, was that she wasn't able to wear her mother's wedding gown, like she once promised she would when it came time for her to marry, because of the extra pounds she had put on during the last few months. Stress always seemed to increase her appetite. But fortunately, the last minute, Felicia and Allyson found something suitable and very beautiful for the occasion. The beautifully tailored outfit fit her perfectly. Thank goodness, because they were getting married no matter what, nothing was going to deter them from what they had wished for for so long.

Felicia and Aunt Edith assisted her into her white on white satin brocaded redingote. A small train of vines and roses ran through the dazzling satin fabric. Then she completed her riding garb with her white chiffon riding hat, which was covered with small white sweetheart roses, and her long white gloves.

"You are a vision of beauty," Aunt Edith cried.

"Oh, thank you, Auntie. I can't believe it's me," Allyson said, standing in front of the full-length mirror on her bedroom door, admiring what she saw.

"So," Felicia said, smiling teary-eyed, "when is the prince arriving?"

"Any minute now. And the horses should be here about the same time," she said excitedly.

At that moment, Ben peaked in.

"Wow, Mom! You look awesome," he said, smiling. They all laughed at Ben's response.

"I'm glad you approve, son," she said, smiling down at him.

"You are the prettiest lady in the whole world," he said, extending his arms horizontally–as far as they would go.

"Well, I do feel rather pretty today. Plus, I know I have the two best guys in the whole world."

"Yup. I'll wait outside for Marc," he said, scurrying off, smiling from ear to ear.

In a short time, Ben had grown to love Marc immensely, and right after they were married, Marc planned to adopt Ben. They wanted to wait for the right time, but there was no better time. The love was there between them, along with the yearning to be father and son.

"Come here you two," she said, gesturing to Felicia and Aunt Edith. When they got close to her, Allyson put her arms around their shoulders. "I want you to know that I love you both. What would I've done without ya? I'm really lucky to have you," she said, with tears filling her eyes.

"Knock it off. Your mascara will run," Felicia said, with tears in her own eyes.

"We love you too, darling," was Aunt Edith's reply.

"We sure do. You've been a great friend to me, and I'll never forget it. If it wasn't for this nice lady," Felicia said, smiling at Aunt Edith, "bringing you here summers…I'll always be grateful to you, "Aunt" Edith, for that."

Seconds later, Ben rushed in to inform them that the horses had arrived. And Marc and the photographer had come in the meantime. The Justice planned on meeting them at the beach. Suddenly everything was happening at once, but at a leisurely pace. There were their loved ones hovering around them with smiling faces and tears of joy streaming down their cheeks.

Marc looked utterly handsome in his long, gray-and-black tailored tux and his black top hat. His eyes revealed a dreamy passion of love as he focused on her. They mounted their horses and together trotted to the beach.

"You are beautiful."

"And you look like a prince, Counselor."

Mr. Alden, the justice of peace, was already waiting for them when they got there. The water, the sand, the sun, the horses and the people they loved made the setting memorable. Ben stood gleaming, holding the little white satin pillow, which held their wedding bands—the small keepsakes of their new and wonderful beginning. A gentleman with a guitar sang, as he played their favorite, "The Wedding Song." His voice was poignant—and it thrilled them, with an ethereal harmony. When the song ended, the preacher took his prayer book and read a few versus from it. They were viewed by a handful of spectators, other than their family and friends, but that didn't distract their concentration from the vows they carefully chose to say to one another.

Marc began first.

"I, Marcus Kelsey, ask you, Allyson Porteus, to be my lawful wedded wife, through sickness and in health, for richer or poorer, until death do us part. Ali," he continued, looking deeply into her eyes, "you are a courageous and witty woman, whom I adore with all my heart. Your compassion for others reveals to me—the beautiful person you are.

I promise to love you beyond the heavens, and protect you the best way I know how—from any danger or pain that you may endure, through our years together. I will be near you—always, supporting you. I want to be a part of your dreams. I pray that our love will continue to grow stronger throughout our lives. For I love you, Allyson, with every breath that I take. Please accept this ring," he said, leaning over and placing it on her finger, "as a small token of my endless love for you."

She had to wipe the tears from her eyes, after hearing his beautiful words, before she could start.

"I, Allyson Porteus, promise to honor you as my lawful wedded husband, and to obey, over and above, all the rules suggested in the common vows. You, Marc Kelsey," she said, looking deeply into his eyes, "are my world. You are my best friend. And you were my strength when my weaknesses prevailed—and I'll never forget that. Your timely patience, your infinite caring and your heart-warming love have taught me so much.

I intend to devote my life to you, giving back all the cherished and unforgettable moments you have given me. I promise to be the best wife I know how to be—by not disappointing you, and by showing you with my actions, as well as with my words—how much I truly love you."

Then she placed the ring on his finger, and they kissed for a long time. The guitarist sang, "Endless Love." As they galloped down the beach, confetti was thrown at Marc and her.

She knew, at last, she had found her true love. Her authentic love. She intended to hold on to Marc and cherish him for the rest of her life. Even more, she knew that Marc would be a wonderful father to Ben.

0-595-28759-X